ALSO BY J. S. LAW

Tenacity

THE FEAR WITHIN

THE
FEAR
WITHIN

A THRILLER

J. S. LAW

A HOLT PAPERBACK

HENRY HOLT AND COMPANY   NEW YORK

Holt Paperbacks
Henry Holt and Company
Publishers since 1866
175 Fifth Avenue
New York, New York 10010
www.henryholt.com

Henry Holt ® and ® are registered trademarks of
Macmillan Publishing Group, LLC.

Library of Congress Cataloging-in-Publication Data

Names: Law, J. S., author.
Title: The fear within : a thriller / J. S. Law.
Description : First edition. | New York : Henry Holt and Company, 2018. | "First published
   in Great Britain by Headline in 2017"—Verso title page.
Identifiers: LCCN 2017022487 | ISBN 9781250173676 (trade pbk.) | ISBN 9781627794596
   (electronic book)
Subjects: LCSH: Women sailors—Fiction. | Great Britain. Royal Navy—Fiction. | Missing
   persons investigation—Fiction. | GSAFD: Mystery fiction. | Suspense fiction.
Classification: LCC PR6112.A983 F43 2017 | DDC 823/.92—dc23
LC record available at https://lccn.loc.gov/2017022487

ISBN: 9781250173676

Our books may be purchased in bulk for promotional, educational, or business use. Please
contact your local bookseller or the Macmillan Corporate and Premium Sales Department at
(800) 221-7945, extension 5442, or by e-mail at MacmillanSpecialMarkets@macmillan.com.

First published in Great Britain by Headline in 2017
First U.S. Edition 2018

Designed by Kelly S. Too

Printed in the United States of America

1   3   5   7   9   10   8   6   4   2

To my family and friends who
supported me on this journey—thank you

THE FEAR WITHIN

PART ONE

1

"Boss, just wait."

Dan felt her shoulders tense at the name.

There was only one person in the Royal Navy, and possibly the whole world, who called her that and got away with it.

It felt like a man's name, something the boys called each other as a compromise between the formality the navy required of them and the friendship they developed from social outings to the local pubs and clubs.

"Boss. Wait!"

The second time it sounded like a command.

Dan stopped and paused, then turned slowly to face him.

John Granger had called her Boss when they'd first worked together on the Hamilton investigation, too, but that seemed like a lifetime ago.

In the beginning, she'd felt too new, maybe too young and inexperienced, to call him out on it. She hadn't wanted to rock the boat with the more experienced master at arms; and she may have liked it, too, a little, but not much. Now it'd just gone on too long to try to change it, and it also signaled that he was starting to relax around her again, that things were returning to whatever normal had once been. Dan wanted that.

She waited for him to realize that she didn't like his tone, but he stared back at her, defiant.

"I'm going to go and look," she said.

Dan saw a flash of anger spark in John's eyes, watched his lips set hard and his eyebrows furrow.

"Just wait for backup. He's dangerous," said John through gritted teeth.

"You go and call in the cavalry. I'm only going to confirm they're here."

Dan crouched and ran along a fence that separated the open parking area from a small wooded copse. She could no longer hear the cars that were motoring down the main road through Hampshire's New Forest, and the sound of her feet crunching on the loose stones and broken asphalt of the parking lot seemed amplified against the near silence around her.

After a moment's pause, John moved in the other direction, heading back down the lane that'd led them to this place, to where they'd parked the car and where they'd last had a signal on their mobile phones.

Dan chose to ignore the little shake of his head just before she'd turned away.

Single-story industrial units framed the parking area on three sides, and Dan ran low across the mouth of the large courtyard, heading toward the corner lot and a vacant shop set on the very end of the row.

She hugged the fence that ran next to her for what little cover it might offer. She reached the building and walked slowly across the short gap between fence and brick wall.

The slatted shutters of the shop were down and locked, the shop and all the other units around looked long unused, abandoned.

Dan peeked around the edge of the grimy shutters and looked through the slim gaps into the shop. She could see no movement, not at first, then Dan saw her; almost naked, utterly filthy, with streaks of darkness running down her pale skin. Only the rusty red tinge when the light caught her just right showed what the smears were.

The woman's hands were bound behind her back. Her skinny shoulder bones pushed against her skin, tenting it, prodding out at impossible angles.

Dan checked behind her.

John was several hundred meters away now, across the parking lot. He was moving quickly and Dan knew he wouldn't want to be out of sight for long.

She looked back through the shutters.

Evelyn wasn't moving, and her husband, David Simmons, was nowhere to be seen.

She turned again just in time to see John disappear from view.

The sky was a dull gray and the light was leaving, the sun ducking behind the building opposite and presenting it to her as a silhouette.

She looked along the wall, toward the back of the shop.

There was a small red hatchback car parked off to one side. Only the back end of it was visible, sticking out from behind some bushes and a rusted metal dumpster that was overflowing with building debris and other rubbish. The car had been well hidden, would be almost invisible unless you were there specifically to look for it.

It'd taken time to find the car since the moment of pure fate when a half-dressed child ran out onto the road and nearly beneath Dan's tires while she drove to work; the girl had stood crying and staring back toward a house set into a terrace almost identical to Dan's.

The child was hysterical. Dan managed to talk the girl into the back of her car. Another worried passerby waited with her while Dan went into the house to see what had happened.

The social worker would have had no chance.

Amanda Collins, a naval petty officer and Armed Forces social worker, had been sent to investigate concerns of domestic violence in one of the military families that lived in the small housing development near Dan's own home.

Dan could see from the patterns of blood that Collins had been set upon as soon as she'd stepped into the kitchen. She'd later learn that David Simmons was supposed to have been at work but that he'd hidden in the garden shed, suspicious and watching, before entering the house by the back door and beating Amanda Collins unconscious with a claw hammer.

When the sheer volume of blood made it impossible to grip the wooden shaft, he'd continued to bludgeon her with his bare hands.

He'd dragged her limp body to the raised threshold of the backdoor and had used the concrete step to stamp repeatedly on her head. By some miracle she had yet to succumb to her injuries.

Then he'd fled, taking his new wife with him.

The hunt for David Simmons had spun up quickly, a multiforce effort to track him down.

He had a prior record, but the law meant that Evelyn may not have known about it. He also had served in the British army for five years, joining relatively late, when he was already in his midtwenties.

With nothing else to go on, Dan had pulled his service records and found the address—not of a house, but a shop.

It was listed as his next-of-kin address at the time of his joining.

His family still owned the unit. They'd sold food and general supplies to the seasonal RV crowd, complementing the other units around them, which had also catered to this trade.

Now the place was deserted, and it looked as if nobody came here at all anymore, except those who'd plastered the graffiti over the walls, doors, and shutters.

Dan looked back at Evelyn and then around in John's direction.

He'd raise the alarm and be back any second.

She ran again, crouched low, and made for the red car. She looked through the windows, felt the hood for heat, and decided it hadn't been driven recently.

The leaves strewn across the windshield and the beginnings of spiderwebs growing out from behind the sideview mirrors and fenders showed it'd been some days since this vehicle had been moved; he must have come straight here after the attack.

She bent down and screwed the dust cap off the rear tire. She pulled her house key from her pocket and used the end to compress the valve, gritting her teeth at the noise the air made as it hissed out and the wheel moved slowly toward the ground. When it was done, she moved around to the other side and did the same, until the metal of the rear wheels was separated from the gravel only by the layer of flat black rubber. He wouldn't be driving away from them this time.

She stood up, nervous, looking at the building and then checking behind her. Then she went back toward the fence to wait for John.

He was on his way, running along the fence line toward her, trying to stay low.

"I'll kill her."

The words echoed around the silent spaces, vibrating off the walls and disappearing into the trees.

"Stand still."

The voice was loud, violent in its delivery, and Dan saw John stop, stand straight, and look up toward the roof of the shop unit.

Dan froze, unsure if she'd also been spotted, whether the sound of the escaping air had given her away, then she moved quickly away from the fence and pressed herself against the wall, hoping that she couldn't be seen.

"If you move any closer, I'll flay her."

"I won't move," said John. "Relax, David, just relax. I only came to talk to you."

"No, you didn't. You want to arrest me for sorting out the interfering bitch who accessed my house without my permission. Even though she was trespassing. Even though she was trying to talk my wife into doing things she didn't want to do, trying to break up my family for things that aren't any of her business. It was self-defense. Defending myself, my home, and my family from her."

"Amanda's in a bad way, David, I can't say different; you really hurt her."

"She was trying to hurt me," said Simmons. "Trying to take what's mine."

Dan couldn't see Simmons and he hadn't yet addressed her, so she assumed she hadn't been seen.

John was looking up toward the roof. He wouldn't dare glance at Dan and give her away. But his right hand, the one nearest to Dan, was at his waist and held flat toward her. He was telling her not to move.

Dan ducked away and followed the line of the shop wall toward the back, past the car.

The front door of the shop and all the windows were locked and shuttered, Dan had seen that. They were padlocked from the outside, so Simmons hadn't been using them for entry or egress.

She turned the corner, leaving John out of sight, and saw a rear entrance.

The door had been blue once but was now dull gray with cracked paint flaking down from it, the undercoat showing through where the paint had conceded to time and weather. The wood was buckled at the bottom, sticking out three inches, so that Dan could see the dark inside through the gap. Much of the black paint on the handle was still bonded to the metal, though it looked gray, dirty, and worn—most of it snuggled in thick cobwebs. In the center of the handle, however, she could see that the debris had been cleared away. There were marks, greasy fingerprints, where a hand had touched the dry, cold metal.

Dan reached out and leaned down on the handle. She was determined to open the door slowly, soundlessly. She could see that the wood was swollen, could see on the floor that there were marks where the metal weatherstrip had dragged repeatedly against the concrete as the door was opened and closed.

"David. Evie and Eric are safe. I thought you'd want to know that," said John, his voice echoing around the space.

Simmons laughed in a way that broke Dan's concentration and made her shiver.

"I think we both know I couldn't give a shit about them kids. They were ninety percent of what was wrong with their bloody mother. Always fussing around them, wrapping them in cotton wool, neglecting what should've been her priorities. That boy would've grown up a fag if I hadn't taken them on. I was the only chance he had of becoming a man, and look where that got me."

The handle resisted and Dan had to go up on her tiptoes, leaning with all her weight to force it. Then, once the handle was down, she pulled back with her whole body, moving the door open just an inch so that the lock couldn't reengage.

The noise made Dan freeze, gritting her teeth. It was more of a pop than anything else, and she waited for a reaction.

"What was that?" Simmons shouted.

"It could be the police coming down the entrance road, David. My partner's at the car now, calling this in. But you know what, if we sort this out now, between you and me, if you were to let me come and get Evelyn and walk her out here, safe and sound, then it'd go much easier for you, David, much easier for us all."

Simmons laughed again.

"I don't think Evelyn feels like moving at the moment," Simmons shouted. "We're married now, remember? We consummated our union until she could barely walk, the lucky lady. She also found out what happens when you shoot your mouth off about private family business. She's knackered after all that excitement; she's just chilling out for a while."

Simmons's voice echoed off the walls of the other units.

Dan was still waiting, not wanting to make another noise so soon after the last. She looked down at the marks on the floor where the door had rubbed against the concrete, and then she hooked her forearm under the handle, standing up to try lifting the door, reducing the weight of it on the ground as much as possible before leaning backward and slowly walking the door open without making a sound.

The door moved, the rubbing against the ground low and soft, lost in the wind, and Dan pulled it open just wide enough for her to squeeze her small frame through the gap.

Her senses were heightened and she couldn't help but look behind her again before she entered the dark interior at the rear of the shop.

She was alone now, felt alone, as she so often did, but John's voice carried to her, and the threats that Simmons had made against Evelyn were enough to give her the confidence to continue, to recognize that she had an opportunity while the two men talked, and that time could be running out.

She pulled a small flashlight from her pocket and shone it around. She was in a storeroom. She panned her beam, taking in high shelves and stacked boxes.

Large shelf racks lined the walls along three sides of this area. Directly across from where she stood by the door, the fourth side was a glass window running along the whole wall, from waist height up to a false ceiling. Through the glass, Dan could see an office, a computer chair, and a dusty monitor set against a backdrop of filing cabinets and a number of children's drawings pinned to a corkboard. She wondered how many, if any, were drawn by David Simmons.

The shelves around her looked full, as though the business hadn't died slowly, the customers coming in smaller and smaller numbers, but had instead been deserted without warning, as if some attack or event had driven people to leave in an instant.

The storeroom felt cold and damp, and the boxes that were left on the shelves looked as though they had begun to droop and disintegrate over time.

She moved farther into the room.

The shop was silent. She could no longer hear John and David Simmons talking outside.

There was a door at the far end of the room on Dan's left, framed by shelves.

Dan walked quickly toward it, looking around, realizing that she couldn't see the roof access and wasn't sure what route David Simmons had taken to get up there. She reached into her other pocket and pulled out a telescopic military-issue police baton.

It was heavy and hard and could extend quickly at the flick of a wrist, as it did now.

She scanned the door again with the flashlight. There were bolts top and bottom, extra security in case someone broke into the shop, perhaps, but they were unlocked. Dan looked for gouge marks on the floor, but there were none. She reached for the handle, pushing down steadily, and opened the door.

The shop floor on the other side was brighter than the storeroom, some of the retreating light from outside making it in through the slatted shutters. It was also cold, like a room with a door left open, and Dan knew that the access to the roof was in the main shop somewhere, maybe a fire exit toward the back.

She stepped inside.

The shop was larger than Dan had expected. It was at least as long as a basketball court, and aisles ran the full length of the shop floor.

To her right she could see a fire escape sign. The cold breeze was coming from that direction.

The door started to close behind her and she grabbed a bag of pasta from the shelf next to her, wedging it quietly between the door and the jamb to keep it open.

She scanned her flashlight in both directions again, wondering whether she might be able to secure the fire exit from the inside, locking Simmons on the roof while she tended to Evelyn. She listened carefully, heard Simmons's voice as a few words echoed down to her before the rest were lost to the wind; he was still talking to John. Then she heard a rasping, gurgling sound. Dan moved quickly to her left, toward the front of the shop, where she saw the tills.

There were two of them, side by side, and behind them were empty shelves where cigarettes would once have been; somebody had remembered to come and take those away when the shop had stopped trading.

She heard shuffling behind her, was sure she had, and spun around, turning off her light and listening for Simmons's footsteps coming into the shop.

Silence again.

She looked at the shutters, then moved toward them, turning right and looking down at the spot where she knew Evelyn Simmons had been lying when she'd looked only a short time before.

Evelyn was gone.

What was left was an area smeared with dark fluids, blood, and urine, as though someone had tried to clean up a mess with a blood-soaked rag.

"Evelyn," Dan whispered, hoping that the woman might be conscious and had moved herself.

She turned her light back on and saw the trail of dirt disappear deeper into the shop. She could see now that it could've only been made by dragging a bloodied body along the floor; Evelyn hadn't moved herself.

Dan followed the trail, walking beside it so as not to get the slippery blood on the soles of her shoes. She held the flashlight in her left hand, her right gripping the baton, which was raised, cocked, resting on her shoulder as she walked and listened, aware of every sound around her. She reached the junction, the point at which the shelves running lengthwise met others that crossed the store, and she stopped.

In front of her was an old gift section beneath a sign that read GIFTS 4 THOSE U LOVE.

In the center of the gift section was a rocking chair, an old wooden classic, and on it was a large teddy bear, huge in fact, the kind of thing that her sister, Charlie, had loved to try to win at the fair ground when they were kids. She remembered how they'd often walk back with something like it, Charlie smiling, clutching some enormous soft toy as tightly as she could, barely able to carry it, and her dad looking a bit grim as he wondered where on earth they were going to keep it.

"Evelyn," Dan whispered again, but there was still no reply.

On the floor, the trail of human fluids was no longer as clear as it had been, instead the whole floor was dirty, and Dan moved farther into the shop, shining her light along another aisle as she moved away from the gift section.

The noise was there again.

She heard it, no question this time, a shuffle, a rasp, the rattle of labored breathing. It was near her, behind her, and she turned quickly, shining the light and almost losing her balance.

Then she saw it.

Next to her was a large double-door fridge with a bright handwritten sign declaring that this was the Last Chance section.

Dan could already see that inside the fridge on the upper shelves were the remnants of rotten produce, probably so long gone that there wouldn't even be a smell, but at the bottom, curled up and not moving, was a body. Evelyn Simmons. Dan could see every single vertebra of the woman's spine as it pushed against her thin, bruised skin.

The fridge was big, as big as a wardrobe, with two glass doors as wide and tall as the shelves around them.

Dan pulled at one of the doors to open it, but it didn't budge.

The fridge wasn't powered on and she spotted what looked like a bike lock at the very top of the door.

It was looped and locked through two security eyes.

Dan tried the other door and was sure she saw Evelyn breathe as the glass door opened a tiny bit, until the bike lock at the top prevented it from going any farther.

"Evelyn, can you hear me?" whispered Dan.

Evelyn didn't move, though Dan was sure she heard the sound of breathing. She was alive, at least.

Dan wedged the end of her police baton into the gap and tried to lever the door wider. The bike lock looked solid, but the eye loop it was fed through looked weak, as though it were only riveted in place to stop the doors from falling open in transit and maybe to dissuade a casual thief.

With all her strength, she forced her weight against the end of the lever again and again, bouncing against it, and she felt the door move a little bit farther each time.

The eye at the top of the door gave way with a crack and the door flew open.

Dan stepped back, her foot hitting a patch of fluid, and she slipped and stumbled, falling against a shelf of canned fish and knocking several cans to the floor.

"Shit," she said, but she knew she had no time.

She stood up, the flashlight beam spilling across the floor, illuminating the dirt in a rusty red glow. Dan collapsed the baton and put it back in her pocket. Then she picked up the flashlight and held it in her mouth, gagging at the taste of the dirt that covered the handle. She reached in through the open door and grabbed Evelyn's body, reaching under her arms and dragging her out of the refrigerator.

The woman was emaciated, but even so, she was bigger than Dan's five-foot-two-inch frame, and as she dragged Evelyn out, she was unable to stop the woman's skinny legs from slapping against the floor with a crack that made Dan wince.

She laid Evelyn on her back, straddled her, and gritted her teeth as she lifted her under the arms into a sitting position. Then she took one of Evelyn's arms, wrapped it behind her head, and tried to heave the woman's unconscious body up onto her shoulder in a fireman's carry.

Dan knew that Simmons might well be on his way, but she also knew that that meant John would be, too, and she had to trust him to be here so that she could get Evelyn out of harm's way.

It took her three attempts to lift Evelyn's naked, unconscious body, and she staggered at first, struggling to find her balance beneath the weight. When she finally did, she turned to head for the front of the shop, just in time to see David Simmons jump at her.

He was already in the air, flying toward her, and he landed a two-footed kick to her stomach.

The blow doubled Dan over and collapsed her, throwing her back hard against the fridge and shattering one door as both she and Evelyn crumpled to the floor.

Dan was dazed and winded. Her arms and legs seeming to be tied together with Evelyn's bare limbs. She barely registered Evelyn's body being dragged off her in a single movement and being tossed out of the way, flying through the air, the limbs as loose and free as a child's rag doll, before landing with a sickening wet thud on the floor more than six feet across the aisle.

Dan was convulsing, the wind knocked out of her, and she wasn't able to fully avoid a blow that caught the front of her face, skimming her cheek and catching the side of her nose hard enough to make her head flick over her right shoulder and blood start flowing.

Her nose was blocked in an instant, her eyes filled with reflexive tears, and instinctively she leaned away again, her head moving into the space that would have been blocked by glass as another wild punch whistled past her head.

Even in her dazed state, Dan knew she was in big trouble. The ferocity of Simmons's attack had left her winded, her airways blocked at her throat, her nose numb and pouring blood, her vision obscured. The fear she now felt was intensified by the fact that in her mind, the images flashing faster than anything she'd ever seen, she replayed the result of his animal aggression on Petty Officer Amanda Collins.

Dan felt a sickening pain on her left shin and knew, though she couldn't properly see, that he'd stamped down on it with all of his weight.

Simmons wasn't trying to win a fight, he wasn't trying to subdue her or keep her down, he was trying to break her bones, to disable her, to kill her if he could.

There was a loud crash and through her tears she saw the shadow before her disappear.

John Granger, her partner and friend, had arrived.

Dan blinked repeatedly, clearing the tears from her eyes and trying to calm herself so she could recover her breath.

John had tackled Simmons to the floor, was on top of him now.

She could see that John wasn't trying to restrain Simmons, the violence she was watching had gone too far for that, John was fighting for everyone's safety, and she watched as Simmons drove his hand up into John's face, keeping his fingers there and reaching to gouge at John's eyes.

Both of John's hands were trying to fight off this attack, and Simmons, a former soldier who was physically fit, large, strong, and aggressive, reached out with his other hand, grabbing a large tin of fish, ready to use it as a weapon.

Dan willed her body into action, though it was slow to respond. She tried to stand, the leg where Simmons had stamped her giving way, and she hurled herself at Simmons, catching his thick forearm, unable to stop him, but diverting the direction of his arm and forcing the weapon to bounce off John's shoulder just a split second before it would have slammed into his temple.

Simmons was strong, very strong, easily a foot taller than Dan and more than twice her weight. He had the overdeveloped forearms of a man who loved lifting weights and training hard, and he turned to Dan, his teeth bared. In the instant that he looked away, his attention divided, John

Granger leaned back enough to free his face from Simmons's grip and sweep his other arm aside.

John dropped forward fast, driving his elbow down onto the bridge of Simmons's nose.

Simmons didn't make a sound. He easily ripped his arm free of Dan's grip, dropped the can, and grabbed John's head in both of his hands, drawing John's skull down toward him at the same time that he drove his head upward, head-butting John in the center of his face.

Dan watched John go limp for a second, watched as Simmons easily reversed their positions, and in what seemed like an instant, John was rolled onto the floor, Simmons atop him, and Dan saw Simmons again drive his head down into John's face.

She grabbed her baton and extended it quickly, the cracking sound drawing Simmons's attention. He reached for her, looking away from John, who immediately swung a punch at Simmons's head.

Simmons looked back at John, grunting for the first time and torn between two opponents. His arm was still outstretched toward her, and Dan, taking her chance, whipped the baton down hard onto Simmons's forearm, feeling the vibration travel up the length of it to her hand as it impacted. He screamed in pain as the loud crack of his radius bone breaking rose above the other sounds.

John looked as though he was spent, was on the edge of losing consciousness, and Dan looked at Simmons as his arm hung limp.

Simmons stood, leaving John on the ground, and swung his good arm at Dan, missing, but making her stumble backward. He seemed to take in his surroundings, unsure what to do, and Dan saw the first flashes of blue light as they touched his features and glinted in his eyes.

He looked at her and then at Evelyn, sneered, and then headed for the unconscious woman.

Dan rushed him, swinging the baton, but he ducked.

The baton glanced off his shoulder and he swung at Dan again, catching her clean on the side of the head and knocking her back against the broken fridge.

She was confused. She looked across at John, who was out cold, his face like road kill, and then she saw Simmons dragging Evelyn into the middle of the aisle.

He was making a sound under his breath, that same one again and again, and it took Dan a moment to realize he was repeating the word "bitch."

He laid Evelyn flat and raised his foot above her head.

Dan knew exactly what he was going to do. She'd been the one to find Amanda Collins, her skull almost split open from where he'd repeatedly stamped on it. He meant to crack Evelyn's skull before he was taken.

Dan pushed herself up and threw herself at him. She swung the baton, aiming for his lower back, but he was ready, a trained fighter, clad in muscle and pumped with adrenaline.

The baton landed, but not hard enough, and this time, instead of striking Dan and pushing her away, he clubbed her to the ground.

She slumped at his feet and he smiled down at her.

"Bitch," he said. "Her first, so you can watch, then you."

He moved his feet, placing one next to Evelyn's head as he raised the other. His broken arm was hanging limp at his side and Dan forced herself up off the floor, reaching for that hand and grabbing it tight.

With everything she had left, she pulled hard on the broken arm, twisting her whole body so that the arm contorted, too. Then she reached up for his elbow and bent his forearm as far back on itself as she could.

He howled, stumbled back, swung at her, but missed, and he fell away, Dan hanging on to his arm like a terrier. He fell to the ground and only then did she let go. He was sitting against some shelves, his breathing heavy, sweat pouring from his brow.

Dan could hear more people in the shop now, could see flashlight beams.

She willed them to come.

He looked at her, was close to enough to push himself forward and grab her one last time. The word was coming out again, "bitch, bitch, bitch." He heaved himself forward and Dan felt a hard object in her hand.

She'd swung the can of fish at his head before she even realized what it was.

It struck him on the temple, hard, and he slumped to the floor in front of her just as the first of the military and civilian police appeared round the end of the aisle.

2

Dan felt her phone vibrate and grabbed it from her pocket. She checked the screen, then smiled at the military assistant behind the desk, who simply looked irritated, and then stepped outside the door of Captain David Harrow-Brown's outer office.

"Charlie," said Dan, hearing her sister sigh as soon as she heard the tone. "I can't really talk now."

"You can never talk," said her sister. "Where are you?"

"Cheltenham, broadly. If I'm to be exact, I'm at GCHQ, outside Captain Harrow-Brown's office."

"Really? What does that cockblister want now?"

Dan snorted, caught out by her older sister's unusual use of foul language.

"Charlie!" said Dan.

"Yeah, sorry. I just learned that one yesterday. I know swearing doesn't really suit me, but, you know, he feels like someone it's worth having a go for."

Dan smiled, looking away from the assistant and feeling like a naughty child outside the headmaster's office.

"What're you there for, anyway? Have you got a big book stuffed down your pants again? I mean, you did what he wanted, saw the shrinks, got the clean bill of health, what more can he possibly want from you? Blood?"

Dan was silent as she thought about that.

"Seriously, Danny, what are we now, January? He's been on your case since you got off that stupid submarine in October. That's three months, almost four. At what point does it become bullying and harassment?"

"I don't know," said Dan, looking at the assistant and turning away a bit more. "At the point I start to give a crap, I guess."

"Well, start. He makes me mad and Dad wants to pull his arms and legs off."

Dan laughed again, keeping the volume low but glad for the smile it put on her face.

"Look, I really need to go. I'll call you back."

"Do. It's important. Oh, and we didn't manage to get a hard copy of the story on your latest heroics, but Dad printed it off some of the newspaper websites from down there. They're saying that your actions saved the social worker's life, which is a reason why you should be going in there for a commendation, not a bollocking. Anyway, I know you won't do this, but I said I'd ask you to get a proper copy for Dad; he collects them."

"You're right, I won't. It'll be a load of crap and it's probably why I'm here needing a book down my pants. Plus, he needs to ease to a frenzy. It's like he's stalking me since I got off *Tenacity*."

"He loves you and he's worried about you," said Charlie, ever calm. "I'll tell him you said you'd try your best, and I also need you to plan a trip back home, we all want to see you and your place isn't big enough for us all."

"It's big enough for us two," said Dan.

"Love you. Call me back later," said Charlie, and ended the call.

Dan stepped back into the office and sat down on the chair opposite the assistant. Her bum had barely touched the seat when the door off to her left, the one that led into Captain Harrow-Brown's office, opened, and Roger Blackett stuck his head out.

He didn't smile, just grimaced and nodded toward her.

"You're on, Danny," he said, and leaned out of the way to let her pass into the office.

Dan didn't make eye contact as she brushed by, she just tried to ignore the serious frown etched onto his face as though she hadn't noticed.

"Ah, Lieutenant Lewis. So often do I wish that I could start a meeting with you by stating what a pleasure it is to see you again, and yet I feel we both know it just never seems to be the case."

Captain Harrow-Brown stared at Dan as he finished speaking, his eyes cold and gleaming as he looked at her from behind his large, very clean, sterile-looking desk.

Dan had a flashing vision of Harrow-Brown alone, flicking his tongue out like a lizard and licking his own eyeball; Charlie would've loved that, and Dan suppressed a smile.

"Morning, sir," said Dan, meeting his stare and holding it.

He looked at her now in a way familiar to anyone who's ever seen a cat watch prey. His eyes were fixed, unblinking, looking through her.

Her dad had once said something to her about the family cat as it lazed on Dan's lap, gazing up at her as she stroked him. He'd said, "He may love you, but only because he can't eat you. If you were small enough, I can assure you he would." That's how Captain Harrow-Brown looked now, predatory and bleak, as though if he could do Dan harm, he would, but he was compelled, for the moment, to tolerate her.

Harrow-Brown sighed, deliberately loud, and looked at Roger Black-ett, who was sitting in a chair off to the side; he didn't invite Dan to sit down.

Roger nodded at Dan again.

She nodded back, looked at the two men in turn, then let her eyes settle back onto Harrow-Brown.

Roger Blackett, her immediate boss and the man in charge of the military investigators across the United Kingdom, was a man she'd known for years, since she was a child; he was also a good friend of her father's. Thickset and ruddy, he was less than a year away from retirement now, a whisky drinker and die-hard Scottish rugby fan, and he had the stocky look and red nose of someone who'd partaken regularly in both, often to excess. He'd always been Dan's strongest ally in the Special Investigation Branch, and Dan hoped that would continue.

Captain Harrow-Brown might have been the polar opposite of everything Dan admired about Blackett. He was a tall, thin, slimy man who made Dan's skin crawl if she thought too much about him. He reminded her of a spider furled up in his chair ready to expand outward, as though he would lengthen his long delicate limbs if he were to stand up and fully reveal himself. He was pale, looked like the typecast baddie in a children's movie, with slicked-back black hair and pallid skin. He was, it was fair to say, Dan's strongest detractor in the Special Investigation Branch, and unfortunately for Dan, he was also the head of Investigative and Intelligence and so her boss's boss. One step higher than Harrow-Brown and you were into the military men who'd become bureaucrats, joined the executive, and transcended specialization. That was where Harrow-Brown would be headed in short order.

Dan knew that he was changeable, adaptable, he was everything he needed to be to succeed in this world. He was a survivor who could catch the eye and leave his mark just as easily as he could slither along the floors of power, his mucus trail drying behind him and leaving no trace. He mixed effortlessly with both the military leaders and politicians; her foe was only going to grow in strength while her ally went out to pasture.

Judging by Harrow-Brown's look and tone, he'd not come to like her any better since they'd bumped heads shortly after she'd left the submarine HMS *Tenacity*.

"I believe we can be honest in that I wasn't enamored to hear that you'd returned to active duty," he began, reaching for a file in front of him and just touching it, sliding it toward her, not so that she could read it, but just so she could see what it was.

It was the report that had been written about her by the psychiatric assessment team at Catterick; Dan could see the crest on the front of the buff-colored folder.

"And yet it seems that those who are reckoned to know, after a few months of talking to you, believed you ready to do so."

He left the folder alone and leaned back in his chair.

Dan was still standing, had expected as much, and watched him touch the fingertips of each hand to the fingertips of the other, steepling his fingers and resting his chin against them.

"And now, lo and behold, we meet again in another situation where your judgment has to be called into question. Where you've colluded again with our friends in the British media to further your celebrity."

"I can't control what the press publish," said Dan. "I never even spoke to the—"

"The reports from the medical staff are clear, sir," interrupted Roger, forcing his way into the conversation and cutting Dan off, but supporting her. "Had Lieutenant Lewis not gone in and attempted rescue, and had the situation ended in a standoff, the most likely outcome was that Evelyn Simmons would have died from her injuries. The medical—"

"Thank you, Roger." Harrow-Brown cut Blackett off. "I read the reports, too, and while I saw that, I also noted that it was not a firm conclusion, but a hypothesis that supported Lieutenant Lewis's actions. The report also mentioned that Mrs. Simmons was further hurt in the ensuing struggle, that Master at Arms Granger was badly concussed and is recovering from a broken nose, among other injuries, and indeed, though some may say they were well deserved, our very own Lieutenant Lewis still bears the bruises from her encounter. So it was hardly what one might call a resounding success."

Roger made to speak again, but Harrow-Brown raised a hand and silenced him.

"Indeed, if I may continue, Roger, I often lament the fact that we have only Lieutenant Lewis on our military police front line, only Lieutenant Lewis willing to venture into such dangerous places. Perhaps we should consider recruiting some more people? Perhaps we could train some of them up to deal with hostage situations, or have some specialists whose job it is to breach buildings and rescue those who are trapped within them." He looked at Blackett. "What do you think, Roger? As the senior investigator for the Special Investigation Branch, do you think you could use such skills?"

Roger just looked at Harrow-Brown, refusing to be drawn into his sarcasm, and Dan was again glad of his support.

"Silence, Roger? I would have thought these would be useful men, though we can also seek help from our civilian counterparts if needs must, can we not?"

Roger didn't look at Dan, but she could tell from his profile, the way he was squaring himself toward Harrow-Brown, that he was getting angry at the needless sarcasm.

Blackett was reddening. His proximity to retirement meant he would advance no further, had little to prove, and cared less and less for the bureaucracy and snobbery of Harrow-Brown, something he occasionally voiced to Dan when they were alone.

Roger leaned forward.

"She was on the ground. She was faced with a choice and she made a decision," he said, his voice low.

"The wrong decision," said Harrow-Brown.

"Not according to the reports from the first responders and medical teams at the University Hospital, Southampton," said Roger.

The two men looked at each other and Dan had the sense, for a while at least, that she'd been forgotten.

"Indeed," said Harrow-Brown, breaking the deadlock. "And yet while the reports will *protect* Lieutenant Lewis, they do not fully *exonerate* her. I have been given reason, once again, to question, to lose faith, in her decision making and her confidentiality concerning the press and media."

He looked back at Dan and tilted his head as though unsure what she was.

"You are an honest person for your faults, are you not, Lieutenant Lewis?"

Dan looked at him, clenching her jaw and refusing to reply.

"Indeed, I believe that too much honesty has been a problem in your past, but will it be a problem in your future, I wonder? So answer me this. After you closed the *Tenacity* investigation and were ordered to move on and make no further inquiries into anything or anyone involved in that unfortunate series of events, have you, or have you not, been spending your own private time, inasmuch as a serving member of the British Armed Forces has such a thing, trying to track down Able Seaman Ryan Taylor?"

The question hung in the air, and both men were looking at Dan.

She watched Harrow-Brown carefully, thinking about her answer and about the young man who'd gone missing without a trace shortly after she'd escaped from the nuclear submarine HMS *Tenacity*. He was presumed to be on the run, presumed to have been part of the conspiracy that had been allowed to fester on board there, and yet Dan still believed him to be a key pivot in unlocking a larger conspiracy that she'd not yet been able to break. She had indeed been looking for him, had spent evenings and weekends researching his family history, trying to figure out where he might go or who he might run to, walking around areas he and his family had frequented throughout Taylor's life, and showing pictures of him to people there, hoping for sightings; to date, she'd found nothing.

"And what am I to understand by your silence, Lieutenant Lewis?" said Harrow-Brown.

Dan looked at Blackett.

He looked both angry and hopeful, maybe not in that order. He'd be hopeful that she hadn't and already angry because he knew she probably had, though she hadn't told him. It was something that was against his orders, against his advice, and against military protocol.

"I have," said Dan.

Blackett turned away and slumped back in his chair.

"Well, I appreciate your honesty on this occasion, Lieutenant Lewis," said Harrow-Brown, smiling at her and then at Roger like a child proved right.

"I'm a police officer in the Royal Navy," said Dan, hating how sanctimonious it sounded. "I don't believe that *Tenacity* could've been an isolated incident. The network required to move and process the quantity of narcotic that was found on *Tenacity* has to go beyond the sailors we know about. How could they distribute it and sell it? Finding Ryan Taylor is central to answering these questions."

Harrow-Brown smiled triumphantly and looked at Roger as he gestured toward Dan. He said nothing, as though there were nothing to be said, as though his point were twice made.

Roger was watching Dan now.

She knew him well enough to see the waves building beneath the calm water.

"And while I'm sure Commander Blackett will impose sanctions and court further discussion about your 'off the record' investigation, I'm also sent this."

Harrow-Brown raised a file and showed it first to Roger and then to Dan.

The file bore the mark of the National Crime Agency, and Dan frowned.

Roger hadn't mentioned it when they'd met in a café a few hours beforehand, even as he'd told her, "Keep your mouth shut and your ears too, if it helps," and cautioned her to say nothing, "absolutely nothing," while she received her "bollocking from Sparrow-Frown," one of the many names Blackett privately reserved for his boss.

"We should discuss that separately, sir," said Roger, and Dan detected a change in his voice, some stress, maybe, a weakening, as though he were asking Harrow-Brown to listen to what he was saying. "Once Lieutenant Lewis has left."

"No, Roger, not at all. Lieutenant Lewis must hear this."

As Harrow-Brown opened the folder, his eyes on the pages within, Roger looked at Dan, and again she couldn't read his expression. It could have been an apology for something that was coming, or maybe a warning to keep her mouth shut awhile longer, but there was anger in it again, that was for certain.

"So, we're all security-cleared here, and I need to call upon your advice, Lieutenant Lewis. We have a request for assistance from the National Crime Agency, no less."

Dan felt her stomach flip.

"They believe they've discovered evidence of a series of disappearances with a possible single offender, and it seems they've decided there may be a current or former link to the Armed Forces. They've asked for a liaison to support them. I can't really say too much more about it, except that the target demographic seems to be women between the ages of twenty and forty-five and that they've found very little at all, except that these women are no longer where they should be."

Dan opened her mouth to speak, but this time it was Roger who raised a hand.

"Sir," he said, "I would very much appreciate it if we could discuss this in private." He turned to Dan. "Danny, would you please wait outside?"

"No, Roger, not at all. Standing before us at this very moment, we have the preeminent Armed Forces mind for cases such as this. Why would we eliminate Lieutenant Lewis from our discussion?"

Roger turned toward Harrow-Brown and Dan again saw something pass between them. He'd always been a consummate professional, but lately, as his retirement neared, he seemed to be hastier in his decisions, more willing to stick his head above the parapets.

"Sir," said Blackett, the word a warning in its delivery.

"Commander Blackett," said Harrow-Brown, his voice casual, the use of Blackett's rank reminding Roger of his subordinate position. Harrow-

Brown's eyes gleamed at Dan. "She will stay, and we will listen to her advice."

"I'd prefer to stay, please," said Dan, looking from one to the other.

"Good," said Harrow-Brown. "So, with this small amount of knowledge in mind, I need to ask you this, Danny. Whom should we attach to this case? There are few candidates in your branch qualified to investigate loss of life, a skill set required for this type of investigation. Only two of you are left in the navy, eleven in the army, and three Royal Air Force, so the pool is shallow."

Dan reddened as she realized why Blackett hadn't wanted her here.

"Captain Kevin Sharpe from the army investigative team could be a good choice, don't you think, Danny?" said Harrow-Brown, his use of her first name adding insult to the growing knowledge that he was going to block her appointment to this case. "He gained good experience working in the Iraq Historical Allegations Team, among other assignments. He's an officer who has always shown excellent judgment."

"Sir," she said, looking at Roger and then at Harrow-Brown, trying to compose herself. "I'm far and away the most experienced and qualified to support an investigation like this, and I'd be willing to do that."

Roger looked away, his head turning as his eyes fell to his lap.

"Indeed," said Harrow-Brown. "You would be eminently qualified, and I have a request here"—he brandished a letter—"that specifically asks for you, by name, but . . ." He paused and let his eyes run up and down her until Dan had to brace herself to prevent a shiver from crawling up her back. "Your judgment cannot be trusted, as we were only moments ago discussing. Furthermore, we aren't able to trust your relationship with the media, a lesson we all learned the last time Commander Blackett saw fit to place you into a role like this one."

"That's bullshit," said Dan, remembering how the dissertations she'd written had been leaked to the press, that in them she'd stated that the man reckoned to be the United Kingdom's most prolific serial killer, Christopher Hamilton, a serving lieutenant in the Special Investigation Branch, who'd twice been seconded as a liaison to the very investigation that was trying to hunt for him, had not worked alone. She'd hypothesized that he'd had help, she was certain of it, and when the national media got hold of that, the subsequent frenzy that another killer might still be out there, traveling around the world under the cover and protection of our Armed Forces, nearly ended her career and still haunted her now.

Harrow-Brown threw his hands in the air in mock exasperation. "And here she proves our point. Foul language thrown at superiors and a disregard for the authority of this office."

Dan was clenching her fists now, her jaw tight, and she could feel rage trembling in her stomach.

"You'd jeopardize an investigation to punish me," said Dan—a statement, not a question.

"Danny," warned Roger.

"Let her speak," said Harrow-Brown, and Dan could tell from his tone that he was enjoying this, was hoping for a further reaction from her.

Dan breathed deep, trying to control her emotion.

"Sir," she began, "I would respectfully ask that you consider me for this role. I'm experienced in this field and was central to the capture of Lieutenant Hamilton. I swear to you now, as I have done before, that I had no hand in leaking those dissertations to the press, which almost ruined my career. I'd take steps to ensure nothing like that happened again, and I have not engaged with the press or media at all concerning the Evelyn Simmons events. But, sir, if people are being hurt, and the NCA believe I may have something to offer, then it's possible that we really could help."

He leaned back in his chair, looked at her for a few moments, and then clapped his hands several times, a snuffling laugh escaping from his lips.

"Bravo, Danny, bravo," he said. "I knew you'd eventually learn to control yourself, if you only had the right motivation, but I'm afraid my mind is made up."

"Then why include me in this at all?" asked Dan.

"Several reasons, Lieutenant Lewis." Harrow-Brown's voice had regained its usually hard edge. "Because you will now know that there is a team of well-trained and trustworthy investigators around you, who have sound judgment, and, as such, you are not indispensable, as you currently seem to believe."

He leaned forward in his chair, his hands on his desk, as he watched her.

"You will also know that you cannot continue to live off of, and be protected by, your single success, that you seem to drag around behind you, drawing it like a gun whenever you feel undervalued."

He stood up, raising himself to his full height and looking down his nose at Dan.

"And finally, you will realize that in this branch and in this profession, we do not tolerate, or reward, those who do not conduct themselves as full and valued members of our team."

Dan stared at him, watching the vein on his head push against his pale, almost translucent skin as he forced the words out.

"You will know that I have reached the end of my tether with you, and whilst this last debacle isn't enough to allow me to dispense with your services, it does give me sufficient reason to consider whether you are the best face for this branch to present to our civilian counterparts when they ask me for help. I am utterly certain that you are not."

He stared at her, and Dan looked back at him.

"Do you understand, Lieutenant Lewis?" he asked, his voice even.

"Yes, sir," said Dan, swallowing hard. "Are we finished?"

"Yes, Lieutenant Lewis, you very nearly are."

3

Dan pulled into the communal parking area outside her house and killed the headlights. Her phone buzzed in her pocket and she answered it immediately.

"Lewis."

"Ah, also a Lewis here. Well, I *was* a Lewis, and like to think I do have many of the family traits, though I lack the stubborn pigheadedness of you and Dad, and I definitely got mum's looks, social skills, and charm."

Dan laughed.

"Hey, Charlie."

"So, you got some time for your wittier, prettier big sister?"

Dan laughed again.

"I'll concede prettier, but not much. I just got home and Felicity's coming any minute. What's up?"

"It's okay. I just wanted to see how today went. Call me when you've got time for a proper chat, but soon, okay? I mean, like, tomorrow, or the day after for definite. I'll send Dad to visit you for two weeks if it goes any longer. Or"—Charlie paused—"I'll just mention to him that I called your home phone and a man answered. I'll tell him it might be a boyfriend, but I couldn't be sure . . ."

"Call you back. I get it," said Dan, unable not to smile.

"And book to come up for a visit soon, too. Or I'll tell him how you'd love it if he just came down to meet your new man and help get the garden straightened up for the summer."

"What's with the threats and coercion?" asked Dan, laughing

again. "Do you know he calls me weekly now? After no news being good news for years and years, he calls me every week without fail. He's got nothing to really say, so he just babbles. He's getting worse with age."

"Not if you like the stories and fables from his time in the marines. If you like those then you're quids in, but honestly, if I have to sit through—"

Dan heard a noise in the background at Charlie's end and her sister stopped talking for a second, then there were muffled sounds as she covered the handset and spoke to someone else.

"I have to go," Charlie said when she was back on the line. "The man of the house"—Charlie paused and giggled, and Dan could hear that she was fending off her husband—"is deploying for a few months. So I'll be home alone and he wants something from me before he goes. I'm not sure what, but he's dragging me in the direction of the bedroom."

There was more giggling and Dan waited, not sure what to do, or say.

"Okay," she said after a break. "I'll leave you to your . . ." Dan paused. "Bedroom," she finished.

"Love you," shouted Charlie. "And you're pretty, witty, and wonderful, don't ever think otherwise."

" 'Bye, Danny," shouted Charlie's husband in the background and the line went dead.

Dan looked at her phone. There was a missed call from Felicity a little while ago and five missed calls from Roger. She touched the screen and called Roger back.

"Ryan. Bloody. Taylor," he said, as soon as he answered the phone.

"Why didn't you tell me about the NCA?" asked Dan.

"Why did I not tell you? You made us both look like fools. If I'd even thought for one second you'd continued the *Tenacity* investigation, I could have had some response ready, but no, I knew nothing, because you told me nothing. The fact that he knows and I didn't is double worrying and makes me look stupid and incompetent. I just had my ass handed to me in there."

He trailed off now, his temper starting to cool and the line falling quiet.

"You know, Danny, I don't have much time left. I leave the service in less than a year. With resettlement and termination leave, I'll be gone in less than nine months. I applied for my own job in a full-time reserve role, but they won't do it, so I really am going."

"I know," said Dan.

She looked over her shoulder, scanned the road and treeline around her, turning back and shaking her head when there was no one there.

"You there, Danny?" said Roger.

"Yeah. I'm sorry I didn't tell you," she said. "I just can't let what happened on *Tenacity* go."

She let the words hang, then continued.

"There's more, Roger. That quantity of drugs, how were they going to sell that? How were they going to move it and manage the money they got? And they were well off, but not that rich, not almost-a-ton-of-cocaine rich. Where's the real cash? There's more there, I know it, and it eats away at me that they're getting away with it."

Roger sighed.

"You're going to stop now though, right? Because I just gave my word that you would and that I'd make sure of it."

"I'll stop getting caught," said Dan.

He laughed.

"Well, we'll need to discuss this later, then," he said. "Because that's not going to work for me."

"So how come you kept a secret?" asked Dan.

Roger was silent for a few moments.

"I couldn't tell you, and Sparrow-Fart shouldn't have either, you know that. These requests come in and they're treated with total confidence. I'd planned to talk it through with him today and see if we could support the recommendation."

"He used it as a stick to beat me with," Dan said. "That's not right."

"He's a petty man, Danny, and he has no love for you, but I won't dress it up, you gave him all the ammunition he needed. You can't do the things you do and then feel wronged when someone else uses that as permission to step out of line as well."

Dan looked around at the front of her little terraced house set back from the road with her new security door, cameras, and lights.

"So there's no way?" she asked.

"Danny," said Roger, his voice softer now. "The Hamilton investigation requested military assistance five times, or maybe even more. That was before you came along and broke it. This one, I can't say much—to be honest, I don't know much—but it feels early to me. It feels like they're seeing patterns up at the NCA, but they're not even certain what they're looking for yet; I think this will have a time to run. And, for what it's worth, I thought you did the right thing going in there to get that young woman. I like to think I'd have done the same. I believe she's alive because of you and your willingness not to give a rat's ass about your own welfare, or indeed that of anyone who's around you."

"I do give a rat's ass," she said. "I knew John would be in there the second Simmons disappeared from view. It was a calculated risk, and he's tough."

"Calculated risk," Blackett repeated. "Calculated on what? Do you know, Danny, I've been in the navy over thirty-five years, and I don't think I've managed to really piss off more than a handful of people in that time. I wonder if you should 'calculate'"—he emphasized the word—"how you might go for a few weeks without pissing off ninety-five percent of the people you interact with. What do you think?"

"I think I need to go, Felicity's on her way over. We're going out for dinner."

"Send my regards. We'll speak tomorrow," said Roger, and the line went dead.

As if on cue, Dan heard a loud voice rising into earshot, the words coming in a steady cadence. She knew she was hearing one of Felicity's audiobooks.

The narrator was speeding up now, the words coming quicker, as though an action scene were reaching its climax, and as Dan watched Felicity park next to her car, she wondered if she'd get out straightaway or sit in her car and listen until this part was done.

The narrator's voice stopped, cut off, as Felicity's lights went out.

"Hey," Dan said, as Felicity opened her door.

"Hi," said Felicity, hauling her bag and briefcase out of the car and edging down the small gap between hers and Dan's.

She looked flustered when the belt of her coat caught on Dan's sideview mirror, but a broad smile spread across her face a moment later. "That damn book is too good, Danny," she said. "I got to the venue this morning and was nearly late for my workshop because I couldn't go in until I'd listened to the end of the chapter. Honestly, you should try one. It might help you to relax a bit."

Felicity approached and leaned forward, kissing Dan once on each cheek.

"I'll bear it in mind," said Dan, giving Felicity a pointed look. "Anyway, I'm running a bit late, in fact I was almost really late. Crappy day. How did your meeting go?"

Felicity sighed.

"Dull, dull, dull," she replied. "Everyone's seen too much television, Danny. You try to brief these police on profiling and offender psychology and they've all read the books, seen the films, watched the box set. It's like dealing with teenagers; they really think they already know everything there is to know."

Felicity was smiling as she spoke.

"Your name came up, as usual," said Felicity. "Impossible for me to talk profiling without Hamilton getting a mention—nice mention for you in the papers over that Simmons character, too. I know it's unprofessional to say, but I hope the lads in D-wing are looking forward to his arrival; they don't like wife beaters and child abusers inside."

Dan nodded.

"What were you doing when I pulled in?" Felicity continued, looking stern. "You looked shifty; all guilty-like."

"Not guilty, m'lord," said Dan. "Charlie called, then Roger, then I saw you coming and decided to wait for you. Well, I heard you coming, really, the Felicity Green equivalent of a teenage girl-racer with the loud *thump, thump, thump* of crap music, except it's some old guy reading a book at the top of his voice."

"Don't you knock Ludlum, Danny," said Felicity, an eyebrow raised. "His thrillers are literally the only thrill I get these days."

Dan laughed and turned to unlock her front door. She walked inside and dropped her bag onto the floor at the foot of the stairs.

"Do you want to stick the kettle on? I need to grab a quick shower and then we can head out," said Dan, reaching down to pick up the mail that was scattered on the floor beneath her letter slot.

"I swear my postman hates me," said Dan, setting aside a small parcel. "I ordered that a while back, it should've been here days ago."

She sorted through the rest of the mail, separating junk from bills.

"The sins of the father will be visited upon the children," Dan said, holding up a printed piece of paper with the words on it. "Getting loads of this stuff lately, but if you're trying to encourage people into religion, you'd go for something more cheerful than that, eh?" She tossed it to the side.

One letter at the bottom stood out from all the others.

This envelope was cream-colored and expensive-looking, embossed with a marking that Dan recognized. The address was handwritten onto the envelope in a beautiful flowing script of deep, black ink.

Dan rolled her eyes and tossed the envelope into the pile for shredding.

"What's that one?" asked Felicity.

"Nothing." Dan sighed, watching Felicity's face and then relenting. "I told you before, Hamilton's solicitor writes to me, on behalf of his sick and deranged client, every eight to ten weeks or so."

Felicity picked the envelope up and turned it over in her hands.

"I told you about these letters, remember?" said Dan. "I shred them in case anyone finds them and they end up in the papers."

Dan was in the kitchen now, flicking the kettle on and grabbing a mug out of the cupboard.

"Green or builder's?" she asked.

"Decaf?" asked Felicity. "No milk."

Dan looked back in the cupboard, found some Redbush tea, and dropped a teabag into the mug.

"Interesting," said Felicity, tapping the envelope against the heel of her hand.

Dan looked at her friend and knew what was coming.

"I know you're dying to open it, so you can, but I don't want to know what it says, okay?"

Felicity smiled, but it was awkward, an apology of sorts. "Okay. Only it would be interesting to just see what he says, don't you think? To see how much of it's just legal nonsense and how much is actually coming from Hamilton. I know there must be part of you that's still interested in him; the kind of link you had doesn't just go away."

"I really don't want to go there, Felicity."

Felicity nodded, putting the envelope down and walking into the kitchen. "I'll finish making this. You go and get ready," she said.

Dan was watching her, the way she moved with hesitation, the way her eyes darted away when Dan had spoken and the way she'd only half smiled.

"You okay?" asked Dan, feeling as though there was something unsaid.

"Sure. I'm fine," said Felicity.

"Did you know?" asked Dan.

Felicity was silent for a moment.

"I do know stuff, Danny, but specifically what?"

"That the NCA was requesting an assist from the military."

"I did know that," said Felicity, her voice hard to read, as though she wasn't sure whether Dan was going to be happy or annoyed about it. "In fact, I made a recommendation to the case lead about who I thought might suit the role."

Now Dan was silent.

"Your recommendation was taken up and passed along, but was ignored," she said.

"Really?" said Felicity. "That's quite unusual. I don't think I've ever heard of the military police not following one of our recommendations. Do you know why?"

"Well, it's happened now," said Dan, not willing to answer the "why."

"Look, Danny," said Felicity, reaching out to touch Dan's arm. "These investigations are marathons, ultramarathons really, not sprints; the unfortunate truth is that we most likely have time, far too much of it. I know you'll want to know and I can't tell you much. What I will tell you is utterly confidential and really quite speculative."

"Discretion goes without saying."

"Well, firstly, I know you must be devastated not to be seconded to us," said Felicity. "I'm stunned that your boss, or boss's boss, or whoever, decided not to meet our request for you to be loaned to us."

Felicity paused.

"Can you tell me what's going on? Anything at all?"

Felicity nodded but said nothing.

"You don't have to if you don't feel comfortable," said Dan, trying not to flush red in annoyance at Felicity's reluctance.

"Oh, I feel absolutely comfortable talking to you. It's just, it's very early and very upsetting. I actually spoke to the lead investigator and to Trish Campbell, my boss, about telling you, so they know I'm going to seek your thoughts, and I assured them both that we can trust you to secrecy, but, well, when the press do eventually get this, and goodness knows they will . . ."

"Okay," said Dan, frustrated at the buildup.

Dan had been on the Hamilton investigation team, had ultimately caught him, and had seen what images there were of the few victims that were ever found. She'd also seen many times, and firsthand, the horrendous things one human could do to another. She couldn't think what it could be that might make Felicity so unusually careful about what she was going to say.

"Danny, it feels important to say that we had no clue at all about this current investigation. We weren't looking for anyone; we weren't monitoring suspicious activity in an area; we had nothing."

"Okay. But something must have happened for you to pull a team together. You must have something now."

Felicity poured the boiled water into her mug and stirred the tea bag, then began to crush it repeatedly against the side of the cup with her spoon.

"We found some body parts," she said, not looking at Dan.

Dan made to ask a question but had so many she wasn't sure which should be first.

"We didn't find them as such. They were posted."

"Sent to you? At the National Crime Agency?"

Felicity nodded, not looking at Dan. "Not to me, specifically, but yes, you could say that."

"Jesus, Felicity, would you just come on and tell me?" said Dan.

Felicity finally turned to Dan, warming her hands on the mug as she raised it to her lips and took a sip.

"We received a ring finger taken from the left hand of a female victim. The victim was already dead when the finger was removed," said Felicity.

Dan watched her, saw the way Felicity swallowed and hesitated.

"It was old, several years old, but in very good condition, preserved, likely in formaldehyde. We believe that most of the degradation that had occurred happened during the time it was in the post; it had, for want of a better word, seeped."

"Did you identify it?"

Felicity nodded.

"We did, but we received several more, starting on the twenty-first of October last year. We received them at intervals, and now we have seven in all."

"Seven?"

Felicity nodded.

"We haven't identified them all yet, but they look as though they've been deceased for varying lengths of time, though all of them are well preserved."

Dan made to speak, but Felicity cut her off.

"We don't know how. Not yet, anyway. We have ideas; as I said, formaldehyde is most likely, or some kind of very cold storage, maybe periods of both, but we don't know for sure yet. Anyway, we identified the first, and it belonged to a young girl who went missing on the twenty-first of October 2009."

Dan froze, feeling the color drain from her face.

"Sarah Louise Sharples," said Dan, realizing now why Felicity had been acting the way she had, why she might have been given permission to speak to Dan. "You received it on the anniversary of her disappearance."

Felicity nodded and Dan felt her stomach lurch.

"But we were certain that Sarah was one of Hamilton's," said Dan, hating the phrase, the words implying that Hamilton in some way owned his victims, even in death. "We were positive of it. He had access and we put him in the area. She was a slam dunk for the victim profile he favored during that period."

Felicity drew in a deep breath and hesitated before speaking.

"We're fairly sure that the other six were also considered to be Hamilton's. We're not certain, but four of the others, the ones we successfully identified so far, were disappearances that were put to Hamilton with a high degree of certainty, though, as you know, we were never able to convict."

Dan leaned back and drew in a deep breath in turn, then let out a long exhale as she gathered herself.

"So my hypothesis . . ." began Dan, thinking back to the paper she'd written in the aftermath of capturing Hamilton, the paper that had been leaked to the press and had almost destroyed her career overnight, the paper in which she'd asserted that Hamilton had not worked alone, that he had to have had help throughout his relentless extermination.

"Yes," said Felicity. "There are only two ways that this could work. First, if Hamilton wasn't responsible for their deaths, in which case we have another, potentially prolific and almost undetectable, serial killer to find; or second, if Hamilton had an accomplice, someone who knew what he did with the bodies and still has access to them. We've found very few bodies to this day and, frankly, we haven't the slightest clue where to start looking. Of course we're looking into each woman's disappearance again, reinterviewing, reviewing files, but we've nothing. Nothing from the body parts that were sent to us, nothing from the packaging they were in."

They were both silent for a long time.

"I can't tell you much more, Danny, because I don't know much more."

"Why post the fingers at all?" asked Dan, maybe to herself.

"I don't know, maybe something is coming up that's triggered it. An anniversary, or some other significant date? Maybe he—"

"Or she," interrupted Dan.

"Or she," agreed Felicity. "Maybe they hate that Hamilton gets the glory and they're unknown, unhunted, unnoticed. Who knows what might trigger someone to do something like this?"

Dan nodded but didn't speak for a few moments. Then she wondered aloud, "Why not just tell the military that there's a Hamilton link? Then they'd have to release me."

"I don't think we're prepared to do that at the moment," said Felicity, letting the words hang as they both considered the breach of trust that went with Hamilton's appointment to the investigation to hunt himself down.

Felicity reached into her pocket and pulled out a piece of paper with a list of dates. She handed it to Dan.

"We've formally identified some and put our best thoughts against the others, but we'd be willing to hear other theories if you'd take a look."

Dan took the piece of paper.

"I appreciate you and Trish trusting me with this," Dan said, trying to be calm, though her mind was whirling as she thought about all she'd heard. "I'm going to take a quick shower. You still want to eat out?"

"At the moment, I'm not sure I could eat at all," said Felicity. "But we should try. Go get ready. When you're done, we do need to talk a bit more."

4

Dan closed her bedroom door and sat down on the bed.

The shopping list of dates, the name of a dead woman marked against most of them, was hanging loosely between her fingers.

She looked at the piece of paper again, examined the dates, and lowered herself onto the bedroom floor, turning slightly so that she could reach under the bed and pull out the lockbox where she kept her notes from the Hamilton investigation.

It took her a moment to notice that her hands were shaking.

Memories of Hamilton were jostling to the front of her mind. The image of the bodies she'd found in his garage, the snapshot that regularly visited in her dreams, seemed now sharper with hindsight, her mind having filled in gaps and enhanced the detail, until all that she knew of their injuries and the horror of their deaths was in high definition, a perfectly presented study of torture and death.

Her breathing deepened and then quickened, and she placed a hand to her chest as she remembered fighting with him in his garage, remembered his eyes, his smile, the strength of his hands, the sound his blood made as it seeped across the floor and soaked into the dry concrete.

Dan looked away from the lockbox, tipped her head back against the bed, and blew out a long breath through rounded lips. She ran her hand through her hair, closed her eyes tight, and then pinched the bridge of her nose, trying to squeeze the memories away.

Then she remembered the parking lot, a year after Hamilton had been jailed for life. She remembered the men who had been waiting there for her, their ruthless attack. As she did, the scars on her back, long since faded but never fully gone, seemed to burn behind her, painful again, the agony fading only as she clenched her teeth and counted slowly to ten.

The hunt for Hamilton had been one of the longest and most uncertain manhunts in British criminal·history, and Dan had ended it when she'd found three women stacked like firewood, their bodies broken and their skin mottled, underneath a tarpaulin in the corner of Christopher Hamilton's garage.

But even though he was now locked away, there was so much that she didn't know.

He'd been convicted of the murders of the three women, but he was widely considered to be the most prolific nonmedical serial killer in British history. The number of possible victims reckoned to have suffered and died by Hamilton's hand over his relentless thirty-year massacre reached over one hundred, with some estimates at double that, but what confounded police, and Dan, to this day was the absence of his victims' bodies.

Dan knew that everywhere Hamilton had ever lived, or spent any serious amount of time, had been searched, X-rayed, and excavated, but with no trace as to where the bodies of his other victims might be.

Theories raged that he carried his victims' bodies on board naval warships and disposed of them at sea, though Dan knew that the risks associated with this undertaking would have been simply too high. Also, she knew that there were periods of years when he wouldn't have had access to seagoing vessels, and so this theory was ruled out.

Dan had never come up with a satisfactory answer to this question. Where does a killer hide so many bodies so well that they are never found?

She'd assumed the location of these murdered women would be something Hamilton would take to hell with him, or that one day someone would discover a collection of bones while walking on a moor somewhere, and the mystery, or some part of it, would be solved, the families allowed some modicum of peace and closure.

But what Felicity had just told Dan changed everything.

That someone was now sending well-preserved body parts to the police, that the body parts were arriving on the date of the victim's disappearance, that each of these victims was firmly believed to have been abducted and murdered by Christopher Hamilton—all of these things made Dan's head spin.

Dan rested her head forward in her hands and opened her eyes, looking down now at the lockbox.

Could there have been a completely separate, unconnected killer all along? A second killer working in parallel with Hamilton?

The thought seemed unlikely.

Flashing light caught Dan's eye, and she heard her phone vibrating. She ignored it at first, then fumbled around on the bed until she found it and looked to see who it was.

She paused and took a moment to settle herself.

"Hey, Dad," she said, leaning back against the bed and letting her head rest against the mattress.

"I was just thinking about you and thought I'd check in," he said. "Are you okay? You sound tired."

Dan couldn't help but smile.

"I'm okay, but I am a little tired. I can't really talk at the moment, though; I'm in the middle of something."

There was silence at the end of the line.

Her dad, who was so loud and gregarious in person, was crap on the phone. He hated using it, much preferred the face-to-face approach, and could never seem to settle into being himself on a call.

"I was thinking I might come down south for a few days next month," he said. "I don't have to stay with you, happy to get a hotel nearby, thought I might go for a beer with Roger and catch up with some old friends."

Dan closed her eyes and sighed.

"You know you can stay here," she said.

"Are you sure? I could fix some things for you while I'm there. That shower needs replacing, and the extractor wasn't working properly, either. I could get those sorted out, and I bet the garden's looking grim. I'd tidy that up for you, too."

Dan noticed how much more easily he talked when it was about functional things, things that needed to be done, problems that needed to be solved.

"That'd be great, Dad. Thanks."

He paused again.

"Okay, well, I'll get Mim to text you the details and I'll let you get on."

"That's great," said Dan.

"Love you," he said.

"I love you, too. Tell Mim I said her, too."

She ended the call and dropped the phone on the floor beside her. She wondered how it must seem to someone like her dad, who loved her, there was no doubt about that, but who didn't really know what was wrong with her.

He knew that the events on *Tenacity* had taken something from her, knew that something else had changed in her before that, but in the absence of someone to confront, an enemy to fight on her behalf, he simply didn't know what to do.

Dan knew that there was nothing he wouldn't do for her, but he was completely unequipped to deal with what had happened, so much so that she could never tell him all of it, because the weight of it, the weight of knowing and not being able to fix what she'd been through, would destroy him, as surely as it was slowly destroying Dan.

She pulled the lockbox toward her and set the combination to open it. She steeled herself for the first picture, the one she always kept on top, but she managed to set it aside without lingering on it; there was no time for self-flagellation now.

The other files and papers were there, her notes and the laptop that she kept solely for her research into Hamilton's relentless slaughter.

She reached for the small laptop and stopped. She didn't need it. She recognized all of the dates on the piece of paper, and she recognized the names that would go with them, too. She could have recited each of them from memory.

Felicity knew this.

Dan leaned back against her bed and looked at the picture of her family on her bedside table.

Felicity and the National Crime Agency didn't need help with theories or identification. Felicity wouldn't be in any doubt at all about who these women were or who had been abducted on which date. Nor would she have any doubt that Hamilton was responsible for their disappearance.

No, Felicity needed something else, something that she hadn't been able to ask for, something that she'd needed to let Dan work round to. She wanted Dan to go and face him again, she wanted Dan to meet with Hamilton.

5

"Boss."

Granger caught up with her, slowing from a jog to a walk as he saw she'd stopped.

His nose was swollen and out of line, and the bruising around his eyes was a deep purple.

"What's up, Chi Chi?" she said, turning to face him properly.

"Cute, but my kids are saying I'm more raccoon than giant panda," he said, smiling, though between the swelling and the dark bruises, he looked a bit more like a bulldog snarling.

"They're being sensitive to your feelings," Dan assured him.

"They're teenagers, so I genuinely doubt that. Anyway, we've got a call. MISPER on *Defiance*. Young Stores Assistant. She checked in for work on Friday, was seen by the armed sentry and the quartermaster, and was pegged in on the ship's name board all day."

As he said this, he motioned with his right hand, as though inserting one of the small plastic pegs into a hole on the wooden peg boards that were used by ships to show whether sailors were on board.

"No one saw her leave. Her line manager assumed she'd gone week-enders early, though no one saw her at the weekend, either, and so she's just been reported missing now, after the Monday musters."

Dan frowned. "They just assumed she'd gone on leave? That's poor," she said.

"It is. Her divisional officer knew about it, too. The commanding officer's kicking ass and taking names as we speak. They did a thimble hunt on board today, but she's been gone three days, so they weren't likely to find anything. They've contacted her family, who made it clear they couldn't care less where she is, so *Defiance* is confident she isn't at home. The duty watch spoke to as many of the ship's company as they could; no one's seen her, no one knows anything about this."

"Okay," said Dan. "And they're bouncing it straight here?"

He nodded.

"*Defiance* knows full well that sailors do this all the time and that they usually turn up after a few days. They take their punishment on the chin and move on. But her former fiancé, a civvie lad who moved down here with her after she joined the mob, well, he's been calling the ship saying he's not happy. Apparently, he was getting blocked all the way up the chain, until he finally got hold of the commanding officer. The ex, Jason, says she still talks to him a bit, even though they split a while back. He says she wouldn't just run and says she's got nowhere to run to if she did. The ship thinks she was happy, no problems; he says different. He turned up at the gate this afternoon asking to see you."

John smiled again at that, just as Dan sighed.

"Am I the only name that comes up when you search 'navy police' on Google?" asked Dan.

"You're the poster girl for the branch," he said cheerfully, "your exposure to the Great British public knows no bounds, nice picture in last week's paper. I have to say, though"—he gestured at the marks on her face—"you look a bit more like a poster girl for a cage fighting franchise at the moment, to be honest."

"Where's Jason now?"

"I sent him off home," said John. "The investigation's just been passed on to us. I said that once the famous Danielle 'Drew' Lewis had cast her eye over it and solved the whole thing, she'd give him a ring back. I said you were a busy woman but it wouldn't take you long."

Dan rolled her eyes and then looked sternly at John.

"Actually, I'm double sorry," he said. "You're way more Salander than Drew."

"Stop pretending you can read books, Master at Arms," said Dan, grinning at him as she walked into her office.

He followed.

Dan dropped her stuff onto her desk.

"So break it down for me," she said, grabbing a half-full bottle of water and taking a drink. She looked down at the papers on the desk; the corner of a note she'd been reading poked out the top, Ryan Taylor's name now visible, if John were to look.

Dan's eyes were drawn to it.

"You listening, Boss?" asked John.

"Sorry. I am. Go from the top again. I get that she's been gone the weekend and that her former fiancé is worried, but—and I mean this nicely—if she's shacked up with a colleague somewhere, then he's not likely to know where she is, is he? She might have dumped him, or gone elsewhere to get away from him."

"True, but he called the civvie police, too."

"They refer it to us?" asked Dan.

John shook his head.

"She was last seen at ten thirty on Friday just gone, the thirtieth. She'd had a meeting with her divisional officer but then missed a meeting with her line manager after that. They weren't too worried, lots going on and she'd jobs inboard she could've been getting on with. Then she missed the muster after lunch. She never met with any friends for lunch. No one knows where she is or even where she might've gone. With it being a Friday, and with things slowing right down in the afternoon, her line manager, the section petty officer, decided that there might have been a miscommunication between him and her divisional officer, and he assumed she'd gone off on early weekend. He called her mobile, got no answer, but it was he who raised the alarm this morning when she didn't show up."

Dan looked at her watch, it was gone four o'clock. The ship's company of *Defiance* would shortly be leaving at the end of the working day, making it pointless to go down, as there'd be next to no one there to speak to.

"Is she a junior?" Dan asked, needing to know if the missing girl was under eighteen years old, which would mean a different duty-of-care requirement and an escalation in the response.

He was shaking his head.

"She turned eighteen a few months ago, not long after she left basic training in Raleigh."

Dan looked at her watch and said, "Just wish we'd got it earlier. There'll be no one down there to talk to at this time."

She sighed and looked back down at the notes she'd been reading through before John called on her.

"Are we sure she's not just run home? You said the parents didn't seem to care, but they wouldn't be the first ones to cover for their kid."

Again, John was shaking his head.

"I don't think so, and the ex really doesn't, either. Apparently, the stepfather was dead set against her joining up in the first place. Because she was seventeen at the time and needed a parental signature, she pressured her mum to sign the forms behind his back. Jason's opinion was clear; she wouldn't go back there under any circumstance, and the stepdad wouldn't have her in the house anyway. I got the impression her upbringing wasn't reminiscent of the Waltons', if you catch my meaning."

"All this from the former fiancé, who'd be a central suspect if this escalated into a full missing persons search."

John shrugged and then nodded.

"Anything to indicate she's come to harm? Anyone think she might want to harm herself?" asked Dan.

John reached up to scratch his face, moving his hand delicately, wincing as his finger touched his bruised skin.

He'd never mentioned it, not once. Never even joked about it being her fault or anything like that, but Dan would be a liar if she didn't admit to thinking it'd been her responsibility, her decision that had put him in harm's way.

Ever since last Thursday's meeting in London with Harrow-Brown, she'd continually replayed what'd happened at the small, disused industrial park on the edge of the New Forest. She'd worked back through it, each decision, trying to see which one had been the wrong one. Whether it'd been the initial decision to go out there once she'd found the address, the decision to take a look once she'd seen the car, or the decision to go into the shop and try to get Evelyn out. Each and every time she looked, that decision, the last one, the one that took her inside the shop and ultimately put John into conflict with Simmons, that decision seemed the soundest of them all.

"You drifted off again?" John was saying.

Dan looked up.

"I was just thinking it all through. Sorry."

He didn't look convinced.

"Look, there's a few things I don't like. Her bike's still down by *Defiance*, locked up in the sheds near the jetty. Also, some of the ship's company have nipped back to her flat to check, but there's no sign of her there. Still . . ." he said.

John sighed and paused.

Dan knew what he was thinking.

Sailors going APOD, or Absent from Place of Duty, was commonplace, and investigations like this one, ninety-nine times out of one hundred, ultimately led to their finding the sailor with some friends in a local bar, at home with their folks, or shacked up with a new squeeze that they hadn't found time to mention to their former partner.

"When are they due to sail?" Dan asked, acutely aware that sailors might see an impending deployment as a stressor. The prospect of a lot of time away from family and loved ones could often cause sailors, young and old, to run, or head to the doctor with a story that might get them medically downgraded and pulled off the ship, in much the same way that Evelyn Simmons had tried to do, though her need had been real and it still hadn't helped her.

"Not for weeks," he said. "They're going into a refit period. What d'you want to do?"

Dan shrugged.

"We'll head down and take a look. Has the commanding officer stopped leave so that we can talk to people?"

"He has where he could. It's Commander Stuart Ward, he's a good guy, so we'll get full cooperation, but a fair proportion of the ship's company are already gone. He hasn't begun a recall, not yet."

Dan wasn't surprised to hear that John knew the commanding officer; there seemed to be no one in the Royal Navy that John hadn't crossed paths with at some point. She picked up the file from her desk, spared it a glance, and locked it in her desk drawer.

John was watching her closely as she did, but she ignored him.

"Pictures?"

John shuffled in a file that he was carrying and pulled out a photo of a very young, very pretty blond woman. He held it up for Dan to see.

Dan took the photo from John and moved closer to the window to get some more light onto it. She furrowed her brow.

"I recognize her, I think," said Dan, looking back over to John. "Don't you?"

"I thought that, too, at first, but we've checked and she's never been in any bother, so I can't think where it'd be from."

Dan nodded and thought hard. "Definitely familiar," she said, handing the image back to John. "Let's go, then. Who saw her last?" said Dan, grabbing her foul-weather jacket and tricorn hat. "In fact, just fill me in on anything else in the car."

She walked to the door.

"What was her name again?" asked Dan, as they walked together toward the exit.

"SA Moore, Natasha Moore."

6

Natasha drove her small, beat-up Clio toward Portsmouth Dockyard's Trafalgar Gate. She was pleased to have passed her test, but still didn't like driving in heavy traffic. Cycling would be her preference in the future, but for the first day, she needed to bring in a lot of gear, so Jason had grabbed a lift with one of his new colleagues, and Natasha couldn't help but remember the flash of long auburn hair as "Susi" had leaned over to open the car door for him. Still, she'd cycle as of tomorrow and he'd have the car back, then Susi could travel to work on her own again and all would be well with the world.

She smiled at her own thoughts, knowing she wasn't the jealous type; maybe Jason was rubbing off on her.

The traffic was a nightmare even though she was approaching the naval base from within the city. The road coming the other way was even worse, total gridlock, and with so much traffic, Natasha was pleased she'd done a dry run with Jason the night before; she knew where everything was and how to get there.

She pulled into the Pass Office, grabbed a car pass, and sat through her briefings—don't touch high-voltage stuff or you'll evaporate into a cloud of flesh dust and bogies, got it—then headed off into the dockyard looking for Fountain Lake Jetty.

She saw *Defiance* from a distance, and it was every bit as big as she'd imagined it would be. She'd done some ship's visits during training, a Type 23 frigate in Plymouth and a minesweeper here in Portsmouth, but she'd known that the Type 45 destroyer was a much bigger warship than both of those, and as she looked up at it, she smiled. She'd always wanted to serve on one, always wanted to get away from her crummy housing development in the midlands to do something different. She'd fancied the army, too, had done selection, but they'd offered her a joining date a full seven months after the navy would take her, and the navy was her first preference anyway, so it was fate, a done deal, and off to basic training at HMS *Raleigh* she'd gone. The rest, as they say, was a very short period of stressful history.

She'd argued with her stepdad when she'd needed permission to join the navy. She'd had to beat a retreat from him before changing tack and slowly wearing her mum down.

There was literally no reason at all why they wouldn't let her go.

Her stepdad barely spoke to her at all, and she knew full well that her mum was working her own plan to escape from him, this time with Brian Shaw from two streets over. So why they didn't want her to leave was a mystery, except of course that her real dad was a sailor, and though she'd never seen him much, her mum and stepdad hated that he'd done well, hated that she might find him, spend time with him and maybe get to know him, even follow in his footsteps. One day, one thousand years or so from now, when she finally went home again, assuming someone physically forced her to, she'd see them again, and she'd have done well, and they'd likely hate her for that, too.

She'd turned eighteen now, earned more money than both parents and her fiancé, and didn't need permission from anyone for anything.

She looked up at *Defiance* again. She liked the name—Defiance. She loved all of those types of names: Invincible, Illustrious, Dauntless, Daring, Intrepid, Conqueror, Tenacity. A warship should sound like it was a warship. She could even live with HMS *Spiteful*—it sent a message— but *Defiance* sounded perfect to her, and it was a destroyer, too. She hadn't fully understood what a destroyer did, but that would come, and it sounded great.

She parked the car and grabbed her bag out of the trunk.

The navy-issue bag was almost as big as she was and she had to pull the rucksack straps as tight as they'd go to stop it bouncing off the back of her legs as she walked across the parking lot.

The plan was to just bring in clean, ironed stuff after this. Her clothes were small, and an ironed and folded shirt and trousers fitted neatly into the laptop pouch in the back of her rucksack, so this was a one-off mass delivery, the shock and awe of naval uniform.

It was early, still only 10:00, and the ship wasn't expecting her until 10:30, a late arrival because of all the additional briefs. It meant she'd allowed herself some time to get sorted, and if a good sailor was always five minutes early, then she'd be a great one. Hopefully someone would show her to her bunk, so she could drop the bag off somewhere safe; she'd only walked twenty paces and it was already hurting her shoulders.

She rested twice as she crossed the large main parking lot en route to the ship.

The gangway, when she finally reached it, looked as though it continued upward forever. She waited at the bottom for a moment, looking at the steps and taking another breather.

"You want help?"

Natasha turned to see who'd spoken. She saw the man's shirt buttons first, around the level of his upper abdomen, before leaning back to look up at his face as she took a pace away from him.

He also stepped back and looked down with an almost smile.

"Accident," he said. "I didn't realize you were going to wait."

Natasha wasn't sure which was bigger, the ship or this guy.

"Sorry," she said. "I'm okay, though. I'll manage."

He definitely smiled this time, an odd smile, shy with his head tipped slightly to one side, as though he didn't do it often, then he held out a hand.

"We don't let little people carry big bags up gangways on *Defiance*, not when big people are going that way anyway," he said, his cheeks flushing a little bit. "It's not a gender thing. It's just common dog."

Natasha leaned back slightly as he reached farther out, his forearm thicker than her thigh, and grabbed the top of her bag.

He held it at arm's length, taking all of the weight, as Natasha stepped forward and slipped her arms out of the shoulder straps.

"Thanks," she said, watching as he changed the bag around in his hand, gathering the rucksack straps together and using them as a handle.

He moved it so easily that it looked as though the bag were empty, or stuffed with foam packing to keep its shape.

"Come on, then," he said, and gestured for her to start walking up the gangway.

The gangway was a long plank of wood with wooden strips screwed across it at intervals, so not quite like stairs. The angle of it, coupled with her short legs, meant that Natasha needed to use the steps, but they were too far apart for her to stride from one to another, and she found herself doing a check-pace between each one—step, check, step, check—like a toddler just learning to do stairs.

Behind her, the enormous bag carrier was walking up the steps with ease, pausing every few strides when he got close behind her.

At the top, she stepped onto the flight deck and turned to take her bag.

"It's fine," he said, switching it into his left hand and extending his right. "I'll take it down to your bunk for you. I reckon your name's Moore?"

Natasha nodded, a little taken aback. She also noticed that he spoke with a slight lisp, that seemed to make his speech sound softer, more child-like.

"I'm Gary Black, the POSA. We'll be working together." He smiled, again looking shy, as Natasha shook his hand, her tiny fingers getting lost up to the wrist inside his thick palm.

"Thanks. I'm a little bit early, but I can take my own kit down, honestly."

He shook his head and waited.

"Go check in with the QM," he said. "I'll wait here and then take you down."

Natasha hesitated, not sure what to say, and then accepted that possession was nine-tenths of the law and there was absolutely no way she'd be able to physically wrestle the bag from him.

The quartermaster was watching her and raised an eyebrow as she walked toward him.

"Checking into Her Majesty's Hotel *Defiance*?" he said. "Step right this way, please."

He gestured to a book and asked her to sign in, watching her as she did.

"Right, that's you sorted. You need to get your joining routine from the killick writer, down at the ship's office on two-deck. I'm supposed to call PO Black to come get you, but as he's already here, I'll just leave you be."

"Thanks," said Natasha, and walked back over to PO Black.

"Thanks for waiting, PO," she said.

"It's okay. Just call me Gary," he said, and led them into the hangar.

"What do I call you?" asked Black.

"Natasha. Well, most people just call me Tash, or Tasha."

He smiled, or maybe grimaced, at that, then nodded, opening a bulkhead door and leading her inside the ship's superstructure.

"I'll take you to your cabin and show you your rack, then I'll show you where the stores office is. After that, I'll take you to meet the boss in her cabin."

Natasha said nothing, just followed on behind him, watching how he filled the whole gap when he passed through a bulkhead door and how he had to duck to miss obstacles that she hadn't even seen.

He carried her bag the whole way, hauling it easily in one hand, the way a toddler carries a teddy bear, and Natasha felt a bit conscious that she was just following behind him doing nothing. Fortunately, for the most part, they didn't pass anyone else, and so she was able to feel embarrassed only to herself.

He led her along 2-deck, suddenly ducking aside as a small chief petty officer came toward them from the other direction.

"Gaza," said the chief, greeting PO Black.

"Hey, Polly," said PO Black, his voice quiet.

The chief stopped and looked down at Natasha.

"Aye, aye. This yours, Blacky?" he asked.

"Joined today," said PO Black.

The chief examined Natasha carefully, deliberately, as though she was a bug in a jar.

She looked away.

"Sorry," he said suddenly, in a deep Scottish accent, "but I have the ability to tell things about people as soon as I first meet them, just from looking at them." He looked earnest. "Could I ask you a question?"

Natasha looked to PO Black, and then, when he gave no sign, she nodded. "Yes, Chief."

"When you're in bed, do you sleep on your stomach?"

Natasha looked at him for a moment, took in his stern face as he waited for an answer.

"No, Chief," she said, swallowing hard. "And neither can you."

He bellowed with laughter and slapped her on the arm. "Heard that one before, eh? Love it. You'll fit in here just fine."

He laughed again, way louder than was necessary.

"Look after this one, Blacky, she's a feisty little filly," he boomed, and continued on his way down 2-deck, laughing as he went.

"Apologies," said PO Black once the chief was gone. "Chief Pollack can be a bit of a dick."

Natasha shrugged, trying to be nonchalant, but her heart was beating hard and she felt flushed and embarrassed.

He led her farther on and they dropped down a steel ladder onto 3-deck, where they eventually turned into a flat, a lobbylike area with multiple doors and cabins leading off it.

"You're in the one down the end there. It's all mixed up. You're in with a couple of clanky girls, mechanics, and some others in that cabin. Heads and bathrooms are down there. Girls use the starboard heads."

He pointed to a door at the end of the flat, and Natasha could see, just from the change in flooring and darker blue color on the bulkhead, that it was a wet area.

"I'll show you the mess-deck later on, it's back up on two-deck, we passed it on the way here," he continued, making no move to return her bag or to move toward her new cabin. "It's a shared mess-deck on here, so you have all the junior rates, male and female, and the detachment of bootnecks in there, too."

"Sounds interesting," Natasha said, with a deliberately forced smile.

PO Black nodded.

"I should drop my kit off, then?"

He nodded again, turning away from Natasha as she stepped forward for her bag. He stepped round her and carried the bag along the flat to the cabin at the end.

She watched as he knocked gently on the door, which was open just a crack, and then pushed it open when there was no reply.

Then he stepped inside and she saw her bag being swung upward and out of view.

Natasha followed along and looked inside the cabin.

It was bigger than she'd imagined, six beds, four along one bulkhead and two along the other, with lockers taking up the remaining wall space.

PO Black had put her bag on the top bunk nearest the door, and Natasha had been warned to expect that. She didn't care, either. She was serving on one of the navy's most powerful warships, and her friends at home, who pretty much all made sandwiches for distribution to petrol-station minimarts, would think it was amazing wherever she slept. So would Jason, though he'd prefer she slept at home, of course.

"Come in. Take a look around," he said, gesturing with his arm and hitting one side of the cabin.

Natasha paused, looking at what space was left with him in there.

"Ah'm not shore this town's big enough fer the both of us," she said, a nervous laugh following her terrible Texas accent.

"Apologies," he said, frowning and blushing as though she'd shouted at him. "I didn't think."

He stepped out immediately, moving away from her and waiting.

"It's okay. I was just kidding," Natasha said.

She hovered for a moment, the awkward feeling of having done something wrong and not knowing what it was making her unsure what to do next. Then she stepped into the cabin.

It was bigger and more spacious and had loads more storage than the only other ship she'd ever slept on overnight.

She wanted to move her bag and climb up to try out her bed, see how comfy the mattress was and maybe stick some pictures up. She could send a picture of her bunk space to Jason, with pictures of them together in pride of place, and unpack some of her stuff before she met the other girls. But she was aware of PO Black outside, watching and waiting for her.

He seemed nice, if a little odd, and he was utterly enormous.

She wondered if the lisp that she kept picking up on was what made him seem a bit shy. She'd noticed it straightaway, of course, it wasn't easy to miss, but she noticed it even more in the way he tried to avoid saying words with the *s* sound.

He'd said "apologies" several times instead of "sorry," and there were other times when she'd also spotted odd word choices.

She thought about his face when she'd said that people called her Tash, or Tasha. Taking a deep breath, she stepped out into the flat and smiled at him.

"It's great in there," she said. "Thanks for carrying my bag. I bet it'll feel different once we've done some proper time at sea, though."

He smiled back and nodded.

"You know, my gran always called me Nat instead of Tash. You could call me that if you wanted to."

He smiled so broadly that she thought he might step forward and hug her.

Natasha stepped away, although she laughed as she did so, raising her hands.

"That's sorted, then," she said.

7

"You going to tell me what's up?" asked John as he pulled the car onto the main drag and headed for *Defiance*.

"I'm okay," said Dan, looking out the window at the high dockyard walls and the sheds that towered over them.

There was so much going on, so many things floating around her head, that she couldn't imagine what she would, or even could, tell John. The fact that she'd told Felicity that she would go to see Hamilton again was there, right at the forefront, niggling away like a headache on the build, but there was more.

She wanted to be part of the new NCA investigation. Knowing that some of Hamilton's presumed victims were involved, that in some way her hypothesis, her belief that he hadn't worked alone, might just be true, made her want it so badly. She wanted desperately to be there to prove it. The feeling of genuinely wanting to help, to do the right thing, mingled with the thought of being proved right, and she was angry at her own selfishness for even allowing that to be a thought at all.

Then there was her *Tenacity* investigation, and it was hers and hers alone, as no one else wanted it. If she was seconded to the NCA, the reality was that she'd need to drop it. There wouldn't be time to continue as she had been doing, working alone and offline. As much as Dan wanted all that came with the NCA investigation, she wasn't sure she could give up what she needed to do for herself after what'd happened on board *Tenacity*, wasn't sure she could leave it now and ever find closure.

That final thought, filled with more selfishness, added to her anger at herself.

"So, obviously I didn't spot the name Ryan Taylor sticking out of your file earlier then, no? I couldn't have, because I'm certain that you've let that investigation drop, am I not right?"

Dan looked at him, the name jarring her out of her thoughts, but he was watching the road, being deliberately conscientious, avoiding her eyes.

"I take it Commander Blackett spoke to you, then?" she said, making sure the annoyance was clear in her voice.

"He did. We are partners, after all, you and I, and the last time you kept me out of what you were doing, well, it could be said that things very nearly didn't end well."

John said this as a joke, in a lighthearted way, but Dan knew there was still something behind the words, a disappointment that she hadn't trusted him all those years ago when she'd chosen to go alone to investigate Christopher Hamilton. She'd nearly died that day, as had their trust and friendship.

"I've dropped the *Tenacity* investigation now. I didn't tell you because I didn't want to get you in any trouble," she said. It was as close to an apology as she was willing to go. "It was just legwork anyway. If I'd come across anything, I'd have told you and asked for company. I promise."

He nodded but still didn't face her.

"I assume Blackett asked you to let him know if you saw that I was still pursuing Taylor and the *Tenacity* lot?"

"Of course he did."

"You need to do what's right, then," said Dan, turning to look out the window again.

"Of course I do," said John.

Dan watched his reflection in the window, saw him steal a glance at her when he thought she wasn't paying attention; there's no way he'd tell Blackett what he'd seen, no way at all, and it made Dan smile inwardly that she could feel so sure about him.

"Doesn't it bother you a bit, too?" she asked, turning toward him. "You're a good copper, you know what they're getting away with."

He shrugged. "I guess the job's hard enough when you have the command imperative and the support of the Armed Forces police behind you, but when they're not, sometimes you just need to move along. If what you think's true, then we'll get another crack at them. You can't move that much gear without it showing up again."

"Yes," said Dan. "Exactly. If it's *Tenacity*, then why only *Tenacity*? Look how few people had to be involved on board to bring in almost a metric ton of cocaine. Why not bring it in on an aircraft carrier? A bigger ship? How many shipments came in before we got it? Where does it go after it gets here?"

"I don't see that it's worth it," he said.

"What do you mean?"

"You could argue that it's low risk, no one was checking submarines, but it isn't really, is it? Bringing it through the naval base, letting people in on the supply line, and for what? A ton. These folk are shifting fifty tons, a hundred tons, why all the risk for just one ton? It makes no sense to me. There's money, but not enough for my liking. There'd have to be something way more valuable for me to be taking that risk."

Dan was thinking.

"You're right, I hadn't really thought about it like that," she said.

He was smiling as he drove.

"What?"

"You're never going to let it go, are you?"

Dan leaned back in her seat and couldn't help but smile again.

"I'm going to try," she said.

"How hard will you be trying?"

"Not very," she replied quietly.

"Do you feel bad for lying to me a second ago, then? When you told me you'd dropped it?"

"No. It's not a proper lie if we both know full well I'm doing it."

They both laughed as the dockyard passed by beside them.

"I do feel bad about what happened in the New Forest, though," said Dan. "At the shop, with Simmons."

"Ah, don't think about it again. I won't. You got your bollocking from Harrow-Brown, so I hear, and these things happen. I'd have done the same thing as you did."

Dan looked at her hands and wriggled her fingers as she thought about what else to say. She knew she wasn't able to tell him about the request for a liaison from the National Crime Agency, and that was bothering her, too.

"Silence?" he said.

Dan sighed and turned to him.

"I guess I'm just not sure the navy's where I want to be," she finally said. "I'm not sure it's able to take me where I want to go anymore."

He turned to look at her.

"You're serious?" he asked, frowning as though expecting her to be joking.

"Yeah," she said. "The lack of drive to really investigate *Tenacity*"— she paused—"and some other things, decisions made for the wrong reasons and with the wrong outcomes. Personalities and sad little vendettas being put before making the right decision."

John appeared puzzled, and the silence drew out between them. Then, without warning, he snorted, laughing as though what she'd said had finally hit home and he'd found it ridiculous.

"How's that funny?"

"Look, Boss. You're one of the navy's great deniers, okay? You like to think you rebel against the system and that it, in turn, fights against you. Maybe bumping heads with Harrow-Brown again has made you feel a little bit tender, but if I were to cut you open, you'd bleed dark blue. You're like a stick of Blackpool rock, but with an anchor running right the way through you. The navy, the system you think you fight against, is actually what defines who you are. Who'd you be angry with if you didn't have the Royal Navy? You and the mob, the Senior Service, the Andrew, whatever you want to call this fine organization, you're symbiotic. I think you'd find it harder to be on the outside than you might think."

She looked at him.

"Symbiotic? That's a big word for a master at arms."

John laughed and slapped the steering wheel.

"And you might be a lifer, Granger, but I'm not."

"We'll see," John said, still grinning. "Time'll prove one of us right. But either way, don't go it alone on the *Tenacity* thing, okay? Keep me in the loop."

8

"Call me Gary," PO Black said again.

He smiled at her over his shoulder as he led her forward along 2-deck.

"Sorry, PO—I mean, sorry, Gary," said Natasha. "So." She paused. It just felt awkward to call a senior rate by his first name, because when she'd been in training, only days before, everyone was strict, always using ranks and rates to address the instructors, divisional officers, and other trainees. It felt like a hard habit to break and one that maybe shouldn't be broken. "Gary. My divisional officer is Lieutenant Cox, right?"

"Yup." He flushed as he spoke, then opened a bulkhead door for her to pass through.

"Shouldn't we wait till eleven? It says on my joining letter to meet you at ten thirty and then come up to her at eleven. We're going to be forty minutes early."

"No. Ma'am told me to bring you up the minute you came."

Natasha shrugged and followed him.

He had it all planned out and he was her line manager, so it wasn't like Lieutenant Cox could be annoyed with her.

"Stop right there, young lady."

Natasha froze, turning quickly to see a guy who could've been only a few years older than she was.

He was dressed in black slacks with a white vest under the pristinely ironed white jacket of a naval physical training instructor. The crossed clubs were embroidered on the left chest.

Natasha stood still.

"Yes, staff," she said, using the formal term she'd learned at HMS *Raleigh* for physical training instructors.

His rate would be leading hand, so one level above Natasha, but she'd learned in training that not doing *exactly* what a PTI wanted you to do could be a painful and exhausting proposition.

He laughed.

"Love it," he said. "Can't remember the last time someone called me that on this pusser's war canoe, but keep it up. Who knows, it might catch on."

He held out his hand to Natasha.

"We're going to see Lieutenant Cox," said PO Black before the PTI could say anything more.

Black's tone was low, but the PTI seemed to ignore him, smiling even more broadly.

"We shouldn't keep her waiting," Black added.

The PTI seemed to forget Natasha, withdrawing his hand and looking at PO Black.

"You sure you don't fancy the Navy Power Lifting Championships, Gaz? I could still get you an entry, and your warm-up lifts would probably place you in third, straight off the bat."

Natasha looked at PO Black; he didn't seem to take it as a compliment.

"I bet you could win it," said Natasha to PO Black.

PO Black softened a bit but still shook his head. "I don't do competitions anymore."

"Shame, big man. Could be another article in the dockyard dandy and a trophy for *Defiance*; you know how the Old Man loves both of those."

The PTI turned back to Natasha now and reoffered his hand. "LPT Mark Coker, Ship's Morale Officer. An important duty and one I take very seriously indeed."

"Tasha Moore. I just joined today."

"Perfect," he said, still holding her hand. "Are you a fittie?" he asked, then paused and shook his head as if he'd made an error and only just realized it. "I mean, I can see that you are definitely a fittie, but do you work out, too?"

Natasha laughed, feeling a little taken aback, but she could see he was joking.

"That isn't appropriate, Coker," said Black from behind Natasha.

"Aw, come on, big man, I was only kidding. It was a compliment if anything."

Coker held out his hands, palms up, as though pleading forgiveness.

"Tell him you forgive me, Tash, please," he asked, still smiling. "If you do, I'll do you a grat-issue training and nutrition plan and give you two further hours of one-to-one training absolutely gratis, free of charge, no cost at all, except your forgiveness."

Natasha watched him closely. "Aren't you supposed to do all that anyway?"

He stopped pleading and looked guilty. "Well, yeah, most of it, but not the one-to-one training sessions, that was the apology."

Natasha laughed and turned to PO Black.

He looked angry and was frowning at Coker.

"It's okay, Gary," she said. "I'll take two hours of free one-to-one training and accept an apology. And yes, I do work out. I run and I'd really like to do a triathlon. Me and my fiancé both fancy it."

"Fiancé. Nice," said Coker. "And triathlon, too. Well, we can help with that for sure. I'll dig out details on the Royal Navy and Royal Marines Triathlon Association and find out which events we can cover on the ship's sport budget. We're in refit for a while after this next trip, so you'll have time, and we might be able to get some triathlon gear from the ship's funds, too. It's always worth a shot and always good to have the ship's name out there."

"Cool," said Natasha.

"Yeah, cool. Circuits are on the ground floor of the old Sail Loft gym on Monday to Friday, except Wednesday, which is bleep test. I run from the ship most lunchtimes, so if you want some company on a run, just holler at me. I got to shoot, catch you soon."

He turned to go, switching back quickly and pointing toward PO Black.

"So it's a definite maybe on the power lifting, right?"

Black just stared at him, until he smiled again and winked at Natasha. "Have a good time with Sucks," he said, and was gone.

Natasha looked back to PO Black.

"Sucks?" she asked.

"It's what he calls Lieutenant Cox. He shouldn't do that. He's a wanker," said PO Black, quietly. "Nothing to say and always saying it far too loudly."

Natasha waited, unsure what to say or do next.

"Come on, we shouldn't keep Ma'am waiting, and you don't want to do training with him," said PO Black. "He's one to avoid."

Natasha nodded, still without a clue what to say, and pursed her lips. She also wondered how forty minutes early would be keeping someone waiting, but she was silent.

"Okay?" said PO Black.

Natasha waited for a second. She wasn't sure whether he was waiting for her to agree that she wouldn't train with LPT Coker, or whether he was checking she was okay to carry on up to Lieutenant Cox's office.

"Sure. I'm okay," she said, after a pause.

He smiled, seeming to relax, and started back along the deck.

They moved forward, passing compartments and walkways, Natasha knowing that she'd figure out how to get around the ship in time but feeling utterly lost for now.

It seemed so big, every corridor seeming the same as the last, spaces and compartments everywhere. She decided that if they all played hide-and-seek, she wouldn't be it, not for a while, anyway.

Eventually they entered another flat, longer and narrower than the one she'd been on previously, but still with a row of doors leading off it.

Many of the doors were closed, and this area of the ship was quiet.

Black walked along to the cabin at the very end.

The door was slightly ajar. He knocked and waited, standing to attention as he did.

Natasha did the same, waiting off to the side. She heard noises as someone moved around inside the cabin and then approached the door.

The woman who opened the door was tall, easily five feet eleven inches, and very broad across the shoulders.

Natasha immediately wondered if her new boss was a swimmer; she looked fit, but broad and powerful, like many of the good swimmers she'd seen when she watched triathlon events.

She was wearing a white short-sleeved shirt and black trousers, and her hair was tied behind her in a French plait. She looked at PO Black and then smiled as she saw Natasha.

"Hey," she said, stepping out of her cabin and offering her hand. "Relax. You must be Natasha?"

"Yes, ma'am," said Natasha, shaking her hand.

"Cool. Very cool. Come in."

She stepped back and waved Natasha into the cabin.

"Shall I come in, ma'am?" asked PO Black.

"No, Gary. I'll call you when we're done here. Wait at the stores office."

"I could just wait out here if you wanted," he said.

Cox turned and looked at him until Natasha saw his eyes drop away.

"Stores office will be fine. I'll call you when we've talked, and you'll be able to come and show her around some more."

Natasha watched as Black hesitated, then turned and walked away along the flat.

"So," said Lieutenant Cox as she came back into the cabin. "Grab a seat."

The cabin was long, with a bed down one side of it, which was currently made up to be a sofa. It wasn't hugely dissimilar to Natasha's new cabin in shape and size, except the extra space was filled with a desk, more cupboards, and a sink area near the door.

Natasha sat down on the sofa and looked around.

The place looked pretty. Loads of pictures were set up on the desk and against the walls, and Natasha looked at them as she waited.

"You found us okay, then?" said Cox. "No problems getting into the base or parking, or what have you?"

"No, ma'am."

Cox sat down on the chair, turning on it to face Natasha.

"You know, we're a small ship's company, and there aren't loads of girls on here, so when it's only us, we do have to be careful, but I'm happy for you to call me Sarah; we all have to be friends, right?"

"Yes, ma'am, I mean, yes, Sarah."

"It's quite different from basic training, isn't it?"

"It is," agreed Natasha.

"Well, you've met Petty Officer Black, and he'll be your line manager. We run quite a relaxed team here, and we all pull together to get the job done. Who else have you met?"

Natasha thought back to the names of the few people she'd spoken to, the quartermaster and the chief in the passageway, but she couldn't remember them with certainty.

"Just a few others. I can't remember their names.' She smiled an apology. "I met the PTI, LPT Coker. He seemed keen to get me involved in sport, and I like running a lot. I'd also like to try out some triathlon."

"Did he indeed?" Cox was smiling, though her eyes seemed to narrow slightly at Coker's name. She looked at Natasha very closely, enough to make Natasha look away. "And did he offer you some one-on-one to improve your fitness?"

Natasha nodded. "Yes, ma'am."

"I thought he might have." She looked Natasha up and down. "But we'll be keeping you way too busy to be mixing with the likes of Mark Coker."

9

Defiance was bigger than any of the ships that Dan had sailed on previously, much bigger, several thousand tons more, and the form factor was different, too. Where traditional ships had a hull and a superstructure with walkways running all around the outside so that sailors could go from the very front to the rear without entering the ship's superstructure, *Defiance* had smooth sides, the hull continuing upward and merging into the external bulkheads.

The shape meant there were few pronounced angles, the form factor being designed to confuse enemy radar, and it made the Royal Navy's new Type 45 destroyer look modern, intimidating, and secretive.

The commanding officer, Commander Ward, was on the flight deck as Dan and John arrived. He waved down at them, then waited, still talking to the sentry and quartermaster as they walked up the long gangway to the ship's flight deck.

Dan saluted before she stepped down onto the deck and looked around.

"Lieutenant Lewis," he said, stepping forward, accepting her salute, and then offering her his hand. "It's good to see you, thank you very much for coming down so quickly."

Dan shook his hand.

He reached out and shook John's hand, a broad smile on his face.

The two men exchanged some words as Dan watched, but she tuned the sound out.

John was smiling, genuine and open, speaking to yet another person who knew him and liked him.

It seemed as though when she and John walked into any setting, they started from different points and needed to follow different routes to get to the same place.

John was always already halfway there, instantly respected. The way he looked, spoke, and acted, the way he held himself, all courted respect and, more than that, demanded that he be taken seriously.

Dan felt she had to earn all of these things time and time again. She looked at the commanding officer now and wondered how much of this greeting might be a former friendship and how much was because Commander Ward was simply seeing someone who looked like him, a form he recognized—a tall, broad man, someone easy to trust and easy to listen to.

Commander Ward was shaking his head now though, his expression turning grave. "I'm really quite worried," he was saying. "And I'm very hopeful it's not your main area of expertise that we're going to be calling on here," he said, referring to Dan's Loss of Life credentials. "But it just doesn't feel right at all. Her bike's still on the jetty, no one saw her go, and we've looked everywhere and phoned everyone we can."

Commander Ward had guided them away from the quartermaster and the armed sentry as he spoke, and they were on the seaward side of the flight deck now, only John and Dan within earshot.

"What bothers me most is that if she wanted to go AWOL," he said, "then why go from here? She could have gone home once we'd piped leave and just not come back in on Monday morning. She's got plenty of leave outstanding, too, so if she needed to get away, she could have. I've actually been pushing quite hard for the ship's company to use up their leave in this next refit period, as we've been deployed a lot and so too much is just being carried over from one leave year into the next."

He looked from John to Dan.

"It's the act of her sneaking out that bothers me. She's young, fairly new to the ship and it just . . ." He looked at Dan with his eyebrows slightly raised, an expectant look on his face as though waiting for her to deliver an answer to the problem.

"Okay, sir," said Dan. "Let me have a chat with the people that saw her last, and we'll see what we can do."

Commander Ward nodded.

"You know, sir," said John, "ninety-nine times out of a hundred, we know how this ends."

Commander Ward nodded. "Yes, John, of course I know you're right. I know she's probably safe and sound somewhere and she'll come back when she's ready."

He started to walk back toward the ship's citadel, gesturing for Dan and John to do the same.

The main hangar door was open, the Merlin helicopter that would usually be put to bed in there long since departed back to the air station at Culdrose for maintenance.

He passed through the hangar and entered the ship using a bulkhead door on the port side, pulling on a large metal lever to open the water-tight door.

The single handle operated multiple thick metal locking bars to let the heavy door to the citadel swing open into the hangar.

He stepped through, holding the door until Dan had her hand on it, and then moved inside the ship's superstructure.

A long walkway ran ahead of her and there were pipes running down the walls and along the deck heads. Firefighting equipment was every-where and the green linoleum flooring was marked with black scuffs from the soles of sailors' protective boots.

The last time Dan had been to sea was on board the submarine HMS *Tenacity*, and the space around her now hammered home how compar-atively cramped and confined that had been. If *Tenacity* had felt close and claustrophobic, then this felt large and eerie, as though there were too many places you could go where no one might find you, or even hear you.

They moved along 1-deck, heading toward the front of the ship to drop down onto 2-deck and the area that housed the officers' cabins.

Commander Ward and John were talking, but Dan struggled to focus on what they were saying. It was her first time on board one of these ships, and she took in all the surroundings. But her mind kept jumping back to the file in her desk, to the fact that if you could hide significant quan-tities of narcotics on a tiny cramped submarine, then who knew what could be done with a vast floating superstructure like this? Surely, the larger the ship, the fewer people would need to know, as there'd be less chance of discovery. That might make it worth it.

On board *Tenacity*, only the Old Man, the submarine's captain, had had his own cabin, and that was small, a fraction of the space afforded to officers and senior rates on *Defiance*.

Dan had seen that many cabins had pictures hanging on the walls and enough desk space for family photographs and trinkets from home. It looked to be a far more humane environment, not the hard function of the submarine, but a place where people might actually want to live.

"SA Moore's divisional officer is the deputy logistics officer," said Commander Ward over his shoulder as they walked along, passing a few more cabin doors. "Lieutenant Sarah Cox. She's been with us for well over a year, almost two in fact, and was here when Moore arrived around four months ago, so she knows her quite well. She's on board at the moment and should be . . ." He paused outside a cabin door.

The door was open just a crack, light coming from inside, and the sound of quiet music.

Commander Ward knocked, waiting to hear a reply before he called out that it was him, and then opened the door fully.

"Here she is. Sarah, please, meet Lieutenant Dan Lewis and Master at Arms John Granger, both from the Special Investigation Branch; they're here to talk about SA Moore."

Sarah Cox stood up, shutting down her laptop screen and killing the music as she did. She nodded a greeting to Commander Ward before she offered her hand to Dan first and then to John, introducing herself as she did.

"Thank you both for coming down," she said, her accent posh in a way that Dan hadn't quite expected, almost faux posh, as though she were teasing someone from a wealthy background.

She was tall, maybe even a full foot taller than Dan, but Sarah was also broad-shouldered, making her look imposing, and she had the air and confidence of someone who'd been raised with money.

There was camera equipment stacked underneath her desk, and on the desk was a large portrait photograph of a man whom Dan felt she recognized; Cox was sketching the picture onto a large pad using charcoals.

There were a lot of completed sketches on the walls, some in pastels and some in pencil, and they were excellent, really excellent.

Dan looked at the picture of the man on the desk again, partially re-created on the sketchpad beneath it. She admired the strokes and shading.

"My father," Cox said, in answer to Dan's lingering look.

Dan nodded and smiled.

"They're all really fantastic," said Dan, looking at Sarah Cox and then at the other pictures. "You're very talented."

"I mainly do family and friends," said Sarah. "I sometimes get asked to sketch or photograph them, sometimes I just do it for practice or fun. This one's for Daddy's birthday."

"Well, you've got a real eye for it."

"I'm a people watcher," admitted Cox with a resigned smile.

"I need to go," said Commander Ward, "but I leave you both in good hands, and John, please call on me before you leave. Just to let me know what you think and what we're going to do."

He made to leave, then turned. "I've kept everyone on board at the moment, though I appreciate days have passed, but I've stopped short of recalling those already gone on leave . . ."

He looked at Dan, the question as to whether he could let his ship's company go home for the night clearly implied.

"I think we can let people go home soon," said Dan, looking at her watch, "but if you could just hold off for a short while, as I'll want to talk to a few of them, people that SA Moore knew best, and anyone who saw her on Friday. Can you let me know the list of names soonest?"

Commander Ward nodded. "Good, that's fine. I think Sarah's already identified who they are. I'll make sure they stay."

The room had one chair next to the desk that Cox had been using and another, a folding chair, resting against the wall.

Sarah pulled it out and offered it to Dan, gesturing to her bed, currently made up as a couch, for John to sit.

"I'll be all right standing," said John, moving into the corner next to the door to give them space.

Sarah sat down and Dan opened the chair and did the same.

"You did well to catch that abuser," said Sarah.

"I'm sorry?"

"I saw the article in the papers. What you did up at that shop in the middle of nowhere. You did really well. The paper said you might have saved the woman's life."

Dan didn't know what to say.

"They said he put her in a fridge, in a shop his parents owned? The place sounds absolutely awful."

"I can't really discuss it," said Dan, "but suffice to say, it's somewhere I'll never go again, physically, or in my memories, if I can help it."

Sarah nodded in understanding.

Dan pointed to another picture of Sarah Cox, standing on the deck of a white-hulled yacht.

"Is that Port Solent?" she asked, changing the subject as she looked at the background and tried to recognize the landmarks.

"It is. I'm keeping the yacht there while I'm Portsmouth based."

"Nice," said John. "On a lieutenant's wage, too? Do you not eat?"

Sarah Cox turned away and flushed crimson. "I do eat, but I guess you already know who my family are?"

Dan raised both eyebrows, surprised at the response.

"I honestly don't," said Dan.

"If you don't, then I'm sure you'd have found out soon enough. Everyone does. My grandfather was the First Sea Lord, and my father made vice."

"Vice Admiral Bobby Cox," said John from behind Dan. "I knew I recognized him from your picture. I knew him when he commanded HMS *Gloucester*. Good man."

Dan looked at the picture on Cox's desk and realized why the man had seemed familiar to her.

Cox looked resigned.

"Yes. They were both great men, everybody says so, all the time."

"Tough footsteps to follow?" asked Dan, thinking about the respect her own father, the retired major "Taz" Lewis, commanded within the Armed Forces, the Royal Marines particularly, and understanding something of the pressures that it could bring.

"You have no idea. I didn't even want to join the navy. I got a first in law from Cambridge, and of course I love art, photography, and cinema.

I wanted to join my uncle's law firm and specialize in privacy law, use that to fund me until I might be able to make some money from the creative arts, but my father and Grandpa were adamant. In the end they bribed me. If I did an eight-year commission in the navy, 'see the world and grow up a bit'"—she made air quotes as she said this—"then they'll support me while I spend two years sailing around the world and building up a portfolio to sell, and after that, if I want to, my uncle will still take me on at the firm."

John whistled. "Sweet deal if you can get it."

"It is," laughed Cox, "and I wish I'd never told a soul. I let it out once, to one person, and the whole fleet knew within about thirty minutes."

"It's always a secret as long as you only tell one person at a time, eh?" said John.

"So the saying goes, Master. But despite what everyone thinks, I seriously doubt anyone would turn down an opportunity like that, and I'm certainly not going to. I know Dad and Grandpa really hoped I'd get bitten by the navy bug and that I'd love it so much I'd never leave. They really thought I would, but in truth, I can't wait to get out. I've less than a year left, and regardless of what either of them says afterward, I'm holding them to their word."

"I don't blame you," said Dan, unable to think about her own future, wondering whether John had been right, whether she'd been bitten by the navy bug, was infected and just didn't know it.

She looked at Cox, thought about how she stood out physically, about the self-deprecation in her confession, about being defined by something beyond your control, about being different from so many of those around you.

"Are you looking for crew?" Dan smiled and turned to look at John. "I reckon I could cope with a few years sailing round the world. I'd be happy to mix your paints and cart easels around to wherever you want them."

Sarah smiled again. "Going solo, I'm afraid, but I'll keep you in mind."

Dan laughed, then sat up a bit in her chair. "So, I understand you saw SA Moore at around ten thirty on Friday, is that right?"

Sarah nodded. "I did, yes. We had a meeting."

"How was she?"

Sarah shrugged and at the same time shook her head, as though she were apologizing in advance for how little she was going to tell them.

"She was fine, really fine. We had a normal divisional meeting," she said. "We spoke about how she was getting on, how the last deployment had gone for her. That kind of thing. Catching up, really."

Dan was still looking around the room, taking in the trinkets and pictures, the expensive-looking photography equipment.

The sheer quantity of photographs and drawings of family, home, and treasured things all made sense to Dan now, seemed obvious: this was the refuge of a woman who was where she didn't want to be, doing something she didn't want to do.

"So she never mentioned anything about being unhappy, stressed about work, about home life . . . ?"

Sarah was already shaking her head. "No, not at all. It was a good meeting, positive. She's a young one, only just eighteen, and so I do chat with her more than I perhaps would with the more experienced sailors. The last deployment was her first since she joined the navy, and she knew we were coming back in for some prolonged maintenance afterward, so she had time before we started deploying again; she was happy enough. And I did ask if anything was going on. She wouldn't have to tell me, of course, but Tasha often did talk to me."

"Tasha being Natasha Moore?"

"Yes, she's called Tasha on board, or just Tash."

Dan looked at Sarah and said nothing.

"I don't call her that in one-to-ones, of course," said Cox, "but we have to get along. There's only thirteen girls on board *Defiance* and so we do have to make it work professionally, and often socially, too."

Dan nodded. She got that, remembered her own situation on board ships well enough to know how isolated you could feel and how much you craved some female company, if you craved company at all.

"You guys are only just back in Portsmouth. Did anything happen on this deployment that might've been a stress raiser for SA Moore?"

Sarah shook her head again. Until this moment, she'd seemed strong and businesslike, but now she suddenly looked teary, as though she might cry. She was silent for a moment as she breathed and recovered herself.

"Were you and Tasha quite close?" asked Dan, deliberately using the girl's nickname.

"Not really," said Sarah after a moment. "I just hate that she was in here a few days ago. We were chatting, ate some biscuits, had a brew. If something was wrong, she could've spoken to me then, couldn't she?"

"She could, but we need to ask some questions, and it seems like you're best placed to answer them."

Dan's eyes met John's and she knew that he would pick up on what she wanted him to do.

This was where he would step in, asking the direct questions, some that might seem insensitive and intrusive. He would do this instead of Dan, leaving her to maintain a relationship with Cox that she might need to draw on later.

"I need to know a little bit about SA Moore," John said immediately. "Was she seeing anyone on board?"

"No, I don't think so. She'd been recently engaged when she joined us, but she ended that a while ago. It wasn't amicable, I don't think, but it seemed to be very much in her past. They did try to be friends, I think, but it didn't work out. I know that Tasha actually had to get a different e-mail address to stop him from contacting her on board."

"That sounds stressful," said Dan.

"It was at the time, but it was a while ago now and we've talked it through many times. It's old news."

"Did she have boyfriends on board?" John asked.

Sarah looked at Dan and then back up at John. "I don't think she was seeing any of the guys. She sometimes worked out with the leading physical training instructor, LPT Mark Coker. They were friends, used to hang around a fair bit."

"And the girls?" asked John.

Sarah frowned.

"I'm not sure exactly what you mean by that," she said.

"We have to ask," said Dan, softening her voice. "There's a number of things that increase risk when we consider a missing person, and sexuality is, unfortunately, even in this day and age, still one of them. Particularly if it's not widely known or the person isn't out."

Sarah nodded. "Okay, well I'm pretty certain that SA Moore was straight, though I wasn't that close to her and I wouldn't ever ask."

John nodded.

"Were you aware of any problems at all? Did she ever talk to you about feeling depressed, or stressed? I don't mean just that day, I mean ever, at any time?"

"She had her moments with her line manager, Petty Officer Black, but don't we all. They work closely together in the stores office, so occasionally there were grumbles, but who doesn't fall out with their boss from time to time?"

"So nothing you'd call significant or recent?" asked Dan.

Sarah seemed to think about this before looking back up, her lips pursed. "No, I don't think so. She was always quite happy and bright. She seemed to like it here, and the ship's company warmed to her quite quickly, so far as I could tell."

"Has she ever been absent from place of duty before?" asked John.

Sarah drew in a deep breath and pursed her lips again. Her eyes dropped away from John and down to her desk.

"Sarah?" said Dan.

Sarah was still not looking at her, and Dan prompted her again.

"Kind of," said Sarah. "Look, I don't want to get her in any more trouble, but we have to look after each other, don't we? There's not many girls on board, and I'm the most senior."

"What happened?" asked Dan.

"Nothing like this, but she didn't show up to work one day. I called her and she didn't answer her phone—well, not straightaway."

Sarah paused.

"And?" said Dan.

"Well, she eventually called me back a few hours later, apologized, and headed back to the ship."

"So what did you do?"

Cox looked sheepish.

"I completed and authorized a leave chit in retrospect," she said, looking away when she saw Dan raise an eyebrow. "People have problems. Sometimes things just happen. If it became a regular thing, taking the piss, then

I'd take action, but it didn't seem worth seeing a young girl who'd just joined the ship go under puns for the sake of a day's leave. Things on board are hard enough, we were due to deploy and I didn't think the commanding officer's first proper meeting with her should be when she was marched into his table to be weighed off."

"Does Commander Ward know?" asked John, his voice grim.

"No."

Dan thought for a moment. "Okay, well, no harm done, but thank you for telling us now."

Sarah looked at Dan, grateful for that response.

"You know I'm going to have to tell your commanding officer, though," said Dan, watching Sarah's eyes drop again in acknowledgment. "He'll need to know. It's important."

Sarah's shoulders drooped, but she seemed to accept it, looked as though she'd known when she'd confessed that this would be the case.

"So, Sarah." John's voice had also softened. "Talk us through all you know that happened on Friday. Do it in chronological order if you can. I need to know her movements, as you understand them, and I need to know who else you think we should be talking to. Who saw her? Who knew her? Who were her friends?"

10

Natasha had headed to the ship early. She wanted to drop her stuff on her bunk and maybe check in with Beverly Shott and Sam Derbyshire, two of the girls who shared her cabin, before they went off to work for the day.

They both worked in the Marine Engineering Department, and so she wouldn't see them until at least lunch and maybe not then.

She wanted to see what the plans were for the night, and she knew if she went down to the stores office, Gary Black would have her down there talking for hours and she'd never get away from him ever again, would never see another human being until the end of time, or the end of the day at the very least.

Sometimes, when she was trapped down there listening to him talking and telling stories, the end of time and the end of the shift could feel very similar.

Jason carpooled again that morning and now Natasha couldn't shake the feeling she had about "Susi."

She didn't do jealousy, it wasn't her thing, but she felt like she knew the girl because Jason talked about her so bloody much. At first it hadn't bothered Natasha. She was making new friends, so why shouldn't he? It also crossed her mind that it might be worse if he never mentioned her, like there was some secret to be hidden, but it'd worn a little thin this last day or so and the fact that it was still on her mind now proved it was becoming a problem.

Her mum and her various stepdads had spent their whole lives lying to each other, cheating on each other, scoring points and knocking lumps off each other every Friday and Saturday night.

Natasha remembered her and her sister standing between them as kids, still in their nightdresses, crying and trying to hold their parents apart as the screaming and shouting raged back and forth like mortar shells flying overhead. She'd be damned if she'd let her life go that way. She looked down at her phone, which had a tiny bit of signal, and sent a quick text.

> Can't wait to be home in bed with you tomorrow night xx I'll make sure you'll be glad to have me home too ;-) xx

She watched it send and then pocketed her phone and walked into the ship, dropping down to 3-deck and heading for her cabin. She checked her watch, had loads of time, and climbed back up the steel ladder to head for the junior rates' mess.

The mess was a large area, three large areas, actually, all joined together, but with dividers that could be dragged across if needed. It was shared by all the junior rates on board, and she knew that Bev and Sam sometimes went in there after they'd had breakfast to grab a coffee.

She walked along 2-deck, humming to herself and checking her phone when she thought it vibrated in her pocket. It hadn't, and she popped it back in.

As she approached the mess she could hear voices, more of them and louder than she'd heard before, but then a lot of people were staying on board tonight, so it made sense that a lot of people would've come in early to drop off gear before the daily routine really got going. She was sure her phone buzzed again, sure she felt it vibrate in her pocket, and she stopped to dig it out again. This time it had, she must have picked up a tiny bar of signal, and there was a text from Jason, his name displayed on the screen. She unlocked the phone to read it.

"It'll be tonight, I'm telling you," came a loud voice from the mess. "My money's on tonight for sure."

Natasha smiled as she heard laughter, fumbling to read the text quickly so she could go and join in.

"Mate, she's not the sort. I'm telling you. It'll take way longer."

Natasha read the text—Jason loved her too—and walked into the junior rates' mess.

The noise carried on for a few more seconds, then stopped as people saw her.

"What?" she asked, frowning at them.

No one answered.

"What's up?" she asked, starting to worry.

"Totes awks," said someone she couldn't see.

She looked around.

Bev and Sam were sitting together on the long green-cushioned bench seats that ran around the perimeter of the mess. They were smiling, but awkwardly, Bev not quite looking at her, but Sam having no problem meeting her eye.

She looked to her right, where a noticeboard hung full to the brim with papers and flyers. One of the other marine engineers was standing there.

He was looking sheepish, a pen in his hand, his eyes flitting around the room; he'd been caught doing something that he knew he shouldn't.

Natasha walked over to him and looked at what he was doing.

On the noticeboard was a piece of A4 paper with a table printed on it. The title at the top of the page was TASHA'S PASH and the table was broken down into three columns. The first was a date, starting with today, the next column was headed THE PASH, and the third was a selection: HJ/BJ/HWS/BW—BONUS RW.

Natasha grabbed the piece of paper off the board and looked at it.

"You're betting on when I'll do the dirty on my fiancé?" she asked, to no one in particular.

"It's just a joke," said Sam. "We do it when all new girls come on board all loved-up and getting married."

"How much is it for me to take 'never,'" asked Natasha, crumpling the paper up. "You lot are idiots."

There was silence, but murmurs started again when instead of storming out, she walked over and sat down next to Bev.

"It's just a daft joke," said Bev, as soon as Natasha sat.

"Yeah, well, Jason wouldn't laugh if he found out," Natasha said. "He's really pissy about me staying out tonight."

"I thought you said he was shagging some bird from the hotel he's working at," said Sam.

Natasha let her jaw drop.

"I did not say that," she said, and slapped Sam gently on the leg. "Bitch."

They laughed together.

"You know," whispered Natasha, looking around to make sure no one else was paying attention to them, "I don't even know what all that stuff on the form stands for. It looks like the letters written on the side of pencils."

Bev chuckled and leaned forward, as did Sam. They were the only three girls in the mess, and someone shouted, "The coven convenes!" from behind them, but they paid no attention to whoever it was.

"Well," began Bev. "It goes: HJ/BJ/HWS/BW, which is, hand job, blow job, hot-willy sex, brown wings, and the bonus was the red wings."

Natasha sat back from them both, recoiling.

"That is really gross."

"It is a bit," agreed Bev, "but these morons think it's funny."

She gestured to the male sailors around them.

"Really?" said Sam, looking at Natasha closely. "We got them to leave off the green wings because you didn't strike us as the sexually transmitted disease type."

"Thank you, I think," said Natasha.

"It's just sex," said Sam. "You're engaged; don't tell me he's never needed some home comfort while the red flag's flying?"

Natasha felt herself flush.

"No," she said, trying to laugh it off and now wishing she was anywhere else but here.

"Really?" pushed Sam. "You've never thrown a dark-colored towel on the bed and just gone for it?"

"Oh my god, Samantha Derbyshire," said Natasha, her mouth open again in not-so-mock shock. "No, we have not done that."

Sam was watching her closely and it made Natasha blush more and look away toward the door.

"Tash," said Sam, hushing Bev, who'd made to speak. "Have you and your fella done, you know, anything?"

Natasha looked around the room, alarmed, but no one was paying any attention at all to what they were saying. She looked back.

"We've done . . ." she paused. "Stuff."

"Stuff?" said Sam and Bev in unison.

They were both leaning in closer now, hanging on Natasha's every word.

"Oh my god," said Natasha again. "Yes, stuff. Things."

"Like?"

"Like, none of your business, stuff," said Natasha.

"Like hide the sausage stuff?" asked Sam.

Natasha's eyes were wide open, she could feel it, and she knew her face and chest would be flushed red.

"No. Not that stuff," she said quietly, looking away from them both. "Other stuff that keeps us both happy."

Sam laughed and Bev followed suit. It didn't sound like a horrible laugh and Natasha relaxed her shoulders and leaned into the group again.

"You two are awful," she said. "Honestly."

Sam was laughing a bit louder now and wiped a tear from her eye.

"Look, chick, you're going to have to help me out here, because I'm trying to figure out how you're going to stop your fella from shagging this slapper from the hotel by giving him the occasional hand job."

Natasha stopped herself from saying "Oh my god" again and tilted her head at Sam, as though she was telling her off.

"I do other stuff, too, and he's happy enough."

She watched Sam laugh again, felt irritated at how Bev seemed to not be finding it funny, but was laughing anyway.

"But are *you* happy enough?" said Sam, her voice rising.

"Shhh," said Natasha. "It's no one's business but mine."

"Ours," said Sam.

"Sam!" said Natasha.

"Don't worry, I won't tell anyone," Sam said, smiling and crossing her fingers. "I promise."

"Sam!"

"Kidding, Tash, kidding. We girls have to stick together. Your secret's safe with me."

Sam pretended to lock her mouth shut and tossed the imaginary key over her shoulder.

There was a loud knock at the door and the three of them turned.

Chief "Polly" Pollack was at the door and regarded each of the girls in turn.

"Bloody hell," he said, his voice loud and the mess silent. "Where's the Big Bad Wolf?" He waited as the other sailors looked at the three girls on the bench and then laughed.

"Right, come on, you two," he said, pointing to Bev and Sam. "I need my two little piggies down in the engine rooms early. I'm afraid gossip'll have to wait."

Sam and Bev stood up and walked quickly to the door.

"And you, young lady." He pointed at Natasha. "Blacky was looking for you. I can only assume he needs a cup of tea, so off you pop and get him one."

He turned and left, Natasha's two friends falling in behind him, both looking back at Natasha with a smile and a wink.

11

Dan and John left Sarah Cox in her cabin and walked back along the route they'd previously taken.

It was quiet now, the commanding officer having piped leave for the majority of the ship's company, meaning the passageways were clear and there was little noise from running machinery and equipment.

As the ship emptied, it felt eerie and vast.

John stepped into an empty cabin and Dan followed.

The cupboard doors inside the compartment were still wide open, likely from the search earlier in the day, and the bedding and mattress had been thrown back and not remade.

Dan took a deep breath that she blew out with some force.

"Well," she began. "What do you think?"

"I agree with Commander Ward and Lieutenant Cox," he said. "It's odd that she went like she did and that she didn't peg out, and no one recalls her leaving and such like, but at the same time, it doesn't change anything. You saw the state of the jetty when we arrived. There's equipment and personnel going on and off this ship all the time, she could easily have been missed, particularly if, for whatever reason, she wanted to be."

"CCTV will confirm that, though," said Dan.

John nodded his agreement.

"I don't want to sound like the manual," said John, looking at his watch, "but we have a happy, bright, non-drug-using, straight, eighteen-year-old girl, with no known hang-ups or problems, who was fine at ten thirty on Friday, and who's jumped ship without notification in the past . . ."

John let the words hang out there.

"There's nothing at all to indicate a raised risk profile," agreed Dan.

"No, there isn't," said John. "Chances are high that she'll show up tomorrow, go to the commanding officer's table for absence, get weighed off, and get fined. She'll be back on board and working in the stores by the weekend. The money that'll be missing from her bank account will be the only thing reminding her of it all."

Dan nodded. "You know, I agree, but there's something that bothers me about this scenario. I can't shake it. If you do get a call from home, or whatever, and you know your divisional officer covered for you before, then why not just go back again and tell her?"

John was nodding.

"Cox strikes me as a bit of a soft touch. I don't want to judge her on her round-the-world boat trip from Daddy, hell, I'd do it if I could." John paused. "But I really don't think she's bought into the navy culture, do you think?"

Dan shook her head.

"No, she hasn't, but then has the navy bought into her?"

"What?" John frowned.

"Never mind," said Dan. "I'm not sure you'd get it anyway, but she's an outsider, the rich admiral's daughter, remember? She might not have bought into the navy, but I don't imagine the navy's been easy for her, either."

John made to reply, twice opening his mouth and then saying nothing.

"Forget it," said Dan. "I'm just saying that I think she'd have let Moore go, in fact, given that Moore has a good amount of leave still to take, I can't see why anyone wouldn't. Natasha Moore had a soft-touch boss who's not a stickler for enforcing the navy's will and who'd covered for her before. So why not turn there? And if it's an emergency, why not take your bike home? She could've cycled home in the time it'd take her to walk across the dockyard and get a taxi. I just don't know. The ex-fiancé bothers me, too. You said he seemed straight-up and worried, but Cox says it wasn't a peaceable falling-out. It's one of those things where lots of tiny bits don't feel right."

"I know," he said. "Well, why don't you go on and speak to the ex-fiancé? I'll wander around here and see if there's anyone worth a chat. We can swap notes in the morning. I'll talk to the section petty officer and then to the trots, or whatever the skimmers call their sentries. I'll also get Josie to sit at the office and check through some of the CCTV to see if we can spot her leaving. Then we can see what tomorrow brings."

"Okay, let's do that," said Dan.

12

"I feel really odd."

Natasha looked over her shoulder again, scanning the streets behind them.

"Tash, relax," said Sam, giggling and waving to a large group of lads who were walking parallel to them across the other side of the road. "Hellooo, boys," she shouted, waving and then bowing to their applause and whistles.

Natasha looked away.

"Doesn't that bother you?" she asked.

"No," scoffed Sam, looking to Bev for support. "I just spent hours making myself look this good. Least I can do is get a little appreciation."

Natasha shook her head and looked to Bev, who just turned away from her, as she always did when the other option was to challenge Sam.

"Wait until we get to Joanna's," said Sam, still grinning at one of the boys across the road.

"You ever been to the Royal Naval School of Dance before?" asked Bev, speaking for what seemed like the first time in ages.

Natasha shook her head; she'd never been, but she'd heard of it.

"Carpets that make your feet stick to the floors?" Natasha asked. "A half-hour slot for ska and dance music so that all the blokes grab each other and jump up and down until fights start?"

"Sounds like you've been properly briefed, if nothing else," said Sam. "If never fully debriefed."

Sam and Bev looked at each other and then burst out laughing. They'd drunk a fair bit more than Natasha had; she wasn't much of a drinker at all, really. They'd stayed behind when the ship's company crowd had moved on from the last bar, chatting to some young guys they'd met near the Guildhall walk. They'd decided the guys weren't right for them, before downing their drinks in one go and leaving to try and catch up with *Defiance*'s ship's company. They were getting louder by the minute as they led Natasha to the next pub on the crawl.

Sam had toppled over once already, her skirt riding up and three young lads shouting, "Aye, aye!" as soon as it had.

Natasha had offered to walk behind her until they got to the next pub, but Sam didn't seem to care and flipped the boys the finger before carrying on her way.

"Joanna's is . . ." Sam paused, sucking her teeth as she looked at Natasha. "Not a bad place to get yourself laid, you know."

Sam and Bev fell about laughing again, and Natasha walked on, ignoring them.

"I'm just saying," continued Sam, "if you wanted to try some hot sausage and never see the guy again, then you could do a lot worse than there. Just make sure you bag up."

"Twice," added Bev, immediately looking at Sam and then laughing again.

Natasha walked on. "I'm fine, honestly. Thank you."

She was walking slightly behind the other two now and was relieved when they turned a corner and caught sight of some familiar faces gathered on the pavement outside another pub. Mark Coker was among them, and he smiled as soon as he saw her.

"Back in a mo," said Natasha, not waiting for an answer and heading straight for him. "Hey, you okay?"

He smiled.

"Yeah. You don't half scrub up well," he said as he approached.

His hair looked wet from the shower and he had a red graze across his cheek.

She waited till he was close enough and punched him on the chest.

"Don't be sassing me, Coker, or I'll give you another bruise to match that one," she said, brandishing a fist at him.

He laughed and held up his hands in surrender.

"Surprised you'd have the energy for a fight. You were struggling to keep up on the run at lunchtime."

Natasha turned to Sam and Bev, who'd caught up with her, her mouth dropping open as she made eye contact. "He. Is. Lying," she said. "I whooped him like a naughty puppy and his excuse was"—she pulled a face and made her voice go high-pitched like a whining child's—"'I have to take it easy, because I have rugby training tonight.' Honestly, it was embarrassing."

"I did have rugby training. And you never whooped me, although, if there's a whooping to be had . . ." He moved closer and put his hands on Natasha's waist.

"Get. Off," she said, jerking away from him, but still smiling.

"Looks like Tasha might have found a new squeeze after all, Bev," said Sam, a group starting to form around her.

"Hardly," said Natasha.

Natasha watched as Sam and Mark Coker eyeballed each other. She looked at Bev, who rolled her eyes and looked away.

"Come on, Bev, let's go," said Sam, and she stalked off into the crowd without looking back.

Bev trailed off behind her, only briefly glancing back to smile at Natasha.

Natasha looked at Mark Coker, eyebrows raised, waiting.

"Bit too long a story for tonight. I could fill you in on our next run, if you like, but it's way duller than I bet you're thinking."

Natasha shook her head. "I don't want to know," she said, then craned her neck to look in the direction that Sam and Bev had taken.

She turned back to look at Mark just as something flashed past her eye.

His face changed in an instant and it took her a second to understand what was happening. He seemed to be smiling at her one moment and then she lost focus.

It was getting dark and the artificial light wasn't great out here on the street, but Mark's cheek was obscured for just a second before it exploded into a fountain of red. Before she knew it, Mark's whole chin and chest where seeping with the same glistening color.

He looked dazed, wobbled a bit as he blinked, then staggered back a few paces.

A swell of people surrounded her.

Natasha heard shouting—"Someone's glassed Cokes!"—and then there was fighting all around her and she was knocked to the ground. She was narrowly missed by a glass herself as it smashed on the pavement next to her, and she crawled away from the legs all around her like a child lost in a thick forest of adults.

She looked at her hand, it was bleeding, a small splinter of glass jutting out of it, picked up from crawling on the pavement. Her vision wavered and then she heard someone talking to her.

"Come on, get up."

She looked up and saw a face she recognized.

"Come on, Nat. Get up."

Hands grabbed her under her armpits and she was picked up like a toddler and carried out of the melee before being placed on her feet.

There was still fighting outside the pub. The number of people seemed to have tripled and the noise was deafening as sailors, locals, and door staff clashed and shouted.

She was being dragged away now, a firm grip on her wrist guiding her away from the noise.

"You okay?"

She looked up at Gary Black and nodded.

He moved around behind her, putting his huge body between her and the trouble, and walked her farther away.

"It's just a little cut, I think," said Natasha, looking back over her shoulder, hoping she might see Mark Coker and know he was being helped.

Black looked down at Natasha's hand. His eyes went wide.

"You're hurt," he said, squinting down at the glass. "You're not supposed to be hurt."

He scanned behind them and then turned back to Natasha.

"I think I'll be okay," she said.

"You'll need stitches in that."

He was holding her hand out, twisting it slightly, and Natasha winced.

"You're hurting my arm," she said.

His eyes met hers as he twisted it just a fraction more, seeming to take a moment to understand what she'd said before he let her go.

"I didn't mean to," he said. "I'll get us a taxi and we can go to the sick bay and get this stitched up."

"Honestly, I just want to go home, but thank you."

Gary Black was shaking his head and fumbling in his pocket as he looked around.

"What are you looking for?" said Natasha, blurting the words out, annoyed at the way he was acting.

"Nothing."

"I need to find Mark before I go anywhere," said Natasha, still peeved. "He looked like he was in a bad way. He didn't get glassed—well, he did, but someone threw the glass. I saw it."

"You saw who threw it?" asked Black, watching her closely.

"No. I saw it hit him in the face. It looked really bad."

Black was dialing a number on his mobile phone now.

Natasha listened as Black told the operator where they were and where they were going.

He was taking her back to the sick bay at HMS *Nelson*, probably to get a few stitches.

The cold was starting to catch up with her and her hand was throbbing. The pain felt as though it had always been there, but she was only just noticing it, and as she did, it grew in intensity.

She shivered, clutching her arms around herself and turning quickly. She had a feeling, a tingle down her spine as though someone was watching her. She looked all around.

There were still a lot of people behind her. Sailors milling about, some police cars that had turned up, and bouncers standing on the pavement ready for more action. Some of them looked as though they might start some if nothing exciting was forthcoming soon.

Aside from Gary Black, no one seemed to be paying any attention to Natasha at all.

She scanned the scene again, glancing back to a pub doorway where she could have sworn she saw someone step back out of sight.

"Anyway," said Black, as he dropped his phone back into his pocket, "there's a lot of people who would think Mark Coker deserves anything he gets."

13

"Can I help you?" Dan asked to the man's back.

He turned slowly, calm, unbothered at being questioned.

"Oh, hi. No, I'm okay, thanks. Well, actually, yes, you probably could help me. I'm looking for Mountbatten Close? There's a house for sale. I'm thinking about viewing it, and I thought it was here, but, as you can see, it's not."

Dan looked at him.

He had current, or former, military written all over him. The way he stood, the way his hair was cut and his neck was shaved. The way he looked, confident and sure, and the way he spoke; friendly, but clipped and businesslike. There was no doubt in Dan's mind that civilians often possessed these traits, too, but there was something in the way that they combined in someone with military experience and training that just stood out if you knew what to look for.

"You're one street too early," said Dan, returning his smile. "Mountbatten's identical to this, but one street over."

She pointed over the top of her own house.

He looked behind himself, at Dan's house, as though he might be able to see through the terrace to where she was directing him.

"Oh, great, thanks," he said, moving up the small hill toward the road.

"The signs for all these small closes get lost in the bushes," said Dan, pointing to the thick greenery where the street name for her close should be. "But it literally backs onto these houses, so it'll be easy to find."

"Well, excellent," he said, stepping toward Dan and extending his hand. "Maybe we'll be garden neighbors?"

"Maybe we will," said Dan, shaking his hand.

She watched him leave and couldn't help but vividly imagine what Felicity's expression would be now.

Her friend would almost certainly have raised eyebrows, wide eyes, a gleam in her eye, and a broad smile on her face. She'd very likely be mouthing "Handsome" as the man walked away.

Dan headed straight to her front door. She shut it quickly behind her and went to the kitchen window to check that he was gone. She pulled her phone from her pocket and searched houses for sale in her area. Sure enough, she found an end of terrace in Mountbatten Close for sale, just as the man had said.

She watched the small parking lot outside for a while, knowing she was just spooked but feeling that to dismiss her instincts so easily would be a mistake.

The last time she'd been here, looking out the window for something that wasn't there, she'd ended up on the phone to Josie, asking her for a favor, asking her to check where Aaron Coles was.

He was at sea, redeployed onto HMS *Torbay* and gone for several more months; still she'd watched and waited for an hour or so, the lights off, peering out from the darkness of her kitchen to the darkness of the world, until fatigue had forced her to bed.

There was nothing there, no one watching, and the man was simply on the wrong street.

She felt herself relax and flicked the kettle on before she wandered upstairs to her room.

The lady on reception at the hotel where Jason, Natasha Moore's former fiancé, worked had been helpful, but she hadn't known where Jason was.

Dan had left her card and asked for him to call her, talked the woman into giving her his home address, and left another card there when the small flat had been empty. She'd hoped for a callback soon but suspected it'd be morning now before she heard.

Her phone rang and she snatched at it, wondering if she might be able to speak to Natasha's former fiancé tonight after all, but it was her dad again.

"Be honest with me," she said, without any other greeting. "And I mean super honest. Do you set an alarm to remind you to call me?"

There was silence for a moment.

"Well, yes, but not to remind me to call—to remind me not to call too often."

Dan chuckled.

"Then you set it wrong, because I'm in-date for Dad calls from yesterday."

"I just wanted to remind you to call your sister back," he said, ignoring her teasing. "Don't tell her I rang, and she's out for dinner tonight now, but call her tomorrow, okay?"

"Is something wrong?"

"No, not at all. I think she just gets bored being the one who always has to deal with me."

"Hey," protested Dan. "When the time comes, I'll pay my share of your old folks home."

"Bet you don't do your share of the visiting," he said.

"I will," said Dan. "I'll come and sit and listen to your stories, but I'll secretly nap, and you'll be too old to notice."

He laughed at that, and the sound made Dan smile; he had an infectious laugh, loud and honest. He'd have slapped her shoulder if he could've reached it.

"You used to try that when you were little," he said. "You'd hear me coming upstairs and switch off your flashlight and hide your book, then pretend to be asleep when I came in to check on you."

"You didn't know," said Dan. "You're just guessing."

He laughed again.

"Believe it or not, Danny-bear, I've known you and your sister all your lives. I remember when all you wanted to be when you grew up was a boy. And I can tell without fail when you're lying to me, when you're pretending to be asleep, when you and Charlie are rolling your eyes behind my back . . ."

Now Dan laughed.

"We don't do that, Dad. We wouldn't, not to you!"

"Yeah, right," he said.

"I have to go, Dad," said Dan, glad of the distraction he'd brought.

"You always do," he said gently.

"I'll call Charlie tomorrow, and I'll call you next time, okay?"

"Okay," he said.

They said their good-byes and Dan sat down on her bed and then stood up again, hearing the kettle boil and switch itself off downstairs. She remained in her room.

Her sister would soon be facing several months alone while her husband, Liam, deployed with the marines. Dan thought about how cheerful Charlie was at the moment, even as the time for his leaving approached. Dan wondered if she'd be able to be that positive if her partner was leaving for so long; though she also wondered if she'd ever be able to have someone in her life who meant as much to her as Charlie and Liam did to each other. She moved to the window and looked across her garden at the back of Mountbatten Close, then went back to her bed and kicked off her shoes. She let herself slump onto the floor and instinctively pulled the lockbox from beneath her bed. She hesitated, not sure why she wanted to look at it tonight, then set the combination and opened the lid.

She looked at the picture on top for the first time in a long time. She'd become used to palming it out and flipping it facedown as soon as she opened the lid, hiding it from view so she wouldn't have to deal with the guilt that it spawned, then putting it back on top so that she'd never forget what had happened, as if that was possible. Now she let her eyes scan over the image and down the words before she set it aside, faceup; she was proud that she was able to look at it today.

Tucked to the side was the letter her father had given her a few months before, still unopened, though she had no idea why.

There'd been something in the way it'd been delivered, passed to her by Roger, by hand, that meant that Dan knew it was important and would know when to open it. Now so much time had passed that she didn't open it for fear it was something so important that it shouldn't have been ignored, or maybe too mundane, something that should have been dealt with long ago but had now changed and become more complicated.

She'd spoken to her dad many times since she'd received the letter and he'd never once mentioned it.

The envelope felt cool in her hand; it was plain, boring, and functional, everything her father wasn't.

She set it aside and looked at her files.

The *Tenacity* files were on top—she'd been looking at those last—and she flicked through them again now, looking at notes and pictures, names and theories. Ideas as to where Ryan Taylor might have gone since he went missing after the *Tenacity* investigation ended.

He'd hold the key to understanding what had happened on board *Tenacity*. He'd have some information about the quantities of narcotics that were being brought in and where they went. When and how the sailors passed it along and how they were paid for their efforts. If he could be found.

She dug in her lockbox again, to the files and laptop a few layers down.

There were years of files generated from investigating Hamilton, and Dan wondered how she'd end up as the years passed by. Would she one day come home to the house and have a huge filing cabinet of all the different cases and investigations that she couldn't let go of? Maybe she'd work away into her old age, poking into crimes that only she cared about, unable to move on and not totally sure why.

The files on *Tenacity* covered those that were about Hamilton, and Dan was glad. Some of the images toward the bottom of the box were hard to look at, but they also tempted back more vivid ones, ones that were locked away inside Dan's mind.

"Not tonight," Dan said out loud. She put the files back, locked the box, and pushed it under the bed.

She'd read a book tonight. That might clear her mind, stop her from dreaming about crimes and wrongdoing, stop her from dreaming about Christopher Hamilton and all the terrible things he'd done.

14

Dan Lewis—Early September
(ten years before)

"Roger," Dan said, still whispering and ducking down behind her car.

"Where the hell are you?" said Roger, not bothering with a greeting. "Four more members of Carson's old troop are missing and you've gone swanning off. Is Chris with you?"

"We've got them. Chris found them. I don't know how, but he did. We're up near Aldershot at the British Army Storage Compound on the outskirts of town. I've had visual on three of the missing persons, all alive. Chris is in there now keeping watch. We've not spotted Carson yet, but it looks like they've had it rough. We need armed response and you need to come in quiet. If he hears you there'll be a bloodbath; he'll slaughter them all."

Blackett was silent for a moment and Dan knew he'd be making notes, gesturing for people to gather around him and be ready for instruction.

"Get Chris and get out of there. We're inbound, but armed response is at least twenty minutes away."

Dan could hear him running now, heard him take the phone away from his mouth as he barked orders and demanded that the armed response team be connected immediately.

"Roger, we can't let the military response know. If they get here, he's dead."

"We're inbound. It's the civilian police I've called in, now get out and prevent entry until we get there," barked Roger.

Dan heard him muffle the phone, probably a hand over the mouthpiece, as he spoke to someone else.

"Did you hear what I said?" he asked, when he came back to her.

"Get Chris and get out," repeated Dan. "Got it. I'm in the lay-by on the north side, you'll see our cars as you take the first turning before the main compound entrance."

"Get Chris and get out," Blackett said again. "And keep your phone near you."

The line went dead and Dan leaned back against the car.

It was a nice day here, out in the open, and it jarred against the cold shadows that lay trapped between the high storage buildings she'd walked around with her partner, Chris Hamilton. She looked at her phone, checked that it was switched to silent, and reached into her car, collecting two heavy navy-police-issue telescopic batons. She tucked one into her pocket and kept the other in her hand as she headed back into the compound.

Dan retraced her steps as she made her way back to where she'd left Chris. She had to look down the alley between the two storage units twice, and then check through the window she'd found him looking through, before she was sure she was in the right place.

Chris wasn't there.

She looked through the window again, recognizing the broken segment of glass from before, and peered between the machinery; she could see the men, kneeling, bound, bloodied; she was in the right place.

She turned and crouched, her back against the wall, and before she could even curse, she looked up to see Matt Carson, who towered above her, a Browning 9 mm pistol in one large hand. It was pointed directly at her face.

"Up," he said.

Dan didn't move.

"Up, now," he said, his eyes on her, hard, but blinking, repeatedly blinking.

He stood straight, broad, not so much confidence as outright challenge in his posture; a fighter gone bad. He was dressed in full combats and had an SA-80 rifle slung across his chest. His face was pale between the stripes of green camouflage cream, and his eyes never stayed still, never locked onto her, as they repeatedly ducked behind his eyelids, pointing somewhere else when they resurfaced.

Dan still didn't move as her mind worked through all the different ways she might handle this, but Carson didn't wait.

He grabbed her with his free hand, gripping her navy blue coat around the shoulder and digging in hard against her collarbone, as he easily heaved her to her feet.

Dan winced as his fingers dug in deep and then again as he released her and pushed her back against the wall.

"Give that to me," he said, pointing at the baton.

Dan did.

"Phone," he said.

Dan dug into her pocket and passed it to him, watching as he dropped it into a pocket on the thigh of his combat trousers.

"Turn that way." He pointed along the side of the unit. "Walk."

Dan hesitated and made to speak, but his hand whipped out more quickly than she could have thought possible.

He was wearing black leather gloves and the whole flat palm of his left hand slapped her cheek, rocking her brain inside her skull and making her knees almost give way beneath her. Her head swam, lights flashing, her eyes opening and closing as she tried to regain her senses.

"Walk," he said. "That way."

Dan staggered, used the wall to steady herself, and stumbled along in front of him, waves of nausea ebbing and flowing as her head slowly cleared. She could hear his footsteps behind her but was unsure whether the faint echo was the sound vibrating off the brick walls or vibrating in her head.

"Others are on the way, Matt. My partner has already gone to call for help," she said, immediately stumbling forward and falling onto all fours as a blow to the back of her head knocked her to the ground.

"Get up and don't talk, just walk," he said, and she felt the hand on the scruff of her neck again, pulling her jacket tight against her neck and choking her as he dragged her to her feet.

They walked between the two units for another ten or so meters before the light began to change, brightening as they stepped out of the shadows and into an intersection, a crossroads where the corners of four identical units met.

The road that ran across Dan's path was big, wide enough for two trucks to pass each other and for armored vehicles and tanks to be stored or collected.

"Go right," he said.

Dan hesitated, only then realizing how disoriented she was. She heard him move, flinched, and brought her hands up to cover her head, but he didn't strike her, just grabbed her and pushed her in the right direction.

They walked down the wide road and he stopped her outside a huge hangar door that covered the whole front of a unit.

Set into the door was a smaller entrance.

"Open it," he said, throwing a set of keys onto the ground.

Dan picked them up, almost toppling as she did, and then fumbled at the lock, unlocked the door, and pushed it open.

"In," he said.

She stepped inside the storage unit.

It seemed to go on forever and there were crates and boxes stacked in huge piles and, next to them, the green metal panels of Land Rovers and armored personnel carriers.

"Put the keys on that box," he said, tapping a rough wooden pallet and then stepping away from it.

Dan did as she was told. Then she turned to face him, trying to make eye contact, to connect with him, this man who they now believed had killed seven men from his initial entry troop, the group of soldiers that had joined up with him at the Guard Depot in Pirbright many years before.

"Turn away," he said, raising the gun again.

Dan didn't. She looked at him.

"These men aren't responsible for what happened to you," she said.

He raised the gun until it was leveled at her forehead.

"You're responsible for your life, and you're responsible for the seven other lives you took."

He stepped forward, and Dan closed her eyes tight as she felt the cold metal barrel push against her skull.

"Stop talking!" he shouted. Dan's head jerked back as the pistol pressed harder against her with each syllable.

Dan kept her eyes closed.

"I don't believe you meant to kill Victoria, though," she said, hearing her voice shake. "I really don't believe you meant to do that."

"Shut up. Shut up. Shut up!"

Dan felt the barrel pull away and relaxed her eyes, though they remained closed.

A ripping, tearing sound echoed around the open space.

Dan opened her eyes and saw him advancing toward her, a strip of thick brown packing tape held out in front of him.

"I won't speak again," she said.

"I know."

He pushed the tape hard against her face, the edges of it touching her hair.

Her head rattled around as he did it, his hands slapping her skin as he smoothed the tape down.

"Don't move," he said, and went to lock the door.

He turned back and pointed at her.

"Over there."

Dan turned, but not quickly enough, and he pushed her again, making her stumble deeper into the storage unit.

They walked, the barrel of his gun occasionally touching the small of her back as he urged her along.

Dan looked around as best she could.

There were few entrances, the ones that there were, metal and heavy, easily locked or booby-trapped. Any team that tried to breach the doors could be taken down before Carson was neutralized. At the very least he'd have time to kill his three or four hostages; this situation had the makings of a massacre, and Dan was now in the center of it.

She wondered where Chris was, and how long it would be before help arrived.

As she passed some equipment, her eyes widened. Kneeling off to the right in a neat semicircle were eleven naked men. She could see that each was held in place by multiple bonds, their ankles zip-tied together, the thick plastic biting into their skin, their arms bound by what looked like wire behind their heads, and more thin rope that ran from their necks to their ankles keeping them arched back and kneeling upright, preventing them from even daring to lean forward. All of them were dirty and bruised, blood seeping from their bonds, their faces swollen and grazed.

Dan had to look again, count them again.

There were supposed to be four, four missing men, the last four that made up Carson's entry troop. How could they have been so wrong?

He pushed her so hard that she fell forward onto the floor.

Then he was on her, his knee on her back, pulling her arms behind her so hard that she was sure he'd dislocate one of her shoulders.

She tried to cry out but the tape stuck tight and she began to struggle for breath. She looked around, her eyes wide, and then she saw him.

Chris was leaning back against a wooden box, blood running down from his temple, his hands out of sight behind him. He looked completely still, his eyes shut, his body crumpled in a way that looked lifeless and limp.

Dan felt tears well up in her eyes as she saw her partner slumped and still. She looked for any sign of life, anything to tell her that Chris Hamilton, her partner, friend, and mentor, wasn't Carson's ninth victim.

15

"Don't expect too much," said Felicity, leading Dan into a small, plain observation room in a secure area of Broadmoor Hospital.

The color of the paint, the smell of the corridors, the architecture and décor, a mix of original Victorian and redeveloped modern that already looked worn, all added to Dan's deep-seated feeling that she was somewhere she didn't want to be.

"His solicitor's been very tight on the agreement to speak, so we'll have video feed to ensure you're safe, but we won't have audio. It's all we could get, and we won't know what's said until we debrief you afterward. It also means anything he says will be your word against his, but it's a start, and you're the first person he's ever agreed to speak with."

"He didn't agree. He asked," said Dan.

Felicity stopped and looked at Dan. She looked worried, a bit tired, had seemed uncomfortable since Dan had agreed to do this.

Dan was sure Felicity hated asking for this, hated herself for being the messenger, but she was right, if Hamilton was willing to start talking, then someone needed to take that opportunity.

"You're right, he did ask," said Felicity after a pause. "And we don't know what he might say, probably very little at first, these things tend to build slowly. We also don't fully understand his . . ." Felicity paused. "Obsession with you?" she offered. "I don't think that's the right word, but there's something more there and it makes me uncomfortable."

"He gets his solicitor to write to me, but that's it, really; hardly an obsession."

Felicity looked down at the floor and seemed to think about that before she looked back up at Dan.

"I said it wasn't the right word, but he's got some kind of fixation on you, so don't feel the need to push anything, just see what he says and get a feel for him. This conversation happening at all is already a great outcome. When you think about what success looks like today, it's simply his consent to another meeting." Felicity paused again. "And yours," she added.

Dan nodded and put her hands into her jacket pockets, worried that they might give her away. She'd believed that she'd never have to face Hamilton again, and yet here she was, that solid truth no longer holding firm, and her confidence was shaken at how quickly it'd broken free from its mooring.

"Are you sure?"

It was Roger speaking now, from behind her.

He'd followed them into the room, had been with Dan from the second she'd called him, insisted on being with her when she came, tried to insist on being in the room with her, though Hamilton, or his solicitor, blocked that.

She was glad to have him near and to have his support, though he was vocally against the meeting taking place at all.

Dan thought of John Granger, how he'd been so quiet when she'd called him this morning to say she would be in very late and couldn't say why. She'd need to tell him soon, regardless of how secretive this whole meeting was, she'd need to tell him because she needed him on her side, realized now that he was one of the few who always was.

"And there's no way we can get comms in there?" said Roger, speaking to no one in particular, though it was Felicity who made to answer.

"No way," said a fat, bald man, cutting Felicity off before she could utter a word.

He entered the room quickly and sat down on the chair in the corner.

Dan looked at his expensive suit, fat gold jewelry, and leather briefcase that looked as though it cost more than a month of Dan's wages.

"No way at all," he said.

Roger turned to look at the man, making no attempt to hide the utter contempt he felt for anyone who sided with Hamilton, defended him in court, and ran his errands.

"I'd almost forgotten you were coming," Roger said, with a fake smile.

"Well, don't forget again," said the solicitor, immediately looking back down at a file he'd pulled from his briefcase, ignoring them all.

Roger looked at Dan, his eyes blazing, and Dan smiled at him and mouthed "Calm down," though she knew it would've been good advice to take herself.

"Okay, then," said Felicity. "Let's go. He's in there now. He'll be in wrist and ankle restraints, as agreed." She nodded to Hamilton's solicitor, who didn't even look up from his paper. "And you have as long as you like, though he's asked that you agree to stay for at least thirty minutes."

"If you want to get out, you get out," growled Roger, his face fixed in an unhappy frown. "No one'll have anything to say to you about it. I can assure you of that."

Dan smiled at him again.

He was acting like a protective uncle, and though it often annoyed her when this side of him came out, today it felt reassuring to know he meant it.

"I'd suggest that we pull you out if it starts to go near to an hour," said Felicity. "That would be a very long chat, and we want you to remember the salient points."

"I'll remember," said Dan, and walked to the door.

An attendant was waiting outside, and he nodded to her and walked with her along an institutional corridor with linoleum floors, magnolia walls, and dirty bars on every window that had once been painted cream.

Dan followed the guard, her eyes down, watching his heels as he walked, noticing how he favored the outside of his right foot when he stepped and how this caused his sole to wear significantly more on that side, only a few millimeters of rubber separating his flesh from the hard floor.

"We're here, miss," he said, stopping abruptly. "Knock twice when you want out and I'll come. It'll only take me about thirty seconds to get here, but I'll be watching you on the screen and if anything happens that shouldn't, I'll be in that room with you a damn sight quicker than that, okay?"

Dan nodded. "Thank you."

He reached out and opened the door, his hands moving in slow motion as he pressed the handle down and pulled the door open.

Dan took a deep breath, making sure she didn't pause for more than a few seconds, and then stepped into the room to face him.

16

"Hey, Gary," said Natasha as she entered the stores office.

He turned round quickly, startling Natasha and making her step back.

"Hey, Nat. Where you been?"

Natasha looked down at her watch. She was ten minutes earlier than she needed to be.

"Just stopped for a chat with the girls in the mess. You okay?"

He nodded and put some papers away in his desk drawer, locking it before he looked back up.

"What's up?" she asked, moving across the office to her desk area.

"Nothing," he said.

"Okay."

Natasha sat down at her desk and for a moment, staring at her screen, wished there was someone else there that she could look to, pull a face, maybe wink at, do anything to break the tension.

The phone rang next to Gary and he snatched at it.

"Black," he said.

His body language immediately changed.

"Yes, ma'am," he said, "I'll send her up now."

He placed the phone back down quietly and looked across at her.

"Ma'am wants to see you in her cabin," he said.

Natasha blew her jaws, stood up, and shook herself out as though she'd just finished a run. Then she walked toward the door.

"Best I go, then," she said.

As she passed PO Black, he slammed a finger down hard into his keyboard and then stood up, the back of his thick arm pushing against her chest, lightly, but not moving away quickly.

Natasha jumped and stepped away from him.

"You okay, Gary?"

He shook his head.

"Apologies, it's just this dumb machine won't let me log on."

He leaned forward and hit the keyboard again in frustration.

"I just need to get onto the system for a minute. I'll have to call someone and get my password reset or something."

"I could find someone for you."

"It'll be too late by then. I just want to check a few things and it's urgent; Ma'am wants it. Don't worry."

Natasha nodded and walked to the door.

"Unless."

Natasha stopped.

"Would you mind logging on to your account for me? Just for a moment. I only need to go on the system quick. I'll log off straightaway."

She hesitated. She'd only recently signed the information security paperwork and sat through the IT security brief; the rules were fresh in her mind.

"It's okay, don't worry," he said, watching her and seeing her hesitate. "I don't want you to get into any trouble, I wouldn't tell anyone—it'd be my head on the block, too, but Ma'am Cox wants some stuff right now."

He smiled for the first time that morning.

"It's fine," she said, and stepped forward.

He moved aside, waving her onto his seat.

Natasha began to type in her password and login details.

"Just log off when you're done and I'll change the password later on. Then we'll both avoid almost certain prosecution, electrocution, and possibly even execution."

He leaned over her as she typed, and she tensed as she felt his breath on her neck, the gentle brush of his chest against her shoulder.

"Thank you," he said, and waited while the computer signed her in.

"No probs," she said, standing up and heading for the door.

She was around the corner and out of sight when her body shook uncontrollably, a big shiver that ran up her spine and around her shoulders.

COX'S OFFICE DOOR was open a crack, as seemed the norm, and Natasha knocked gently and waited to be called.

"Come," shouted Cox from behind the door.

Natasha pushed the door open far enough to stick her head through.

"It's SA Moore, ma'am. You asked for me?"

Cox smiled as soon as she saw Natasha.

"Come in, Tasha. Grab a seat."

Natasha opened the door fully and walked to the bunk-cum-sofa.

Cox was doing some paperwork, and was making a show of hurrying to finish.

"So," said Cox, turning on her chair to face Natasha. "How's things at sea?"

Natasha nodded. "Good, ma'am."

"Sarah. We're alone, remember."

"Sorry. Good, Sarah."

Sarah Cox paused and looked at her, as though trying to figure out whether she was lying.

"I understand there was some unpleasantness in the mess a few days ago, before we sailed, on the night of the infamous ship's company run ashore? Bets being taken on whether you'd cheat on your fiancé?"

Natasha tried to hide her surprise.

"Word travels," said Cox, but she was still smiling, and Natasha relaxed a bit.

"It was nothing," said Natasha. "Just some of the lads thinking they're funny."

"Are you sure? Because the commanding officer's policy on bullying and harassment is to take a hard line. So if you want me to take action, then I'll do so. You just have to talk to me about it."

Natasha looked down at her hand, the small scar from the stitches she'd received still clearly visible. She was unsure how this had come to Cox's attention and she felt embarrassed about it, but also she felt she'd dealt with it herself and done okay. She'd thrown the stupid piece of paper into the wastebasket. It was done, over, and was the least of the problems from that day.

"Honestly, ma'am. I'm fine. It was nothing I can't handle."

Cox smiled again. "Okay. But if you do find you're getting any trouble or unwanted attention, then come and speak to me, sooner rather than later. That way, we can nip it in the bud."

"Okay. Thank you."

Natasha stood to leave.

"One more thing," said Cox. "You look tired. Are you sleeping well on board? Not doing too many workouts with our PTI?"

The questions sounded casual, interested, but Natasha was still caught out by it. She paused for a moment, thinking.

"I'm fine, ma'am, honestly," she said.

"Okay, but this is all new, so take it easy. It'd be nice to have a girl on board start and finish her time as a virgin. So, we'll keep an eye on you."

Natasha stopped and her mouth dropped open.

"Sorry, ma'am," she said, her mouth dropping open and her cheeks flushing.

"Don't be, and also, Natasha, your shirt has a mark on it."

Natasha looked down, numb, and spotted a tiny stain on the breast pocket.

"You need to change it. You can go and do it now. If you're late down to stores, just tell PO Black you were talking to me. He'll be fine with that."

Sarah Cox turned back to her desk and began to type on her laptop.

Natasha waited, already doubting what she thought she'd heard, but once it was apparent that Cox wasn't going to say anything more, she left the cabin and headed for her bunk.

17

Dan was struck by how normal Hamilton looked, how unchanged he seemed after the years in prison. Dan wasn't sure what she'd expected, or even hoped for. Maybe that he'd look skinny, malnourished, pale, and tired, with big dark bags under his eyes. Maybe some signs that he'd been attacked, a black eye or a new scar on his face.

Instead he looked exactly the same as he always had.

She saw that his hair was still short and tidy.

It looked clean, slightly wet, as though he'd only recently showered.

His blue cotton shirt was tight around his sinewy biceps, and his forearms looked as honed and powerful as ever.

He was smiling at her, broad and warm, an old friend excited and happy to greet someone he'd missed and was delighted to see again. He made to stand up, the restraints at his wrists stopping him from rising fully, and instead he almost bowed to Dan, nodding, his shoulders hunched toward the table.

"Danny," he said. "It's fantastic to see you."

He was gushing at her, and the sound of his voice saying friendly things, coupled with the way he looked, made Dan feel dizzy.

She'd thought about this moment in the car on the way here, thought about all the different ways the first time might go, but she'd never considered for a second that it might be like this.

"Take a seat, please," he said, gesturing to the chair across the table from him, the restraints meaning that as his right hand moved forward, his left had to move back toward him and this had the effect of tipping his shoulder toward her as though he were deferring to her and submitting.

Dan walked to the seat and sat down, watching as Hamilton did the same.

He was still grinning like an idiot, and Dan tried to remember the days when they'd been friends.

They'd been partners—well, he'd been the senior man, her mentor really, but they'd had lunch, grabbed a coffee, once even gone Christmas shopping in Oxford Street together when they'd had time between meetings.

These memories came to Dan as though new, as though she'd shut them away so deeply that she was experiencing them again for the first time.

She looked at him now and tried to think of what to call him.

Chris had been his name before, but now everyone referred to him as Hamilton, had done so since he'd been caught and his crimes revealed. It was as though the world needed to rebrand him so it could see him for what he was. It was as though, while surnames were often used in the Armed Forces, by calling him Hamilton, it distanced them all from the person they knew. He became a thing, an object, something that people knew about but didn't actually know.

Sitting in front of him, though, it felt odd to call him Hamilton, the name that had come to mean so much to so many people, the name that had ended lives and destroyed families, that was a bogeyman that people read about, wrote papers about, watched documentaries about.

Hamilton no longer felt like the name of a person she'd ever known.

She'd always called him Chris when they'd served together, but looking at him now, knowing what he'd done, that name no longer fit.

"Hey," she said.

"So, how've things been?" he asked, and Dan blinked at how surreal the whole situation was.

"So-so," she said. "And you?"

"Well, where to start? They don't let me out much, as you can imagine. I'm starved of decent conversation. That's for certain. I'm allowed some access to the Internet and Twitter now, so I get the news from the lefties, but how is anyone supposed to form proper opinions from social media? When we came through training the navy prided itself on intellectual challenge, forming and defending opinions through verbal sparring, arguing and counterarguing. I don't get any of that at all, and so, from what contact I do get with the outside world, it seems to me that we're in an age of bite-sized news, stories being absorbed in a single sound bite. Opinions being formed from short headlines. No one thinks for themselves anymore, certainly not in here."

He was smiling and thoughtful, his expressions calm, but reacting as he spoke.

"And I really don't get to speak to many women, that's for sure, not ones of passable intelligence, anyway. I get letters from quite a few who want to marry me, something that confuses me, I'll be honest. We've talked before about how I feel about women in general, but really, marrying me? Even you must agree that's stupid."

He stopped speaking and it took Dan a second to realize that he was waiting for an answer.

"I certainly wouldn't marry you," said Dan, unsure what else to say.

He looked at her, mock hurt on his face and his bottom lip curled over like a child about to cry.

"Would you really not, Danny? Because there was a time I thought you had a little twinkle in your eye for me. I'm just saying."

Dan watched him, refusing to be drawn, seeing his eyes darken as the real Hamilton skulked back into view.

"I can assure you that was never the case," said Dan, offering him a smile of sorts.

There was silence between them for a few moments, each watching the other.

"You know, Danny," he began, his voice regaining the light and welcoming tone, but his eyes failing to follow it. "I saw a huge thing on Twitter a little while ago about victim blaming. Posters saying how a significant percentage of women who are raped had consumed alcohol. The Internet was up in arms. This was blaming the victim, they said. Then someone started a hashtag thingy—no rape without rapists—and they all said how there should be no blame for the victim, and all efforts should be targeted at the perpetrator."

He waited, but Dan said nothing.

"Well, I'm not allowed to interact on Twitter, just read articles and stuff, but the whole thing struck me as dumb and counterproductive; it was all working against women. You see, the posters weren't blaming the victim, they were educating them, and what they said is true. As a rapist of some eminence, I can assure you that alcohol makes it very much easier to abduct and do harm to someone. They're so much more trusting and pliable, so to my mind, the poster was good, no?"

Dan watched him, expressionless, refusing to answer.

He nodded and continued anyway.

"I felt that that part of the argument really insulted women, implying they can't be provided with information without feeling they're in some way to blame, activating some kind of innate guilt complex. Then, the whole idea that we should abandon warnings and focus solely on the perpetrator is laughable, though it's no longer polite to laugh about rape; I get that. But, say if a young man was heading out for a drink in Southampton and wanted to wear his Portsmouth football shirt, you'd warn him, wouldn't you? You'd say, 'Mate, if you go over there wearing that, you'll get your head kicked in. It won't be your fault. The fault will lie with the prick that batters you, but just take reasonable precautions.' Wouldn't you say that?"

Dan shrugged and leaned back in her chair, her hands still thrust deep into her pockets, settling in for what could be a long speech.

"I mean, how is that different from telling a woman to 'stay with her friends'? Believe me, Danny, there's strength in numbers. I always liked the loners. Or saying, 'Don't drink too much, keep your wits about you'? Is it just me, Danny? Honestly? Is there a reason I think this victim blaming is such a load of bollocks?"

Dan sighed and looked at him, forcing herself to meet his dark eyes.

"Because you're a misogynistic, murdering bastard?" she offered.

He laughed at that, belly-laughed, and the sound of it echoed around the room.

It made Dan feel ill to hear it.

"But who better to advise women on how to be safe than me?" he said, still chuckling. "I think I could be a simply fantastic trainer, an educator, a motivator, really. I was your mentor once, after all, and look how well you've done."

He smiled.

"You know, Danny, they say some of the best coaches and mentors in the world, take football as an example, they can spot a child playing the game at only nine years old and tell you whether he's likely to ever play at the professional level. Imagine that, for just a second if you will, imagine someone with my talent mentoring others."

He looked at her.

"Imagine that," said Dan.

"I could teach you a lot. More than you might think," he said. "But the point is really this, you can't stop rapists by doing what's currently being done. And you have to advise people to take care, because the threat is real and it's not going to go away anytime soon. I mean, how would they have tried to target me, Danny? No one even knew I existed. How can you target a perpetrator if you don't even know he's out there? No, the potential victims must take action. They must take precautions."

Dan watched him, unsure what to do or say next.

"You're speechless, Danny," he said, tilting his head as though examining her, trying to understand why that might be. "Have you no opinion on this?"

"I do, but it's not really what I came here to talk about."

"Is that because the idea of being a victim makes you uncomfortable?"

Dan watched him, at first refusing to answer.

"It's never the victim's fault," she said, after a few moments of silence.

He smiled and nodded.

"I knew you'd be one of them, Danny. I just knew it. But sometimes, people, victims, do bring it upon themselves. Some of them do ask for punishment time and time again. It's only when they eventually do so within earshot of a punisher, a predator, that they get what *they* think they deserve."

Dan rolled her eyes, looking as though she was bored listening to his tedious ramblings, but actually just needing a reason to break away from his stare. She looked around the interview room, wondering whether he was referring to the attack that she'd suffered, one year to the day after he was convicted, an attack she was sure was arranged by him.

"Are we done with the chitchat?" she asked, looking down at her hands, realizing they were out of her pockets and in her lap.

He tried to throw his arms in the air in mock exasperation, but the restraints stopped him, making it look like a halfhearted gesture. "Always with the getting down to business. You know, that's why I asked that you stay for a minimum of thirty minutes, because I wanted to chew the fat awhile first, shoot the shit, put the world to rights with my old friend and nemesis, Danielle Lewis."

"I think I remember our relationship a bit differently than you," said Dan, tilting her head to match his. "I always thought you were an arrogant prick, no more so than many of the other guys, to be fair, but you loved yourself, thought that everyone should listen to what you said. So I really don't look back and see this friendship you keep talking about."

"Come now, Danny, don't let events change the past," he said, smiling again, straightening his head, and leaning toward her, resting his forearms on the table.

"I'm not," said Dan.

"Okay, if you won't discuss victim blaming with me, what about male privilege? Do you think I could have stayed undetected for so long if I hadn't been a white male?"

Dan shook her head slightly, not saying no, just trying to catch up with the question and the change of direction.

"No, in truth, probably not," she said.

"Exactly," he said, holding up a finger.

Dan let out a long breath and placed her hands, palms down, on the table. She made to speak several times, each time stopping, unsure what to say.

"Look, if you're trying to communicate to me that you're a racist, misogynist rapist, then you're preaching to the choir," said Dan at last. "Honestly, I'm already there, utterly convinced of it."

He sat back and took in a deep breath. All traces of humor melted from his face and he looked at her hard, his eyes cold.

"I thought you'd be more fun than this, Danny, I really did. Tell me, did you get my mail? Why've you come now?"

Dan steeled herself and looked back at him.

His eyes were what unsettled her.

Hamilton's eyes were so changeable—one minute they were full of life, shining and bright, and then they'd cloud, the life running out of them like water off a windshield, and they'd be dark, black, reptilian, pitiless, and she was sure she'd glimpsed the man who'd murdered again and again.

"I thought you might be ready to talk," she said, a preprepared answer to this anticipated question.

"I'm trying to talk now and you don't want to."

"I do. I just don't enjoy having feminism and equality mansplained to me by a male I believe to be responsible for the deaths of hundreds of women."

He snorted.

"It wasn't hundreds," he said, like a petulant and pedantic child correcting a parent.

"How many was it?"

He looked at her and smiled.

"As if it would be that easy, Danny."

Dan shrugged.

"So why did you want me to come here?" she asked. "I won't lie, I didn't read your letters after the first or maybe second, once I knew what they were and recognized them. I just shredded them."

He raised his eyebrows at that, a little taken aback.

"Shredded my letters? Really? I feel a little bit hurt by that, Danny. It would've only taken a few moments to read them."

"Pace of life, things to do, not much time for serial-killer mail. You know how it is."

"Any other interesting mail that might be worthy of a mention?" he asked.

"Not unless you've been sending me a load of religious stuff, trying to draw me into a local church."

He nodded. "You'd be surprised what I'd send you, Danny," he said, and smiled.

"So why do you want to talk?" she asked again.

He moved in his seat, settled himself, and placed his hands on the table in front of him.

"I want to help you, Danny."

"Why?"

"Is there any answer I could give that would satisfy you, really?" he said.

"No, but it'd be nice to think you'd spent some time coming up with a convincing lie."

He smiled at that, the corners of his eyes creasing, and it occurred to Dan that a man like this didn't deserve to have laugh lines, didn't deserve to have had the moments that led to them.

"I've decided not to lie. I have my reasons, and they will remain my own, but I have decided to help you, Danny, not the National Crime Agency or local police, but you, specifically you."

"And if I tell you to shove your help up your ass?"

He laughed again, louder, slapped the table with one hand.

"Ah, I've missed your winning ways, but I doubt you will, such is your sense of right and wrong."

"So tell me how many people you murdered and start telling me where we can find their bodies. Once I confirm what you're saying's the truth, then we can really start to build up trust and move on from there, but you'll need to give me something."

He drummed the tabletop with his fingers, four solid, quick beats in a row, then a pause before he did it again. It was all that broke the silence.

"I don't think that's how this is going to work, Danny. You see, I want to help you, but first I need you to understand how I can help, and in order to do that, we'll need to go on a journey together, figuratively, I mean, I doubt they'll let me actually come along with you, but I need to establish value."

Dan sighed, making sure it was loud and obvious.

"I knew you'd react this way," said Hamilton, smiling. "I even prepared myself for your actions, but I need you to be honest with me, for just a moment. Someone has to go first, right? So tell me, truthfully, why you decided to come now."

Dan weighed it, looked around the room as she thought about what she could say, the lies she could try, the lines they'd prepared this morning, but Hamilton, though he seemed simple in many ways, was far from it. He was an expert in reading body language, reading people's intentions while hiding his own.

"The NCA received some evidence. The evidence, which hasn't ever been seen before, comes from murder victims that we believe you abducted and killed. They really have very little to go on at the moment and they hoped you might be willing to help."

She watched his reaction, trying to read it and failing.

He listened without reaction, not even a flicker of his eyes, and Dan couldn't help but wonder how much he already knew.

"Well, I did say that I'd help you, Danny, not the NCA."

"Then help me here."

"You're not on the case yet, though, are you? Someone else has taken your spot."

Dan hoped that she'd managed to conceal her surprise at his knowing that; the slight smile that crossed his lips told her she hadn't.

"No, I'm not at the moment, but I am assisting."

"By speaking to me?"

"Yes, by speaking to you."

He drummed his fingertips on the tabletop again and again.

"That's very irritating," said Dan.

He stopped immediately.

"You're a dogged investigator, Danny. You're a dogged person, really. So I'll say this. You need to find out about a gentleman named William Knight. I think if you take that all the way to its conclusion, then we'll be able to have a much more fruitful conversation when you visit next time."

Dan nodded and stood up to leave.

"Until next time, then," she said, and headed for the door.

"That's it, Danny? You don't have any questions for me at all? We're supposed to do a minimum of thirty minutes."

Dan stopped and turned back. She looked at Hamilton.

"Okay, one, maybe two."

"Fire away, Danny, I live but to serve you."

"How did Matt Carson find you when you were outside that storage hangar up near Aldershot? How did he know you were there? Everyone he wanted to kill was there, so why would he come out looking for you? For anyone?"

Hamilton smiled and nodded, like an old man remembering a fond liaison.

"You know, next time, why don't you bring a chess set with you? I know it's a cliché for archrivals to be playing chess, and I know you're not a player, but I'd be happy to teach you. It'd also give you somewhere to look when you can't bear to look me in the eye anymore."

"I'll mull it over," said Dan. "And my question?"

"I'll mull that over, and I'll let you leave early without penalty while I do," Hamilton said. "But don't forget what I said about victims, Danny," he said, as Dan neared the door and reached out to knock. "Take precautions. I very much doubt that any victim of a brutal rape feels much better knowing it wasn't her fault."

She knocked twice before turning back to face him.

"I won't forget," she said.

"And find out who the evidence was sent to at the NCA. There may be a clue in that alone."

Dan nodded, waiting for the guard, and the silence stretched out between them.

"How's your back, by the way?" he asked.

Dan felt the blood drain from her face. The only other people who knew about the attack she'd suffered and the injuries to her back were Felicity, Roger, and the people who'd carried it out. She'd long known deep inside that Hamilton had been responsible for the attack, that he'd ordered it, requested it, paid for it, but however he did it, he was behind it, and now he admitted it to her.

Dan forced herself to smile at him.

"It's okay," she said, "it's not like someone opened me up with garden shears."

The door opened, and she left without looking back.

18

"I'm so glad to be alongside again, aren't you?"

Natasha looked over at Gary Black, who was hunched over his computer.

He tapped the keyboard a few times and then turned to face her.

"Definitely," he said.

"I know you've done loads of sea time, and I've just finished my first three weeks, but I really feel like I've earned a night out tonight."

She saw him smile as she waited for her account to log on.

"I found a used condom in the phone booth on X-deck," said Natasha, shivering a little bit at how gross it had been when she'd looked down and seen it next to her boot.

Gary looked round and shook his head. "Not nice," he said.

"Yeah, I think one of the bootnecks is seeing one of the other girls in my cabin. I'd heard they were having alone time there, but he should at least clean up after himself."

"Royal Marines," said Gary, as though that explained it all.

"Thing is, I told Jason about it, and now he's being . . ."

Natasha tried to think about how Jason was being. He was like a teenager, grunting at her when she spoke, despite the fact that he was twelve years her senior. He was also mentioning Susi all the time, as though her name was a weapon to hurt Natasha with, to score petty points in a game Natasha didn't even want to play. She'd always liked that he was older, seemed more confident and settled. She'd liked that he didn't play the games that the boys her age did, that he didn't pressure her to do things she didn't want to do yet. She liked how he'd support her in everything, without question; he always backed her, made her believe she could achieve anything, go anywhere, even when it meant leaving his job and bringing her down to Portsmouth to join the navy. He was there for her, always. He was the only person who ever really had been.

"He's being . . ." repeated Natasha, still not sure how to put it.

"A dick?" said Gary, without even turning away from his screen.

Natasha looked at his back, thought that she should defend her fiancé, then didn't, because he was being just exactly that. For the first time ever, he was being a dick. She was going for a night out and she didn't want to call him before she went, because she knew he'd stress her out and ruin the night for her.

Her account was taking ages to log on. Though she didn't feel like speaking to Jason, she'd e-mailed him a long letter last night, explaining how he was making her feel, and she was anxious to see whether he'd replied.

She'd been honest and open, about her being away at sea, about him mixing with this Susi woman. She'd told him she didn't want to be like her parents, her mum particularly, ignoring problems for as long as possible before running away from them to find the next one. She was hoping to catch his reply before she left work to get ready, assuming he'd been able to reply.

Black was looking at her, she could feel it, and she turned back to him while she waited.

"I was thinking, if you wanted," he began, pausing and looking away as he often did, his cheeks flushing red, "we could hang out or something on this stop? Maybe after work today?"

Natasha was shocked and must have looked it.

"I just mean, like, grab some food and wander into town or something," he added quickly. "You know, just to kill some time or something."

Natasha couldn't help but notice how he'd used several words that he normally wouldn't and how it made his lisp so much more apparent when he did. She looked at him carefully.

He was a decent boss, and Natasha liked him well enough. He was a little unpredictable, almost huffy at times, a bit too tactile on occasion, and that could feel creepy, but he seemed like a decent guy.

Now she couldn't tell if she was being asked out on a date by him, something she'd definitely not want to do. She paused and saw him blush again before he stood up and approached her.

"You've got something in your hair," he said, and reached out.

She felt his hand run across her hairline, brushing her cheek.

The awkwardness in the compartment was palpable and she knew the longer she waited to answer, the worse it was going to get.

"Thanks," she said, as he moved, brushing against her shoulder as he flicked something away that she couldn't see. "But I can't tonight."

He looked at her and walked back to his computer.

"What about nipping out for lunch or something tomorrow or the day after?" Natasha asked.

He nodded but didn't look back round, instead becoming quickly engrossed in his computer.

"I could use a day hanging out with a really good friend," she said. "So if you fancied it, we could nip into town. Though I'm not sure you'll like the shops I'll want to visit . . ."

Natasha let her words to trail off, hoping for a smile from him, as they'd often talked about his hatred of shopping, and crowds in general, but he said nothing for a moment, not even turning around.

"Who're you going out with tonight?" he asked after a long silence.

Natasha tried hard to keep it conversational and upbeat.

"I'm going to see if Jason's e-mailed me back. Then I'm meeting Mark for a quick run, before we all head into town." She watched him, hopeful of a positive reaction. "You should come," she added quickly. "There's a load of us going."

"You won't get anything from lover boy. He's gone out," said Black quickly, before tapping on his keyboard again.

Natasha watched for a moment and turned back to her screen, frowning and unsure what Black meant, but not wanting to get further into anything that might lead to her night, or mood, being ruined. She double-clicked on the mail icon.

"We're heading out pretty much straight after work. So you can come along if you want," she said. "But everyone's keen to get going. I'm literally doing a fifteen-minute, high-intensity session and then getting ready and I'm out of here."

Her e-mail opened up and she saw a message from Jason, immediately clicking on it.

Can't chat. Heading out. Agree with what you say and will reply properly when back later. Love you. x

Natasha's stomach seemed to flip as she read the message. It was a massive brushoff. She'd no issue with his going out, of course she didn't. She was going out tonight herself, and he couldn't be expected to stay in for three months, although he was supposed to be saving money while she was away so they could get a deposit and move out of the flat they were renting and into something that they'd own, something that was really theirs, to work on, build up, and improve together. They'd both agreed that they wanted to get a place with car parking if possible, maybe a garage in case Jason was ever able to start mobile catering, something he'd really fancied for a long time.

She read the message again, and then again. She'd poured her guts into her e-mail to him. Had come clean about how she felt about their separation and how they could get through this together while she carved out a career for herself in the navy. She'd already talked to Lieutenant Cox about selection for the commissioned ranks through the Upper Yardman scheme. That'd mean more money, better promotion prospects, a better future for both of them.

She'd told him all of that. She'd made it clear that she could only do it if they stayed strong; both of them had come from nothing and only had each other. And after that, all he'd had to say was that he was going out . . .

Natasha turned to Black.

"How did you know he was going out?" she asked.

Black turned to look at her, confused.

"What?"

"You said I wouldn't get much from lover boy because he was out. That's what you said, just a few minutes ago. But how did you know?"

"I don't know what you mean." He shook his head as though she was being daft and turned back to his computer.

"That's what you said. When I said I was going to check my e-mails and then head out, that's what you said to me."

He was shaking his head, but not looking at her, acting as though he was engrossed in the work he was doing.

"Gary," Natasha said, knowing she sounded exasperated and speaking louder than she meant to.

He spun to look at her, his face red, his sudden action making her jump.

"I don't know what you're on about and I don't know who you think you're talking to," he said, his breathing deep. "Honestly. I was probably talking about Coker. He's going out, isn't he?"

Natasha blinked a few times.

Black was big, but over the short time she'd known him he'd nearly always been friendly, benign even. Now, with his voice raised and his fists balled as he leaned forward in his chair toward her, he was really, really intimidating.

"Okay," she said, knowing she was on the verge of tears. "Okay, it's just that . . ." She paused, not knowing what to say next and feeling tears start to fall. "I'm just going to go to the heads."

She got up and walked quickly to the door.

Gary Black stood up, too.

"Nat," he said, reaching out to stop her, his fingers catching her breast as he seized her arm.

"Let go," Natasha said, spinning to face him.

He kept hold of her arm, easily controlling her, using his one hand on her arm to turn her toward him.

"Let go!" cried Natasha, her voice breaking.

He looked down at his hand on her arm, at his fingers, which easily went all the way around it. There was something in his eyes, something that frightened Natasha as she realized he had forced her up onto her toes, that if he jerked now, he could dislocate her shoulder as easily as he'd carried her bags.

"Apologies" he said, and stepped away from her. "You looked upset. I didn't want you to be upset." Natasha froze for a second, confused, then looked at her watch, numb to what had happened.

It was getting late, she didn't have much time before the working day would be over and she could do some exercise and chat with Mark or Bev, or even Sam, about all of this.

"I'm going," she said, and turned to leave.

"I'll need you back," said Black before she was clear of the door. "Ma'am called down just before you came in. We've had some stores arrive that need to be booked in and sorted through. She wants them done tonight, wants me to show you through the process."

Natasha turned back to look at him.

"But there's loads," she said. "That'll take hours. I thought we were going to work on them in the forenoon tomorrow and get them all done in one go."

He was smiling again now, his whole demeanor changed. He reached out to wipe a tear from her cheek that she hadn't realized had escaped until then.

Natasha pulled away, flinching, but he looked friendly again, tolerant, Gary as she normally knew him to be.

"I know, and I'm unhappy, too. I'll stay with you and we can do it together, but it needs to be done. Ma'am told me literally two seconds before you came in."

Natasha could feel herself shrinking with disappointment.

"But we had plans," she said, not sure if she was even speaking to him, or just speaking her thoughts out loud.

"Yeah, well, you'll need to let Coker know that you'll meet him later. Okay?"

Natasha nodded, numb. "Okay."

She turned and began to walk out of the stores office and into the stores flat.

He followed her, put a hand on her shoulder, and turned her back toward him.

"Look. Once we get done, I could take you out for a beer. Make up for it a bit. We'll be a few hours, so we probably won't catch the others up, but we could grab food somewhere local. What do you think?"

Natasha looked up and him and smiled as best she could.

"Sure. That'd be great. I bet we could catch up with the others if we try, though. I'll find out where they're going."

He smiled again, though she was sure something changed in his eyes.

"Okay," he said. "Go and let people know. I'll wait here for you and then we can get going. I'll stick the kettle on and we can have a quick brew before we start."

He nodded at her and turned away, bustling over to the kettle and starting to whistle.

19

Tuesday, February 3

"No, I'm going in to speak to someone now." Dan looked at her watch. "I'll call you back, Roger, we can talk more once I'm done here, okay?" She listened to him grumble agreement and ended the call.

Dan rubbed her eyes, which were gritty and sore after a sleepless night. They felt heavy as the postadrenaline slump that followed her meeting with Hamilton and the subsequent debrief began to take their toll.

Roger had been present for the debrief but had remained silent and brooding throughout, calling as soon as Dan had left, as though she might have more to say when it was just the two of them, as though she'd held something back from Felicity.

Her phone rang again and she was sure it would be him.

"What!" she barked.

"Nice. Bad time?" Felicity asked.

"It is, actually. I'm just about to speak to someone about another investigation I'm on. I'm dead on my feet and I'm already running late."

"No worries. Call me when you're done."

"Hang on, just tell me quick now, what's up?"

"Well, that gentleman that was to be loaned to us for the investigation, an army investigator with some experience in Afghanistan and Iraq, working in the historical allegations teams, he had an accident this morning when cycling to work, and from what I gather, he won't be fit to join the team for quite some time now."

"It was Stewart Mackenzie," said Dan. "Is he badly hurt?"

She didn't know quite what to do. She was genuinely disappointed and concerned that Mackenzie was hurt. Though she didn't know him well, she'd met him, and he was a decent guy. He'd also been one of the few to congratulate her on Hamilton and to drop her a message of support when the papers had begun to devour her. But Dan also felt excitement tingling deep in her stomach. If Mackenzie was out, then the slot to join the NCA's new investigation was open again and she might be back in the picture.

"He was knocked off his bike, it was a hit-and-run, the driver never stopped. He's in a bad way," said Felicity. "But he'll recover, we're told. We've requested he be replaced, and though I shouldn't say, the lead investigator has reiterated her request for you to join our team."

Dan breathed deeply. She wanted it. But she knew Harrow-Brown would relish denying her the role again.

"I also wanted you to know that we've begun to dig into the William Knight name that Hamilton passed to you. He was one of yours, navy, reckoned to be responsible for a string of very nasty rapes around the Portsmouth area several years ago, had a penchant for slight, young-looking blond girls. Only he's been off the grid for years. No one's seen or heard of him and he's assumed to be either on the run, or possibly even dead."

"So it might be a good lead, then?" said Dan.

"Well, not really. We've already ruled him out of two of the seven cases that you know about, and I'll have more soon, but my feeling is that he has nothing to do with our current investigation. Time will tell, though, and we'll keep digging."

"He might have helped Hamilton, though. Might have known where to hide the victims?"

Felicity paused, the silence stretching out across the line.

"It doesn't feel likely, to be honest, Danny," she said, her voice soft. "He and Hamilton could have known each other, but only briefly. I think Hamilton threw you a time waster. Who knows why. Who knows why he's so obsessed with messing with you at all, but we'll keep at it. I thought you'd want to know."

"Thanks. Did you find out who the parcels were addressed to?" asked Dan.

"No. Not yet. I have asked, though. As soon as I know, and am able to, I'll tell you."

Dan ended the call without another word. She knew Roger would need to talk to her about joining the NCA investigation, even if it was only to tell her that she was being passed over.

She checked her watch. This would all need to wait.

Jason Goulding, the former fiancé of the missing Natasha Moore, had answered Dan's call on the first ring that morning, even though it was only just gone 0630 when she'd set off to her meeting with Hamilton.

She'd expected her call to go to his voice mail and fumbled her greeting when she realized it was actually him speaking to her.

He'd been pleased to hear from her and had agreed to meet her at 1500, during his break; he had the afternoon shift at the hotel in Portsmouth.

DAN LOOKED AT him now, watching his eyes as they flitted around the room. The man seemed exhausted. He had black bags beneath his eyes and his skin looked pale and waxy, with faint acne scars on both cheeks.

He wasn't an ugly man, but neither was he handsome. He also looked more like Natasha Moore's father than her fiancé.

"Thanks for meeting with me so quickly," said Dan, sipping at the cup of green tea he'd made for her.

"I would've met you three days ago," he said, staring at her for a few moments before he looked away.

In that moment Dan realized that he was even older than she'd first thought.

Natasha Moore was just eighteen. Dan had assumed that Jason would be a similar age. But as his face turned and he retorted with more than a hint of anger, she saw the age in his eyes and guessed him to be thirty or more.

Dan ignored his comment for now. There would be a time for apologies, but this wasn't it.

"How old are you, Jason?" she asked.

"Thirty-three," he said. "Next Tuesday."

"And how long have you and Natasha Moore been in a relationship?"

"Four years, just over that," he said.

Dan looked at him, saying nothing.

"Yeah, I get it," he said, starting to bounce his left leg up and down on his toes, making the table bump and jostle. "She was fourteen when we met and I was twenty-nine. We've heard it all before. No, I didn't commit statutory rape; we waited, and in fact, we never got there. But I can't see how this goes any way to finding her now."

"The thing is, Jason, though we can't find Natasha, we also have no indications that she might be in trouble or hurt. She's an adult, and if she wants to go somewhere and not be found, then that's up to her. She can make that choice."

Jason made to speak, but Dan raised a hand.

"Just one second, Jason," she said. "Please."

His leg bounced harder and his hands clenched on the table.

Dan registered that he must be under enormous pressure, but she also detected an air of something else, an undertone of violence, maybe.

His hands seemed to ball easily into fists and small white scars stood out against the hard, thick skin of his knuckles.

Dan reached for her phone as though it had just buzzed in her pocket.

"Sorry," she said, pulling it out and pretending to read a text message.

She raised her eyebrows and typed a message to John.

He was in the dockyard, not five minutes away, and she told him she'd like him to come along after all and to get to the hotel as quickly as possible, then she put the phone away and flashed Jason an apologetic smile.

"There's a number of reasons that people go missing," Dan continued. "And in more than ninety-nine percent of these cases, the missing person is found again safe and sound. Some of the key reasons that make people go can be problems at home, problems with their partner or former partner."

He was shaking his head.

"You're just another one of them," he said.

"I'm really not, Jason, but I'm going to tell you things straight."

He leaned forward quickly, bumping the table toward Dan and making the tea slosh and almost spill out of her cup.

The movement caught Dan off guard and she recoiled from him, annoyed at herself, but wary.

"Sit back," she said, her voice elevated and firm.

He did, his chest heaving as his breathing accelerated.

"I can't help you if you act like that. Do you understand?"

He was glaring at her, his fists clenched and his breath whistling through gritted teeth. Then, slowly, Dan saw the breathing change, go deeper, down into his stomach, and his eyes filled with tears. He slumped, his shoulders relaxing and his mouth dropping open as he tried to take deep breaths and control himself.

"Take some time, Jason," Dan said, still staying away from him but letting her voice soften. "I'll try to help you, I promise."

"No one's helping me," he said, the words distorted. "No one's helping Natasha, either."

"Can you tell me if there was any reason why Natasha might run away, Jason?"

He tensed again, looked as though he might lunge, but it passed.

"Not from me," he said. "Back to me, yes, but not away from me."

Dan watched him wipe his eyes on a blue-and-white towel that was tucked into his chef's apron.

"What do you mean?"

"I told you lot all of this stuff already. She was e-mailing me, long after we broke up. I was the only person she could talk to, and then even that stopped."

"Talk to about what?"

"What was going on there. She hated it. I know she never told me everything, but what she did tell me was enough. Other girls picking on her, that guy she works with touching her, brushing against her, turning up at her house. She'd try to laugh it off, mention it like it was no big deal, a big joke, but it was bothering her. That's Natasha, see, she doesn't just come out and say things, she dances around, waiting for you to pick up on what she wants you to know. You have to coax things out of her."

"Who came to the house?"

"That massive one. Black, I think."

"Uninvited?"

"I don't think he was invited. He was sitting in his car, watching. I went round to collect some of my stuff and he threatened me. Told me if I ever went round there again, well, he'd hurt me."

He looked at her, furious, tensing again, and Dan was glad when his eyes flicked off over her shoulder and she knew that John Granger had arrived and been sent through.

"Why did you and Natasha break up, Jason?" asked Dan, ignoring John as he sat down beside her.

"What the fuck is wrong with you people?" he said, his voice rising. "Natasha hated it on that ship. *Hated* it. She was being bullied, she was isolated. She wrote to me about it. She told me how she was struggling to cope with it. Those bitches in her mess never let up on her, and that guy she worked for, he needs to be fucking locked up."

"I asked you why you broke up, Jason. Will you tell me?"

He stared at Dan.

"I know what you're thinking. Older guy, younger girl. Did I try to control her, did I not like it when she joined the navy to work with all the men. You're wrong. It was me that encouraged her to join. It was me that told her she could start at the bottom and work her way up—she wanted to be the captain of a ship one day—I told her she could do it. She'd never have left that shit-hole town and her idiot parents if I hadn't supported her. I left my job to come here with her, so she could follow her dreams."

"And then she ditched you?" said John.

Jason stared at him now, and Dan saw the threat in his eye fade.

"No. I broke it off," he said quietly. "And I'm not proud of it. I met a woman here and we struck up a relationship while Natasha was away. I tried to hide it from her, just till she could get settled in the navy, but she never got the chance to settle. I think she was outgrowing me and I hated that, but I was too stupid to realize that it didn't have to happen that way. I hooked up with someone else, someone my age, who was here and not away, someone who didn't want to wait, and I regret it."

Dan watched him closely as he spoke, believing what he was saying but letting the silence draw out so he'd speak again.

"I know what I must look like to you," Jason continued, "but it's not like that. I wanted to be a friend to her, to help and support her for as long as she'd let me. No one knows her better than me, no one, and I'm telling you, something ain't right."

Dan felt an emptiness rise up from her stomach.

"Who did you speak to on board?" asked Dan.

"Loads of people. They all brushed me off. Except that woman that she worked for—Cox, maybe? They seemed to be quite good friends, well, Natasha seemed to think she could count on her. She's listened, but she hasn't helped. None of them were interested."

20

Natasha Moore—Mid-November
(two months before disappearance)

Natasha walked down the gangway, enjoying the breeze of the cool afternoon wind as a weak sun shone down through the clouds. It felt great to be in another port, God knows the last one had sucked, with Gary keeping her at work late on two out of the three nights.

She'd managed to catch up with the ship's company one night, but, by the time Gary had let her go, they were so far gone with the drink that she'd just walked back, bumping into Gary, who'd pretty much frog-marched her into a quiet bar for a drink with him. On the only night she'd actually made it out with everyone, Sarah Cox had ruined it—it was like they were working as a bloody tag team.

On that night, Cox had been at the gangway, waiting.

Natasha remembered vaguely saying in passing that they might walk into town together, it was nothing firm, but Cox had been there and then had just refused to leave Natasha alone.

She was grabbing Natasha's hand and pulling her onto the dance floor. Then she'd be taking selfies and pictures. Once, she practically dragged Natasha into the toilet with her and God forbid Natasha tried to go to the loo, talk to someone else, dance with Mark, anything without her shadow looming over her shoulder. Cox was a bit pissed, and Natasha knew that officers were allowed to cut loose and relax, too, and there were no other female officers on board to be friends, but come on . . .

Basically, because of her, no one came anywhere near Natasha the whole night.

Cox was literally close enough to reach out and grab Natasha at almost every second, and even when they got back to the ship she wanted to sneak some wine into her cabin, but Natasha had had way more than enough by then.

Sam had taken the Mickey out of Natasha for weeks afterward, with Bev laughing on cue, whether she thought it was funny or not. The port stop had been awful—but this one wouldn't be, Natasha was going to make damn sure of that.

THE DOCKSIDE WAS fairly clear and not many of the crew were around. Many sailors had already left to meet their loved ones. *Defiance* was down to a small skeleton crew of essential personnel, and there was minimal activity.

Natasha wandered along the jetty.

Jason had calmed down a bit once she'd gone back to sea. They'd decided not to fly him out to this stop, so they could save some money. Besides, it was her first deployment; she hadn't been away much before now.

Defiance might be stopping in Rio before Christmas, and he was going to save up and fly out then.

Natasha had seen some of the sailors with their other halves and children. It'd made her tummy flip to think about how fun it would be if Jason had flown out after all, even just to surprise her.

Her phone had a signal and a few hours left on her international roaming package. She found a low concrete wall at the harbor's edge and sat in the fresh air with her back to the water and dialed home.

Jason answered immediately.

"Hey, babe," she said. "You okay?"

"Hey," he said, his voice low and dull.

Natasha remembered how he'd acted the last time she was in port and about to enjoy a night out. She assumed this was more of the same. She closed her eyes, took a deep breath, and decided the only thing to do was to push on through, there was no way he was going to ruin tonight, she needed a release.

"I'm really missing you. Did you get my e-mail about my boss? He's really starting to bother me; what do you think I should do?"

He was silent, and at first Natasha thought the line had been lost, then she heard a rustling at the end of the phone and another noise.

"Jason?"

There was more rustling and then he was back.

"You got some signal on the phone?" he asked. "Decent signal, enough to pick up an e-mail?"

She frowned.

"Not really, babe. If I turn on my e-mails, they'll all download. I was going to do that at a café or something later, when I have Wi-Fi."

More silence.

"What about a picture message? Could you get one of those?"

"Jason, what difference does it make? I just want to talk to you. I can get whatever it is later, or just tell me about it."

"Look. Just turn on your data, I want to send you something; it's important. When you get it, call me straight back."

Natasha shook her head and looked at the clock on her phone. She was okay, had some time until she was due to meet Mark for a workout before they headed into town with the others.

"Okay," she said, resigned. "Send it by picture message now, then. I'll wait. Love you."

"'Bye," he said, and the line went dead.

Natasha sat and waited, flicking on her data and ensuring that only her messages were able to use it. She waited for what seemed like an age, her gaze drifting over the water and the large American aircraft carrier that was berthed at the other side of the dockyard. She was about to dial again when the first message arrived. She opened it and felt as though she'd been punched in the stomach. Another text message accompanied the image.

Call me if you want. Don't bother if you don't.

Leaning forward and retching as her breathing accelerated and her heart thumped, Natasha flicked back to the picture. She was in it, central, smiling, in a small white tank top with thin straps, and behind her, his hands resting on her tanned shoulders and his lips planted firmly against her neck, was Mark.

He was shirtless, standing really close, and the rest of the ship's company partying and drinking around them had been cropped out, so that they looked like a young couple having fun in the sun.

"No!" said Natasha.

She didn't even remember him kissing her like that. It'd been a flight deck barbecue, everyone was having fun, playing deck hockey, drinking beer, enjoying burgers. He'd jumped on her back, she remembered that, but did he really kiss her? She certainly wouldn't have reciprocated. Even in the picture she wasn't kissing him back.

Her hands were shaking and she dropped the phone on the broken edge of the dark tarmac as she tried to dial Jason's number. Eventually she managed to hold it steady, waiting while the phone rang again and again, finally switching her through to voice mail. She dialed back immediately and waited while the same thing happened again. Then she typed in a text.

Answer the phone!!! Please!!!

She sent it immediately, gave it a few seconds, then dialed him again.

"What?" he said as he answered the phone, and though she hated herself for doing it, her breathing barely under control, Natasha started to cry.

"It's not what you think," she said, and realized how much of a cliché that was, how ridiculous she must sound. "I didn't kiss him. He's just a friend. I wouldn't have kissed him. If I'd known he'd kissed me—even on the cheek, let alone the neck—I'd have told him to get off."

The words were tumbling out, short sentences, between clipped breaths.

"I love you. I haven't done the dirty on you and I never would," she said.

"Really," he said, and the silence drew out between them.

"After all we've been through, you don't believe me?" Natasha said. "I love you, I really do."

"I believe one thing," he said, and his voice was so cold that it chilled Natasha even as the sun disappeared and the wind began to do the same. "I believe you're just like your slut mum. A cheat. Making me wait, but putting out to anyone else who's nice to you. I've always backed you. Everyone said I was too old, you were too young, I wasn't good enough for you, not handsome enough, too much of a loser, but we said 'fuck them,' because we were happy and you knew you'd be able to do all the things you wanted to do while I was behind you. Now this . . ."

The silence on the line was unbearable, and Natasha realized she was holding her breath.

"Don't call again," he said. "I'll be gone when you get back."

"No!" Natasha shouted so loud that she surprised herself. "No, don't go! Please don't. It really isn't what you think. I promise. Fly out today. Take the money from my savings and fly out on the first flight you can get."

He snorted at her.

"What? Fancy a threesome?"

"What?" she said. "What does that even mean?"

"It means that your new boyfriend e-mailed me the picture and laid it out for me. Asked me not to tell you what he'd sent, but told me that apparently you quite like the jolly old thing, eh? We're saving it until we get married, but for him you'll take it any way you can?"

"I don't know what you mean. I haven't slept with anyone."

"Yeah, well, you tell Mark he can keep you. You're a proper Moore now, a chip off the old block, a dirty, slutty little whore—your mum'd be really proud of you. Don't call back."

"Wait!" Natasha cried again, sensing he was going to hang up the phone, but she didn't know what to say.

"Tell the little slag to do one," said a girl's voice from Jason's end of the line.

Natasha heard Jason say something, try to shush the other voice, and then she heard the line go dead. She retched again. Only bile came up, there was nothing else in her belly, and she spat it out onto the ground and wiped her mouth, her head spinning.

She heard footsteps but couldn't look up as someone approached.

"Hey, T-t-t-t-tashaaaaaaaaaa."

She heard the words, the greeting that only Mark used, clicking out the start of her name as though he was stuttering and then singing the long *aaaah* for as long as his breath could keep it going.

"You ready to run? And then we need to get ready to P-A-R-T-Y?" He spelled the word out, prolonging the last letter as though it were a question. "Because we have to."

She saw his feet. He was dancing a little jig to imaginary music while he waited for her to answer. She looked at her phone; now that the call was gone, the screen had switched back to the picture of them together, Mark planting a kiss on her neck. She heard Jason's words again: "Your new boyfriend laid it out for me," he'd said. "Apparently you quite like the jolly old thing."

"You okay, Tash?" asked Mark. "Is something wrong?"

She turned to him, tears streaming down her face.

He recoiled at first, then his mouth opened and he rushed toward her, his arms outstretched.

"Tash," he said. "What's going on?"

He got close to her and without thinking, she swung a punch at him. It was wild, she didn't like fighting, but where she grew up, and with her mum and dad to learn from, she knew how. She connected with his eye and felt her teeth clench as the pain shot through her hand, but she swung at him again with her other hand.

"What the—!"

He stepped back, stumbling, his legs crossing, and fell onto his backside.

Natasha didn't follow him; she knew better than to go to ground if she could help it. She waited until he went down and then swung a kick at him.

He rolled away from her, getting back to his feet quickly and holding his hands in front of him in a defensive posture.

"What's going on?" he said, sounding a little less frightened now, still worried, but he'd overcome his initial shock and some anger was creeping into his voice.

"You're what's wrong," she said, and feinted a punch to his head, watching as his hands and eyes moved to protect it, and then swinging a hard kick at his groin.

Her foot missed, glancing off his thigh, and she lost her balance, turning a bit and showing her side to him.

He was on her in a flash.

Natasha flinched, her teeth clenched and bared as she anticipated the pain of a slap or a punch, but instead she was wrapped up as he threw his arms around her, gathering hers against her own body and lifting her off the ground.

She kicked and threw her head back, trying to head-butt him, but he was muscular and strong, and she had little hope.

"Stop it," he said, his voice firm. "Pack it in. What's wrong with you?"

She ignored him, still wriggling, even as she felt the energy start to drain out of her.

"Natasha. Stop," he said again. "I don't know what's happened, but whatever it is, I know one thing for sure, I'm on your side. Okay? Whatever it is, I'm with you. I've got your back, whatever it takes until we get it sorted. Okay?"

Natasha heard the words and felt suddenly exhausted, the adrenaline dissipated and her limbs heavy and sore.

"You happened," she said.

He'd grabbed her almost from behind, slightly from one side, and he was holding her tight, his head just behind hers, his cheek pressed against hers.

"What?" he said, speaking almost directly into her ear.

"You happened," she said again. "You told Jason we'd slept together. You sent him pictures of when you jumped on me at the ship's barbecue."

His grip loosened, but he didn't let go.

"What?" he said.

Natasha would have hit him again, but she'd nothing left in the tank, no energy left to do it.

"You heard me, and now he's dumped me, because he thinks I'm sleeping with you."

Mark released her, slowly, putting her back down on the floor and then turning her around to face him.

"Tash, whatever you think I've done, I can tell you now, I haven't. I like you. I like you a lot and I feel close to you. But you know what, I want you to want me because you like me, too, not because you've been dumped.

I'd never do that. I'd never do anything like that. I can't believe you think I would."

She couldn't look at him as he spoke, but as she thought about what he'd said, she knew he wasn't lying.

"Someone sent this picture to Jason," she said, and picked her phone up from the floor where it had fallen, thankful that the screen was still intact. She showed him the image.

"Tash, it wasn't me. I swear it. I haven't even seen this one before. Who took it?"

He handed the phone back to her.

"Did he say what e-mail address it came from?"

She shook her head.

"Well, look. It's someone on the ship, right? Because those pics are only on the ship. As far as I know, they're all in the same folder on the shared drive."

Natasha nodded.

He reached out and gently touched her arm.

"I wouldn't do this to you, Tash," he said again.

She looked at him, reached up to move his hand, but squeezed it as she let it drop.

"Ask him how he got them, what the e-mail address was, or whatever, then we'll go to the ship's regulator and tell him."

Natasha sniffed and wiped her sleeve across her face. "He said they were e-mailed, that you e-mailed him and told him we were having sex."

"I'd be more likely to, you know, high-five people than e-mail anyone," Mark said.

Natasha looked at him and sighed, her face stern.

"Too soon," he said, bowing his head and apologizing. "Definitely too soon. My bad. But seriously, I don't even know your fella's e-mail address. I don't know his surname. I wouldn't even know how to find him on social media or anything. I mean, who'd know what e-mail address to even send it to?"

21

"What do you make of him, then?" asked John as they walked back into the SIB offices.

Dan stopped and turned to look at him.

"You know, I believe him. I didn't like him at first, not that that matters, but I didn't. He felt aggressive, but now I'm more inclined to think he's a mixture of worried and feeling plain guilty for being a dirty doer."

"Yeah, maybe," said John.

Dan started to walk again.

"But you know, I do feel like someone isn't being truthful," she said. "I think we should go back to *Defiance*, kick some butts and take some names."

John grinned as though nothing would be more fun.

Dan walked past a cluster of desks in the main office, but only one of them was currently occupied.

The area she was in now, just along the corridor from her own office, housed the majority of the regulators who made up the Special Investigation Branch in Portsmouth Dockyard, but Dan's team was small: herself, John, and a shared resource of two petty officers and four leading regulators, who all had other varying full- or part-time responsibilities.

It wasn't official, but over time this had come to mean that during normal working days, Dan had "first dibs" on one of the leading hands, while the remainder worked on other assignments under different command chains.

Leading Regulator Josaia "Josie" Nakarawa looked up from her screen and smiled as she saw Dan arriving.

"Anything on the young girl from *Defiance*?" Dan asked.

"There is, ma'am, but not much," she said.

Josie looked bright and awake, as she always did. This despite the fact that she was nearly always in the office first and worked tirelessly throughout the day, often staying back after the base had been secured; Dan envied her energy, especially today.

"I called all known contacts and family for the MISPER last night, but there's still no news. They say they haven't seen her, and you know what, ma'am, I believe them. Not one of those people seemed to care a damn that she was gone, honestly, not a one of them."

"It's sometimes the way," said Dan, remembering how little interest she'd aroused from Ryan Taylor's parents when she'd managed to speak to them again, not all that long ago. She wondered if they were the ones who'd called in and told Harrow-Brown that she'd been to speak to them, that she was still pursuing their son.

"Well." Josie shook her head.

The word "well," when spoken by Josie, could often be regarded as its own sentence. It meant a multitude of things depending on context and how she pronounced it. It could also serve to end conversations when she had nothing more to say.

"I also called the officer of the day on *Defiance*, ma'am, and they still haven't seen her. I know they'd call if they had, but it doesn't hurt to check."

"No, it never hurts to check," agreed Dan.

"Whose turn is it to get the tea?" asked John.

"Yours," said Dan and Josie in near unison, and John's face changed to a hangdog expression. "I swear I did it last time," he grumbled before heading through to the small kitchenette.

Dan heard the kettle go on, then he came back out to grab her mug from her office and then Josie's from her desk on the way past.

"Going okay, Josie?" he asked, looking over her shoulder at her screen.

"Yes, Master," she said. "But, you know how you thought you recognized the picture of that girl from *Defiance*?"

John nodded, and Dan raised an eyebrow.

"You mean *I* thought I recognized the picture," said Dan.

He smiled. "I did, too."

"Well," said Josie. "Either way, I was checking and I think you're both mistaken. I think the picture you're thinking of is this one."

She pulled a photograph out of a brown folder on her desk. Josie held the picture up and Dan and John looked at it.

"That's the one," said Dan, stepping forward and taking it, then handing it to John.

"Not the same girl," said Josie. "This young lady, Stephanie James, went missing, lost overboard a year or so ago, when *Defiance* was coming back alongside. She fell overboard at night when the ship was maneuvering; body never recovered."

Dan looked at John.

"What do you think?" she asked.

"What should I think?"

"They look very alike."

John scrunched up his nose.

"Natasha Moore didn't fall overboard. The harbor's crawling with people during the day, and the Queen's Harbour Master has confirmed that the seaward footage is clear."

Dan looked to Josie.

"You know, just find out as much as you can about that. I know a link's unlikely, but it won't hurt to take a look."

Josie took the picture back and tucked it in the file.

"Did you get someone round to check her flat?" asked Dan.

John nodded. "I went and did it myself last night," he said. "It was empty. I checked through the letter slot too, as far as I could. There was one of those free papers still wedged in it and I could see a load of mail on the floor, so I doubt anyone'd been home for a few days, at least."

"I really thought she'd be back today," said Dan.

"I'm not done," said John. "While I was looking, a lady from across the road came to see what I was doing. She keeps an eye on the place for the landlord. So we chatted awhile, and she told me Moore had lived there with her fiancé until a few weeks or months ago, when he moved out. This was before Moore got back from sea."

"Okay," said Dan, reaching up and massaging her temples. A headache was starting to form, and she knew it was from lack of sleep.

"She also said that a large chap had been by the flat a few times, sitting in his car out on the street. She noticed him because he was, and I quote, "fucking huge." She saw him talking to Moore's fiancé; she didn't think they were friends."

"Black," said Dan.

"Look," John interrupted before she could say anything more. "I was thinking about this last night, a lot. Her bike's still there at the dockyard. She hasn't been home for any clothes so far as we can tell . . ."

"And I came in early to get through some of the footage from CCTV around *Defiance*," said Josie. "I can see SA Moore going onto the ship. It's easy. I can see her moving all through the dockyard, but I haven't been able to see anyone like her coming off the ship. The picture is pretty good from one of the dockside cameras, too, but there are occasional blind spots because of the cranes moving stores or stuff like that. So I crossed the timings and looked at other camera angles to see if she'd come off during that time. I'm not finished yet. I started at around eleven o'clock, so just before her divisional officer last saw her, and I've found nothing. I'll keep at it."

Dan and John exchanged an appreciative look. Josie was good.

"Okay, well, if in doubt, there is no doubt," said Dan. "If we're genuinely worried and we believe what Jason's telling us, then let's go back down there and do something. We do need to remember that her peers weren't overly worried about her. That relaxes me a little bit, because you often get a feel for that, and if they're worried, you can tell. If they aren't, then possibly this isn't a major problem, but we'll see."

"The vibe I got was that they were covering for someone, or something," said John. "Just a thought."

"And you don't think they were covering for her?" asked Dan.

"I don't know. Maybe," he conceded.

Dan pursed her lips and thought.

"Okay, well let's find out, then. I want to speak to the PTI who was mentioned. Josie, can you fix that please? I also want another chat with the divisional officer, the section petty officer, and some of the girls from the mess. Especially the more senior girls she was sharing a cabin with."

Josie was scribbling notes, and John was nodding.

"Okay," he said.

Josie ripped a piece of notepaper off her pad and handed it to John.

"So you don't forget," she said. "I'll call ahead now and make sure they know what you want to do."

John put the mugs down, accepting that there wasn't going to be time for tea.

Dan took her mug and walked to her office. She felt him follow her and stopped inside, turning to face him.

"What's up?" she asked.

He gestured back through to Josie. "She's good, really good. You know, before she was recruited by the commonwealth recruiting teams, she was working for the police in Fiji, not as an officer, but in and around the main station."

"I didn't know that."

"Well, she's definitely one to watch, isn't she?"

"She is," agreed Dan.

"Did you know she specifically requested to come here to work with you? I think you're her hero."

"Heroine," said Dan. "But that's not what you came here to say, is it?"

He shook his head.

"No. I want to know what's going on with you," he said. "You look absolutely ball-bagged, like you haven't slept in weeks. I want to know that you've stopped with the Ryan Taylor thing, at least for a while, and that if you're going out for nocturnal trips, you'll be calling me to come along with you. Safety in numbers and all that."

Dan looked up at the ceiling and closed her eyes tight. She hoped the headache might slide to the back of her head, away from her eyes, or at the very least drain to a different part of her skull.

"I'm fine, John. I didn't sleep well and I've got a headache."

"And . . ."

Dan opened her eyes as wide as she could and then closed them again.

"And I need a couple of aspirin and a few minutes where I'm not under interrogation."

"And . . ." repeated John.

"And I . . ." She paused, opened her eyes, and looked at him closely. He was watching her, checking for any sign of a lie.

"And I'm taking some time off looking for Ryan Taylor. Okay?"

He nodded. "So nothing more about Ryan Taylor from the civvies, then? I see you constantly checking your phone. Any news at all?"

Dan sighed. "No. Nothing." She looked at him and knew she couldn't hold out on him, not again. "Look, I'm involved, sort of, in another investigation that the NCA is running. It's only a light touch, but it involves Hamilton."

John shut the door.

"I'm not allowed to say anything to anyone," said Dan, "so I can't answer questions and you can't speak a word of it, but that's where I was this morning."

"You were talking to the NCA about Hamilton?"

"No. I was talking to Hamilton."

John made to speak but seemed not to know what to say. His cheeks flushed red and his eyes darkened.

"Okay," he managed, finally. "I won't push and I get the secrecy that'll be around this, but I want you to talk to me about this as much as you can, share the load a bit, okay? Don't try to take it all on yourself."

"Deal," said Dan, and she meant it.

22

Natasha persuaded Mark to leave her alone for a while after they'd talked at the dockside. Then she headed down to the stores office, a route she'd walked so many times now she could do it in her sleep, and it was a good thing, too, because she was filled with rage, and as she moved closer to the office, she could feel it clouding her vision as much as her judgment.

The flat outside the stores office was silent and she'd encountered next to no one on her way down, which was definitely for the best. She hesitated for just a second before she turned and stormed into the office area.

Gary Black was nowhere to be seen.

She'd been sure he'd be down here and was ready to confront him, but his absence knocked the wind out of her sails. She stood there unsure what to do next.

Then she heard a sound among the shelves and storage racks.

He was humming quietly as he moved around. Then he started to sing a song in a voice that sounded just a fraction too high-pitched for someone his size. He was singing freely, had no idea he was being listened to, and he wasn't quite hitting the notes, though he was giving it such effort that Natasha was certain he'd never have the confidence to act like that if he thought anyone was around.

She looked around the office again, looked at his desk and filing cabinet, and then at his computer screen.

It was unlocked, the window for his e-mails up and available to her;

he must have nipped outside only a few minutes before. She moved forward quickly, reaching for the mouse just as the automatic screensaver appeared and she was locked out.

Natasha's hands tensed and she felt frustration and temper build as she balled her fists and resisted the urge to scream.

Then she looked at his filing cabinet.

He never allowed anyone to go in there, guarded it as a child guards a favorite toy.

She quickly reached for the top drawer, pulled it a tiny bit, and winced at the grating sound of the old metal runners. She stopped, waited, could still hear his singing, and tried the next one down.

It opened far more quietly, and she looked inside. Sweets and nutty, some stores labels, but nothing of interest.

She'd no idea what she was looking for, but she opened the bottom drawer anyway.

This one was filled with suspension dividers.

She looked down and used her fingers to separate out the first divider, then stopped and stared, frowning.

Inside the divider, stored neatly, was sheet after sheet of handwritten notes and lists, all jotted down on scraps of paper and yellow sticky notes. They were in random order, just thrust into the divider, and every one of them that she could see, no matter how mundane the words, was written by her. She flicked through them, shaking her head as she looked at one after another.

> Gone to lunch. Nat

"What the . . ." She fished through and pulled out another one.

> Going to canteen. Text if you want anything. Nat

There were loads of them.

She dug deeper and found a small pile of crumpled sheets stapled together. Pulling them out and smoothing them flat, she instantly recognized what they were.

On the sheets she saw attempt after attempt, and version after version, of what her signature might look like after she and Jason were married. She'd done it one day at sea when things were quiet, remembered it now, tried to see how it might look when she was Mrs. Goulding. She'd tried her full name—Natasha Goulding—tried it in several different ways with a large curling initial G and with a long tail on the final g, flicking the nib back and underlining her whole name. She'd also tried her initial with the surname, practicing it several times, big and small, writing it quickly, as though signing a check, and sometimes slowly, as though signing an important letter. She remembered doing all of them, and then she remembered crumpling them up and throwing them at the bin from across the room; she'd gotten it in on the first try, and Gary had cheered the shot.

She tucked the sheets under her arm and opened the next divider.

"What're you doing?"

She stood up, stunned to see Black just inside the door. She couldn't read his face—anger, shock, embarrassment—but she wasn't scared, either. She held the sheets up so he could see.

"What's this?" she said.

He seemed to hesitate, the muscles twitching around his mouth and his hands flexing, as though he wanted to both speak and act but wasn't sure which to do first.

"I found this in there." She turned to point to the drawer and stopped.

In the divider that she'd just opened, she caught sight of hair, her hair, in a photograph. She couldn't see her face, but she knew it was her. She looked at it and then back at Black. Then she leaned down, reaching for it.

He was next to her in no time. He pushed her aside, not hurting her, but easily moving her off balance and sending her reeling across the compartment.

She fell against her own desk and looked up at him.

He pushed the drawer shut with his boot and turned to face her. His face looked on the edge of angry, flushed and humiliated, as though he might either tear her apart or break down and cry. His lips were moving again, but no more words were coming out.

"Did you send an e-mail to Jason?" she said, her voice low.

He was shaking his head before the words even left his mouth. He seemed to calm, breathing slowly.

"No, Nat, I don't know what you mean."

"Did you send pictures to my boyfriend from the ship's barbecue?" she said, and she instantly remembered why she recognized her hair from the tiny fragment of photo she'd glimpsed in the drawer. The picture was from that day, the day of the ship's barbecue, her hair was down and loose and she had colorful earrings on, neither of which happened during a normal day at sea.

She looked at him, stared in disbelief.

"You've read my e-mails too, haven't you? That day when Jason went out, you'd read my e-mail."

He said nothing.

"You're done," she said, and looked down at the paper with her signature on it, the signature that would now never be. She tucked it under her arm and stormed to the door.

"No, Nat," he said, reaching for her, his huge hands closing easily around her arm as they had done before.

"Don't you—!" she spat the words at him, digging her fingernails into the back of his hand and glaring at him until he recoiled from her as though his fingers had been burned by her touch. "I'm going to Cox, right now," she said.

He said nothing as she left the compartment.

NATASHA KNOCKED ON Cox's door, her head bowed, watching her hands shake while she waited. There was no reply and she knocked again, harder, but already wondering whether Cox might be out.

The door was ajar, though, as it often was, and that would normally mean Cox was at least nearby.

Natasha heard a sound at the end of the officer's accommodation flat.

The layout was similar to Natasha's own, and the door at the end opened, one that Natasha knew led to the officers' shower area, and Cox walked through, a towel round her head and a long dressing gown covering her down to midcalf.

She was holding a long wash bag by a hook and it hung down beside her, almost to the floor, a column of clear pockets filled with toiletries.

Sarah Cox looked at Natasha and walked quickly toward her.

"Are you okay?" asked Cox, moving in close to Natasha and then hesitating, seeming not to know what to do next.

Cox looked round the flat, as though checking to make sure they were alone.

"I'll come back in a bit," said Natasha.

"No, it's fine. Come in now and talk to me."

Cox pushed the door open and walked into the cabin, dropping her toiletry bag into her sink and sitting down quickly on her chair.

"Come in."

"Honestly, ma'am—Sarah—I can wait till you're ready."

"Tash." Cox's voice was stern. "Come in now and talk to me."

She smiled at Natasha and waited.

"Shut the door," said Cox, as Natasha reluctantly stepped inside and sat down.

The bed in the cabin was usually converted into a couch, and that was where Natasha would ordinarily sit, but being alongside in harbor and during a quiet period, Cox hadn't made it up yet, and Natasha felt odd as she was told to sit on the edge of the unmade bed, the duvet gathered up behind her where Cox had thrown it aside that morning.

Cox smiled again and waited. She moved in her chair and crossed her legs, and as she did, her dressing gown parted, revealing the length of her leg up to the top of her thigh.

Natasha looked away. It felt awkward, and she waited for Cox to sort the dressing gown out and cover herself up, but she didn't.

"What's got you so upset?" asked Cox.

Natasha paused, not knowing where to start. She felt more tears coming and looked away.

Cox just watched her, tilting her head.

"Whatever it is, it's okay," Cox said. "Tell me, and if I can help, I'll help."

Cox looked serious.

"It's PO Black. There's loads of stuff. I don't know where to start. He keeps me late at work for no good reason. He does it all the time so I can't go out with the other junior rates. He's done it more than once or twice, just when we were in Gibraltar . . ."

Natasha could see that Cox wasn't listening to her to understand what she was saying, but listening to her so she could reply.

Her lips were already moving, itching to start explaining her thoughts about what Natasha had said.

Natasha pushed on, not allowing Cox to speak.

"And then today, I found this." Natasha put the crumpled sheets of paper onto Cox's desk. "I did these ages ago. I threw them in the waste-basket, but he kept them. He's got a whole drawer full of notes that I left in the office for him, just random things I've written down. It's weird. It's worse than weird. He's got pictures of me in that drawer in his filing cabinet. I saw them, before he slammed the drawer shut. It's not right. He's frightening me."

It wasn't until Natasha spoke the words that she realized they were true. It wasn't just Black's physical size—that, in truth, didn't frighten her; but when she said all of these things one after another, she realized that the sum of the individual parts was way greater, a much bigger prob-lem, than any of the isolated incidents. She hadn't done this before, listed all the different little bits and pieces that Black had done in one go—each one of them, on its own, completely explainable and justifiable, but when put together, like pieces of a jigsaw, forming a picture of something that wasn't right at all.

"Pictures?" Cox looked stern. "Okay. Wait for me outside for just two seconds and let me drag some clothes on. Then we'll go down and check out this cabinet and see what's there. After that, we can talk again."

THEY WALKED DOWN to the stores office together, Cox carrying the sheets of paper with Natasha's practice signatures all over them.

Black was in the office, sitting at his desk typing. He looked up as he saw them, smiling at Natasha initially, then looking worried as he saw Cox behind her.

"Are you okay?" he asked Natasha. "Is everything okay?" he said, look-ing up at Cox.

"Open the bottom drawer of your filing cabinet for me, please, PO Black," said Cox in a firm voice.

He stood up and stepped away from his desk.

"It's already open," he said, gesturing to it. "Nat . . ." he began, but she cut him off with a raised hand.

"This one?" said Cox, pointing to the drawer and kneeling in front of it.

"Yes, that one, but he could've moved it all," said Natasha. "I've been gone twenty minutes or more."

Black looked mortified. "I haven't moved anything," he said. "I don't know why you got so upset. I really don't, but you can look as much as you want. In there, anywhere round here."

Cox pulled out the drawer and then opened the first of the suspension files.

Natasha could see inside it.

Some of the notes were still in there, but now there was other stuff, too, notes and papers and even sweet wrappers that should have been in the trash bin.

Cox held up a chocolate bar wrapper and Black looked sheepish, taking it and ditching it in the bin across the room.

"It's just where I keep my crap," he said.

Cox rifled through, finding some notes that were in Natasha's handwriting, but also many that were from others.

"I think this needs a clear-out. What do you think?" she said.

"Yes, ma'am," said Black.

"Natasha, where did you see the pictures?" asked Cox.

Natasha stepped forward and flicked through the suspension files with her fingers until she caught a glimpse of her hair.

Cox gestured for her to step away and pulled the pictures out. On the top was a photo of Natasha, her blond hair loose and blowing in the wind that was cutting across the flight deck. Next to her in the picture was Gary Black. He was holding a can of beer and smiling at the camera, his massive arm over Natasha's shoulders.

"That wasn't the one," said Natasha. "It was more of a close-up."

Cox flicked through the pile.

They were all of Gary Black with people from *Defiance* or previous ships. Some were of a woman Natasha didn't recognize but suspected was his ex-wife. There were more of him in uniform at parades or military presentations and some of Black with sports teams, several of them at powerlifting competitions when he looked much younger, showing him straining as he lifted a bar with numerous colored disks on each end.

"It's just my memories," he said, his lisp making him sound vulnerable as he spoke. "I thought that that one of us was a nice picture, so I printed it out," he said, looking at Natasha. "It was on the drive. I really didn't think you'd mind. I'm sorry."

Cox looked at Natasha and then at Black.

"Gary," Cox said, and Natasha couldn't help but notice that she had slipped into first-name terms with him. "Why would you fish these out of the bin and keep them?"

She held out the crumpled pages of signatures.

He hesitated, seemed about to stutter.

"I saw them in the bin," he began, looking from one woman to the other. "And I thought Nat'd regret throwing them away. I thought when she got married we could frame some of them for her, a gift from the ship's company, like something to keep and to show Jason how much Nat thought about him when she was away at sea."

He was still looking continuously from Cox to Natasha and back again as he spoke.

"I thought it would be really thoughtful," he said. "I thought you'd really love it, Nat. We could've got a nice frame, given it to you and Jason from all of us."

Natasha was shaking her head. She made to speak, but Cox silenced her.

"Gary, would you please go outside and close the door? In fact, would you meet me in my cabin in ten minutes, please?"

Black nodded, looked at Natasha, and then walked out of the stores office in silence.

Cox waited until the door was shut and then sat down on Black's chair.

"Sit down," she said to Natasha.

"I can't," said Natasha, her body charged with adrenaline. "This isn't how it should be. It's not right."

"Look. You've had a really shitty day. What happened between you and Jason, and then coming down and seeing this. It's easy to see how you've gotten yourself into a state."

"No," began Natasha, but she was told to be silent again.

"I believe you, Tasha. I believe that something isn't right. I'm going to speak to Gary now and sort this out. Okay?"

Natasha's shoulders slumped. She sat down on her chair, spun around to face her desk, and put her head into her hands. She didn't know what else to do, who else to turn to.

Black had rearranged the stuff in the drawers, had moved things to make her look stupid and paranoid, a troublemaker. Natasha was certain of it.

23

Commander Ward, *Defiance*'s commanding officer, was somewhere on board.

Dan hadn't seen him, but she could tell by the tight atmosphere, people moving around with purpose.

John was making some calls on the flight deck, standing at the edge of the ship next to the collapsible barriers. In port, they were always up—safety first—and he leaned against them, his form black against the scene behind him as he looked out on the seaward side of *Defiance*.

Dan was just inside the hangar. She checked her phone repeatedly, a bad habit that was becoming an obsession. She wasn't sure what she was waiting for, whether it was an update from Roger about the NCA investigation, or from Felicity perhaps, telling her some news about what Hamilton had said. She knew she really did need to take a break from Ryan Taylor, too, needed to leave him be, wherever he was, unhunted for a few weeks at least—Harrow-Brown would be watching.

She thought about the fingers that were turning up at the NCA, about the missing women they belonged to. She looked across at John as he wandered across the deck toward her.

"Sorry, Boss," he said. "So, Josie's working on finishing off the CCTV footage back at the office. She's top-notch and she's on duty tonight so she'll stay late if it takes longer than we think. She's rechecking the seaward cameras, too, just in case we missed an overboard, but I don't think that's likely."

"Did we find her bag?" Dan asked.

"No. Well, I guess she must have had one."

Dan managed not to roll her eyes.

"I don't mean a handbag, John. I mean she was carrying a bag when she arrived, wasn't she? The image that was on Josie's desk this morning showed her carrying a bag over her shoulder, a little daysack, but no one's mentioned it yet."

"Okay, I'll check her bunk space and ask around. Where're you going now?"

"I'll try to find this Petty Officer Black. You can meet me down there when you're done."

John laughed. "He's not hard to find, they call him the Silver-Black Gorilla."

Dan did roll her eyes this time.

"Exceptionally hairy?"

"You'll know why when you see him." said John. "I'll meet you at the stores office in a little while, then. You know where it is?"

"I'll find it."

Dan left him and walked back onto the ship.

Defiance had a subtly different layout from that of Dan's previous ships, with a central passage, 2-deck, that ran more or less the length of the ship from bow to stern, as opposed to the ring-road arrangement of her previous ships with a deck that ran down each side and linked at either end. In various different places there were hatches and ladders that let you move up and down the levels.

Dan walked along 1-deck and then took a ladder down to 2-deck.

She looked down a passageway that was eerily familiar to the last, and then turned around on herself.

"Lost" felt like too strong a word to use, as she thought about where exactly she might be.

"You looking for me, ma'am?"

Dan turned around again and immediately stepped backward, moving away from the sailor who'd spoken to her.

The man in front of her was enormous. He reached out a hand.

"Gary Black," he said. "I think you've gone a section too far. The stores office is back in 3-Gulf, you've come into 3-Hotel."

She was well aware that the ship was divided by numbered decks from top to bottom, and by lettered sections forward to aft. She looked around at the markings in the compartment; he was right.

"I must have been in a bit of a daze," said Dan.

Dan took his hand, hers disappearing inside it, and shook it.

He shook gently, firmly, but not squeezing as some men tended to do, and then he stepped back, and Dan was grateful for the space.

She could see now how he'd earned his nickname. He was easily six feet six inches tall, but his real size was in his build. Everything about him was oversized, and he must've been three hundred pounds or more of nearly solid muscle.

Dan introduced herself.

"I'll take you to the office," he said.

He spoke with a slight lisp, then turned away, gesturing for her to follow.

She noted how considerate he seemed, stepping back so as not to crowd her when they went through hatches and bulkhead doors, and not trying to "prove" anything in the handshake.

Eventually they ended up in the stores flat, a lobby-type compartment, and off to their left was the large main storeroom.

Black led her through, and Dan saw row after row of silver-colored stores racks, all numbered and lettered and many with items in cream-colored cotton bags placed on shelves next to bigger items, all of the equipment and spare parts that would be needed to keep *Defiance* operating at sea.

She followed him through a door and turned left into the stores office.

She was surprised at the size of the space.

Cupboards and desks ran around the compartment on three sides, and there was enough space and computers for three or four people to work comfortably. There was a calendar up on the wall, Harley-Davidson motorcycles, but the woman atop the bike had been colored in, censored with black marker pens, and had a large black mustache and a sombrero drawn on her for good measure.

"Got girls working down here now," Black said, nodding at the pictures. "But we all like the bikes, so we just censor the pictures so no one gets offended."

Dan tried not to think about how that would make her feel.

He looked back at her. "Tea, ma'am?" he asked, his soft voice sounding odd coming out of such a large man.

"No, thank you."

Dan looked for a seat and Black immediately grabbed a chair for her, clearing some coats off the back of it and dusting it down before stepping back so she could sit.

Dan waited for him to sit down first, not wanting to feel even smaller than she already did.

He seemed like a nice guy, aware of his size, and she felt sure that his lisp in some way dented his confidence, but it was still hard not to be intimidated in a space like this with someone who so clearly dwarfed her.

"So, ma'am, you want to talk about Nat?"

"I do, yes, please, but I thought her nickname was Tasha."

He smiled and his cheeks flushed red.

Dan immediately caught on.

"I don't say that word very well," he said. "We agreed I'd call her Nat."

Dan nodded an apology. "Of course."

"Well," he began without prompting, "Nat works for me and has done since she joined *Defiance* about four months ago. She was supposed to come to work on Friday and she did. We had a cup of tea in here at about eight. Then I needed to go and do some stuff at the main stores offices, inboard. Nat was supposed to be chasing up a load of maintenance stores for the engineers, as well as starting to audit our sea stock."

Dan watched him speak, noted how he talked about Natasha so easily, almost as though they were partners, rather than her working for him.

"I knew she had a meeting with Lieutenant Cox at ten thirty and I wasn't expecting her back for at least an hour."

"At least an hour?"

"Yeah, those two can really talk when they get going. You know"— he paused, looking at Dan and thinking—"what people are like."

"I do," agreed Dan. "Some people love to talk, but it still seems a long time for a simple divisional catch-up. Do you know what the meeting was about? Did SA Moore tell you?"

"No, but she had regular meetings. Lieutenant Cox liked to talk to her."

"Go on," Dan prompted him.

"When she didn't come back by twelve, lunchtime. I called up and Ma'am said she'd left her cabin a good hour or more ago. We normally eat lunch in here together on a Friday, right before we go weekenders. So I was surprised when she didn't show up, but I thought she might have nipped inboard, maybe met a friend and grabbed lunch there. So I just ate mine on my own."

Dan almost felt sorry for him when he said this, imagining him sitting in the chair like a massive lost child, eating his sandwiches in silence.

"But then she didn't show up for the thirteen hundred hours muster either, and that's not right. Nat always shows up on time, and so I started looking for her. I called around and checked the main stores in the dockyard. I made some pipes over the ship's main broadcast and I called her mobile and stuff, but she didn't answer. No one had seen her."

He seemed to be speaking more quickly now, his lisp less prevalent.

"By fourteen hundred I knew something was wrong. It's just not like her. So I spoke to Lieutenant Cox. We decided that Nat'd gone weekend and not managed to say good-bye. I wasn't happy. Nat didn't answer my calls all weekend, and she wasn't at home, either. Then she didn't come in on Monday. That's when I went back to Ma'am and then to the skipper, Commander Ward. He took it serious from the off and we searched all the compartments, you know, in case she'd been looking for something and got hurt or trapped or whatever. But nothing, nothing at all, and I'd already been round the stores areas anyway, so I knew she wasn't there."

"How was she when you saw her on Friday morning?" asked Dan, wondering if she could get that question recorded and play it on a loop.

"She was fine," he said. "Just normal, we had a cup of tea together, chatted and stuff, she was just like she always is."

"Has she ever done this before?" asked Dan.

"No, never," said Black, surprising Dan with his certainty.

"Are you sure? I understood that she'd missed a morning muster once, but that Lieutenant Cox had sanctioned retrospective leave."

He looked genuinely surprised, but Dan wasn't sure how honest he was being. It was clear from the way he spoke that he was fond of Moore, and it was highly likely he'd cover for her if he could. Also, as Dan well knew, senior rates could be wilier than younger, less seasoned officers like

Sarah Cox, less likely to show their hand if they knew they couldn't be discovered, less likely to come clean and face unnecessary music.

"I never heard of that," he said. "But I'm sure Lieutenant Cox is right. I mean, Nat's been a few minutes late before now, but who hasn't been, right?"

Dan nodded agreement.

"A moment ago you said she's never late. What do you do when she is, then?"

He shrugged.

"Nothing. Everyone has the odd bad morning. It's no biggie, and she makes the time up, no problems."

"But wouldn't she get pulled up on the gangway for being adrift?"

He smiled again, the same shy smile, his eyes dropping away from Dan.

"Well, ma'am, you know the score. We all know each other on here. Got to look after each other, right?"

"Right," agreed Dan.

There was a knock at the door and she turned to see John coming in.

She watched the two men shake hands, noting yet again that there weren't many men around who dwarfed John Granger, but Black did. She watched how John reacted to it, seeming to lean into Black, invading his personal space, whether consciously or subconsciously, forcing Black to be the one to move away.

John looked at Dan, and she knew there was something he needed to tell her, but he looked around and grabbed another seat to let her finish.

"Were you due to be here, in office, all day on Friday, PO Black?" she asked.

"No, ma'am, I was going to be in and out fairly often. I was supposed to be inboard most of the morning. I did have to pop back and forth in the end, though. Loads of stores to move on and off, it's easier if I'm there to supervise."

"Okay, thanks, PO," said Dan, standing up.

Dan turned to the door to see Sarah Cox standing at the entrance to the office.

"Hello," said Cox stepping inside. "All okay?"

"Yes, ma'am," said Black.

Dan watched the interaction between Sarah and Black.

It was odd, the way Sarah, who seemed relaxed, put Black on edge as soon as she arrived, his body language changing, tensing. It wasn't odd that he called her "ma'am"—she was his boss, after all—but Dan doubted that Natasha had called her that. It was also the way he did it that caught Dan's eye, as though Sarah Cox had just sucked all of the wind out of his sails.

There was a moment's pause, no one speaking, before Dan nodded at John and they made to leave.

"Just one thing," said Dan, turning to look at Cox and Black. "I understand that I should speak to the club swinger. What's his name?"

"LPT Mark Coker," said Cox.

Next to her, PO Black's eyes narrowed and he looked hard at Dan.

"He's away on tour with the command rugby team," said Cox.

Dan nodded. "When did he leave?"

"He flew off a few days ago," said Cox. "The rugby tour started before we were due to get back alongside, so Commander Ward let him helo-transfer back as soon as we were close enough to land, so he could travel with the team."

"Was he a good friend of SA Moore's?"

"No," said Black, his eyes dark.

Cox turned to look at him but said nothing.

"So Moore wouldn't be likely to be with him?"

"I really don't think so, not on a rugby tour," said Cox.

"Okay, thanks," said Dan.

She left the office and followed John out of the stores flat.

"I want to show you something in the girls' cabin," said John, as soon as they were alone. "Might be nothing."

Dan followed him up and over, climbing ladders, heading aft along 2-deck until they dropped back down to Natasha's accommodation flat.

"It's so different from how I remember," said Dan.

"It is," agreed John. "I bet you remember the days when you had a wrens' mess, with its own mess square and loads of gulches leading off it with six or more pits in each?"

"I do," said Dan, feeling old.

She remembered her time on board one of the carriers when she was a young trainee. The darkest gulches—spaces that were lined with bunks—always went to the oldest and most senior sailors. They got the bunks that were farthest away from the door, with less through traffic and less chance of disturbance from people walking past outside, or from parties and television noise in the communal mess square. The newer sailors did time in the bunks closest to the mess square and would suffer the noise and disturbance as messmates gathered, shared a drink in the evening, or watched movies and played games.

Now there were small rooms with plenty of locker space to make it comfortable.

"Which was Moore's?" asked Dan.

John pointed.

Moore's bunk was the one closest to the door; some things didn't change. She had her own duvet cover, plain, dark purple, and her bed was made, but messy, the cover pulled up and over but no more.

Dan looked around at the other bunks, and it took her a moment to recognize why Moore's was different from those around it.

All of the other bunks had pictures pinned to the wall, odd letters or small posters.

Moore's walls were bare, not even a notebook or personal item tucked down in the space between the mattress and the bulkhead. Nothing at all.

John was standing quietly, knowing to wait and let Dan think before he spoke.

She turned to him.

"It's a bit bleak, isn't it?" she said.

He nodded.

"It is, but come over here."

He pointed to a spot back out of the cabin, farther into the accommodation flat, then he moved his head as though trying to find a certain way that the cabin's lights would reflect onto Moore's bed.

Dan moved to where he pointed, and looked.

"See it?" he asked.

Dan was looking at Moore's bunk at an angle, almost facing the entrance to the cabin.

"I can't see anything," she said.

John moved closer to her, lowering his head down right next to hers, his chin almost touching her hair.

Dan held her ground.

"Step back a bit," he instructed.

Dan did, and then she saw.

As the fluorescent glow from the cabin's light glinted off the side of Moore's bunk, some marks became visible. Words on the empty wall next to where she slept.

Dan squinted and moved her head to catch the light. There, on the wall next to Moore's bed, appeared the word SLUT. It looked as though it had been written there but had been cleaned off. The whole area had probably been cleaned, but the lines where the ink had been were just a little cleaner, had seen greater effort or more chemical, and the outline of the letters was still visible.

"Nice find," said Dan. "How?"

He tapped his nose and smiled. "I'm afraid a wily old master at arms can't reveal all his secrets."

Dan rolled her eyes.

"Fine. I had to tie my shoelace," he said.

"Still, well spotted, but . . ." Dan moved her head to get a better view, moving in close and touching where the letters had been. "There's nothing to say how long ago this was done, or whether Moore was in this bunk when it happened. She's been here, what, four months. It could've been done before she arrived."

John acknowledged that with a nod. "Still a question worth asking, though, eh?"

"It is, and I think I know who should be able to answer it, too," said Dan.

24

Natasha Moore—Mid-November
(two months before disappearance)

Mark Coker had called her no fewer than eight times, and he'd also sent her fourteen text messages.

She'd read them all but hadn't replied. She just lay motionless on her bed, facing the bulkhead, trying to figure out how everything could be going so wrong.

She felt utterly powerless.

There were things happening at home when she was so far away, things that couldn't be easily dealt with by phone, or even a video call. She needed to be there, to look Jason in the eye, hold his hand, and show him that things weren't the way he thought they were.

How do you deal with that?

She almost formed the thought into words, her lips moving but no sound escaping.

How do you hold your world together when you're so far away that you can't reach out and touch it?

Jason had always had doubts about the navy. He'd never said it—the opposite, in fact—but she felt sure of it. It wasn't as though he'd wanted her to stay at home and work in the sandwich factory, he'd wanted her to leave home and do something better with her life, but to do it somewhere close to him, not where they were apart all the time. He'd been the first person in her life who seemed to want nothing from her, but only wanted to give. He told her she could do anything, be anything, and he encouraged her, not pressured, encouraged her to take chances. He treated her like an adult when she was still just a child, and she knew that now. He'd given her somewhere safe to go, away from her stepfather and the way he looked at her. He'd given her space and privacy, but at the same time he was there for her. He'd agreed to move to Portsmouth, to give up his job at the hotel near home so he could be with her, but despite what he said, she was sure now that he'd never really loved the idea.

She'd really thought they'd make it. She'd really thought they loved each other enough, had been certain that she loved him enough, enough for them both, but one person can't love enough for two people; it just doesn't work that way. She thought about him now but Mark Coker jostled him aside in her mind. In the years she'd spent with Jason, she'd never felt the physical buzz, the butterflies in the belly, that she felt when Mark touched her.

It was confusing, conflicting, her worldview changing, but not slowly, being ripped away like a magician revealing that the rabbit was gone; the box was still there, but everything else had changed.

What would have been a cute huff when she was at home, easily solved with a cuddle and a kiss, became an irritation that could ruin a night when he did it now that she was not there to soothe him. What might have been a joking comment or a tease when she could see him sounded more cutting when read in an e-mail.

And then there was the female voice before he'd ended the call today, no doubt the "Susi" who annoyed him when they carpooled, and who'd probably be annoying him in their bed tonight, the new bed and mattress that they'd bought with money from her second-ever Royal Navy pay packet.

Her phone beeped again and she looked at the message.

> I only sent this message so I could watch you read it and know you'd ignored all my others. Look behind you. M xx

She frowned and then rolled over on her bunk.

She hadn't heard him approach, but he was standing at the door, dressed in jeans and a tight-fitting dress shirt.

"You're sweating," she said.

"Don't look so disgusted. I'm sweating because I just walked all the way back from town to come and get you. Well, I ran some of the way; time's a-wasting."

She smiled at that.

"I'm not feeling up to it today, Mark. Sorry."

He came into the cabin and leaned on the edge of her bed.

She was on the top bunk, so he could comfortably lean on his elbows and look at her as he spoke.

"See that prick there?" he said, pointing to a picture of Jason.

Natasha made to speak, but he raised an eyebrow at her.

"Let me finish," he said. "That prick there was engaged to one of the smartest, funniest, most ambitious, and most smoking hot girls ever."

She smelled alcohol on his breath as he spoke.

He didn't seem to be drunk, just a little tipsy, and she rolled her eyes and shook her head at him.

"No. I'm serious, and I'm not done. You see, he got some pictures sent to him that didn't look great, I'll give him that, but they weren't damning, either, and you know what he did? He shacked up with some tart from work and had her there while he dumped you."

"I don't know why she was there," said Natasha. "I don't want to jump to the wrong conclu—"

"Bollocks," he said, cutting her off. "Big fat hairy bollocks. He's been winding you up about her for weeks and months, and he invited her in so she could watch while he embarrassed you and ditched you. That's what he did, those are the facts of the case. So, I put it to you, that this man is a prick, a dick, a penis, a trouser snake of enormous proportions, and that he isn't worth spit. He definitely isn't worth another tear, or another minute of your time, not even another second."

Natasha sighed again, frowning as she waited for him to finish.

"He dumps you and treats you like muck and still gets your time. I'd be delighted just to spend some time with you as a friend. To go out for a drink, see you smile and forget about this for a while. You know, all this shit'll still be here tomorrow. Come on, Tash, we never got to have a beer in Gibraltar, not properly. Come out with me now. Let's have some fun. Don't make me have walked all this way back for nothing."

"It's not just him. It's Gary, too, he's weird, he's freaking me out."

"Your whole section are freaking weird," Coker said, pulling a face that said it was obvious. "Apart from you, of course," he added.

"What do you mean?"

"They just are. Come on, come out with me."

"Cox seems okay most of the time," said Natasha.

Mark snorted.

"She's the queen of the weird, the fruitiest cake of them all."

"What do you mean?" said Natasha again.

He was shaking his head now. "Come on, forget them, let's go out."

"You can't drop that bomb and then not tell me," said Natasha.

"I will tell you, but later."

"Tell me now, and I might come out with you."

He sighed.

"I don't know, she's just weird. When she first joined she used to train with me a lot, but I never really thought she enjoyed it; it's my job, though."

Natasha felt a small flip in her stomach and blushed, no idea why she'd feel like that just because Mark had spent a lot of time with Sarah Cox.

"Another admirer?" joked Natasha.

He shook his head.

"No, she just got a bit weird. She offered to help me with my court case to get visiting rights with my little girl, her uncle runs a law firm and she said he might do me a deal, maybe free. I didn't want charity, but my ex's parents are loaded and I can't afford to take them on."

Natasha watched him closely, again feeling odd inside.

He'd often talked about his daughter, but she realized now that he'd always done it without ever mentioning her mum.

"That's not weird," said Natasha. "That's really nice."

"Yeah, it was, but then she decided I would have to pay"—he paused and sighed—"and I couldn't afford it."

"So she just took the offer away?" said Natasha, leaning forward on her bunk as she spoke.

"Basically, yeah. She's weird and well worth avoiding. Now come on, let's not talk about this anymore; let's go."

Natasha dropped her head back onto her pillow and closed her eyes.

She could feel that he was still there, leaning on her bed, close to her, waiting.

"Okay," she said. "Just a few drinks, but if I mope, you don't have to hang with me, okay?"

"Okay," he said. "Now get ready. Make yourself even hotter, because the night is young and the party's waiting."

"I'M GLAD YOU came out," he said as they walked away from the dock-yard in Naples, *Defiance* dropping out of view. "We'll have a really good time and it's always good to have a few beers when you need to unwind."

"And this excellent nutritional health advice is coming from the ship's full-time fitness and well-being expert?" said Natasha, shaking her head as though deeply disappointed.

He laughed, and it made Natasha smile to hear it.

"I'm full of good advice," he said. "But I like to look after your body *and* soul. A few drinks with your mates isn't great for the first, but the benefits to the second massively outweigh it."

Natasha heard a loud roar go up from around the next corner, and although she couldn't make out what was said, she knew, just by the accent and tone of it, that it was made by a group of British sailors. They'd found some of *Defiance*'s ship's company.

Mark leaned toward her and she felt his breath on her ear as he spoke. "Ready? Because if you want to leave, just let me know and I'll go back with you, or at least get you a taxi if you want to go back on your own."

She looked at him and smiled. "I'll let you know."

They were met by a small cheer as they approached the crowd.

The cheer was more for Mark than Natasha, and there were shouts of "Grab some straws, the Coke's arrived" as people slapped Mark on the arm and someone placed a pint in his hand.

"I'll grab us some drinks," he said, sipping at the beer.

"You've got one. I'll get my own."

Natasha moved through the crowd on her way to the bar. People greeted her and smiled, but nothing on the scale of the welcome that Mark got.

He'd been on the ship a long time, played rugby for the navy and command teams, ran almost all of the physical training that went on. He knew everybody and was definitely "one of the boys."

It was only now, as Natasha walked away from him, still able to hear people calling his name and making jokes with him, that she realized how intimidating it felt that he'd come back for her. All the people here that would gladly drink with him, and he'd come all the way back to get her.

She made it to the bar and looked at the drinks. She didn't particularly like the feeling of being drunk, hardly drank at all, but as the barman smiled at her and waited for her order, she decided that tonight she fancied a few; tonight, she'd earned them. She ordered a brightly colored alcopop and watched the barman drop a straw into the bottle.

"Careful with those, my lady," said the barman in broken English. "The drunk creeps up on you from out of nowhere."

He laughed and gave her the change before he moved on to the next customer.

"You decided to drink tonight, then, Nat?"

She spun to see Gary Black looming over her.

He stepped back, bumping into a stranger, who spun around angrily but then saw the sheer size of Black and nodded as though he'd only been kidding and turned back to his friends.

Natasha took a swig of her drink and stared up at Black.

"Only you always say you don't like drinking," he said.

"I don't like people who creep me out and make me look like a liar," said Natasha, having to raise her voice to be heard above the chatter and not caring that she did.

He looked around quickly, flushing as he always did, and then back at her.

"I wasn't being creepy. I promise. And I didn't mean to put you on duty that night, or keep you at work late, it was just the way it panned out; we've all got a job to do. Honestly, Nat, I'm sorry."

He looked genuine, but Natasha was still seething, and even as he spoke to her she could see the bottom drawer of his filing cabinet and what was in it, but more than that, even if she'd been wrong about what was in there, it'd changed by the time Cox came down. If he had nothing to hide, then why change stuff?

She took another sip.

"Same again?" said Mark, putting both hands around her waist as he maneuvered past her toward the bar.

"You shouldn't have too many," said Black, leaning in. "He'll get you drunk, that's what he does. He smooths his way into people."

Natasha leaned away from him and frowned.

"I can get myself drunk," she said, shaking her head at him. "But you know what, for tonight, just stay away from me, okay?"

Mark was now standing beside her, seeming to have caught the last few words.

"Everything all right?" he asked, though he was openly staring at Black.

"All good," said Black, turning away and walking through the crowd toward the door.

"I saw him come over," said Mark. "Thought you might want a bit of moral support."

Natasha leaned in close to make herself heard.

"Thanks. I'll take another drink, too," she said. "These are really nice. It doesn't even taste like there's alcohol in them." She laughed and then looked back over toward the door to make sure Black had done as she'd told him to.

"You sure?" Mark pointed to the bottle in her hand, which was still quite full.

"I'm sure," Natasha said, raising the bottle and finishing the drink in one long swig.

25

Sarah Cox was sitting sipping from a cup of tea and sketching aimlessly on a pad when Dan stepped through her cabin door without knocking. She closed the pad and looked at Dan, saying nothing, but her eyes narrowed, almost quizzically, as though she were waiting for Dan to explain herself.

"Sarah." Dan grabbed the second chair from against the wall, set it up, sat down, and leaned forward, closing the space between them. "It's a stressful time for anyone who knows someone who's gone missing, but I'm a bit concerned that not everyone's being entirely honest with me."

Sarah's eyes shot away from Dan, looking first behind her at John and then away from them both and back down to her cup.

"I think more's been going on than you're telling me. Or maybe you've covered for SA Moore again. Anyway, I'm certain that you know something else, something that you haven't been willing to tell me."

Dan waited now, saying nothing, but still leaning in, her eyes on Sarah even though the woman was looking away.

"If you know something, ma'am, if you know anything at all, then now's the time," said John. "Here and now, because if we find out later . . ."

He let the words hang.

"There are some markings on the wall next to Natasha's bunk. They've been cleaned off, but I can't believe you don't know anything about it."

Sarah Cox's lip trembled and she rubbed her eyes with her free hand.

"Tell me what I need to know, Sarah," said Dan. "Tell me the truth, because if you don't, and I find out, and I will find out, then Daddy,

Grandpa, and anyone else you know won't be able to help you. Do you understand what I'm saying?"

A tear dropped from Cox's eyes onto her trousers, disappearing into the rough black material.

Dan pushed harder.

"And now we're only chatting in your cabin, informally, but I'm happy to take this down to the SIB interview room, because I think you're hiding something from me. I think you know what it is, and if SA Moore doesn't show up soon, then this is quickly going to become something very serious."

Another tear, and a small sniffle.

"I'm not covering for her."

"Okay, but what do you know? Where is she?"

"I really thought she'd be back by now. I really did."

"Okay, but she isn't. So why don't you tell us where she is, or who she's with, and we'll go and get her. You'll be doing her a favor, because the quicker we bring her back, the less trouble she's going to get into."

"I don't know where she is," Cox said.

Dan watched her speak through her tears, and believed her.

"There were some problems that I didn't tell you about. I'm sorry, but they were done with, in her past, and I didn't want to dredge them back up again for her. I didn't want everyone on the ship to know."

"Tell me," said Dan.

"She got into a thing with the ship's PTI," said Sarah. "Early in the last deployment, shortly after she'd joined the ship."

"Okay, go on," prompted Dan.

"Well, he's been a bit of a problem on board before."

"Mark Coker?"

Sarah nodded.

"So what happened?"

"I don't know everything, but after she joined, she started hanging around with him, flirting with him. I think he had been seeing one of the other girls in the mess, but he'd ended it. Natasha took a liking to him and they started hanging around. I saw them sometimes on the NAAFI flat, waiting to buy stuff from the shop or just sharing a drink, you know, a soda or whatever. I think they did that to avoid hanging around the junior rates' mess too much, because the girl that Coker used to see would be in there and they probably didn't want to cause problems."

She looked at Dan as though needing some encouragement to continue.

Dan nodded.

"Moore was new and young, and both PO Black and I actually spoke to her about it, though she didn't seem to care about what we'd said and she wasn't actually breaking any rules."

"Did you speak to Mark Coker?" asked Dan.

"PO Black did," said Cox. "He spoke to him about hanging around Moore so much, and about the problems that can arise with relationships on board a warship and when a young girl gets a bit fixated."

"Okay," said Dan, a little confused as to why PO Black would be the one to do that but hoping to keep Sarah on topic.

"Well, I think they may have slept together one night on a port visit to Naples, though there were rumors that they'd also slept together on board a few times, while we were at sea."

Dan raised an eyebrow at that.

"There was no proof, and I spoke to her again after that. No one wanted her to get a name for herself."

"What happened on the port visit?" asked Dan.

"They came back on board together in the early hours and were spotted walking hand in hand, disheveled and tipsy. You know what gossip's like on board a warship, and within a short while everyone knew, or at least decided they knew."

"That's not illegal, though," said John.

"No, of course not, as long as they obey the 'no touching' rule while on board, then we don't really mind. Commander Ward doesn't love relationships between sailors on board *Defiance*, but as long as they conduct themselves properly, he can live with it."

Sarah was looking at Dan now, and Dan said nothing, letting her talk.

"Well, after a while, certainly by then, something had happened. Moore had broken up with her fiancé, and good riddance to him, too, he was a nasty piece of work from all accounts."

"How so?" asked John.

"Really pushy and controlling. She'd talk to me about it and tell me how weird he'd get whenever she was in harbor. He'd want to talk to her when she was going out, or try to convince her to go to an Internet café to Skype, or whatever, so she couldn't be with her crewmates. I think he hated that she worked with so many men. Once they split up, I advised her to just cut him off for good."

"Do you know whether she ended it?" asked Dan.

"I believe she did, though I only know what she told me. He was pretty cut up and angry about it, from what I could tell," said Cox, looking Dan in the eye.

"And LPT Coker helped her through this?" asked Dan.

Sarah nodded. "Yes, I believe so. But it caused a number of problems. Tasha was very upset about the breakup, and I think it caused her and Coker to argue, too. They fell out. This is why relationships on a warship can be so damaging. He's a big personality on board *Defiance*, always around the place, running circuits a couple of times a day. He knows everyone and everyone knows him. He's been here for almost two years and he's well established and almost universally liked. He's also quite a controlling personality himself, though, so things became a little bit awkward for her."

"And you never thought to tell us this yesterday?" said Dan, not even trying to conceal her annoyance.

"It'd all blown over," Sarah said, her voice irritating Dan with a pleading whine. "It'd all settled down and was in the past. Tasha was happier—seemed to be happier, anyway. She seemed to have made friends with some of the other sailors and she was doing well."

Dan waited, watching Cox closely.

"Look, I'm sorry," said Sarah, her wheedling voice sending an irritated shiver down Dan's spine. "I didn't want to air her dirty laundry in public. She was getting over all of this, seemed to be feeling better. I wanted to leave it in the past where it belonged. I didn't want to dredge it all back up again. I really thought she'd come back. I really did."

"Why don't you think that now?" asked Dan.

Cox licked her lips as she thought about what she'd said.

"I do," she said, looking angry at Dan. "I don't know why I said it like that, and I think you're being pedantic, but I do think she'll come back, and I really don't think this is why she's gone. It was all done, finished with. There's no reason at all why it'd all come to a head now."

"Anything else?" snapped Dan. "Is there anything else you didn't tell us?"

Sarah looked frightened, or maybe just wary now, leaning away from Dan and watching her carefully, as though considering everything she might say.

"There is one more thing," she said quietly, "but I don't know if I'm even allowed to tell you. It may not be directly relevant, and I could well fall foul of the law if I do."

Dan couldn't help but feel angry as she heard Cox speaking these words, concentrating on covering her own backside. She remembered that Cox had a law degree and that she'd be going to work at her uncle's law firm once she'd had her two-year all expenses-paid trip around the world. Now, to Dan, Sarah Cox sounded like a spoiled rich kid, surrounded by pictures of horses, expensive cars, and pretty friends and family. She sounded like someone for whom the navy was nothing more than a hobby, the sailors in her charge just inconveniences that she had to tolerate. What was a career for Dan was something Cox would do only to "prove" herself. Dan had thought she'd understood a bit about Cox, her relationship with the navy and the environment; now she was certain she didn't.

"I'm not convinced you could be in any more trouble at this point, Sarah," said Dan, her voice cold, "so if there's more, then I suggest you get it out."

Sarah Cox was looking away, her cheeks red. She looked like a petulant child being forced to confess to some wrongdoing, and Dan was struggling to keep her temper in check. What Sarah Cox had told them in the past few moments had changed everything regarding the way that Dan had assessed the risk involved in Natasha Moore's disappearance, and now Cox seemed unwilling to help shed any further light on the matter.

"Well, when Natasha first joined, she had some other problems, too."

"Go on," said Dan, as Sarah paused again.

"She had some problems with Petty Officer Black."

Dan was listening intently but didn't want to continue to prompt Sarah. She wanted this to come out without being forced, lest Cox forget something or simply omit more detail.

"She felt that he was"—Sarah paused—"crowding her."

"Crowding her?"

"Yes, like turning up when she went out, following her around in the nightclubs, warning other people to stay away from her."

"You mean stalking her?" said Dan.

"I don't know. I think at first she thought he was being friendly, kind of fatherly-like, looking after her because she was new, but after a while she began to think it was more than that. She said he'd follow her when she went on nights out, be everywhere she went, watching her. Sometimes he'd be with some of the other senior rates, but often he'd be on his own, she said. She said that he threatened LPT Coker when they started becoming friends." Sarah paused again, shifting in her seat and looking uncomfortable. "She also said that the night she slept with LPT Coker"— Cox paused and thought about her words—"was believed to have slept with LPT Coker, well, she thought he might have been there, that he'd followed them down to the park and was watching them."

"She told you that? She said that she went to the park and had inter-course with Coker? And that Petty Officer Black was there, watching?"

Dan tried to keep her face as calm and straight as she could, though she was certain it'd be flushing now, as her temper reached bursting point.

"No, not exactly," said Cox. "She told me that she and Coker went for a walk and sat and talked in a park on their way back to the dockyard."

"If you could just keep to the facts, unless I specifically ask for your opinion, then I'd be grateful," said Dan. "Continue."

"After that, she complained that Petty Officer Black started keeping closer tabs on her. He runs the duty watch bill for the stores team and she said he'd deliberately plan it so she was on duty when Coker wasn't and vice versa so that their duties weren't aligned and it would limit the time they might have together."

"Was that true?" asked Dan.

"There were occasions when their duties were offset, but we don't write the watch bill based on one person, as you know."

The last three words irritated Dan, but she let it go for now, making a mental note to look at the duty watch bill herself.

"She also said he'd keep her working needlessly late," continued Cox. "He'd make her wait down in the stores office with him, not for any good reason, until she'd missed the others going out, and then he'd offer to take her out for a beer with him, or to buy her dinner or something like that."

Dan turned to look at John again.

He, too, looked serious, stern, angry, though he was better at keeping it under wraps than Dan was.

"So SA Moore had problems with the ship's PTI, broke up with her fiancé, and told you she was being stalked by her section petty officer?" asked Dan.

Sarah's eyes went wide.

"She didn't say it was stalking. I mean, is that stalking? I only had her word for all of this. She's not the first junior rate to ever feel she was unfairly treated on the watch bill, or who got pissed off because they had to work late," said Cox. "I spoke to Petty Officer Black about it, he's been here since before I arrived, we interact a lot, and he had reasonable explanations for everything she'd said. He's a respected member of the ship's company and had good justification for when he'd asked her to work late. We're always very busy when we're alongside in foreign ports. If stores are arriving late, then we do have to wait for them, so none of it's unreasonable or even unexpected. Life in a blue suit, really."

"Good explanation for following her around bars?" asked Dan.

"The ship's company often go out together, you know that." Sarah was becoming a lot more defiant now, answering back quickly and with some anger in her voice.

"What was his explanation for watching her have sex?" asked Dan.

"He wasn't there," replied Sarah, her eyes also blazing now as she stared at Dan.

"He told you that?"

"Yes, he did. And frankly, he's a very well known and well respected senior rate and was with another senior rate that evening, too. You can check that with Chief Pollack—I did. Natasha Moore was going through a hard time brought about, at least in part, by her own behavior. She'd come to enjoy being up here talking with me, and frankly, I think she enjoyed the attention from all the men."

Dan had to take a second before she could speak. The urge to reach over and slap Sarah Cox was so strong that she worried if she opened her mouth at all, it might just be the lapse in control needed for it to happen.

"Anything else?" said Dan, her voice stony.

"No."

"We'll need to speak again, at the SIB offices," said Dan, standing up. "I'll also be speaking with your commanding officer very soon."

Sarah was staring at Dan, her eyes boring into her, a spiteful look on her face.

"I want to speak to Petty Officer Black."

"He's gone for the day," said Sarah.

"Well, get him back. I want him on board this ship, now."

26

Natasha saw Mark behind her on the edge of the dance floor. She could see his lips move but could barely hear him over the music.

She was dancing with a load of sailors from *Defiance* and she noticed how Sam turned away as soon as Mark arrived, and Bev dutifully followed.

Natasha looked down at his hands.

He was gripping her waist again as he danced behind her.

It felt nice, warm, his hands gentle but strong.

Natasha sighed, not minding his hands on her but not liking it here, where everyone could see.

"Hands off, cowboy," she shouted, leaning close to his ear so he could hear her above the music.

He let go, looking mock-sheepish, but he continued to dance close to her.

"Hold this," she said, passing him her umpteenth bottle of bright blue alcopop. "I'll be back in a second."

She continued to dance as she cut through the crowds looking for the ladies' restroom over near the main doors, stumbling as someone jostled past her. She felt her ankle almost go as her heel slipped on the beer-soaked floor, then felt a strong hand catch hold of her arm. She looked up, but she already knew who it was.

"I'm serious, Gary," she said, her teeth clenched. "Leave me alone, okay?"

He looked shocked.

"I was just going to the loo and I saw you fall. I caught you."

Natasha looked at him. He loomed over her, but she felt no fear. She did realize, however, that either she, or he, was swaying gently, and she began to feel a little dizzy as she tried to focus on him.

"You need to take it easy on the drinking," he said, not looking at her as he spoke. "You've had seven bottles now. That's a lot. You're not used to it, Nat."

She realized he was still holding her arm and she ripped it away from him, almost stumbling back again when he didn't resist.

He reached out again to steady her, but she batted his hand away.

"You're watching me drink and counting them?" she said, screwing up her face and shaking her head in disgust. "I trusted you to be my friend," she said, "and you're doing this?"

"I am your friend," he said. "I'm not doing anything to you."

"Stay. Away. From. Me," she said, very slowly. "I'm going to tell people about this, Gary. You can't keep doing this."

She deliberately pushed past him on her way to the ladies' room, glad that he yielded to let her past. She felt unsteady on her feet, knew a few glasses of water were in the cards once she got back out.

"I thought you weren't going out tonight?"

Natasha turned to see Sarah Cox. She'd come into the restroom and was standing at the door, watching her. "Oh, hey, Sarah," said Natasha, sniffing as she did. "Sorry, Mark came all the way back to get me and persuaded me to come out. It all happened in such a rush. I just didn't think."

"He can be a real darling, can't he?" Sarah said, watching her, no obvious expression on her face.

"He can," added Natasha, her eyes starting to fill with tears as the mixture of frustration, alcohol, and stress began to combine.

Sarah continued to watch her, saying nothing, the silence drawing out between them.

Natasha put her hand to her abdomen, felt her stomach flipping and gurgling.

"Shall I go and grab you a drink?" Cox asked. "That blue stuff again?"

"I think I just need a water, please," said Natasha.

Cox smiled and made for the door. "Okay, I'll see you at the bar," she said.

As soon as Cox was gone, Natasha went into one of the stalls and pulled out her phone. She texted Mark, telling him she'd been hijacked; there was no way she was having this night ruined, too, no way at all.

She finished up and washed her hands, smiling at some of the girls from the ship as they came in.

Bev entered just as Natasha was leaving.

"Hey," said Natasha. "You okay? I lost you guys, where are you?"

Bev smiled. She was always way more friendly when Sam wasn't there.

"We're over by the back bar, round the other side of the dance floor."

"Cool. I'm going to come over," said Natasha.

Bev looked skeptical. "You aren't bringing Cox with you, are you?" she asked. "You know Sam can't stand her, and, to be honest, I don't want to hang with her, either."

Natasha sighed.

"No. I'm going to have a drink with her and tell her I'm going with you guys. I'll sort it," said Natasha, and felt stronger for having said it aloud.

Bev nodded and passed her before stopping again and looking at Natasha.

"Maybe don't bring Mark either?" she said.

"Tell me," said Natasha, needing to be blunt. "It's so obvious that there's history between him and Sam, but what happened that's so bad?"

Bev shrugged, then looked behind her as though checking there was no one there, or at least no one that mattered.

"She ditched him, so she says, but I don't know for sure. He comes across like a player, all talk and bravado, no doubt about that, but I don't think that's really who he is. He's a lovely guy."

Bev looked over her shoulder again.

"I can't tell if Sam loves him or hates him; opposite sides of the same coin, you know? And she's never talked to me about what actually happened between them, but there's loads of rumors about him, even about your boss fancying him, though I doubt that, she's such a stuck-up bitch. His little girl seems to be his key focus, he'd do anything for her, and I think Sam didn't like coming second."

"I knew he had a little girl," said Natasha, not sure why she felt defensive and needed to say it.

"Yeah, it's no secret."

"Loving his daughter isn't a bad thing, is it?" asked Natasha.

"No, but apparently he hardly ever gets to see her, something to do with his ex's parents, so if he gets the chance, then no matter what, he drops everything and goes. Doesn't matter what's planned, he goes. Look, it's none of my business and I'll deny I said all of this, because I don't want the hassle, but enjoy hanging with Mark, he's fun, but don't get attached, okay? You'll always come second with him, whether he admits that or not."

"Okay," said Natasha. She blew out some air, a long continuous stream. "Okay, but I'll definitely catch up with you guys. Can you not leave here without me? Please. I'll come and find you, but if you're moving on before I do, just give me a really quick tap and I'll come straightaway."

Bev nodded. "Okay," she said.

Natasha made for the door. She was struggling to focus, and her vision seemed to lag behind her eyes by a few seconds when she moved her head. She knew she'd had far more to drink than she'd probably ever had before, apart from that one time when she was fourteen and some friends at home had stolen a bottle of Caribbean rum from her mum. She and her friends had swigged it until they were so drunk that she'd spent the night in the hospital. Now, thinking about that, she imagined she could almost smell the rum, and a light sheen of sweat appeared all over her skin just at the thought of it. She left the restroom and looked to her right, toward the entrance doors that led to the fresh air outside.

As soon as Natasha realized she needed the air, her need for it became worse, and she staggered in the direction of the doors, her head swirling and her throat suddenly dry. She knew she'd need water soon, but right now it was cold air and to sit down for a few minutes that she needed even more.

"You okay? Where you going?"

It was Mark.

"Need to go outside for a minute," she said, not stopping.

He reached for her arm.

"Tash, you okay?"

He may have sounded concerned. Natasha couldn't be sure, nor did she care.

She shook her arm free and continued toward the door. She was going to be sick, but if she could get out of the pub and into the fresh air, she might not. Natasha had no idea how she knew that, but she did.

Mark was next to her, keeping up with her, too bloody close to her.

"Just leave me be for a minute, Mark," she blurted, trying to get the words out in a way that didn't sound too harsh.

He tried to put his arm round her shoulders, to guide her to the door.

"You're all over the place," he said. "Let me help."

The feeling of him near her, smothering her, was too much. She'd be fine, but she needed some space.

"Just leave me be for a minute," she said again, maybe shouted it this time. She tried to move his arm from her shoulder, stumbled, and almost fell. Someone caught her, picking her up and holding her upright.

"Back off, Coker," said Gary Black in a loud voice.

He sounded angry, threatening, and she looked up to see him standing over her, holding her.

She wasn't sure whether Mark said, "She's fine" or Black said, "She's mine," but it didn't matter. They both needed to just back away and give her space.

"You okay, Nat?" Black whispered in her ear. "Where do you want to go?"

"Just get off me," she said to him, trying to jerk free but failing as he gripped her arm tight. "Get off!"

She was definitely shouting this time, and she twisted, using her free arm to elbow him in the ribs, though it had no impact at all.

"No," he said, leaning down and speaking into her ear. "You're not right and I'm not leaving you alone until I know you are."

"Get off of her, you freak," Mark said.

Natasha caught a blur of movement as Mark stepped forward to grab her away from Black. She tried to push him away, too, feeling like a rag doll between two fighting dogs. She saw Black shove Mark away, kind of a half push, half slap.

Mark came forward again, reaching for her.

Black spun her around, putting her behind him, but Natasha heard two thuds and knew that punches had been thrown.

In a second, she was free, leaning against the wall and turning back to see Mark and Black swinging at each other.

Mark was quicker, way quicker, and he easily dodged Black's attempts to hit him and landed his own strikes at will. The problem was that they seemed to have no effect at all, just bouncing off Black, who continued to move forward, swinging and grabbing for him.

"Get him, Blacky," came a voice from off to the side, and Natasha saw Sam watching the fight, a smile on her face as she looked across at Natasha and mouthed, "Good work" before turning back to watch.

Natasha looked down at the floor, then back at what was now a scrum near the door.

The security from the club were swarming around Black and Mark.

One bouncer was holding Mark back now, gripping him across the chest, wrapping his arms to his side and holding him off balance, while several more seemed to be crawling all over Black, hanging onto his back and trying to hold his arms as he pushed one of them across the dance floor so hard that the bouncer fell and slid on the wet, dirty floor.

The bouncer was up again and ran back to the fray, throwing himself at Black.

One of them had an arm round Gary's neck now, gripping him like a playground bully, and was punching him repeatedly in the side of the head.

Another, the one that had been pushed away, kicked hard at the back of Black's leg, pushing his knee forward and forcing him down onto the ground.

"Stop," shouted Natasha, but then she felt someone grab her hand and looked up to see Sarah Cox.

"Time to go?" Sarah asked.

Natasha nodded.

"I need to use the bathroom again, though," she said quickly. "I think I'm gonna puke."

Sarah nodded and released her, but followed her in.

It took a few minutes for Natasha's heartbeat to slow and the sweats to fade. She was sitting on the toilet, the lid down, her head in her hands, and Sarah was in there with her, leaning quietly against the door. Natasha hadn't been sick, and that feeling had passed, the large glass of water that Sarah had given her had really hit the spot and she was starting to feel a little bit better.

"Gary Black's been thrown out of the club, just so you know," said Sarah.

"What about Mark?" asked Natasha.

"What *about* him?" said Cox.

"Is he okay? Did he get thrown out? Is he hurt?"

Cox folded her arms, Natasha could see it in the shadow that she cast onto the floor.

"I hope so," Cox said. "I bet a punch from Black would do him some good. Knock some sense into him."

Natasha looked up.

"He's bad news, Tash," said Cox, as though answering a question that Natasha hadn't asked. "We need to stay away from him. You need to stay away from him." Cox paused as if to let the words sink in.

Natasha looked away, grabbing her phone from her bag and checking it.

There were some unread texts and she opened one from Mark first.

> Hope you're okay. I'm kicked out. Waiting for you outside, just in case you wanted me to. Text me if you don't and I'll see you tomorrow. M xxx

Natasha looked up at Sarah, who was holding the door open.

"One sec," said Natasha. She typed a reply.

> Where are you now? xxx

The response was almost instant.

> Outside. Look for all night cafe on your right as you leave through the main door. xxx

Natasha looked up at Sarah.

"Look, Sarah. Thank you so much for being there for me tonight, and for being a friend, but I'm going to go and meet some of the others for a while. I hope you understand."

Sarah Cox just looked at her.

"Please be okay with this," said Natasha.

"Sure," said Cox. She stepped back and gestured with her arm for Natasha to leave. "Have a good night."

Natasha made to leave.

"Keep your hand on your ha'penny," whispered Cox as Natasha passed her.

Natasha felt a shiver run down her spine, but she kept walking without looking back.

27

Dan's fists were clenched as tight as her jaw as she walked out of Cox's cabin and into the flat, John following close behind.

She walked back to the empty cabin they'd used before, stepping inside and holding the door until John was in so she could close it herself and they could speak in private.

"How pissed off?" she said, her hands shaking. "I'll tell you now. If that silly bitch lying to me is the difference between Moore being hurt or not, I'll . . ."

She looked up at John, who was listening but saying nothing. That was unusual, he always had something to say.

"What?" she said.

He shook his head.

"Nothing."

"There's something."

"I'm as angry as you are," he said. "I took my eye off the ball, too, and I'm angry I didn't push harder yesterday."

Dan's phone rang and she answered it without saying anything to John.

"Ma'am, it's Josie. Can you talk?"

Dan took a breath, trying not to be short.

"I can."

"Ma'am, LPT Coker didn't go on the rugby tour. I just spoke to the tour leader. He was on the signal to go, but he canceled weeks before they left. The ship was certain that that's where he was, so, in short, no one knows where he is."

"Coker's not on the rugby tour. No one knows where he is," said Dan to John, watching as his brow furrowed at the news.

"Yes, ma'am," Josie said.

"Josie, find him for me," said Dan. "An address, next of kin, somewhere he might go. We need to speak to him urgently."

"No problem, ma'am."

"Also, a petty officer by the name of Gary Black. Find out everything you can about him and bring it down to me on *Defiance* as soon as you can. I want to know if he's been the subject of investigations concerning his behavior toward female colleagues, stalking, harassment, and the like."

"No problem."

Dan ended the call.

"This doesn't feel like we're going to find her drunk in a sailors' bar somewhere anymore, does it?" said John.

"We need to speak to Black and Coker as soon as possible. We also need to speak to Jason again."

"Well, Black's back," said John. "He was stopped at the gate and turned around. I asked him to be escorted down here. He came on board a few minutes ago."

"Let's go see him, then," said Dan. "And let's go get Cox. He may want his divisional officer to sit in with him."

"I think she already is."

28

Natasha Moore—Mid-November
(two months before disappearance)

Natasha left the club and walked out into the night air. She passed the small crowd that was still outside. He was not very far away, sitting on a plastic chair outside a fast-food shop. He raised his hand in greeting but stayed sitting.

She smiled and walked over, her mouth dropping open as she got close to him.

A blotch of red swelling under his right eye spread down onto his cheek and made his fairly recent scar look angry and puckered again.

"Gary managed to hit you, then?" she asked, pulling up a flimsy chair and sitting across from him.

He shook his head.

"It wasn't Gary, it was one of the bouncers. Prick cheap-shotted me during the scuffle. Hurts like hell, too."

He reached up and dabbed at it gently.

"Every time we go out together you get your face injured," Natasha said, reaching over and taking a swig of the beer on the table in front of him. "Maybe we just shouldn't hang out together."

He smiled, more of a grimace, and shook his head.

"Someone's got it in for one of us, that's for sure," he said.

"Did you see what happened to Gary?" she asked, looking at the streets around her.

"Yeah. They threw me out first. I guess he was a little harder to shift. He walked off down that way."

Mark pointed over his shoulder along the strip, in the opposite direction from the dockyard.

Natasha looked where he was pointing, checking out the lights and bars almost as far as the eye could see, but she didn't see Black lurking anywhere.

"Did he leave alone?" she asked.

Mark nodded, picking up his beer and draining the bottle.

"You want one?" he asked.

"I've probably had enough," she said.

He shrugged.

"Want a softie, then? Coke? Lemonade?"

Natasha looked into the café, at the kebab meat browning on the spit and the people hustling around it.

"You know, I will have a beer, but only as long as they're cold, okay? If they aren't cold, like properly cold, then just grab me a Diet Coke."

He nodded and was gone.

A movement off to her right caught her eye. It was a fair distance away and was suddenly lost in the bustle of passing drinkers, loud girls in white heels, and a group of lads carrying long tubelike glasses from the yard-of-ale challenge.

She was almost certain someone had been there, watching her, and then stepped back into the shadow.

"What's up?" asked Mark, placing a beer in front of her.

"I thought I saw someone watching me."

Mark looked around, then back again, shaking his head.

"You are a bit of a hottie. I wouldn't be surprised if people were checking you out."

Natasha rolled her eyes and felt her beer.

It was freezing cold.

"You want me to go and check out wherever you saw them?" he asked.

Natasha shook her head, taking a shallow swig of the beer.

She sneaked a glance at Mark as he looked around. He was handsome and muscular, not overbig like Gary, but in proportion. His pecs pressed against his shirt as he craned his neck, and Natasha watched as his biceps pulled the material of his shirtsleeves tight.

He was everything Jason wasn't—good-looking, funny, lighthearted—

but he was also many things Jason was—dependable and sincere, and he made her feel safe.

She watched him, taking another sip and wondering if Jason could ever be any of those things to her again.

"You think it was Black?" he asked, turning to look again and seeming agitated.

"I don't know. He's pretty noticeable."

"Yeah. He's a big old unit, all right," agreed Mark. "What do you want to do, then?" he asked. "Grab a hotel, chill out together in rampant nakedness?" He flashed her his cheekiest grin.

Natasha looked at him for a long time, smiling, not rolling her eyes as she usually did when he said something like this.

"Will you just walk back with me?" she said.

He nodded, his voice changing, sounding more serious. "Of course I will."

They stood up together, grabbed their beers, and headed back in the direction they'd come.

The night was fully dark now and it felt much cooler.

Natasha's feet were sore, and as they walked, she saw some soft grass running alongside the pavement and took off her heels to walk on it.

Mark looked behind them.

"You okay?" she asked.

"Yeah," he said, but he sounded uncertain. "I thought I heard something." He looked again. "It's you messing with my head," he said, and poked her playfully in the ribs.

She punched him on the arm and he rubbed it, looking wounded.

"People have been hitting me all night," he said. "But your bony little fist hurt the most."

They laughed and walked on.

They'd moved away from the busy strip now, and while she could still see people, there was a long empty space behind them.

The street around them looked empty, but also not empty, and Natasha realized again that she was still quite tipsy.

The grassy strip continued into what looked like a park.

Trees rose up around them and she could see what looked like a playground in the clearing just beyond where the light ended. It was dark, very dark, none of the glow from the poor street lighting making it that far. It was also silent.

"Shall we go play on the swings for a few minutes?" Natasha asked.

Mark snorted and smiled back at her.

"So let me get this right," he said. "Two young, attractive, nubile people—"

Natasha tipped her head and punched his arm again.

"Okay, one attractive person and one total hottie are out walking down a quiet street and think they're being followed."

"We don't really, we're just spooked. It's been a strange night," said Natasha.

He raised a hand.

"They think they're being followed," he repeated. "So instead of sticking to the lit pathway, they head off the road and onto the dark moor, where God only knows what will happen . . ."

He grabbed at her suddenly, barking like a dog and making her squeal as she recoiled from him.

They were laughing, Natasha recovering her breath.

Her phone beeped, but she ignored it.

"Idiot," she said, not really angry. "And there's no one there, but you're right, let's go back."

He took her hand and pulled her toward him.

Her stomach tingled in a way it never had before as he held her.

She didn't fight to make him let go.

"We can go to the park for a while if you want to," he said. "We can do pretty much anything you want to do."

They walked across the grass hand in hand until they came across a wooden bench and Mark sat down. He had his back to the street that they'd left behind and so Natasha, not wanting to turn her back on the light, walked just a few paces farther, to the low metal railing that ran around the outside of the children's play equipment. She leaned back against it, looking at Mark as he sat on the bench, his arms spread out along the back, his legs wide apart.

Behind him, even though the light was dim, she could see everything along the street, apart from a corner of it that was obscured by the line of trees. Standing in darkness, and with the light in front of her, she knew that anyone approaching would be silhouetted for her to see.

"Why are you so nice to me?" she asked.

He looked taken aback by the question.

"What do you mean?"

"I mean, why are you so nice to me all the time?"

"I'm nice to everyone."

"No, you aren't, not like you are to me."

He paused at that, really looking at her.

"Because I really like you," he finally said. "And even if you are with someone else and I can't have you in the way I'd really like to, I'll take what I can get and be your friend, because I love spending time with you."

"Why?"

"You're smart, funny, fit, motivated . . ." He paused. "And you're the hottest girl I've ever met."

She watched him carefully, looking for any sign of a smile or a signal that would let her know he was lying to her, teasing her; there didn't seem to be any.

She looked back out at the road, squinting, not sure if the edge of the tree line had changed slightly.

"How would you like to have me?" she asked.

"I'd like you to be all mine," he said, without hesitation. "I'd like every bit of you to be mine and mine alone."

She looked at him again.

He was handsome even with his face roughed up, she'd always thought it. He was funny, too.

"But would you be all mine, though?" she asked.

She walked toward him, dropping her shoes onto the grass and moving closer so she could look him in the eye. "Because I wouldn't be willing to share."

He leaned back away from her, seeming unsure what she was doing, but his legs moved closer together and she knelt on the bench, straddling him. His head was back, looking up at her, and their faces were close.

"Yes, I'd be all yours."

"You sure?" she asked.

"Yes."

"Absolutely certain?"

"Absolutely certain," he said.

"What if I said you could have me tonight?" she whispered. "What if I wanted you?"

He swallowed and looked into her eyes.

"I'd say no," he said, his voice quiet.

Natasha raised both eyebrows, pulling her head back. Her hands, which had been running across his chest, stopped and balled into fists.

"Really?" she asked.

"Really," he said.

"I'm a little bit confused by that," she said, not moving away, but sinking down a little, relaxing her weight onto him.

"Look, Tash. I really like you. If I'm going to sleep with you, then I don't want it to be on some dirty park bench and when you're a bit tipsy. I don't know if you really want me or not; I don't want to be tomorrow morning's regret. If you're saying I can be with you like that, then let's take some leave together, find somewhere nice and quiet, and do it right, go for some food, talk for a while, then go back to a comfortable bed with clean sheets and no chewing gum stuck to it. Let's do it so we might even want to remember it."

She watched him again, her heart racing.

"I think I want it now, though," she said, and leaned forward to kiss him.

"And what about Jason?" Mark asked, kissing her gently and pulling away. "You told me that you'd made him wait and you've been together for years. What about him, and what about waiting?"

"You and Jason are worlds apart. He's never made my stomach flutter like you do, I didn't even know that ever happened. Maybe I wasn't waiting for Jason, maybe I was waiting for the right person . . ."

She leaned in and kissed him again, then looked up as their faces pulled apart, sure that she'd seen something move in the trees, but she didn't stop, didn't care, leaned back in and kissed him again. She was going to start being with Mark, she wanted to be with him, loved how he made her feel. It would also send a clear message to everyone to leave her alone, that she wasn't a little girl.

He was a great guy. He liked her, understood her, put himself out for her, stood up for her, and she liked him an awful lot.

It wasn't how she'd imagined her first time would be, she thought, as she felt him undoing his jeans, but she felt good about him, felt good when she was with him and near him.

He pulled her close as her breathing quickened.

She watched the shadows of the treeline over his shoulder, watched the way it moved and then didn't. Part of it, the shadow on the end, was out of time with the wind, moving more slowly, and without the natural rhythm of the trees. She watched for as long as she could bear, trying to make out if there was a human shape there, before she lowered her head to Mark's mouth again.

29

Black and Cox were deep in conversation when Dan arrived at the stores office. They were leaning in to each other, Black listening intently to what he was being told.

Cox, in her role as the deputy logistics officer, also fulfilled the role of legal adviser, and this immediately came to Dan's mind as she saw the two consulting. Cox was also Black's divisional officer, and as such he was well within his rights to have her present while he was spoken to.

"Quick word, please?" said Dan, watching as Cox immediately came out.

She was smiling and greeted Dan cheerfully.

"I thought you and I could have a quick chat before I speak with Petty Officer Black," said Dan. "You okay with that?"

Cox nodded. "Sure."

"What were you guys talking about?" asked Dan.

Cox tipped her head as she looked at Dan. She seemed like a different woman from the one Dan had seen only half an hour ago, happier, more self-assured. She almost rebuked Dan with her eyes for asking.

"I'm his divisional officer and the ship's legal adviser," she said. "He's concerned and he wants me to sit in there while you speak to him."

"Concerned? Why?" asked Dan.

"Because he knows that I'll have been required to disclose to you the complaint allegations that Natasha Moore made against him, which of course I have, and because he knows that you'll have found out that he was accused of some indiscretions on his previous ship. He thinks he's going to be held accountable for something he didn't do."

Dan couldn't help but watch Sarah as she spoke, animated and friendly, confident and forceful, not the woman who'd wept at their last encounter just minutes before.

"He won't get into trouble for anything he hasn't done," said Dan, "but that's what interests me. If you know that he's previously been accused of this type of thing, then when Natasha came forward, why wouldn't you have taken it more seriously?"

Sarah Cox looked surprised.

"Oh, I took it seriously. I spoke with Black and really thought I'd resolved the issue. Moore knew that I'd spoken to him, and that she should come back to me if there were any other problems; she never did. In fact, when we did talk again, it seemed that things had improved between them. That was certainly the firm impression I had."

"What did you say to Black just now?"

Sarah Cox's expression turned serious.

"I explained to him that given the previous allegations against him, if another formal complaint were made, then it would likely be the end of his career in the Armed Forces and very probably could lead to a stint in Colchester, or worse."

"And how did he react?" asked Dan.

"He was horrified, and I genuinely believe he hadn't realized how his behavior had been viewed."

"You should know that I intend to search Petty Officer Black's office, cabinets, and all of the storerooms where he holds access. I'd like to think I'll be able to do that now, without delay, or I can have a sentry come down and stand guard until I get permission from your commanding officer."

"Yes, I suspected you might, and of course that's fine."

"Okay." Dan rocked up onto her toes. "Let's go, then."

John and Black were sitting in silence when Dan and Sarah Cox walked into the office.

The four of them made the space feel smaller than she'd have liked.

She moved to the side, allowing Cox to pass her and take the seat next to Black, while Dan sat down in a chair slightly in front of John.

"Petty Officer Black, I'm not going to beat around the bush. I've been made aware of some very serious allegations made against you by SA Natasha Moore. I'm awaiting details, but I believe they may be broadly similar to some allegations that have previously been made against you, on board your last ship. So, in light of this, I want you to be very truthful with me from the get-go, so we can get this sorted out as soon as possible. Do you understand?"

He looked terrified, fidgeting in his chair, his right leg bouncing continually, his tongue wetting his lips every few seconds.

"I haven't done anything. I promise."

"Okay, so tell me about your relationship with SA Moore."

"We weren't in a relationship, we were just friends. Nat was okay with that."

"Okay," said Dan, "tell me about your friendship, then. How did it come about?"

His mouth was already moving before Dan had finished asking the question. He was eager to speak, eager to help.

"She joined the ship, and I was her line manager, so that's how I met her," he began.

Dan felt surprised at how juvenile his language and thinking were, as if he was an enormous man-child, too simple to inhabit his adult body.

Black seemed to be genuinely an open book, spilling out words in hopes of being understood.

"We became friends straightaway," Black continued. "Because we hung out down here, away from everyone else."

"Is that really true, Gary?" asked Dan. "Were you really friends from the start?"

He nodded, big nods.

"Speak up for the recorder please, Petty Officer Black," said John.

"Yes, Master, it really was true."

"Tell me how your friendship went," said Dan. "How did it start and how did it grow?"

"Well, she was very young and new. So I took her under my wing, to help her get settled in."

"Did anyone give her any trouble?"

His face darkened, again childlike in the way his emotions were so clearly changed and broadcast.

"Yes, she had some trouble, but I helped her."

"How did you do that?" asked Dan. "Can you give me an example of how you helped her?"

Black looked at Cox, who simply nodded, as though giving him permission to speak.

"What about LPT Coker?" suggested Dan. "I've heard there was some friction there. Were you able to help her with that?"

He took in a deep breath, seeming to tense his whole body, and Dan felt John do the same beside her. Then Black exhaled.

"LPT Coker isn't a very nice person. He's controlling and manipulates. When Nat came on board, he started sniffing around her. He does it with all of the young girls, but he's bad news. He doesn't want to be with them, to love them, only wants to have sex with them, because he can."

Dan nodded. "Okay, can you tell me what you think happened with LPT Coker and Natasha? Did anything physical happen between them at all?"

"It did. I told him to leave her alone right from the beginning. I told him just to stay clear of her and let her be."

"Did you say you'd do anything if he didn't?"

He shrank back into himself, the frown back in place, then looked at Sarah Cox, who again nodded.

"I told him he needed to leave her alone or I'd hit him," he said, but he looked beseechingly at Dan. "But he's horrible, he only wanted sex and that's what he got."

"How do you know they had sex?" asked Dan.

"Nat told me."

"Really?"

"Yes."

"Gary," said Dan, leaning forward and putting her arms on her knees, as though they might talk with just the two of them able to hear. "You promised me you were going to tell the truth, all of it, and now I feel like you're holding something back from me."

He licked his lips, looking Dan in the eye.

"I saw them," he said, then looked away. "I was in the club, where everyone else was too, and he was pestering her. She was quite drunk, drinking too much, and I'd told her to stop twice, but she wouldn't. So he started sniffing round her again and I told him to back off and leave her alone. She was only eighteen a little while ago."

"And did he?"

Black shook his head. "No, ma'am. There was a scuffle between me and him and some of his friends. I didn't hit him, though, I promise, but the bouncers, they said it was my fault and I had to go, and also Nat was shouting at me, too, saying it was my fault, but I was only looking out for her."

"Then what happened?"

"I had to go out of the club, but she was still in there, and I knew he'd wait for her, because she was drunk. I couldn't just leave her there. I knew she'd been drinking. I'm her friend."

Dan nodded slightly as though she approved of all he was saying.

"What did you do?" she asked.

"I waited outside the club, down the street, for her, just so I could make sure she was okay when she came out, to make sure she got back to the ship okay."

"Did you follow her, Gary?"

He shook his head.

"No, ma'am, I didn't. I saw her meet with him again and then . . ." He looked to Cox, who again nodded her permission. "And then I went for a drink with Chief Pollack."

"Gary, did you know that sometimes Nat didn't like you helping her? That it made her feel frightened?"

"I was just trying to help. Like, I changed her duties so she wouldn't have to see Coker and his mates, and I'd let her stay back here with me so that they'd all be gone off the ship and she could be away from them."

"How did she feel about that?"

"We were friends, so she was okay with it, appreciated it. We became good friends. We had lunch together and stuff."

"Did you ever go to her house, Gary?"

He seemed to shrink back at that question, tensing again.

"Did you?" pressed Dan.

"Only to check if she was okay," he said. "I thought if she was frightened or worried, then she'd feel safe if I was there for her."

Dan felt John Granger readying himself on the chair next to her, but wasn't sure why. She felt oddly calm, as though she knew Black wasn't going to do anything rash, not yet.

"Gary, did you go there before she went missing?"

"Yes," he said, his voice faint.

"And did she know you were there, or did you go uninvited?"

"She didn't say I couldn't go," he finally replied. "So I went there and slept in my car for a few nights, just to make sure no one bothered her."

Dan inhaled deeply and watched him carefully.

"Gary, do you have any idea where Nat is now?"

"No, ma'am, I really don't, honestly. I'm worried sick about her."

"Do you know anyone who might want to harm Nat? Someone who might want to hurt her?"

He laughed at that, a broad smile.

"No, ma'am, she was lovely, I can't think that anyone would want to hurt her at all."

"Gary. I think SA Moore was afraid of you—"

"No, she wasn't," he said quickly. "We talked about it."

"I think she was worried because she knew you'd been outside her house."

"No," he interrupted again. "No, it wasn't like that. We talked about it, she liked me, too."

John Granger was on the edge of his seat now. Dan could see him trying to look casual, but Black's manner was becoming more agitated and erratic as he shook his head and explained himself more loudly.

"Did you take pictures of Natasha without her knowing?"

"Ma'am?" he said, and it took a moment for Dan to realize that Black wasn't talking to her, he was talking to Cox.

"Answer the question please, Gary," said Cox, her voice calm.

"No, ma'am, well, yes. I had pictures of her, but she didn't like it and I stopped. I don't have pictures anymore."

Dan paused, thought about what she was hearing.

"Gary, I'm going to ask you now to stand up and accompany me off *Defiance* and down to the SIB offices so we can talk some more."

He was still shaking his head.

"No, ma'am, listen . . ."

"Gary. I want you to pass me your keys to your lockable cabinets and stowages so they can be searched."

"Nat spoke to me," he said, but he was looking at Cox, his eyes beseeching, begging her for help.

"Do as you're asked, please, Gary," said Cox, smiling at him. "I'll be down to join you very soon. We'll sort this out, okay?"

Gary Black looked terrified.

"There's nothing in my bunk," he said. "I don't have any pictures anymore."

"Stop speaking now, Gary," said Cox, her voice firm and loud. "Just do as you've been asked."

The two looked at each other for a long time, Dan and John frozen, as though time had stopped, the tension thick.

Then Black seemed to relax, and so did everyone else around him.

Dan felt John exhale and turned to look at him, just as Black lashed out.

"No," he shouted, his face changing from confusion to anger and then to rage. "I didn't do anything, we were friends!" He swung an arm to push Dan out of the way as he headed for the door.

The movement of his arm seemed slow, Dan saw it coming, though she wasn't able to do anything to avoid it.

The strength of Black was unimaginable. His swinging arm hit her and knocked her clean off her feet, slamming her against the bulkhead.

She was dazed for a second but saw John Granger move quickly, grabbing Black's arm and trying to twist it into an armlock to control him.

Black spun round before John could apply the lock, twisting away, using brute strength and pushing John hard with his other arm.

John stumbled backward.

Black was shouting "No!' over and over again, and before John and Dan could recover, he darted out the door.

Dan rushed for the door and did a double-take as she saw Josie lying there holding the file Dan had asked for. Black had knocked her over, papers scattering as he barged his way out. Josie rolled over and grabbed at Black's leg, but she was only able to slow him down for a second before he ripped his leg free and fled.

"Shut the gangway," shouted John.

Dan knew he'd been speaking to Cox.

"He's not trying to get off the ship," said Dan, turning for only a second. "He's trying to get to something."

Dan ran out of the compartment and up the ladder, John and Josie close behind her. As she reached the top of the ladder, she stopped and scanned around the flat, then went on up the second ladder.

2-deck was quiet, long, doglegging out of sight, and she listened for footsteps and heard none.

"We should stay together," said John, arriving beside her.

"We don't have time," said Dan. "Josie, with me. John, that way. Don't engage with him, just find him and call for backup."

She rushed off along the passageway.

The ship felt vast, long, and open, so many places to hide, but she didn't think he was going to hide, to leap out and attack her. Dan believed he knew exactly where he was going and exactly what for.

She walked quickly, Josie beside her, and looked into flats and passageways. She recognized where she was, near the officers' flat, and she stopped, thinking of no reason why he would come this way.

Then, as Dan turned to speak to Josie, he was there.

He grabbed Dan by the collar of her shirt and swung her easily behind him, bashing her off a bulkhead and throwing her into the nearby flat.

Dan landed, skidding along the polished floor, and looked up to see Josie with her arms wrapped around Black's waist, trying to push him backward against the bulkhead.

Black raised his arm and brought it down hard onto Josie's back. She slumped to the floor, and Black raised his foot.

"No, Gary, don't!" screamed Dan, sure that he was going to stamp on Josie, but he looked at her, confused, and stepped over Josie's body as he headed back along the passageway.

"Are you okay?" said Dan as she checked on Josie.

"I'm fine," said Josie, sounding angry, already rising to her feet and looking as if she meant business.

They heard a sound from farther along the deck and ran to find John on his back.

"He's heading for the flight deck!" shouted John, struggling back to his feet.

They ran in that direction, Josie at the front, Dan and John catching up behind. They saw Black disappear through the bulkhead door, Josie reaching out instinctively to grab at it.

Dan pulled her back, watching Josie's fingers slip away from the heavy metal door as it slammed shut.

"Thank you, ma'am," said Josie, realizing what might have been.

Dan opened the door again and stepped through it into the hangar, just in time to see Black head left out of the hangar. She followed, hesitating as she realized she'd been right, he wasn't running for the gangway, wasn't trying to get off the ship.

She exited the hangar a second behind him and saw him stopped a few meters along the flight deck.

He turned and saw her.

"We were friends," he said, his voice muffled by the wind.

Dan saw something in his hand, a folder made of thick, buff card.

He held it out in both hands and ripped it in half in a single movement, crumpling the two halves together in one hand as though ready to hurl them away.

Josie pushed past Dan, and John was behind her. She and John surged against Black, taking him off balance and forcing him against the safety railings.

Sarah Cox was there now, watching from the hangar.

Dan saw Black push and fight—not to get free, but to keep the bits of the folder away from them.

He was really starting to fight now and he lashed out with his elbow, Josie ducking out of the way at the last moment, and he was still shouting, "No" like an alarm on repeat.

"Gary!" shouted Dan. "Gary, listen, stop fighting. Stop! I'll listen to you, I promise, but you have to stop!"

He seemed to relax a bit at the sound of her voice.

"Relax, Gary. I promise you, I'll listen and I'll believe you. Okay? I promise you that."

Gary Black stopped fighting, and John relaxed his grip slightly.

Black juddered suddenly, and they all prepared for another fight. Only none came as he started to cry.

He looked at Dan, and then behind her at Cox.

"No one believes people like me," he said.

Dan was stunned at the words, drawing breath just in time to see Gary Black stand up and throw out his arms with all the strength he had.

John Granger was a big man, but even he was launched across the flight deck, landing several feet away.

Josie fared worse, staggering back and bouncing off the hangar before she slumped to the deck.

"No one will believe me!" cried Gary, and Dan leaped forward as she watched him place his free hand on the flight deck rail and kick his legs over it, throwing himself into space.

She grabbed for what she could, her fingers brushing against the card and only gripping a few sheets of the torn paper as she watched Gary Black fall toward the dark water far below.

She heard the quartermaster react, heard the Man Overboard drill commence. She looked down at the paper in her hands, at the dim, grainy pictures of Natasha Moore, taken from above as she washed her hair in one of the junior rates' showers.

30

The lights were off as she waited. That was to make sure there was no warning.

It had been a shitty, stressful few months, and Natasha had taken all she was going to.

She'd spent the leave period in Rio with Mark and it'd been amazing. She'd known that everyone would realize they were together, but everyone seemed to know what they'd done, too.

They talked about it behind her back, whispering all the time, and worse.

One of the girls was shagging a marine in the phone booth, leaving their bloody condoms lying around, and that was just funny.

Natasha has a boyfriend, a proper exclusive relationship, and she's a slut.

She'd had a great time with Mark, finally understood what all the fuss was about surrounding sex. She'd never wanted it with Jason, and she could see now that her relationship with him had been wrong in many ways, not founded on the right feelings; with Mark, it was different.

He couldn't keep his hands off her, and she loved it. But someone was out to get them.

She'd had sex with him on the beach in Rio and everyone knew, but that wasn't the real problem.

Someone had followed them, and there were rumors of some video footage that some of the other junior rates had watched.

Someone was going out of their way to make Natasha's life miserable, and she'd had enough.

Mark had flown off the ship to go on some rugby tour and they'd agreed she'd just tough it out till he got back, but sleepless nights, no appetite, and the word "SLUT" written next to her bed in permanent marker meant that the waiting was over.

She looked at the door.

It was bright, like a portal to another dimension, as she sat quietly and watched it, planning what she might say, how she might say it.

The doorway darkened just for an instant, and then Gary entered, flicking on the lights. He immediately jumped back.

"Nat," he said, recovering quickly. "What are you doing in the dark?"

She watched him, probably three times her size, but she felt no fear, just rage.

"I really thought you were my friend," she said, shaking her head. "I honestly thought we could be friends. You were a bit controlling sometimes, but I put that down to you caring, looking out for me. Then the pictures, and you keeping all my notes . . ."

"No, Nat—"

"Don't, Gary, please, don't. If you'd done nothing wrong, then why did you change what was in your filing cabinet?"

"I . . ." his words trailed off.

"What I really can't understand is why you couldn't just back off. Even if you'd followed me to the park in Naples to see if I was okay, why stay and watch? Why follow me and Mark in Rio, too? I didn't see you, but I knew you were there."

"No, Nat . . ."

"Why videotape me? You're a filthy, disgusting pervert. And even if you'd watched, which is vile . . ." Natasha felt her voice start to break. "Why did you have to tell everyone? Why would you let people have the video?"

The first tears rolled down Natasha's cheek.

"I've been called a slut, a whore, a slag. I've been asked how much I enjoyed the 'cock.' I've been asked if I took it in the ass and how much I liked it. I've had 'back door Moore' scrawled on my stuff, and my locker and bed are full of Cherry Poppers, those chew bars from the naffi, because everyone knows Mark popped my cherry. I've been asked if I'll do more videos and how much I charge. Someone filled out the application paperwork for my ankles to qualify for separation pay. Do you know what I did to deserve all of that?"

"I didn't do it, Nat, I promise."

"All I did was have sex with someone I really like, on a night I was a bit tipsy and I wanted to."

"Nat, I—"

"Stop lying!" Natasha shouted now, standing up, her fists clenched. "Well, I wanted to do you the courtesy that you couldn't do me. I wanted to tell you straight to your stupid, sick, lying face that I'm going to Cox and then I'm going straight to Commander Ward, and I won't stop until I've done as much damage to your life as you've done to mine."

"Nat, I didn't—"

"You're the only one who had my password. You're the only one who could've accessed Jason's e-mail address. I saw the pictures in your drawers, I saw that you kept all that stuff of mine. I know how you touch me whenever you get the chance. I thought it was by accident, but it isn't, you're sick and you make my fucking skin crawl!"

"No . . ."

Natasha stood up and made for the door.

"Don't, Nat." He grabbed for her, gripping her upper arm.

Natasha tried to pull away, but she had no chance.

"I'm going to see Cox to get a meeting with the commanding officer, then I'm going to tell Commander Ward everything. You're done, don't make it any worse."

"No, Nat, don't go up there, don't go to see Cox. Please."

"Get off!" Natasha turned and scratched at his face, drawing blood just below his hairline.

He didn't even flinch. He just looked at her, gripping her arm so hard that she thought she might cry out, and then he began to sob.

"Don't go up there," he said. "Please, Nat, don't. I'll tell you everything, all of it, but don't go up there."

"Let go!" said Natasha again, the pain of his grip making her wince and bend over as she dug her nails into his hand.

He did, finally. He let go of her, stepping away toward the door, closing it and leaning back against it, his huge shoulders wider than the frame as he blocked her exit.

"I'll tell you everything, just don't go up there alone, please," he begged. "I'll tell you about her, and then we can go up together, okay? Once you hear, we'll go together."

31

"How you doing?"

John turned his head and smiled, but Dan could see he was wincing.

"He caught me on the nose again," said John, dropping the smile and shaking his head slowly. "It wasn't even hard, he just brushed by me, really, but by God, he nailed me good."

"He's a big lad," said Dan.

They were alone on the flight deck, the silence after all the excitement settling on them slowly.

"He'll be in the hospital for a while, I guess," she added. "He was unconscious when they fished him out, didn't look in good shape at all. Almost succeeded in drowning himself."

John nodded.

"Tell me about Hamilton," he said. "Why would you go see him? I thought nothing would ever get you back face-to-face with that man."

"The NCA wanted me to talk to him about some missing women. They thought he might be able to shed some light on an ongoing investigation."

John sat up straight and looked energized, his sore face forgotten. He looked hungry for information.

"Easy there, Johnny Boy," said Dan. "Just relax. Nothing particularly interesting doing."

"Well, and did he help you?"

"He was supremely helpful. I really thought he wouldn't be, but he pretty much just gave us the name of the bad guy without too much fuss."

"Really?" said John, surprise on his face.

"No, of course not really. He was an asshole, like he always was. He gave me the name of some ex-navy guy who disappeared off the grid a few years ago. Said he'd be able to help me. The NCA are looking into it, but I think we all know that Hamilton only wants to mess with people."

"To mess with you," said John.

"Yeah, to mess with me. He made a big point about how he'd help me, but no one else."

"What name did he give you?" asked John.

"William Knight."

John nodded slowly.

"You know him?" asked Dan.

"I remember him. A serial rapist. Used to attack pretty young girls. Picked them up from around the pubs and clubs in Southsea, or he'd follow them, pick up the ones who couldn't afford a taxi, and offer them a ride home. They'd regain consciousness somewhere, we never found out where, and he'd rape them and beat them in almost complete darkness. They'd eventually pass out and wake up again somewhere else, naked and battered. He's a proper nasty piece of work, that man."

"What happened?" asked Dan.

"No one knows what happened. The police identified him from some CCTV footage that gave them the plates for his car. They called the military police because Knight was living on board HMS *Nelson* and they wanted to come and get him. In the time it took them to sort themselves out, enter the base, and get to his accommodation, he was gone and hasn't ever been seen again. Disappeared."

"Just gone?"

John hesitated.

"There *is* another story, maybe a theory, about Knight and where he went. You probably wouldn't know this, but back in the day, in the eighties and nineties, it was the navy that ran all the doors around Portsmouth. I mean bouncing in the pubs and nightclubs, even working security at the football stadium. They ran it all. It wasn't official, of course. It started as a group of guys who weren't on operational ships and they'd supply bodies to the local nightspots. It changed all the time, but there was always a supply of sailors looking for cash, and if you use a sailor for security, you're less likely to get trouble from other sailors. They turn up on time, look halfway decent, do as they're told, and they're grateful for the extra money. They'd set up a few guys with radios at the clubs and pubs and then have a minibus driving around as a mobile response team with a dozen guys in it. If there was trouble, the bus turned up and things got nasty. It was like that right up until around 2001, I think, when licensing and the Security Industry Authority came to be. But by then, it was big money. The core of the guys who ran it all had been in the navy a long time and they decided to leave the forces and set up a company doing it properly. They ran the training courses to get licensed, went legit . . ."

"Except?" said Dan.

"Except, well, you know as well as I do, if you control *who* goes in and out of nightclubs, you also control *what* goes in and out of nightclubs."

Dan nodded. "So they took over the drug scene?"

"And with that and the money it brought in, they slowly took over everything else, too. They went from being sailors earning a bit of extra cash and spending it on beer and women, probably squandering the rest, to being a serious criminal organization."

"So they're a gang?" asked Dan.

"Not really. These guys use all ex-military muscle and security, ex-forces logistics guys, ex-forces communications guys. They're massively secret now, but only one of the original group that set it all up survived the growing pains. There were five in the inner circle at the beginning, but the one everyone knew was the only Royal Marine in the group, Jimmy the Teeth."

Dan leaned back and looked unimpressed.

"Master at Arms Granger, are you telling me fairy stories?"

John laughed.

"No, and you wouldn't find it funny if you knew him. He did have a big old set of munchers, though, could eat an apple through a tennis racket, but his surname was Nash, and so he became Jimmy the Teeth."

"Okay, you've still got me listening, but I'm hoping this is going to get somewhere pretty soon."

"I thought you were going to be a new, patient Danny. A new woman who listens more."

"You said you wouldn't like her, so I decided to just stick with Get-to-the-Point Danny."

"Okay, to the point. The last of William Knight's known victims was a young lady named Victoria Nash."

Dan's mouth dropped open as she thought about that.

"So you think . . ."

"Hold on," said John, "let me finish. Victoria Nash was found near the woods, up on Portsdown Hill, and it was horrible. Jimmy wanted to tear the city apart. He used every ounce of influence and fear, trying to find who'd hurt his little girl. Put money up as a reward, hired private investigators to try and get the guy first. The police knew it, too, I bet there were some coppers on the take who would've happily tipped him off, but the rumors were that once Knight was identified, and at some point between the police identifying him and the military police getting to HMS *Nelson*, which wasn't very long at all, Jimmy had managed to have Knight snatched, and as we know, he wasn't ever seen again."

Dan sat back and exhaled.

"And the police?" asked Dan.

"Nothing. They knew the rumors, but Jimmy's not some small-time crook, he's all over the south coast, major links into London and the north. He isn't going to get nailed for something like that. He'd have been nowhere near it—even assuming he had anything to do with it at all."

"But if he didn't, then Knight could be on the run," said Dan.

"That's true," said John.

"And he would've been around at the same time, so Hamilton could've known him. Felicity even said so."

"I guess so."

Dan leaned her head back against the bulkhead.

"So we need to find out if this Jimmy Nash did take Knight, or if he's still out there," said Dan.

"Jimmy won't help you," said John. "I doubt you'd even get near enough to speak to him."

"He won't speak to the police," she said, "but might he speak to some of his navy buddies."

"He won't," said John, "trust me."

Dan was already on her phone.

"Jessie, it's me. Can you speak to the NCA? They're digging around into a guy named William Knight, ex-navy. Can you offer whatever we have, but can you also send me a digest of it—career history, what jobs he did, where and when? Anything you can, really."

Dan waited a second, listening, and then hung up.

"What were you saying?" she asked.

"I'm saying he won't help you."

"How do we find out for sure? How do I talk to him?"

"You don't talk to him," said John. "You stay away from people like him."

"But I need to talk to him."

"No, we just need to pass this information, which is likely not even relevant, along to the people who're dealing with it, though they'll already know that speaking to Jimmy Nash will be an utter waste of time."

"I'll go speak to him myself, then," said Dan.

Dan turned away to leave the ship. She had her phone in her hand, thinking through how she could get face-to-face with Jimmy Nash.

"Look," said John, jogging to catch up with her. "I know Jimmy. I worked some of the doors for him back in the day, so I know him of old, and—"

"Brilliant. Why didn't you say so? Let's go," said Dan.

"And we should stay away from him," John finished, reaching out and touching Dan's arm to stop her.

"Are you coming or not?" said Dan.

They looked each other in the eye for a long moment, Dan looking at the swelling around John's eyes, noting it had begun to expand again, looking soft and puffy.

John looked away first, his chin dropping to his chest.

"Of course I'm coming," he said.

"Attaboy. I can almost certainly promise that no one will punch you in the face on this trip. Though I do understand why people might want to."

John laughed and walked beside her.

"I'll make a call," he said.

32

John was silent as they pulled up outside the glass-fronted building in a newly remodeled industrial park on the outskirts of Portsmouth. The trees and shrubs looked young and sparse, not fully developed, and they were taking up space in the parking lot that Dan was fairly sure would be cleared out for more cars before they ever bloomed.

She checked her phone. Josie had e-mailed her the digest on William Knight, and she scanned through it in the car while John waited in silence.

"Did you know that Knight had worked as a driver for Vice Admiral Cox?" she asked.

John frowned. "I may have known at some point, but I hadn't remembered that, no."

Dan read on, thinking about Knight and about Hamilton.

"I want to help you," Hamilton had said, and now she wondered whether he'd actually tried to do that, without her, or anyone else, realizing.

"Look, just be careful in here," said John suddenly, as though he'd been building up to this for a while now. "This guy Nash, he's no joke. He's a serious villain, so try not to . . ."

Dan looked at him.

"Try not to what?" she asked.

"Try not to do what you normally do. That thing where you piss everyone off; don't do that."

"You cut me deep, Johnny Boy," said Dan, getting out of the car. "You cut me real deep."

The parking area was block paved, and Dan's leather-soled boots clicked and echoed as she walked toward the building.

"McDermott Sporting Goods?" she said, turning back to John.

"Yup. They specialize in minority and growth sports, ones where existing technology can be brought over from other mass sports and used to produce high-end niche equipment. I think they made a killing on some kind of judo fabric a while back, and they make equipment for mixed martial arts, hockey, cycling, and triathlon, and a load of other things. All relatively specialist and expensive, selling to the serious enthusiast."

"Sounds villainous," said Dan.

John stopped and looked at her. He wasn't kidding, his face set hard and bordering on angry.

"Look, you might think his name is cause for amusement, and that it's all a bit laughable and cloak-and-dagger, but if you do, you're wrong, Danny. He's serious, and all this"—John waved his arms up at the building—"should tell you that more than anything else. He was working doors for cash and a cut of the drug takings fifteen years ago. Now I think he does over a hundred million a year just in his legitimate businesses and clubs alone."

"Are you frightened?" asked Dan, only half joking.

John paused and looked at her.

"I know him, so yes, I am, because I've seen him do things and be responsible for things that . . ." He paused. "Bad things. He's a violent man. You don't get to the top of his game without being just that. Jimmy didn't just run the business back in the day, he lived it. Working the doors, front and center when the violence started. And the others, the ones who didn't make it, they weren't soft, weak, or stupid men, it's just Jimmy was harder and smarter."

"Okay," said Dan. "Ease to a frenzy. I was only kidding."

"Well, if it's all the same to you, please don't," John said and walked to the glass door, which opened silently as they approached.

Inside Dan saw the second most enormous person she'd seen in years.

The woman behind the security desk was huge, bigger than most men. Her muscles rippled and stretched the sleeves of her branded polo shirt, and her jawline was square and hard. She was tanned to within an inch of her life, almost a deep orange, and she took a sip of something white from a sports bottle next to her workstation. She looked up as soon as they came in.

"Hi," she said, her voice squeaky, taking Dan back a bit. "Can I help you, please?"

She smiled broadly and stood up, showing the rest of a covered but clearly ripped physique.

"We're here to see Mr. Nash," said John. "I'm John Granger, and this is Danielle Lewis. I called ahead."

"Sure." The woman was smiling again. "We're expecting you, Mr. Granger. And you, Ms. Lewis," she said, slightly overdoing the z sound.

She pulled out a couple of visitor badges that had been preprinted with their names and then showed them a plan of the building.

"You'll be escorted," she explained. "Mr. Lowe will be on his way down to get you, but if you look here"—the woman pointed a finger at a building map—"you'll know where you are, where you're going, and where the fire exits are along the way. Just in case you get separated."

Dan couldn't help but look over at John, who ignored her as he listened to the brief.

"That's it," said the woman, whose name badge identified her as Tina. "If you'd be okay to take a seat over there"—she pointed to a few comfortable-looking chairs among plants and a water cooler—"I'll hustle Mr. Lowe along to come and get you."

Dan followed John over to the chairs.

"The underworld's really working on its customer service and health and safety, eh?" Dan whispered, looking away before John could shoot her a warning glance.

Dan picked a chair but had only just bent her knees when she saw a man approach them, already smiling, already extending his arm toward her.

"Danielle, John," he said, "I'm Marcus Lowe, Mr. Nash's assistant."

He smiled at Dan again. "We've already met, of course."

Dan nodded, recognizing Marcus instantly.

He'd been outside her house only a few days before. He'd been looking for the house that was for sale near hers and had stumbled into her close by accident.

"He's ready for you, so if you're both good to go, I'll take you straight up."

Dan nodded and followed Marcus along the corridor past Tina's reception desk.

"Thanks, Tiny," said Marcus as they passed, and Tina smiled and gave them all a thumbs-up.

A few paces on, Marcus pointed to a picture on the wall.

"That's Tina there," he said.

Dan looked at the picture of the woman from reception. She was on a stage, the lights beaming down at her and showing every sinew of her granite muscles. She was wearing a bikini that looked as though it would've been small on Dan, and she was posing, her back tense and broad.

Dan nodded; it took a level of dedication and confidence to do that kind of thing, a level Dan wasn't sure she had.

"She's one of our level two community outreach sponsored athletes," Marcus said, walking on. "She works here, but we sponsor her equipment, nutrition, gym membership, and coaching. We also support Tiny to take time off for precompetition and the like. It's a great program. It's been really popular. If she wins the nationals later in the year, then she may become a level one, fully sponsored, and wouldn't have to work, though I think she likes it here too much, to be honest."

"Is she ex-forces?" asked John.

Marcus nodded. "She is." He paused. "She's okay with being called Tiny, by the way, we wouldn't use it as her stage name otherwise: Tiny Tina Trathen. Anyway, yes, we do sponsor people without a military background, but usually only if there's a strong link, a parent or sibling, for instance. Tiny was an army dental assistant for seven years before she moved to Civvie Street."

They entered the elevator and traveled up, exiting on the top floor.

"You'd be eligible, Danielle," he said, smiling. "I know your dad quite well."

Dan nodded, hiding her surprise and saying nothing as they stepped out of the elevator. She could see her reflection in the dark sheen of the floor tiles, and all around her were offices, visible through large glass panes, all with just the right amount of greenery to make them look spacious and welcoming. If Dan had been asked to describe what she thought an organized crime boss's lair would look like, she couldn't have gotten it any more wrong.

"This way, please," said Marcus, and led them down to their left and into an area that wasn't glass-fronted.

A young woman sat at a very large oak desk outside an equally large oak door. She looked up and smiled, bustling round the desk to meet them.

"He's ready when you are," she said to Marcus. "I'm just getting him a tea." She turned to Dan and John. "Would you like one?"

"Do you have green?" asked Dan.

"We do indeed. Mr. Nash is a committed green tea drinker."

Dan looked at the young woman and couldn't help but be surprised again. She'd expected the women to be attractive, short skirts, high heels, low tops, maybe some red lipstick so they could be seen to smile as one of the gangsters patted their rump on the way past, but this wasn't like that, not at all. The woman was as stylishly dressed as Marcus, both professional and classy, and Dan wondered if she'd just watched too much television.

"And you, Mr. Granger?" the woman asked.

"Tea please, NATO . . ."

"NATO standard," finished the woman. "Tea, white, two, coming right up."

John smiled.

"Lots of us are former military around here," the woman said over her shoulder.

Marcus knocked on the door but didn't wait. He opened it a crack and looked in, then opened it the rest of the way and showed Dan and John inside.

Dan steeled herself for what she might see this time. A baseball bat on the wall maybe, some golf clubs strategically placed for beating confessions out of people. What she got was just an office, a large and spacious office, with oak furniture that matched the door, and a television on one wall, the volume completely down, that was set to a twenty-four-hour news station.

The man behind the desk stood up. He wore a deep blue three-piece suit and he moved quickly round the table to meet them.

"Irish John, how's it going, mate?" he asked in an accent that sounded like cockney.

He shook John's hand vigorously, smiling, and Dan could see that he did have big teeth, but even that part of the story had been overdone—the naval service was not known for understatement when it came to stories and nicknames. He was a handsome-enough man, though stocky and hard-looking.

Dan would have placed him in his early fifties but got the impression he might look younger than he was.

He turned to her.

"Danielle," he said. "Is it right that you like Dan better? What should I call you?"

"Dan'll be fine, thanks," she said, shaking his hand and smiling. She could think of fewer places she'd been where she'd been greeted more professionally or warmly.

"Dan it is, then," he said, walking back round to the other side of his desk, then stopping and gesturing them to a collection of chairs near the window. "You've got some of each parent in you. More of your old man, if you don't mind me saying."

Dan smiled, felt awkward at not having realized that she'd be known here, that her mum would be.

"I bet we'll be more comfortable 'ere," he said, dropping the *h*. His accent was strong and he made no attempt to hide it.

He pulled up his trousers at the knee before he sat down, but he sat like a boxer between rounds, his legs stretched out and spread wide.

The tea arrived and Dan noticed that hers was in a small, clean, branded cup, whereas Jimmy Nash's was in an old chipped mug with the Globe and Laurel, the crest of the Royal Marines, on the front. Their motto, PER MARE, PER TERRAM—by sea, by land—was just visible, faded through use.

"Well, it's been years, Johnny Boy," he said, once he'd thanked the woman who'd brought the tea. "How you doin'?"

John nodded and smiled.

"Good, Jimmy, thanks. I'm really good."

Jimmy looked at Dan. "I could tell you some stories about this geezer," he said, smiling broadly, his lips pulling back over his gums as he did. "I won't, 'cuz I know you're all police and stuff now, but by God, I could." He reached across and patted John on the knee.

"How's Taz?" he asked Dan. "It's been years and years. He okay?"

"He is, thank you," replied Dan. "I didn't realize you knew him."

Jimmy laughed and looked over at Marcus.

"Not many people in the corps that don't at least know of him," Jimmy said, showing her his teeth again. "I did my commando course a few weeks ahead of him, and we worked together on operations a few times."

At any other time, she'd have been keen to know more, to understand how Jimmy and her dad had met and how good friends they were. It just didn't seem appropriate to ask at the moment. She nodded.

"So, what can I do for you two, then? Always a pleasure to see serving personnel come down 'ere. Is it sponsorship? We're already doing a lot for the ships' sports funds and some of the squads, navy as well as the corps."

"It's not that, Jimmy, but thank you," said John. "We need to ask for some help, about something from a while back, something you might not want to talk about."

Jimmy leaned back in his seat and watched John closely.

Dan looked over at Jimmy's desk and saw some pictures there. One in particular caught her eye.

It was of a petite, very pretty blond woman, who had to be Victoria Nash. She was smiling in the picture, standing in front of her dad, who looked down at her.

"We need to ask about a missing person, Jimmy," said John quietly.

"William Knight," said Dan.

The room fell silent.

Jimmy looked at John and began to tap his forefinger on his thigh.

"This is what you came for, John?" Jimmy asked. "After all this time, no favors, no sponsorship, just bringing all that back up again?"

John nodded.

"Sorry, Jimmy. It's important."

Jimmy took a deep breath and held it for a few moments before releasing it slowly and looking up at Marcus, who'd remained standing a few feet away.

For the first time since she'd been here, Dan felt the stirring of something beneath the surface that might not be wholesome.

"Well, John, we both know I probably owe you a favor for something, so you can ask your questions, but after you 'ave, I don't want to see you, or talk about it, ever again. Okay?"

John nodded.

"Thanks, Jimmy. I appreciate it."

"So, you do know him?" said Dan, growing bored with the theatrics.

Jimmy turned to look at her.

"I don't know him at all," he said. "I know what he is. I know the things he did. I 'eard he'd disappeared years ago."

"He did," said Dan.

She could feel John staring at her, willing her to be more deferential, but she just wanted to get on with it. "But things have happened recently that now lead us to look for him again."

Jimmy paused and looked at each of them in turn.

"Well, I'm afraid you've 'ad a wasted journey. I ain't seen him in years, but"—he leaned toward Dan—"if I did, I'd let you good people know, so justice could be done."

Jimmy stood up and nodded to Marcus as he walked back to his desk.

"Jimmy, wait," said John, his voice strong, fearless again, as Dan always knew him to be. "We're not trying to find out what happened to Knight. That's not why we're here."

"Good, 'cuz I wouldn't 'ave a clue where he was, how could I?"

"Something's going on and we've had it from a good place that Knight knows something about it," said John.

Jimmy seemed to think about this, but he said nothing.

"I'm only asking for your gut feeling, Jimmy, you always had a good gut. What does it tell you about Knight? Could he still be active? Could he still be hurting more young girls?"

Jimmy seemed to bridle at that.

"I'll tell you what my gut tells me," said Jimmy. "It tells me he's not involved. I think he ran, or hopefully came to justice by some other means, who knows, but I really don't think he's hurting anyone. I think he's in hell."

John looked at Jimmy and then at Dan. He nodded, as though he'd heard enough.

"Does your gut tell you if he could be found?" asked Dan.

Jimmy smiled.

"Who knows, Dan? Everyone can be found. Thanks for visiting."

Jimmy turned away and Marcus stepped forward to usher them to the door.

"Someone's harming women again, Mr. Nash," said Dan. "Someone who's been doing it for a long time. It might not be Knight, but he knows something. I'm talking a lot of women too, tortured and terrorized, worse even than your Victoria. It's been going on for a long time, and now, even in death, they're being mutilated and disgraced."

Dan prepared herself, sure that he'd bridle again, become threatening, but instead she saw his eyes soften, as though he were vividly remembering the painful times that'd likely only faded, never passed.

"And you think Knight would know something about it?" said Jimmy.

Dan nodded. "I really do."

Jimmy reached up and rubbed his chin.

"Wish I could help," said Jimmy.

He watched as Dan and John walked toward the door.

"Dan," Jimmy said, as the door was closing behind her.

Marcus stepped back quickly and held the door open again.

"Well done on the *Tenacity* case a little while back and on your collar of that wife-beating piece of shit a week or so ago. You did well there. Appalling, people using the nation's assets for ill-gotten gain. You know, you do us all a service, and I might think of something. If I do, I'll call you. Just so you know."

"Just call me, Jimmy," said John, speaking from behind Dan.

"It's okay, John. You're a busy man, and I might quite like to speak to Dan again one day, who knows." He turned to Dan, his eyes piercing into her. "Always good to see someone else willing to take filth off the streets."

Dan said nothing.

"Do send my regards to Taz," said Jimmy. "Tell him I send my warmest regards. And call your sister, will you, she's pregnant and she's dying to tell you."

Dan froze, her lips moving but no words coming out as Marcus ushered her out and the door closed behind her.

Marcus chatted as they walked back, but Dan said nothing, only nodded and smiled as they handed their badges back to Tiny Tina, and again as she shook Marcus's hand.

John was already walking to the door when Marcus spoke to Dan.

"Would you like to grab a drink with me sometime?" he said, her hand still held in his. "Or maybe a coffee, or lunch?"

Dan was still numb.

"Sure," she said, and turned away to follow John without another word.

She pulled her phone out as soon as she was outside and called Charlie, who answered on the second ring.

"Hey, sister," said Charlie. "Took your time to call back, as usual."

"I did. I'm sorry," Dan said, as she climbed into the car. "How's things?"

"Well," began Charlie, "do you have time to talk? Because I have something I want to tell you."

Charlie giggled into the phone and Dan felt as though an icicle was being pushed into her gut.

"Tell me," said Dan.

"I'm pregnant!' said Charlie, barely able to contain her excitement.

"How long have you known?" asked Dan.

Charlie went quiet at the end of the line. "Aren't you excited? You're going to be an aunt."

"I'm over the moon," said Dan. "I just wondered how long you'd managed to keep it secret."

"I only really confirmed it a few days ago, but I think I've known for a few weeks. It's early yet. Dad and Mim know, and now you, but that's it."

Dan felt sick.

"That's so great," she said. "Oh, Charlie, I can't believe it. Dad must be driving you crazy, trying to do things for you."

"He is," said Charlie.

Dan looked at John, who she could see was listening to the call.

"Charlie, I'm being called into an interview, I'm so sorry. They said I'd have time. Can I call you back?"

She heard her sister's disappointment down the line.

"I'm sorry. I'll deffo call you back in a little while, and I promise I'll have time to chat, and I'm so excited for you. I love you."

The call ended and Dan looked at John, her mind turning over.

"He's right. Charlie's pregnant. How would he know that? Why?"

John shook his head.

"I don't know, but I know we shouldn't have gone in there at all. It was a mistake."

"It was a threat," said Dan.

"Well, stay away now. He knows your dad, doesn't he? And he's Royal Marines through and through, so knowing you come from Royal Marine stock might make sure he leaves you be."

Dan turned away and looked out of the window.

"Yeah, he knows my dad."

She picked up her phone again and dialed a number.

"You weren't kidding when you said you'd call me next," said her dad as he answered. "I'm just on my way out though, so only got a second."

"This won't take long," said Dan, trying not to sound angry, or worried, or however it was she felt right now. "Do you know a guy named Jimmy Nash?"

The line was silent for a while, the static stretching out between them.

"Dad?"

"Yeah, I'm here," he said, his voice quiet.

Dan heard him cover the mouthpiece and talk to her stepmum.

"I know Jimmy," he said when he came back on. "Just surprised you've come across him. Why do you ask?"

"I just had a visit with him."

"Why?" said her dad.

"It's to do with an investigation."

"*Tenacity*?"

Dan stopped trying to take stock of the conversation so far.

"No, something different," said Dan, not sure why she was so annoyed with his questions and short, clipped answers.

"Why did he come to you?" Taz asked.

"He didn't. I needed to speak to him. Listen, Dad, I just wanted to know if you knew him, that's all."

"I do."

Her dad's voice was odd, had lost all its usual humor.

"Do you know him well? Would he know Charlie, and me?"

There was a long pause again.

"He'd know I had daughters, but we weren't close. Why are you asking, Danny? What's happened with Jimmy Nash?"

"Nothing, honestly," said Dan. "He just sends his regards and said he knew you. I have to shoot now. Love you."

She looked back in through the glass-fronted building.

Marcus was still watching them, standing with Tiny and laughing at something as they chatted.

"Hold on," said her dad.

"It's fine, no biggie," said Dan, still watching Marcus and Tiny. "I have to go, Dad. I'll call you later."

"Wait," he said, but Dan was already ending the call.

"He does know him, then?" said John.

Dan nodded and put her phone onto silent, sliding it into her pocket.

"Why didn't you tell your old man what happened? If he knows him, it might all be some simple misunderstanding."

"I don't know if it is or not," said Dan, "But I do know that if it's not, and Nash was threatening me or Charlie, then telling Dad would be a serious mistake. I don't want to sound like a kid in a playground, but Jimmy Nash would only chew food for as long as it took my father to get here and find him, then he'd be using a straw and a nurse for food for a few months. Dad gets a little protective over his girls."

John laughed at that, but he stopped when Dan didn't join him.

"You think Nash does know what happened to Knight?" she asked, trying to move on, though her head was churning and starting to pound as she tried to understand what had just happened.

"Oh, I'd bet my life on it," said John.

33

Dan's phone was buzzing on her bedside table. It was set to silent, but where it was, lying on top of the bare wood, the vibrations were making enough noise to wake her. The light from the screen made her wince, but she didn't recognize the number, and so she let it ring out.

There was another missed call, too, from her dad.

He'd already called her again that evening, fishing for more information about Jimmy Nash, but she'd put him off, refusing to make a big deal about it, telling him that it was standard service police business.

She decided she'd call him again in the morning and try to set his mind at ease, even though hers wasn't.

A glance at the clock showed it was late, but not yet midnight; she hadn't been in bed that long.

She waited for the signal that a message had been left, but instead the phone started to buzz again, vibrating in her hand, and downstairs, she heard a light knocking on her front door. On instinct, she answered the call.

"Hello?" she said, not wanting to give her name.

"Ms. Lewis, it's Marcus Lowe. I'm really sorry to bother you so late, but could you come and open the front door, please? I've been knocking, but I don't want to wake your neighbors."

Dan's eyes were wide open now. Her bedroom light was on, as it always was, and the light stung her eyes as she sat up in shock.

"Are you at my door now?" she said.

"I am," said Marcus.

Dan froze, unsure what to do.

"Why are you at my door, Marcus?"

"It's in reference to a conversation you had earlier, some help you requested from a mutual friend. I'd much prefer we talk in person, if you're willing to."

Marcus had seemed like a decent guy on the two occasions Dan had met him, friendly and educated, ex-forces, and he knew her dad, but Dan knew she hadn't given him this phone number, nor her address, though he'd obviously known that from when they'd last met outside her house, and it made her heart beat fast to think that he was down there right now.

"What exactly do you want, Marcus?" she asked, sounding stronger than she felt.

"I want to show you something that I'm certain you'll want to see, Ms. Lewis. You asked for help, we'd like to offer you some."

Dan knew she'd need to speak to him now or later.

"Okay, I'm coming down."

She ended the call and pulled on an old pair of tracksuit pants and an overlarge hooded top. She picked up a pepper spray from a shelf next to the door and held it ready in her left hand, then peeped through the spy hole.

Marcus was there, illuminated by her security light. He was wearing a plain black jacket and was looking directly at the spy hole with both hands held up, palms revealed.

Dan opened the door and stepped back in case he rushed her.

He didn't. In fact, he, too, stepped back.

"What?" she asked.

"I'd like to invite you to come with me, please."

"Where?"

"I can't tell you that."

Dan watched him closely.

"I'm not going to do that, Marcus," said Dan.

"Then I'm sorry I disturbed you, Dan. Good night."

He nodded to her with a polite smile and turned away.

Dan waited for a moment.

"Marcus," she said, trying to whisper, but also loud enough for him to hear.

He turned back.

"What's going on?"

"I want to take you somewhere to show you something, but you don't have to come," he said.

"Marcus, it's midnight and you want me to come on my own, quietly, with you, to some location you won't tell me, to see something that you also won't tell me?"

"Dan, if we wanted to harm you, it wouldn't be like this."

Dan paused, thinking.

"Do I have to come alone?"

"Yes. No phones, nothing metallic at all, please. If you want to leave a text message with someone about coming with me, if that makes you feel more secure, then that's fine, though I'm not sure how it'll be received at this time."

"Let me get some shoes," she said. "Can you wait out here?"

He nodded. "My car's round the corner, so as not to wake anyone. You grab shoes and a jacket and I'll move it to the top of the road and wait for you," he said.

Dan nodded and pushed the door shut until she heard it click.

She put the pepper spray down. She was tempted to message Roger or John, but she knew that would be a mistake—either would come running, or try to call and overreact when she didn't answer. She typed out a quick text to Felicity. She needed to know whatever it was that Marcus might tell her, and there was only one conversation that he could be referring to.

Felicity always turned her phone off at night, so she wouldn't get the message till morning anyway, and by then, Dan would be back and could explain, or would need help that Felicity could provide.

She redressed upstairs, pulling on some leggings and boots and a warmer top, and then jogged quickly downstairs again.

If Marcus meant to do her harm, then he could've done that already, and why risk letting her leave messages identifying him?

She checked through the spy hole again, but he wasn't there. She opened the door and walked up the small sloping driveway to the dark-colored car waiting at the top.

She jogged around to the front passenger door and opened it, sliding into the warm leather seat.

"I put the seat heater on for you," Marcus said as soon as she'd closed the door. He pointed to a button on the dash. "Just push that if it gets too hot."

The car pulled away steadily. It was a high-end Mercedes with leather interior, and it was immaculately clean, not just kept in good order but shiny, as though it'd been valeted that day.

"Company car?" asked Dan, looking behind herself.

He laughed and looked at her. "Something like that. You okay?"

Dan nodded, scanning the streets.

"Just paranoid, I think. People turning up at all hours will do that."

They pulled out onto the main road and headed for the motorway.

"So where are we going?" Dan asked, watching the familiar road signs as they headed toward Portsmouth.

"Actually, about that," he said and reached down behind him into the rear passenger foot well. He pulled out a black hood and passed it to her. "I'm afraid I'm going to have to insist on this."

Dan looked at the hood and then at him.

"Marcus, I really don't think I can put that over my head," she said.

He looked at her, sensing that she wasn't just being difficult. He tapped the wheel.

"I don't think we can go ahead without it, Dan."

Dan scrunched up the rim of the hood and readied it to go over her head. Her hands were starting to shake.

"Is it having it over your whole face that bothers you?" he asked. "Would you be able to put it down just over your eyes? It doesn't have to cover your nose and mouth."

Dan thought about that, unwilling to discuss it, unwilling to back out, and unwilling to do what was needed. She took a deep breath and pulled the bag onto the top of her head, unrolling it until it just covered her eyes.

"I can live with that," he said. "But can you lean your head forward, please, chin down, and then lean against the door as though you're sleeping?"

Dan did as she was asked, her mouth and nose in the open air, her eyes in complete darkness. She could feel him checking her, looking across to make sure she couldn't see where they were going.

"I'm afraid you'll need to stay like that for around forty minutes now. I'll let you know when you can take it off."

"Okay," said Dan, her throat dry.

SHE TRIED TO remember the turnings and timings as she felt the car lean. She tried to judge where they might be going, but after a short while she gave up. At one point it felt as though he'd gone twice round a roundabout just to throw her, and several times she heard voices, revelers still out and about. They seemed to drive on forever. She was pleased when she felt the car go down a slight incline, and then the light of wherever they were was so bright that it actually pierced the black hood, making her realize that her eyes had been tight shut the whole time.

"We're here," he said, as the car stopped. "I'll take the hood, but I'm afraid you will need to wear it again on the way home."

Dan took it off and handed it to him.

They were in a well-lit area, an underground garage of some sort, though there didn't seem to be enough supports for that. Maybe it was part of a large warehouse.

A low horn sounded nearby. It continued for six seconds and Dan recognized it as shipping. They were near the sea, down by the docks, though it could have been Portsmouth, Southampton, or even farther afield in the time they'd been driving.

The area wasn't huge, maybe big enough to park ten cars, but it looked clean and well maintained.

Marcus got out of the car and walked around to open her door for her. He stood back, smiling again, and waited for her to get out.

"I really like your boots, by the way," he said.

Dan stopped short, thrown by the compliment.

"Thank you," she managed, looking down at them.

"This way, please."

He led her across the small area to a stairwell. He started up the stairs and Dan heard noises, people talking behind doors that came into view as they approached the first landing.

They must have been underground after all, because Marcus looked at his phone as they climbed the next set of stairs and waited for a signal to connect. Then he dialed a speed-dial number and waited only a second.

"We're here," he said, and hung up.

He looked back at her again.

"You okay?" he asked.

Dan nodded and they continued up the stairs.

They must have climbed four or five stories before Dan turned a corner and saw a green metal security door, set back on one side of a wide, dirty landing.

If where the car was parked had been clean, the stairwell and landings more than made up for that. The smell of urine was strong enough to make Dan's eyes water, and there was another smell, too, one she couldn't place, like a deep rot.

"So, you're Jimmy's right-hand man, then?" asked Dan, as they stopped on the landing.

Marcus smiled but didn't answer. He turned to face her and looked her in the eye.

"I want to tell you right now that you won't like what you see in here. You can leave at any time; you just have to tell me you want to. You'll be safe, you have my word on that."

"Your word?"

"Yes, my word," he said.

"And that counts for something, does it?"

"It counts for everything, Dan."

Dan nodded, looking Marcus up and down, the perfect gentleman, well-spoken, well-mannered, intelligent, thoughtful, and observant, and right-hand man to a gangster.

"I'll be with you all the time, and I won't try to tell you how to prepare yourself, because I can't, but I can say, take your time and don't rush anything. If you need a few moments, you can have them, but once you step back out through that door, it'll never open for you again."

"Unless I show up with all my police friends and the big red key," said Dan, with a smile.

"Once you've been in there, I really don't think you'll ever tell anyone about it, but we shall see. You ready?"

"Born ready."

34

The door opened on the first knock.

Past the threshold, Dan saw a dim, dirty hallway that ran straight along to what looked like an ancient, filthy kitchen.

The man who'd opened the door was obese and unwashed.

The stink from both him and from the flat made Dan wince, though Marcus seemed not to notice.

The man didn't speak. He turned around in the hallway, his middle touching both walls as he did, his gut hanging out below a stretched gray T-shirt, and waddled away without a word.

He passed three doors on the right and entered the one at the very end, just before the kitchen. The glow from a television illuminated the hallway for a brief second, and then he was gone, the door shut behind him.

"Marcus, how do you know my dad?" asked Dan.

"We served together several times, I'm proud to say."

Dan nodded, unsure why she'd needed to know that, then pursed her lips.

"Why am I here?"

"Because I'm going to show you something Jimmy thinks might help you, but I need to talk to you first." He paused. "Actually, I don't need to, but it might be easier and more useful for you to understand a little of what's gone on before, you see."

"You've got William Knight here, haven't you?"

He nodded.

"Can he speak?" asked Dan.

Marcus moved his head from side to side, as though weighing the answer, unsure if it was as straightforward a question as it seemed.

"Do you know what Knight did?" Marcus asked.

"I do."

"You know, after he was found and brought here, five years or more ago, before my time, we spoke to him and we found out that he'd lost count of the number of girls he'd abducted and raped, but we were able to get him to describe thirty-seven of them."

Dan's mouth opened but she did not speak.

"Only eleven girls ever came forward to the police. But you know that, I'm guessing. That's twenty-six girls whose lives were shattered and didn't, or couldn't, for whatever reason, come forward. But thirty-seven, at a minimum, who'll live with what was done to them by an external force that destroyed their innocence, their confidence, their intimacy . . ." He shook his head.

"So you got him, and he's still here, after five years?"

Marcus nodded again. "Do you know how he picked his victims?"

"No, not fully, I know he targeted them on the way home from night-clubs, offering them a lift."

Marcus grimaced.

"No. I mean yes, that's how he got them, but his selection method was more than that. He only liked very petite, very young, very pretty blondes. He liked them to be virgins, that was his fantasy, that he was deflowering them. If they weren't virgins—and he asked every one of them—then they got it worse. That's his words, Danny, not mine, I don't believe rape can be worse, or better, but that's what he did."

Dan drew in a deep breath but couldn't speak.

"Imagine having your life wrecked solely because you're young and pretty and your hair's blond," said Marcus.

"He did this to Jimmy's daughter," said Dan, not sure whether it was a question or a statement, or why she'd said it at all.

"He did. And Jimmy doesn't forgive, or forget, but I ought to prepare you a bit. You've seen pictures of Knight, right? Seen what he looked like? Big, powerful, loved to lift the weights?"

"I've seen some sights, Marcus. Let's just go and speak to him. I'll be fine."

Marcus looked at her closely, examining her eyes.

"Okay," he said.

There were three matching doors on the left side of the hallway, each heavily secured with three large bolts positioned top, middle, and bottom. He stopped outside the third and last on the left. He reached down and drew back the bottom bolt first, then the top, and finally he turned to look at her again before he pulled back the center bolt and opened the door.

There was a partition wall only five feet inside the door that ran across the width of the room, wall to wall, as though they'd entered a waiting area.

Light came through the wooden partition at intervals, through a number of small round holes, maybe three feet from the floor.

Dan frowned and Marcus moved along to the left. At the far end of the partition wall, he undid more bolts and pushed against a hidden door into the space beyond. She followed him, slipping past him as he stood back and gestured her through the gap.

Again, the smell made her recoil, each point on her journey here more putrid than the last, and she tried to inhale only through her mouth as she moved into the squalor behind the wooden panel.

The room was dim, the bare low-wattage lightbulb overhead casting shadows all around her. There was an unmade bed in the corner.

Dan saw a bucket on the floor. It'd been emptied, but she could see and smell that it was used for human waste, and she felt her stomach lurch.

The room was dire, disgusting, no furniture except for the bed and the bucket.

There was movement on the bed. As her eyes adjusted, Dan saw the outline of something vaguely human take shape. It was emaciated, like a corpse, its skin a sickening color, light yellow patches between reds and mottled blues.

The last time she'd seen something like this, it had been under a tarpaulin in Chris Hamilton's garage.

She turned and looked back at Marcus.

"Tell me," she said.

"After they got him, it was decided that he should suffer for as long as the girls would. Namely, for the rest of his life. So he lives here now. He's kept alive by our friend who met you at the door."

Dan felt nauseated as she looked back at the near-corpse on the bed.

"If he's very badly injured, or if his life's in danger, then he's taken offline for a while, stitched up and treated, and then it all starts again. He lives in the same nightmare as his victims—the punishment fits the crime, as they say."

"This is inhumane," said Dan.

"Raping young girls is inhumane, Dan," Marcus replied, his voice hard, though Dan noted that he still hadn't come inside the room.

"His keeper, best you don't know his name, is a nasty piece of work, a sadist, and sometimes we have to give them a little time and distance, but Mr. Knight has shown an amazing degree of resilience."

Dan looked again at the holes.

"You need me to explain?" asked Marcus.

Dan looked back at him, not declining.

"If something comes through these holes"—Marcus leaned in just enough to point at one—"then Mr. Knight gets on his knees and uses his mouth. I'm led to believe he was a bit of a biter in the early days, so you'll notice, when you speak to him, that he has no teeth anymore."

Dan realized that she could breathe normally through the smell, though her heartbeat was quickening.

She looked at the shape on the bed, it wasn't moving, and felt tears form in her eyes.

"Don't cry for him, Dan," said Marcus. "He's caused more than enough tears."

Dan shook her head, taking a moment to compose herself.

"You ready to speak to him?"

Dan shook her head.

"Not like this."

"Okay," said Marcus. He gestured for her to leave the room.

"What are we—?"

"It's like this or it isn't happening at all, Dan. He never leaves this room."

She stood, wavering, thoughts crashing through her mind, confused, powerful, uncontrollable. She looked at the living skeleton on the bed, her eyes adjusted now to see what she was sure were burn marks on his face and lash marks down his bruised and discolored skin.

"Can you ask him if he knew Christopher Hamilton?" said Dan.

Marcus hesitated at the door, obviously not wanting to come in, and Dan sensed that he'd made some degree of peace with this but it wasn't a place he was comfortable in.

"I'll get the Keeper," he said.

"No," blurted Dan, unsure why she spoke so quickly but knowing that regardless of this man's crimes, she couldn't watch what might happen if the Keeper came through the door.

She moved closer to the bed, able to see now that Knight was lying on his stomach, his head turned away from her.

He was naked and on his back she could see raised scars, angry and deep, spelling the word RAPIST from left to right, starting at his lower back, the flat line of the R running along where his waistband would be and the T curving up and over his emaciated shoulder.

"William," she said, speaking quietly. "William Knight?"

It stirred and the face turned toward her.

She had never seen, not in history, or on television, or in her nightmares, a human being in this condition and still alive.

He looked at her, his eyes dull and dead, nothing behind them, nobody home.

"William. Will you answer some questions for me? Can you do that?"

A long groan escaped, then a hiss as Dan was certain she heard him say, "Yes."

"Did you know Christopher Hamilton?"

"Yes," he said, barely a whisper.

"Do you know what he did?"

"Yes," he said, forcing Dan to come closer so that she could hear him.

"Did you help him hurt girls?"

"No."

"But you know that he did?"

"Yes."

"Do you know where he put their bodies, William?"

"No," he said, the single syllable exhaled in a long breath.

"Mr. Knight." It was Marcus, speaking from the door. "Do I need to ask the Keeper to come in here and help us to be sure you're telling the truth?"

There was a rasping sound and Knight's skeletal body juddered on the bed.

"No," he said, the voice pathetic, heartbreaking, the embodiment of hopelessness and despair.

"So you don't know where he put those girls?" asked Dan. "You promise that?"

"Yes," he said.

"We've been told that you do know, William. I was told that you could help me."

He moved, quickly enough to make Dan jump back, and she felt Marcus move to her side in a flash, but Knight had just curled up into a ball and was weeping.

"I don't. Please. I don't know. No more today. Please. No more today."

The words landed on Dan like blows.

"Let's go," she said to Marcus, turning away and heading for the door.

"You sure you're done? This is a onetime thing, Dan. It's now or it's never."

Dan looked at Marcus and then back at Knight.

The man was curled up, his knees drawn to his chest, and he looked no bigger than an eight-year-old child. His skin was tight over his bones like leather and Dan could see every vertebra pushing against the bruised and scarred skin on his back.

She recalled what Hamilton had said to her. "I will help you, Dan—not them, you." Then she thought about Knight's file, remembered that he'd been the driver for Cox's family for eight years, during the height of his crimes. She turned back.

"William," she said, moving closer and feeling Marcus back away again, but not as far as the door. "Do you know Natasha Moore?"

"No," he sobbed.

"Do you know Sarah Cox?"

He stopped shaking and turned his face toward her.

"Yes," he said, his voice hopeful, as though glad he could help.

"Did you know her as a child, as a teenager?"

"Yes," he said.

"Did you hurt Sarah?"

"No." He said. "Never, not one time, no. I promise. She was . . ."

"She was what?" asked Dan.

"I don't know. I don't know what she was."

Hamilton had led her here, to Knight, and Knight knew Sarah Cox. Dan knew there was no such thing as coincidence where Hamilton was involved.

"Tell me about her, William. Tell me what you know about Sarah Cox."

"I don't know what to tell," he said.

"I'll go and grab the Keeper," said Marcus. "I hear he's excellent at helping with ideas."

"No. No! I'll tell you."

"Tell me then. I know you drove for her dad. I think you were a friend of their family."

"She watched," he said, and the words caused Dan to inhale as she immediately understood what he meant.

"Explain that," said Marcus, the voice so cold and hard that Dan had to turn to look at him to be sure it was still him.

"She found me with one of them. She followed me out one night, hidden in the back of the car. She followed and watched. After that, whenever she could, I had to let her watch. I sometimes had to let her help me pick them. Then she wouldn't tell."

Dan's jaw was set. She couldn't smell anything, couldn't hear anything, couldn't see anything except an image of Sarah Cox, in her early teens, watching as William Knight beat and raped young girls.

"Why didn't you hurt her?" asked Dan.

He rocked back and forth now, shaking his head.

"Didn't like her. Too big."

Dan thought about Knight's victims, petite and blond—that's how she'd been told he picked them, exactly like Natasha Moore and Victoria Nash. Dan also realized now that Hamilton had never meant to help the NCA investigation. He was helping Dan, playing games with her, showing her that even inside prison, he knew what she was working on and knew more than she did about it. He was establishing value.

"Where did this happen, William?"

He sobbed but didn't answer.

"William," said Dan. "I want you to tell me where you did these things. Do you understand?"

"Yes," he said, his dry sobs disrupting the word, making it seem like many more syllables than it was.

"Where did you take the girls? Where did she go watch you?"

He said nothing for a moment, just cried into his pillow.

Marcus turned to walk toward the door and Knight spun toward them, sitting up for the first time.

"No!" he said. "It was Defiance. She watched me in Defiance. I swear it."

Dan frowned and looked at Marcus.

"That's a ship, isn't it?" Marcus asked.

"It is, but it wouldn't even have been built at that time."

Marcus turned back toward the door.

"No," said Knight. "Listen." He fell out of the bed onto his hands and knees and crawled toward Dan. "Help me and I'll tell you anything. I'll tell you everything."

"Don't move any closer," warned Marcus.

Dan looked down at Knight, the bones of his shoulders jutting out of his skin. She could now see a word she couldn't make out seared onto his forehead in a pattern that looked as though it was made from small round cigarette burns.

"Please," he begged. "Please don't leave me here."

"Here's the only deal on offer," said Marcus. "Answer the question, and on the way out, I tell the Keeper to take a few days off. Don't, and I'll tell him you said he was a fat, lazy, useless prick."

Knight rolled onto his side and lay motionless on the floor.

"Your choice," said Dan, the words sticking in her dry throat.

"It was Defiance," said Knight, quietly. "Not the ship—the gun emplacement, up at the armories on Portsdown Hill. That's where we used to go. That's where we took them."

PART TWO

35

The pencil strokes weren't quite working today.

Sarah looked down at the sketch and screwed up her face. She tried to capture Natasha's expression, just as it was on the screen where she had it frozen in time.

Black had his uses, had done well in this case, almost cupping Natasha's breast as he reached past her.

Moore's face was perfect. A mixture of surprise and shock, a half smile almost, that moment when she felt so uncomfortable she wasn't sure whether she needed to laugh or be outraged, but there was fear there, too, not much, maybe more like discomfort in her perfect features. It was a face mixed with so many emotions and such confusion that it was difficult to draw accurately.

Cox stopped and flicked back through her pad.

There were many better drawings there, ones that captured what she wanted them to. Not just the pain, but the point when it mixed with fear and ecstasy, a sensory overload.

She looked at one drawing, her favorite.

In it, Natasha's perfect, tiny little frame was completely exposed, she was on all fours and William was behind her, waiting to break her in for the first time, though the little slut had fucked that up for them all. The anticipation she'd captured in both of their faces made Cox's tummy tingle, like brushing hands with your first crush, like the first time she'd watched William do what he did best, what he'd never do to her because she was too big and ungainly to interest him.

She brushed her finger over William's penis. She'd drawn it too big, always did, and it threw off the scale of the drawing.

There was a knock at her door, but no one ever entered a female's cabin without waiting, one of the benefits of being a girl. She was expecting Moore for their meeting, loved to see her fresh and in the flesh, so she could compare her to the captured images in her mind.

Cox flipped the page to the drawing of a bat she'd been working on for weeks, and then pushed the lid of her laptop down flat. She stood up, took a moment to calm herself, and walked to the door.

"Tash, hey," she said, smiling broadly, noticing that one collar of Moore's shirt was off center, allowing a clear view of her fine, pale collarbone as it pushed out against the pale, delicate skin. "Come in."

Natasha smiled, only a turn at the corner of her mouth, really, more concerned than happy, and Cox wondered what nonsense the silly little cow would want to whine about now.

Cox watched Natasha move past her, noticed how her trousers caught her hips and bum as she walked, imagined how William's face would have been when he'd driven himself inside her and made her scream.

Natasha sat down on the couch, rested her hands on her thighs, and looked up.

Cox sat down at her desk.

"So how have things been?"

"Not great, ma'am, if I'm honest."

"You should always be honest, Tash."

"Well, it's PO Black," said Moore, and Cox died inside a little bit; what had that fucking moron done now?

"Okay, tell me, what's he done? I did speak to him a little while ago. I thought we'd reached the bottom of it all."

"No, ma'am, I mean, Sarah, it's gotten worse if anything. I found a small camera in the stores office today. He's been videotaping me, and I think he's been deliberately touching me to catch it on video, too."

Cox was silent, the smile dropped from her face, as indeed it should at this moment in this conversation, not least because she'd told Black to take the bloody camera away for a few weeks until things settled down.

"Are you sure? That's a really serious allegation."

"I know," said Natasha.

Cox watched her carefully, Moore wasn't crying, didn't even look like she might. This wasn't good.

"Let me deal with this straightaway," said Cox. "I'll get PO Black up here and we'll find out exactly what's going on."

"Well, ma'am, there's more. He did take a load of pictures of me, too, and he sent them to my former fiancé saying I was sleeping around, which I wasn't. He was intercepting my e-mails, had set up a forwarding function so they all went to him as well as me. That's how he knew the e-mail address to use."

"How could he know your e-mail address?"

"I let him use my log-on once, when his wasn't working."

Cox shook her head and sighed.

"That's serious, Natasha, a breach of the Ship's Security Standing Orders, but look, let's sort out what we can and see if we can't keep that quiet."

"Thank you, ma'am," said Natasha, still not crying, her eyes narrow. "But I think he also followed me at the last stop and taped me having sex with LPT Coker. I think it was him that started all the rumors about me and shared them round the ship."

"Well, this is serious," said Cox, watching Natasha closely, "very serious, and I'll deal with it as such."

"Thank you, ma'am, but I really want to go and see Commander Ward about it, today, right now."

Cox smiled and shook her head.

"Natasha, that's not how it works. The commanding officer might not even be on board at the moment, we're not long back, and he's busy. Also, I'm the ship's legal adviser, and I'll need to do some investigation before I can escalate it. That, and given your breach of security, which I'm keen to keep out of this, means it's going to take a few days at least. And, I hate to do this, but I want you to make sure you don't discuss these allegations with anyone else during that time, in case it damages the case we'll build. I'm not even sure we should do a full statement here—perhaps doing one at my home might be better, where we can talk freely."

Natasha was silent, thoughtful, but she was still not fucking crying.

"Thank you, ma'am," she said, nodding and standing up. "I appreciate you always watching out for me."

"Of course," said Cox, also standing up and moving toward the door.

"Actually," said Natasha, "I just had a thought. Chief Pollack said he was with PO Black after the fight in the club in Naples. He said they had a few beers together and walked back together. So it couldn't have been PO Black who followed me and spread the rumors."

Cox stopped in front of the door and turned, pushing it shut with her foot.

"Indeed," she said, her eyes meeting Natasha's.

"He was also with Chief Pollack in Rio, so that couldn't have been him, either."

In an instant Cox moved from suspicion to certainty: Moore knew.

Black had likely broken and told her.

How could someone so big and powerful be so stupid and weak? He'd had potential, but it didn't matter, the little blond darling clearly had more to say, a prepared speech.

"So if it wasn't PO Black," Natasha was saying, watching Cox carefully, "then who?"

"You should have gone straight to Commander Ward, Natasha," said Cox.

"I will, but I wanted to pay you the courtesy you never paid me. I wanted to tell you to your face that I'm going to ruin your life."

Cox stepped forward and then stopped.

Natasha not only didn't look frightened, she smiled at the gesture.

"Gary," said Moore, as though she were calling a pet dog.

The door opened and Gary Black filled it as he moved into the room.

"You're done," said Natasha.

Now Cox smiled.

"Silly girl," she said. "Close the door, Gary."

He did as Cox said.

Natasha turned to look at him.

"Gary?" Natasha whispered, and Cox watched as the little girl's face flushed when she saw Gary say nothing, just stand at the door watching her, one hand deep inside his pocket, massaging his groin.

"I have copies of Gary's pictures of you, Tash," said Cox, smiling. "He's a big fan. He particularly likes the videos of you that he took in the showers."

"Gary?" said Natasha again, but Cox could hear that her voice had lost its confidence.

She smiled and looked at Natasha.

"Ah, there they are, the tears have arrived," said Cox, as she saw Natasha's eyes fill up as the fear hit her.

She looked at Gary.

"Don't damage her too bad," he said.

Cox nodded, knew that Black's fantasies were about perfect bodies, smaller and weaker than his.

"Okay," she agreed, and swung hard at Natasha, catching her on the temple and watching her stagger back against the bulkhead.

Cox watched her slump, then reached down for her work boot, steel-toe-capped, sitting beneath her desk, and she swung at Natasha again, and again, three times more, until the small girl collapsed unconscious to the floor and lay still.

She was out of breath when she stood up, dropping the boot to the floor and turning to Gary.

"You did well to get her up here," said Cox.

"I didn't know what else to do," he said. "What are we going to do now?"

She stepped forward and touched his cheek.

"Go to the stores and get some masking tape, zip-ties, rags, and your kit bag. Also get some of that chemical cleaner. Bring it all up here now and we'll get this sorted out."

"What?" he said. "We need to get rid of her, it's me they'll come for."

She slapped him, hard, leaving her hand on his cheek and rubbing it gently against his warm, red skin.

"I'll look after you. We'll buy some time first, report her missing on Monday. By then she'll be long gone. I'll take her somewhere for a while until it all calms down, they'll look at you, but we know that, and if you do as I say, and we stick together, we'll be fine. Within the month you can do anything you like with her, anything at all, as many times as you want. I'll even let you keep some of the pictures and sketches for when she's gone. Now go and get the stuff we need and let's get her off the ship and into your car as quickly as possible."

"They'll find out," he said, quietly.

"No, they won't. Not if they have a better option."

36

Dan almost stumbled from the house, doing all she could to resist clawing at the walls. Her skin was covered in sweat and her mind was churning so that she was worried she'd cease to function, cease to be able to reason at all.

"I need to get back, Marcus. I need to get back really soon."

Marcus nodded, but then his eyes shot away to the stairs and Dan turned to look.

Jimmy Nash stepped out of the shadow of the stairwell to meet her.

"Dan," he said, reaching for her hand and shaking it. "Thanks for coming."

"Did I have a choice?" asked Dan.

Jimmy looked quickly at Marcus, his face becoming hard. "Of course you 'ad a choice," he said, "wasn't that made clear?"

"It was," said Dan, now unsure why she'd said that at all. "I'm sorry."

Jimmy smiled.

"Good. So I listened to what you said today, about them girls. Bad times. I thought about it a lot."

He looked away from her, reached into a pocket, and pulled out a pack of cigarettes.

"Smoke?" he asked.

Dan shook her head.

"Good choice. I don't much, either, these days, but the late nights sometimes make me partake."

He lit the cigarette and dropped the pack back into his coat pocket.

Then he inhaled, drew the smoke deep into his lungs, and stepped away from Dan, blowing it away from her into the stairwell.

"You left me with a dilemma, Dan," he said, looking back at her as he took another drag and exhaled it through his nostrils. "You left me with an opportunity to help you and maybe help those girls, the ones like my Victoria, but everything in life comes at a risk. Do you understand?"

"I think I do," said Dan. "But I wasn't interested in anything else apart from finding out what he knows about the girls."

"You 'wasn't interested,'" said Jimmy. "But that's changed now, has it?"

Dan didn't speak, but nor did she look away.

Marcus had disappeared into the background and she could no longer feel him on the landing with them, though she didn't want to look.

"What's happening in there can't be allowed to happen to anyone," said Dan. "It doesn't make anything right, it just makes even more wrongs."

Jimmy tossed his cigarette, only half smoked, into the stairwell and stepped toward Dan.

"Do you know what? My little girl hasn't had a boyfriend since she was fifteen. I often thought that's what I'd want, that any lad would have to be out of his fucking mind to try it with my daughter, but she's in her twenties now, never had a fella, doesn't go out, lost almost all her friends, because they're all living normal lives. They're all out partying, pissing it up, shagging boys that their dads'll never know about. Doing all the things young girls are supposed to do. My little girl doesn't, though, because of him."

Jimmy pointed to the door.

"So you tell me why he shouldn't suffer like she does. Tell me why that's wrong."

"Because you can't make up your own laws, Jimmy. It just doesn't work that way."

He laughed and then seemed to listen as the sound vibrated and echoed around the stairwell, bouncing back at them as it disappeared into the shadows.

"And yet here I have," he said, smiling again.

"You have for now," said Dan.

"And what if I offered a room at my inn to your friend Chris Hamilton?" said Jimmy. "Would it still be wrong?"

"Yes," said Dan. "It would."

Jimmy smirked at her and Dan saw something in his look, deep in his eyes, a flicker of danger, a flicker of what she saw when she looked into Hamilton's eyes.

"You know, you've just seen what I can do, what I can have done. I didn't just do it to help you with your case, Danielle, though it's always nice to help the law, but I did it to show you exactly what I can do. Imagine what I might do to a young lad who went on the run with too much knowledge about things he should be quiet about."

"Ryan?" said Dan, now thinking about the other rooms she'd passed as she headed to see William Knight. There were others, at least two on the left-hand side of the corridor, both locked and bolted just like Knight's room.

"Imagine what I'd do if someone kept poking around into my affairs. Imagine where they might end up, and for how long. Imagine where their family might end up. That flat in there, maybe others like it, they're no places for a pregnant woman."

Dan stepped forward and swung a punch at Jimmy's jaw.

Marcus seemed to materialize from nowhere, firmly grabbing her before the punch could land and pulling her arm back down to her side.

"Don't, Dan," he whispered into her ear, holding her tight as she fought against him.

"You've been warned, Danny," said Jimmy, still smiling. "I've given you a gift, and now I'm giving you a warning. Understand?"

Throughout it all, he hadn't even flinched, the smile not dropping from his face for even a second.

Dan spat at him, watching it land beneath his right eye.

Jimmy drew in a deep breath but left the spit where it was.

"You're honest. I like that. You could do well in my organization, though I'm reliably informed that you wouldn't be well suited from a moral standpoint."

He grinned and shook his head.

"But I think you've got my message. I don't think we'll see each other again, or hear about each other's activities."

"We'll see," said Dan.

He laughed and pulled a handkerchief from his inside pocket to wipe his face.

"Say hello to your dad for me, won't you? If it weren't for him, you wouldn't be walking out of here."

Dan's heart seemed to seize as he said the words. She felt hollow, weak.

"Fuck you," she said, at a loss for anything else to say.

She watched him as he headed up the stairs and back into the shadows. But he stopped and turned back again.

"You know, Dan, you'll have a fixed view of me now, and I'm betting it's changed a lot in the past twenty-four hours. Your view of me and my organization probably isn't great after what you've seen—what we let you see—but I want you to know that however ruthless and remorseless and lacking compassion you judge me to be, however much the violence sickens you, however frightened the threats make you feel, I want you to know, I've got nothing at all on your old dad."

He disappeared from view.

37

They drove back in silence, Dan resting the hood just over her eyes and again trying hard to guess at what direction they were taking before giving up and letting her thoughts run free. There was so much going on, too much to think about, but she needed to prioritize, and for now, Cox had to come first.

She knew she'd need to go and check out the gun emplacement up on the hill, knew where it was and had vague memories of how the old armories up there looked, though they'd been completely redone and modernized as a tourist attraction in the years since she'd been there. But first she needed to get hold of John and get Cox into custody.

Jimmy's words about her father had seemed cruel and pointless, and yet Jimmy didn't come across as a man who wasted words.

Dan couldn't stop thinking about what he'd said and what she'd seen. Thinking about William Knight, inhumanely treated and tortured, she just couldn't reconcile anything like that with what she knew about her father, nor could she focus on it now.

He was a hard soldier, anyone who knew him knew that, but he was also known and well liked for being fair and open-minded, for supporting his troops, and for going the extra mile for those he loved and respected. The implication that he could have any part in something remotely like what she'd seen seemed out of the question. And yet there was something in Jimmy's eyes when he spoke, something that made her believe his words were about more than spite.

She also couldn't stop images of William Knight from flashing across her mind, sometimes making her flinch as though she were see-ing them in a nightmare, a monster revealing itself to her, running at her from the darkness of her closed eyes, though she was wide awake.

His skin like faded yellow leather, his bones pushing against it like tent poles under a canvas. His mouth was cavernous, his teeth gone, and the burns and the bruises . . .

She shook herself.

This had to stop.

Knight deserved to suffer for what he'd done; Dan knew she wouldn't have questioned that, but what he was enduring wasn't justice, it was tor-ture, plain and simple, and she knew she wouldn't be able to let that go. Had it been Hamilton, she'd need to stop that, too.

Finally, the one thought that kept pushing to the front of her mind was worse still.

Hamilton had said he'd help her—help *her*—not the NCA.

She'd been so preoccupied with his nonsense that she'd failed to really pick up on what that might mean.

He'd helped her, but not to answer the question she'd wanted to ask but had refused to. He'd known what she was working on and knew enough to direct her to Knight. He'd also known, or perhaps only guessed, that Knight was still alive, but he'd at one point known where Knight was, and that made Dan want to look more closely at the links Jimmy "the Teeth" Nash had with the Royal Navy. It also made her want to tear Hamilton's prison apart, because someone was talking to him, passing information, and it was accurate, private, and up-to-date.

"You can take that off now," said Marcus, speaking for the first time since he'd asked her to put the hood back on.

Dan stripped the hood back and dropped it onto the floor behind her seat.

They were back on the motorway, past Portsmouth and moving toward the turnoff for her home.

They stopped outside the entrance to Dan's parking area, just behind the trees that prevented her from seeing her front door. It also prevented any of her neighbors who might be up at this time of day from seeing the car.

He gently touched her arm to stop her from getting out.

"What?" she said.

He seemed to be sizing her up. He didn't look angry or aggressive, he actually looked, if Dan hadn't known what he was complicit in, apologetic.

"Do you understand what happened tonight?" he asked.

"Your boss made it pretty clear," Dan said, staring straight back at him.

He looked genuinely pained.

"You wanted this, Dan. It wasn't going to happen, but there was something at stake that mattered to the decision makers, and so what you wanted was gifted to you."

"And I shouldn't complain about it?" she said. "If you want to fight with pigs, then you should expect to get covered in shit?"

He laughed at that.

"Very few people have ever seen what you've seen tonight. The ones who have seen it had no idea what they were seeing, but not one person who's entered that room has ever really needed to be threatened. Not one person's ever needed to be told that they must not speak about it to anyone, friend or family."

There was a silence between them, and Dan held his stare.

"How can you be involved in that?" Dan asked, suddenly desperate to know. "You seem like a good person, how do you allow yourself to be complicit in what we just saw?"

He looked away, out the window into the semidarkness between the dim streetlights.

The light framed his face and Dan recognized again that he was handsome, and yet he was dirtier than some of the scumbags she'd pulled off the streets, the ones that came looking like villains, filthy and spitting angry.

"Good people do bad things, Dan, and bad people do good things. If you tot it all up at the end of each day, and you genuinely believe that, on balance, you've done more good than bad, and if you keep doing that every single day, then over a lifetime, you can do an awful lot of bad, bad things, and yet still be a good person. The world doesn't work in absolutes."

"Are you talking about something my dad did?" said Dan, moving her head so she could see his eyes.

"I wasn't, actually, no. But a man like your dad, who accomplished some of the things he did—you can't do that and be a 'good person' in a binary sense. I believe Taz is a good man, I can see now that he did a great job raising you, but sometimes the end has to justify the means. It takes a great person to see the greater good."

"And what end does captivity, repeated rape, and torture serve?"

"It doesn't. Someone once told me that there's money, power, love, and revenge, and that all evil in mankind is linked to one of them. What's happening to that person, that's all revenge."

"And power," said Dan.

"Yeah, maybe some of that, too."

Marcus reached into his pocket, pulled out his wallet, and took out a card.

"Here, this is my personal number. Call me anytime."

Dan looked at it, not willing to take it, but he continued to hold it out.

"Why would I do that?" she asked.

"If the time ever comes that you need to call me, then you'll know why."

He smiled and placed the card on Dan's leg. Then he turned to get out of the car.

"Why were you near my house the other night?" asked Dan.

He stopped and turned to look at her.

"How did Jimmy know my sister was pregnant when it's the first time he's met me?"

"Jimmy makes it his business to know lots of things."

"Does he make it his business to send his minions to where I live?"

Marcus laughed, then looked serious.

"You know why he's interested in you. If it's not clear yet, think it through. You've got my number, but some things need to be figured out alone. Come on, let's get you inside."

"I can see myself in," she said.

"Sure, but I'll come with you anyway," he said, and walked round the car to open the door for her. "I gave you my word you'd be safe."

"And how long's your word valid for?"

He walked beside her down the hill toward her front door.

"I never break my word, ever," he said.

38

"This one."

Dan pointed to a large town house off to the left. It was set back from the road and accessed through an open black wrought-iron gate.

"How do you know?" said John, braking hard to make the turn and then waving at the driver behind, who sounded his horn and gestured at him.

"I just do," said Dan. "I'll explain, I promise."

The driveway was gravel, with weeds and clumps of grass starting to sprout here and there. There was room for half a dozen cars, but the space was currently empty.

The tires crunched on the small stones and Dan looked up at the tall town house with its painted window frames and flat flaking walls.

"At least tell me what you hope to find," he said, but stopped any reply with a long low "Wow . . ."

John turned to look at Dan.

"How the hell does she afford a place like this?" asked John. "I mean, even if the girl's renting."

"No car," said Dan.

"This is serious cash, Danny. We couldn't afford this place. Not even together."

Dan stopped opening the car door and looked back at John.

"I just meant, you know, it's expensive," he said, turning away from her and climbing out.

Dan walked straight to the front door, an oversized and ornate wooden affair with an arched top and a black metal knocker in the shape of an anchor.

John reached past her and rapped hard three times.

"She's not here," said Dan.

"She's not at the ship, either," said John. "And it's not even six in the morning, so where else could she be?"

"I'm going round the back to take a look," said Dan, jogging off to her left. "And I'm hoping to find her," she shouted over her shoulder as she went.

There was a gap between the house and the brick boundary wall that separated Cox's home from the neighbors. The wall was easily eight feet tall and the alleyway looked dank and mossy, the pathway green due to the cold, wet weather and lack of direct sunlight.

Blocking the way to the backyard was a six-foot metal gate that spanned the gap. It looked sturdy, designed to look nice but definitely to stop intruders, too. It was barred, but somebody had used plastic zip-ties to attach a piece of untreated plywood to it so that whatever was behind it couldn't be seen from the road. The wood looked fairly new but was already starting to break down and degrade.

Dan walked to the gate, immediately seeing the padlock that was hanging from a thick metal bolt. She stepped back and looked up, but at the top of the metal fence was a row of black spikes, not particularly sharp or imposing, but enough to make climbing over the gate a hazardous thing to do.

Dan reached out and rattled the gate. She stifled a curse, kicked at the bars, and turned to head back to the front of the house. She'd taken barely a pace when she heard a clang of metal.

The padlock had fallen to the ground, striking the bottom of the gate on its way.

"Ripping padlocks apart with your bare hands," said John as he rounded the corner. "Nicely done. I'm starting to think that the Legends of the Lewis are true."

Dan bent down.

"It just fell off," she said. "Well, I banged against the gate, but it just fell."

John moved in close.

"It's been cut," he said, stating the obvious. "Maybe put back in place as a visual deterrent? It'd still stop opportunists from even having a go."

"The cut looks quite fresh, doesn't it?" She reached down and picked the padlock up, running her finger over the shiny surface where the metal had been parted. She showed it to John. Then she pulled the gate open and walked quickly along the length of brick wall until she arrived at the backyard.

It was long and elegant. There were well-developed shrubs, some fruit trees and vines, and a number of old-looking stone ornaments littered around the place like remnants of the White Witch's wrath. All of it was well tended and tidy, the grass recently cut, the place neat and orderly.

There was a back door set into the center of the house and Dan peered through the windows as she made her way toward it. There was nothing inside to draw attention at all, except the sheer scale of the place for a young single person.

The solid back door was made of wood and painted red. It was pulled shut, but Dan could see that something wasn't right.

"It's been jimmied," said John.

He pushed the door. It resisted only slightly, and he was able to push with his fingers and watch as the door creaked open, revealing the lock, completely smashed, with shards of timber and mangled metal.

John was already fishing his phone out of his pocket to call it in.

Dan stepped inside the house.

It felt empty, silent, and cold.

"Sarah Cox?" she called, her voice echoing off the tiled walls and granite work surfaces.

She moved through the kitchen, past the appliances on the long dark countertops.

It was spacious, nothing felt cramped, particularly because the house felt so empty.

"Dan, wait," said John, covering the mouthpiece of the phone. "This is a break-in, pure and simple. Just wait and I'll call it in. She's not here."

"All you know is she's not answering," said Dan, moving farther into the house.

39

Dan moved from the kitchen into a long hallway, the walls covered with photos of Sarah and her family. One showed them at a riding stable, each holding the reins of a beautiful horse. Another showed them standing together next to a large Second World War gun emplacement, a black Labrador in the picture this time, his back to the camera as he watched the family.

At the bottom of the stairs was a large collage of the family, showing them in various harbors around the world, standing together, their skin tanned, and occasionally their hair blown back by the wind. In only one of them, Dan recognized Cox's grandfather, another admiral from this family of sailors, but apart from that single shot, apart from Sarah and her mum and her dad, there were no friends, no other family, no one.

Maybe that was the price you paid to be given a yacht and a house that most people could never afford, maybe the price for that was that you had to adorn your walls only with your benefactors, but to Dan the array told more than that.

As Dan looked at the pictures of the same faces over and over, Sarah seemed more alone in each passing frame.

To Dan's left was a long, wide room with high ceilings and, at one end, an ornate dining table with a candle centerpiece. The table wasn't set, but there were some papers strewn about on it.

"Hampshire police are on their way. We should wait outside," said John, arriving next to Dan.

She ignored him and looked up the stairs.

"Go on outside, then," said Dan, not even looking at him.

"Hardly going to let you go up there on your own," he said.

"And I'm hardly going to wait outside," said Dan. "She could be up there hurt. The back door's been forced; her car could've been stolen. We've got a duty of care."

She took the stairs and knew that John would follow.

The thick carpet, held in place on each step with a brass stair rod, softened the sound of Dan's footsteps.

The landing was empty. The light-colored carpet and walls combined with the absence of furniture made it look expansive and barren. The only color came from the multiple doors that led off the landing, heavy wood and dark varnished. All were shut.

Dan spotted John pointing to one in particular.

It was on the end of the landing and was the only one that had a visible lock. Dan could now see that the frame around it had been shattered, and there was a mark on the paint where the door had been forced.

Dan rounded the newel post and moved slowly toward it. The silence was giving her goose pimples and she knew that she should first clear the other rooms, but she needed to see what it was that needed to be locked away.

She heard John's breathing as she edged along the landing and pushed at the broken door.

It swung open easily.

The one window in the room was almost completely obscured by a dark semitransparent material that was layered onto the glass from the inside, blocking a lot of the light. There was a bed in the corner, metal-framed, hospital-like, with a table on wheels positioned beside it.

The smell was repellent, the bed damp with urine, and Dan stepped toward it, holding her breath, and reached down slowly, lifting up the damp red rope that hung at the corner.

John said her name quietly, and she looked.

There was a rope at each corner; he was holding up the longer ones from the foot of the bed, then he motioned down with his head and Dan stepped back. Beneath the bed was a navy-issue kitbag, the stains of blood and feces obvious to her as she saw it in this context.

"Jesus," she said, turning to John. "She carried her off."

John nudged the kitbag over and saw Black's name stenciled onto the bottom of it.

Dan shook her head, speechless.

John leaned forward and rested the back of his hand on the sheets. "Cold, but still quite wet. I don't think it's been very long."

"I need to get out of here," she said. "I'm going to look around."

She left the room and paused in the hallway to catch her breath. Then, when she thought that John might see her, she opened the next door along the hallway.

As this door swung open, all Dan could see was chaos. Clothes were strewn over furniture and cupboard doors lay open. A small chest of drawers next to the head of the bed was empty, all of the drawers removed and tossed to the side, the contents strewn across the unmade bed next to it.

Paperwork and personal items, some headache tablets and nail clippers, lots of pens and a penknife next to some jewelry and a pair of brand-new lieutenant commander rank badges, one above Cox's actual rank; maybe she, or someone else, had been hopeful of advancement.

Dan looked at the papers. Bank statements, pay chits, and paperwork for Sarah Cox's car. She noted down the registration number and details and then carried on sifting through.

"The door being kicked in and the broken padlock gives us ample reason to have come in. To see if anyone was hurt."

Dan looked up at John, saw him standing in the doorway.

"What?" she said.

"I mean, we shouldn't really have come up here."

Dan scrunched up her face and mouthed "Who cares?" to him, lowering her head back down and poking the papers around with the nib of her pen. She turned to the drawers and tipped one over to look inside. Beneath it she saw a few buff-colored folders. They looked like navy issue, straight out of the stationery cupboard at work, and Dan used her pen to open the top one.

She saw a handwritten letter and leaned down to read it.

Please leave me alone you fucking psycho.

Dan frowned and called John over to look.

"Sucks Cox," he said. "Not the world's greatest nickname."

Dan shook her head and used the pen to see the sheet beneath it. There was another letter, same handwriting.

Stop bothering me. I won't do what you want, not now, not ever!

Dan looked to the next folder. It was stiff card stock, impossible to open with just a pen, and Dan used her fingers to touch the edge and see inside.

Sarah,
Thank you for all your help.
Tash xxx

The handwriting was different from that of the previous letters, obviously not written by the same person.

"Those letters look like they're from a guy," said John.

Dan agreed.

She pulled the folder wide open by its edges and laid it on the bed.

Beneath the letter was a sheaf of pictures. Dan stared at them for a moment and then used her pen to jostle them out of the folder and onto the bedsheets.

There were pictures of Natasha Moore on *Defiance*, good-quality focused shots. Next to them there were others like the ones they'd found in Black's locker and bunk space, grainy, taken from social media or cut as stills from video, cropped to make Natasha Moore the focus.

Dan flicked quickly through them. She stopped when she reached a shot of Natasha in the stores office on board *Defiance*, the quality of the image making it clear it was a still from video. Then she saw the next one, a grainy, dark, poor-quality picture, taken from a distance, as Natasha Moore, recognizable by her long blond hair, straddled someone on what looked like a bench.

Dan dropped the pictures, then something else caught her eye: a sketch, like Natasha Moore, but not her. She held it up to John.

"Jesus," he said. "The overboard from *Defiance*."

"Small, blond, pretty," said Dan. "Same tastes as Knight."

She put the sketch down.

"I don't get it," said Dan. "I just don't. The break-in looks professional, padlock cut and replaced, door jimmied open with what's probably a crowbar. Whoever did that came prepared to do it. The inside's worse than the outside, like someone was trying to hide what they were doing. But the inside hasn't been burgled. The room's a mess, but the jewelry's all there." She pointed to an open jewelry box on a table by the window. "The televisions are all here, and look, there's an iPad next to the bed. It's not a burglary."

"What does it say to you?" he asked.

"Honestly?" said Dan, standing up. "If I ignore the broken padlock and the broken doors, this room says to me that she's running. Look at the way it's been done, fast, reckless. She's panicking and taking whatever she thinks she'll need to get away."

John walked to the window and looked out, then down at the jewelry and the iPad again.

"What about the break-in, though?" he asked. "Could she have done it, maybe to try and say . . ." His words trailed off as his idea died. "Where's she going to run to? We'll find her car, she's a smart woman, she'll know that. The Hampshire lot will find her and it won't take them long."

Dan paced toward the door and stopped.

"But why run?" said Dan. "She was fine yesterday. What set her off, what made her go?"

John shrugged.

"If we assume she's running, then we have to assume she knows she's done for," said John. "I don't know how, but she knew we were coming for her. She knows that driving anywhere isn't going to help her." He looked out the window and then moved across to the main dresser opposite the bed.

"I think we have to assume that Mummy and Daddy have some pretty serious lawyers, so she might've gone home, that would be a good place to look, but ultimately it won't help her as we'll get there shortly, she'd know that," said Dan.

"And turning up at even the most doting parent's house with an injured hostage isn't a foolproof plan," said John. "But she may well not be rational at the moment, so she might look for help there. It looks to me like they pretty much ran her life for her."

He was looking down at the floor now, his face twitching and his lips moving a little as he worked through the possibilities himself.

"But if she's really running, then she needs to go far . . ."

Dan looked up at the same moment John did.

"Her yacht," said John. "She's going for the yacht."

Dan was already running toward the door.

"If she hasn't gone already."

"Do you know where she berths it?" asked John.

"The marina at Port Solent," said Dan over her shoulder. "Get Josie on it now. Tell her to call as soon as she knows for sure. I bet someone on *Defiance* will confirm it."

"We'll need to call the locals and tell them what we think," said John, fishing in his pocket for his phone. "You can't just run off on your own."

"I'm not going alone," said Dan "You're coming with me."

"Danny."

The tone of John's voice made her stop and turn.

He was by the dresser, and he pointed to a small red mark on the wall above it.

"You need to come and see this," he said, his face dropping a shade whiter.

Dan walked over and looked at the mark.

"Blood," she said.

"Down there," said John, pointing behind the dresser.

Dan looked down and took a few moments to realize what she was looking at. On the floor beneath the mark on the wall was a small pink finger with two engagement rings on it, one above the other.

40

Breathe, that's what she needed to think about now. It was all going to be okay.

Black was stupid, no question about that, but he also had an awful lot to lose, and he'd shown his hand way too early. If he could've just kept his dumb mouth shut and ridden this out, they'd have been fine, though she'd rather he'd managed to kill himself, that would've been neater.

There was another problem, though, not insurmountable, but that had to be dealt with.

Cox leaned back in her car, fished out her pay-as-you-go phone from beneath the driver's seat, and dialed the number.

"Please don't call me again."

Cox smiled at the greeting.

"Don't hang up," she said, her voice very calm. "I haven't told anyone that you're not on rugby tour. I haven't asked anyone to check the signal. I'm pretty certain I'm the only one who knows what you're doing. Goodness knows, if Sam found out you were shacked up with your ex-wife again, she'd shop you in a heartbeat. I think you broke her heart, you know."

He was silent for a while, but he hadn't hung up.

"Look, I'm not with Sam, and I'm not 'shacked up' with anyone. I'm spending time with my little girl, because she's staying at my mum's for a week, and you know full well why I have to do it."

"It is a little bit sad, Mark, you have to admit it. Running out of leave and having to lie your way to spending time with your daughter without her mummy's knowledge. I mean, it's gloriously heartbreaking that a father would take the risk just to see his daughter, but still, just go to court, for God's sake, and get it sorted legally."

This time he was silent for longer, and Sarah knew he wouldn't speak unless she did.

"I'd help you. My uncle—"

"I'm not doing what you want me to do to pay for your help. You're a fucking freak, you hold your uncle over me like I'll go to prison if I tell anyone, but you know full well that you'd be in the shit, too, just for asking."

Sarah held the phone away from her ear and looked at it.

Coker was such a granny.

She'd really thought he'd had potential, seemed like a bit of a play-boy when she first heard about him, and women definitely liked him, but all she'd suggested, after months of contact involving long and tedious talks about sports training and conditioning, was that he videotape him-self screwing the loud, slutty one from the junior rates' mess.

It'd have been a start, something to get a small, initial hook into him with, something to build on and develop.

She'd seen him on the rugby field, seen him working out in the gym; small, but powerful, driven, and aggressive; he could fuck women for her with the right motivation, just like he could come to see her now with the right motivation.

"What do you want?" Mark said after a long pause.

"I want to talk, not for long."

"What about?"

"Tash contacted me. She's frightened, she's been up home for some reason and it didn't go well. She wants to come back, but she's worried about going to the commanding officer's table. She's coming here. I said I'd call you and get you to come here and talk to her before she goes."

"Okay," said Mark, without hesitation.

"But, Mark, you must tell no one, okay? We'll wait for you."

"Put her on the phone," he said, pausing, then adding, "please."

"I can't, but she'll be here any minute and then you can speak to her face-to-face."

"Okay, I'm on my way," he said. "I'll only be a few minutes."

"Thank you. Tash really needs you," she said, "and park up the side, out of sight, in case anyone from the ship sees your bike; I'll keep your secret for you."

Sarah ended the call and grabbed her bag. She stepped out of the car onto the gravel drive and headed for the side of the house. She had to, because the bloody, stupid front door stuck so badly it was impossible to open these days. She'd asked her dad to have it changed, or at least fixed, but he wouldn't even hear of it, told her to "improvise, adapt, and overcome," to "spend more time on isometrics and swinging clubs to build up that strength." Instead, she'd just started using the side gate and back door. She'd asked for a light to go up there, too, but the response to that had been something about keeping bridge watches in the darkest of nights, in the middle of the ocean, under thick clouds where the light simply didn't reach, or some such bollocks.

She walked along the side and reached for her keys, the padlock falling away in her hand as soon as she grasped it.

Sarah's heart missed a beat.

Her hands began to shake and she thought about running, right now, but it could be nothing, an attempted break-in. No one knew, and even if Black had recovered enough to open his mouth, there'd be police everywhere.

The gate pushed open quietly and Cox stepped through. She was wary, listening, walking slowly, trying not to make a sound as she approached the back of the house and scanned the garden.

Nothing.

She moved to the back door, instantly knew it'd been opened by force.

No way would the police do this. No way would they break in, put a padlock back again, force a door, and try to reset it so it looked normal.

She lowered her bag to the floor and looked in through the kitchen window.

The room was empty.

She pushed the door open and stepped inside, placing her foot down slowly, walking to the countertop area and pulling a large knife out of the block. Then she headed up the stairs.

Her mind was changing now. Was it possible that someone hadn't broken in, but had instead broken out?

If so, she'd need to move fast, to run, but first she needed to know for sure.

She reached the landing and saw the door to Natasha's room, the broken frame from where it had been kicked open from the outside. She ran toward the door, pushing it open and looking to the bed, the empty bed.

"Shit, fuck!" She spat the words out as a wave of rage washed over her, as she tried to process what was going on.

Natasha was gone. Escaped. But if it was escape, how did she get out, free herself? How could she have cut the padlock, forced the back door? Her bedroom door had been kicked in from the outside. No, not escaped—been freed.

"Fucking Black!" she shrieked, clenching her hands and biting so hard that she drew blood from her lower lip.

"No, no, no."

It couldn't be Black. He might have figured she was here, but he was in custody, no way he was getting out of there. Then who?

She turned in circles for a moment, looked up at the ceiling and then down at the floor.

"Who?" she said, the word seething out from her.

She walked into her bedroom, next to Natasha's, and stopped.

Her bedding was white, with small flowers around the trim, and in the center of it, laid in a small pool of dark, crusty red, was a human finger.

Sarah stopped now, her heart pumping.

No one, but no one, escapes and then cuts off their finger to leave as a calling card. She grabbed it, recognized the two engagement rings, each cheap and worthless, then hurled the finger against the wall.

She heard it drop behind the dresser, and then she heard a voice in the downstairs hallway.

She spun, walked toward the door, the thick carpets masking any sound, and waited.

"Tash? Sarah?"

"Up here," she called, listening to his muffled footsteps as he bounded up the stairs.

She watched him through the crack in the door as he stepped onto the landing and saw the broken door to his current love's bedroom.

"What the fuck?" he said, looking around.

"Tash! Sarah!" he shouted now, his voice louder, more urgent.

She saw the panic in his face; he really was one of the good guys, she'd misjudged him.

He acted loud, but he was all talk and no trousers, acted like a player but was just a little boy, idealistic and naive, in love, a waste of a great body; corrupting him slowly would have been a lot of fun, and those muscles of his could've done some serious damage to a handpicked partner.

Here and now, though, she smiled at the panic in his voice.

She stepped out from behind the door and smiled, the knife behind her back.

"I'm okay," she said, a sniff and a sob breaking through as she let her shoulders fall and stepped toward him. "Tash isn't here yet, but I've been burgled."

He hesitated when he should have just embraced her, that's what a good guy would've done, but the discomfort was evident in his eyes.

She hunched down and tried to shrink into him, as though she were not bigger, broader, as though she was a little woman, frail and in need of protection.

He did eventually reach out, wrapping his arms hesitantly around her oversized frame; he obviously didn't feel comfortable with girls as big as her, while he'd been completely natural with Natasha's petite frame.

She leaned her head on his shoulder and slipped her arm around him. Then she drove the knife up, under his ribs, and into his lung.

He shuddered and gasped, and Sarah pulled back so she could see his face as his mouth dropped open.

Her stomach tingled the way it had the first time William had touched her, the first time he'd gently pushed her away, not interested in more after what she'd watched him do.

It was so much nicer when you could really see what was happening, see the pain and pleasure mix in his eyes.

"Don't bleed on my carpet," she whispered as she laid him down on his stomach and ran to get towels.

She stemmed the flow and then dragged him into the bathroom, where the tiles would be easier to clean. Then she stood up and looked around.

What was she doing?

Someone had come for Natasha.

Someone had taken Natasha.

Someone knew.

There were no police here; Black was locked up; Coker was whimpering out his last breaths at her feet; and Natasha was gone.

She looked down at Mark Coker and then leaned over the toilet and vomited.

The plan was shot. Making him vanish and become the main suspect in Natasha's disappearance was no longer viable.

Someone knew, they'd been here, and that meant that more would soon know.

She wiped her mouth and looked at Coker again as though seeing him for the first time.

He was dead, she'd killed him, in her own house.

"Stupid bitch!" she cursed.

She vomited again, then took a deep breath.

It wasn't the fact that she'd killed him—that'd been the plan all along—but here and now, after what had happened? This was bad, a big mistake. She needed to get rid of this body, and she needed to run.

41

John almost mounted the curb as he pulled the car up outside the marina entrance.

Dan was already out the car and running into the office. She pulled out her military SIB credentials and flashed them at the receptionist.

The card meant nothing outside a military establishment, but Dan hoped that the woman behind the desk wouldn't know that.

"Military police," said Dan, making sure her voice was confident, unquestionable. "I need to know if there's a yacht here registered to a Sarah Cox, or a member of her family, and where that yacht is now."

The woman looked stunned, leaned back in her chair, and paused for a second.

Dan was preparing to tell her that the civil police were on their way, but the woman recovered and leaned forward, typing on her keyboard.

"I think Sarah came in to drop some stuff off a little while ago," said the woman.

Dan turned to John, who was waiting behind her. "Go," she said.

He moved past her and jumped the turnstile that led into the marina area, jogging out of view.

"She's on berth seventy-nine," said the woman.

Dan followed John, stepping out of the reception into the marina. Her view was good, and the level of the jetties was such that few vessels were big enough to obscure her line of sight as she scanned the wharves and walkways.

John had run to the far end of one leg of decked jetty and was look-ing around.

"Seventy-nine," called Dan. "John, it's number seventy-nine."

She saw him react, looking around for numbers on the planking and starting to make his way back toward her.

Dan looked also; there were numbers on small signs attached to the railings. She headed right, toward the berths numbered fifty and above, jogging along the wooden deck, alternating between searching for num-bers and scanning ahead for any motion.

There were slots opening up in front of her, gaps where yachts and sailboats should be but weren't, and Dan wasn't able to tell whether Cox's yacht was still there or not.

She jogged quickly, counting up the numbers, seeing berth seventy-nine and exhaling as she saw a vessel berthed there, recognizing it from the pictures she'd seen in Cox's office and home.

Dan stopped and looked around, then listened. There was no noise at all, no sign of anyone moving around.

"Sarah Cox! Military Police! Come out now!" shouted Dan as she moved closer to the yacht.

John was behind her now and she turned to look at him, weighing what to do. He nodded toward the yacht, asking whether she wanted him to go on board.

"Go," said Dan, her voice quiet.

John moved close and jumped across from the berth to the yacht. His weight as he landed made the vessel roll and Dan listened again, won-dering if that might have disturbed someone within.

She watched him track along one side, heading aft, and then saw him look down into the living areas below.

He looked up at her, seemed confused, and then stepped down and out of sight.

Dan never saw Cox step out from behind the superstructure of an empty yacht. She only caught a movement from the corner of her eye a second before she was struck hard across the back with something long and hard. The blow drove Dan to her knees and then forward onto all fours, knocking the air out of her, and she knew instantly, instinctively, that she couldn't stay still. She allowed the momentum of her fall to carry her down onto her belly, where she quickly rolled to one side.

A loud thwack cracked only an inch from her ear as the long wooden boat hook smashed onto the decking where her head had been only a second before.

Dan looked up.

John Granger was there, back out of the yacht and approaching Cox, who turned, swinging the wooden pole hard at John. He tried to step aside and dodge it, raising his arm in a reflexive defense and taking the blow to his elbow with a loud, sickening crack. He yelled in pain, clutching his arm, and staggered back along the walkway.

Dan saw Sarah Cox cock the pole back, ready to swing at John again. She moved quickly, scrambling to her knees and grabbing Cox around the shins, pulling as hard as she could with both her arms to pull Cox's legs together and then driving her shoulder into the back of Cox's knees, trying to bring the woman down. Dan's bastardized rugby tackle worked—Roger would've been proud—and Cox toppled forward, dropping the pole and falling in front of Dan.

Dan released Cox's legs and tried to crawl up the woman's body, trying to get close to an arm she could lock, or to her torso, so she could hold on and secure Cox until help came, but Cox was stronger, and much bigger, and she was desperate.

Cox lashed out, freeing her legs for an instant and driving her knee up underneath Dan's chin as she fought to get away.

Dan tasted blood in her mouth. Her vision blurred as tears reflexively welled in her eyes and her head swam. She dropped her head down close to Cox, grabbing at her legs again and tightening her grip around them, just below the thighs. She was glad she did, as she almost instantly felt an elbow land hard against the top of her head.

"Get off!" screamed Cox.

Dan looked up to see John reaching down to grab Cox's hair. He was using his left arm to force her head facefirst against the decking, his right arm cradled against him.

Dan took advantage of the distraction and crawled quickly up toward Cox's head, reaching out and grabbing one of her arms.

But Cox wasn't done. She arched up violently, twisting her whole body around to face John and throwing Dan's arms loose. Cox grabbed John's hand as he gripped her hair and twisted his wrist, then, as he dropped down to react, she released her grip and grabbed his right arm with both hands, the arm she'd broken with the wooden pole.

Dan knew it was broken, could see it even now, but she could do nothing to stop Cox from grabbing the injured arm and wrenching it toward her, just as Dan had done to David Simmons only a week or so before.

Cox swung off John's arm, twisting and bending it as if she was wringing out a cloth.

The sound of bone and sinew tearing made Dan flinch, but it was soon lost to the animal-like howl that came from John as his legs gave way beneath him.

He swung a punch at Cox with his left hand, connected well, but it was only a mechanism to make her release her grip, and as she did, he collapsed backward onto the wooden walkway.

She knew she couldn't overpower this woman in a wrestling match, and she knew that to win, she'd need to be willing to escalate the violence quickly. She saw Cox shake off John's punch and turn toward her. Dan threw a solid punch of her own, aiming for the center of Cox's face, trying to catch her nose, knowing a good strike there would fill Cox's eyes with tears, send blood flooding back into her throat, and dizzy her senses.

The punch connected, but not well, glancing off Cox's forehead as she flinched away.

Dan followed her punch in, using Cox's own momentum as she flinched to push her back as Dan now drove her elbow toward the side of Cox's head.

The elbow landed more cleanly, and Cox rolled onto her back.

Dan pressed her advantage, straddling Cox and throwing two more hard punches to her face.

Cox's arms were up as she tried to defend herself, and Dan grabbed one of them, gripping the forearm and leaning in, trying to bend it so that she could twist it to apply a lock. She leaned forward harder, feeling the arm start to give beneath her.

Then, before she knew what had happened, Cox had twisted onto her side, driven her hips away from Dan, and used the space she'd created to raise her knees and push Dan away with both legs.

Dan rolled across the decking, sensing that she'd lose this battle if she didn't get some space, but she was fighting a madwoman.

Cox was on her feet in an instant, twice stamping her foot hard onto the walkway, missing Dan's arm and then her head by only a fraction of an inch.

Dan was still rolling as Cox lunged toward her, swinging a kick that caught Dan in the ribs and doubled her onto her back.

It was sheer luck that Dan's head lolled back in pain as Cox's foot swung again, brushing past Dan's hair and narrowly missing her temple; this woman meant to kill Dan if she could.

Dan was aware of John now.

He was slumped back against one of the posts that supported a rope handrail. He was reaching out, though, with his left arm, grabbing at Cox, gripping the material of her trousers near the thigh and trying to pull her away from Dan.

Cox screamed, a mix of rage and frustration, and turned away from Dan. She clenched her fist like a hammer and swung it down hard, twice, onto John's forearm, forcing him to release her.

He did, slumping onto his side as she pulled away from him.

Cox watched John fall and Dan saw her tee up John's head like a footballer about to take a penalty kick, drawing back her foot.

Dan rolled onto her feet and dived forward, driving both of her hands into Cox's lower back and forcing the woman to lose her balance and stumble forward onto her knees. Dan was lying on the decking now, John next to her, and as she saw Cox look back over her shoulder, Dan knew this was a fight she might not win.

Cox reached out for the long boat hook again, standing up with it and turning toward them.

Dan scrambled to her knees, grabbed John's torso, and, mustering all her strength, rolled both of their bodies off the walkway and into the water.

The cold hit her hard, but she knew what she had to do. She held on to John, turning him onto his back and dragging him away from where

Cox was now standing up, the weapon held tight in her hand as she stared at them in the water, out of her reach.

Dan watched as Cox weighed her options.

She must've known that time was limited, that she couldn't escape by yacht, nor could she deal with Dan and John as she'd have liked. So she stood motionless on the walkway, her eyes boring into Dan's as she continued to pull John and herself farther away.

Dan wondered what Cox would do now that this route of escape was blocked.

"You okay, John?" Dan whispered.

His breathing was heavy and he didn't answer.

"She's got to run now," said Dan. "She knows she can't escape on the yacht, not now."

"Okay," John said, his voice faint.

Dan was still kicking her legs but was now holding them in the same place in the water between two yachts.

Cox smiled at Dan and walked back to her yacht.

New sounds were making their way into Dan's consciousness now. Other marina users had seen Dan in the water and were raising the alarm.

Dan watched as Cox disappeared onto her yacht for a few moments and then reemerged.

People were pointing at Dan and John; someone was running down the deck of the nearest vessel to get to them. They spoke to Cox, who pointed at them before walking away calmly, as though nothing had happened.

Dan tried to tell people to stop her, tried to tell the men who were pulling John out of the water that they needed to call security, when she saw the first puffs of smoke rising into the sky.

An older man grabbed her arm, another next to him reaching for her other arm.

Their hands were tanned, the skin rough, but Dan could only watch over her shoulder as she realized what Cox had done.

She pointed to the yacht, made the men look, and then she dragged John behind the cabin of the small leisure cruiser they'd been pulled aboard as a fireball ignited on Cox's yacht. Dan heard the loud *whoomp* of petrol catching fire as the pressure rocked every ship in the marina.

The heat distorted the air above the yacht as the flames engulfed it, and people ran with extinguishers to try to fight the blaze.

Dan knew that the dark billowing smoke meant that a lot of petrol had been used in there, that there was no way they'd save the boat, nor whoever may have been on board it.

42

"I'm okay," John said. "I just wish I'd blocked the boat hook with my left arm, there's certain activities I really need my right arm for, you know, where the left just won't do."

"You're gross," said Dan, shaking her head.

"What? I meant golf and writing. Don't blame me because your mind's in the gutter."

They both laughed, and Dan looked down at John's arm.

It was in a temporary cast to immobilize it after surgery, too swollen to be put in a permanent cast yet.

"How long will you be malingering in here, then?" she asked. "We've got work to do, you know, proper work, and I need you back."

"You *need* me back?" he said, frowning. "I call bullshit on that."

"Well"—Dan paused and looked at him—"I'd really *like* you back."

"Well, they're operating again tomorrow, reattaching some muscles or some such thing, then I'll be in a few more days until the swelling calms down and they put some kind of protection on it," he said. "Then, eventually, they'll let me go home, but I have to come back every day for checks. I can kinda feel my fingers again, so that's good news, so they tell me, and the bone's back in a good place now, like, where it actually should be, so all may yet be right with the world."

"I'm sorry," said Dan.

She slumped down into an uncomfortable blue plastic chair next to his bed.

"No, you're not," he said. "And I wouldn't expect you to be. If things had turned out different, we'd be heroes."

"But they didn't turn out different, did they?"

He shrugged.

"Ifs and buts. I've never met a patient Danielle Lewis, the sort of girl who waits around and does things right. To be honest, if I did meet her, I'm not certain I'd like her much. She sounds dull, predictable, not the sort of person I'd enjoy hanging out with at all."

Dan nodded. "She sounds dull as you like."

"And," said John, nodding toward Dan. "I assume that the panda jokes will all be stopping now, seeing how your chin makes you look like a chimpanzee."

Dan touched her jawline gingerly.

"She got me good. Between us, we'd be like the Elephant Man," she said. "It's like we're heading out to a fancy dress night themed as the guy from *Goonies*."

They laughed.

There was a sound behind them and they both turned to see Roger Blackett come in.

"How you doing, John?" Roger asked, looking down at John's arm but not yet acknowledging Dan. "You know we can bring charges against malingerers in the navy, right?"

"I already did the malingering gag," said Dan.

Roger grudgingly turned toward her and smiled, but she could see he wasn't happy.

"Anything more from the yacht?" asked John.

"Well, she was leaving. It was stored for a long journey. Torching it seems last-minute according to the way the fire spread. Seems she had a jerry can of fuel there and just kicked it over and lit a candle. The fire caused a lot of damage."

He paused, then turned around and shut the door to John's room.

"I'm led to believe that a body's been found on board. It's badly damaged, though they're sure it's a male."

Dan looked down at her hands.

There was silence among them for a long while.

"People'll say she was burying victims at sea," said Dan. "That's still what some people say about Hamilton."

"Well, people, whoever they are, will just need to accept that it's all speculation at the moment," said Roger.

"Anything else?" John asked.

"There was a tattoo on the yacht victim's body," said Roger. "It looks very much like one Mark Coker had; I think we know it's him."

Dan shook her head, at a loss for words.

"Any trace of Cox?" asked John.

Roger shook his head. "She left her mark on you two, but nothing else. We'll get her, though. She can't hide forever, and she's a remarkable woman, she'll be noticed."

"And Black?"

"Awake and saying very little for now. He's a big dumb animal, but smart enough to lawyer up. The Hampshire police are talking to him today, but their, and my, gut feel is that he doesn't know where Cox is. He's saying she was blackmailing him, wanted him to do things he didn't want to. I'll let you know if I hear more."

John nodded and tried to sit up in his bed a bit more.

Dan and Roger both rose to help, looked at each other, and then Roger sat back down as Dan continued to assist John, moving his pillows and helping him settle.

"I could get used to this treatment," said John, smiling at Dan as she adjusted his pillow.

"I wouldn't," she said, sitting back down.

"Dan, might we chat outside for a moment?" asked Roger.

He looked at John, who raised an eyebrow.

"You need your rest, John," said Roger as he stood and opened the door, gesturing for Dan to pass through. "I'll send her back shortly."

They stepped outside and Dan saw instantly that Roger wasn't just annoyed, or even angry, he was furious.

He turned toward her, the rage seething out of him, the words whispered, but through gritted teeth. His eyes were dark and wild, and Dan, though she'd known him more years than she could remember, stepped back in surprise.

"Jimmy. Fucking. *Nash!*" he seethed at her, leaning in close, invading her personal space.

"What about him?" asked Dan, recovering herself and leaning toward Roger, closing the small gap to show she wasn't intimidated by him.

"You went to see him?"

"Yes."

"And never thought to mention it?"

"I was going to. It happened quickly."

"And pray tell, Danny, which investigation was it in relation to?"

Dan paused, thinking.

"I was following up on what Hamilton said to me when I met him. Following up on William Knight."

They both straightened up and smiled as a nurse walked past and entered John's room, then leaned back in again.

"An investigation you're not on," said Roger.

"It was just a follow-up, a favor, John knows him. We didn't go in under official credentials."

"Do you know who he is?"

"Yes."

Roger took a step back.

Dan could see that his anger was dissipating, as it often did with Roger. His temper spiked and manifested in short but visual explosions, then quickly returned to normal, and that was happening now.

"And what did he tell you?" asked Roger, his voice calmer.

Dan considered the answers she could give.

"It ruins your lies when you have to work them out, Danny," said Roger, his anger rising again like a small aftershock.

"I'm not going to lie to you, Roger. But it's complicated."

"I bet it is," he said.

"He did help, though," she said, pursing her lips. "He helped me in a few ways, but you know what, I might know where Cox could go now."

"And where might that be?"

"There's a gun emplacement up on Portsdown Hill. It's called Defiance, I think she used to go there and observe while William Knight used to . . ."

They looked at each other for a long time, neither needing the sentence to be finished.

"Useful information to have," he said. "Makes me wonder how you could possibly have found such knowledge and when you were planning on sharing it."

"I'm sharing it now," she said. "I've been a bit busy."

"After this, you and I are going to have a very long talk," he said, and turned away from her.

Dan waited, watching him go.

"Come on, then," he said, and Dan followed quickly behind him.

43

Dan was standing in the manager's office at the Royal Armouries on Portsdown Hill. She was off to the side, leaning against the wall and huddled into her coat.

Josie was sitting on a small couch near her.

They were both watching the center's manager, who was perched on the edge of her desk, talking with Roger and shaking her head.

"I'm not against you guys having a look around at all, but I really have no idea where the name Defiance comes into it. There are gun emplacements all around the fort, twenty-four in all, but they're just numbered. I'm not the expert on that side of things, but it's not a name I think I've heard before."

Roger looked across at Dan.

"Of course, you're welcome to look round the whole place if you want to," the manager continued. "Barry's on his way. He'll be more than happy to show you wherever you want to go."

Barry was a guide Roger knew and had called as soon as they'd left John at the hospital. He'd agreed to come straight in and meet them at the armories.

As if on cue, an older man—Dan placed him in his mid- to late sixties—approached the office, passing the fire point markings painted onto the wall in bright red, all original from when the fort had served as an ammunition dump in the last war.

He knocked on the door, entered without stopping, and walked straight over to Roger, reaching out to shake his hand and acknowledging the manager and then Dan in turn.

"So, you all want a tour of the fort, I hear?" Barry said, smiling and rocking forward onto his toes.

Roger nodded.

"We do, but Barry, there may, or may well not, be more to it than that. We're led to believe there's a gun emplacement in there called Defiance, and that's where we really want to look."

"Defiance..." he said, as though thinking it out loud. "The emplacements are numbered, not named."

Roger and Dan exchanged looks.

"But, you know what, I do know Defiance. I doubt it's your place, though."

Dan was standing up now.

"How come?" asked Roger.

"Well," began Barry, smiling and touching his temple as he thought, "let me see. These were first built in the 1860s to protect Portsmouth Dockyard from bombardment and attack. Not a lot of people realize it, but the forts are designed to defend against an attack from inland, away from the coast, to stop an enemy that's swept round from another harbor and is coming toward the back of Portsmouth to bombard and control it."

Roger must have spotted Dan's impatience at the way this story was shaping up, and he looked at her, smiled, and asked Barry to continue.

Dan put her hands into her pockets to stop her from drumming them against something as she waited.

"So the emplacements were built, and they were just numbered, and that was fine. There are three underground tunnels that run from the main barracks area, where we are now, out to the far emplacements. They were dug by hand, with shovel and pick, to break through the chalk and seams of hard flint."

"And Defiance?" said Dan.

Barry looked at her and smiled the same smile her granddad used when she was a child and was being impatient, which was almost always.

"We'll get there," he said. "So, in the First World War the fort was used to garrison men, and one such man, an unusual appointment for the time, was a naval captain. At the time the captain was here in post—I forget his name, and this whole thing isn't well documented—a sergeant who was working here under his command was caught in a homosexual act with another soldier."

He looked at Dan and Josie for effect.

"Regardless of how things are now, back then, that was a big problem," he said, raising his eyebrows as though telling a story to children. "They didn't want him held in the guardhouse with the other prisoners, and so they took him down the east tunnel to the gun emplacement at the end and tied him up in there. The rumors were that the naval captain hated the man and ordered each night that some of the soldiers should go down there and whip him, to cure him, you see. The captain would go to watch, taking pleasure in it, by all accounts. They'd try to force the sergeant to confess to what he'd done and promise that he was cured. I think maybe the captain was enjoying it a little too much, maybe he was trying to see something beaten from his own mind. Anyway, the sergeant refused to confess and eventually managed to free himself enough that he hanged himself, or so they say. It was ruled a suicide. When they found him, he'd cut his arm and written in blood on the walls the word "defiance," which was also the name of the captain's last ship. Many thought that the word was more a statement than anything else. After that, and for years and years on, that emplacement was known locally as the Defiance Emplacement, or the Defiance Room, and the ghost of the sergeant is said to haunt it still."

"So can we go there now?" said Dan.

"Danny," said Roger.

"It might be time-sensitive," said Dan.

"Well, the short answer is no, young lady," said Barry. "After the wars, this whole fort fell into disrepair. Kids came up here and played in the forts. The east tunnel became unsafe and now it's the home to three thousand bats, which live in there and are protected under conservation law. So you can't access the tunnel from this end, it's locked, though you could access it from the other, the one where the bats go in and out, though you'd need climbing gear, so that's not likely. The emplacement itself used to be open and kids would go in there to drink and try to contact the ghost of the sergeant. There's all manner of stories about Ouija boards and kids scaring themselves silly, but that emplacement was sealed up three, maybe four years ago. They blocked off all the exits from the top, so you can only get there through the tunnel now and no one goes in there, no one could get into the Defiance Emplacement. The tunnel's locked tight. Even I've only been in there once, when we lost a tourist and had to check everywhere, and I was ankle-deep in bat poop before I'd made it thirty yards."

"So we can go and look," said Dan, working out the timings in her mind.

It was likely that Knight was telling the truth, that he'd accessed the Defiance Emplacement directly, while it was still possible to do so, but now, even sealed up, it still had to be worth a look. Dan had to be sure.

"No one can go in there, I'm afraid," said the manager. "Honestly, it's sealed up, big padlocks, and the conservationists will have a meltdown if we go in there and disturb the bats. Is it very important?"

Dan tried to think of how to phrase what she wanted to say, how to negotiate steadily and keep the others onside as she tried to achieve her goal.

"I suspect that several women were raped in that emplacement and I need to know for sure that no one else has been hiding out in there. So I think that this is more important than a missing visitor, which was sufficient reason for you to enter the last time."

She looked around.

The manager seemed as if she might be sick, and Barry's jaw hung slack.

Roger was half smiling, and it irritated Dan that he'd likely anticipated what she'd do.

"We've got flashlights," said Dan. "So let's get ready and get in there as soon as possible. That way the bats can still get a few hours of shut-eye before nightfall if we wake a few of them up."

44

Thursday, February 5

They walked from the office along a different corridor now as they headed down toward the courtyard. The walls were lined with pictures, both old and recent, of the forts. Sepia-toned, black-and-white, and full-color images mapped the fort from its beginnings until it became the tourist attraction it was now.

Dan could feel Roger behind her, knew that he was also looking at the pictures.

She stopped abruptly and Roger walked into her.

"Careful, Danny," he said, a mixture of worried and peeved.

"Look," said Dan, pointing to an image of a gathering of dignitaries at the formal opening of the new visitor center.

Roger looked and shook his head.

Dan pointed.

Barry turned back and also looked.

"Ah, yes, you may recognize him, that's the former First Sea Lord, Admiral Cox. He, and his son, the younger Vice Admiral Cox, have been patrons here for many years."

Dan looked at Roger and then at Barry.

"Do you know the daughter? Sarah Cox?"

He smiled broadly.

"Oh, yes, lovely girl, she comes reasonably regularly to see us. Sketches the bats and the guns. I think we have some of her work for sale in the shop."

"And when she's here, she'd have access to the back offices?"

Barry paused now, looking suspicious and weighing his answer.

"Yes, I suppose she would, though I've no idea why she'd want to come back here, except for a brew with one of the staff, and I've no idea at all why you'd ask. She's a kind and generous girl, always polite and friendly."

"But she could possibly have access to the keys that you grabbed from the keyboard on your way out?" asked Dan.

He paused again, looking at Roger as though he might get permission not to answer.

"Yes," he said finally, turning away and walking on past more pictures.

Dan and Roger exchanged looks and followed.

They crossed the courtyard behind what had been the barracks and was now the offices and main exhibitions. A long alleyway ran across the fort, and off it were the barred entrances to the three tunnels, each entry point around thirty meters from the next.

The central tunnel was open to the public, well lit and well traveled, and even now Dan could see and hear a group of excited schoolchildren being herded into it, shouting and laughing as their voices bounced back at them off the rough chalk walls.

The west tunnel was locked, shut off to the public, but was otherwise clear and accessible with electric lights.

Dan had decided, though she hadn't yet stated it, that they'd check that one out next.

The east tunnel entrance was where they gathered now, herself, Roger, Josie, and Barry, who either seemed to think this was a tour or had gone into tour mode as a way of coping with what was happening.

Josie had brought headlamps and handed them out.

Dan's phone rang in her pocket and she looked at it.

It was her dad again, but she couldn't talk to him yet, couldn't focus on that until she was ready.

Barry declined a headlamp with a smile and a comment about how experienced he was with his own little flashlight.

The gates were metal, painted black. They looked heavy, but well maintained, and they were secured with a bolt and a large padlock. The entrance was wide enough for two or three people to walk next to each other, but the mouth had been used as a storage space and Dan could see wooden trestles and some kind of maintenance equipment stacked close enough to the opening to be easily seen before the light stopped penetrating.

Barry leaned forward to unlock the padlock and looked back, as though hoping that Dan might laugh and call the whole thing off at the last moment.

She nodded at him, encouraging him to continue.

The key slid into the padlock and it dropped open easily.

He looked back again, as though this were in some way proof that they were on a wasted errand.

"This key is kept locked in the manager's office all the time," he said as he pulled the first gate open and held it for Dan to pass through.

She walked into the mouth of the tunnel; Josie and Roger followed, with Barry at the rear.

"What are you doing?" asked Dan, as she saw Barry turn to lock the gate behind him, sealing them into the tunnel.

"I can't leave it open," he said, looking to Roger for support. "If it's open a tourist might come in. It's health and safety."

Roger looked at Dan and waited for her to respond.

"No. No way," said Dan, looking at them in turn. "Leave it unlocked. Josie, would you please wait at the entrance and make sure no one comes in?"

Josie nodded, looking disappointed, but she took the keys from a reluctant Barry and stepped back outside onto the pathway, pushing the gate closed but leaving the bolt open.

Barry looked pained. He glanced at Roger again, though less hopefully this time, and stepped to the front.

"These tunnels were dug out in 1860 by hand. There's electricity running in the other two, but not this one, I'm afraid," he began. "When we get a little farther in you'll see some beautiful pick marks on the wall where the navvies worked the stone. Also, some of the seams of flint are breathtaking, and you can imagine how hard it would have been to break that out by hand."

He turned to look at Dan, the light from outside still illuminating them both.

Dan raised a finger to her lips.

This time Barry didn't even look to Roger for backup, he just sighed, nodded, and continued on.

"This way," he said quietly, as though there were any other options.

Barry shone his flashlight into the tunnel and began to walk.

The tunnel near the entrance was brick-walled, with a flat concrete floor. The only thing that made the path difficult was the debris stored there.

Dan stepped over it, using her flashlight as she carefully placed her feet into gaps. She couldn't help but look back at the entrance, which glowed dull blue behind her as the light reached out toward her and fell short.

She took a deep breath. If she'd descended into *Tenacity*, she could damn well walk the length of this tunnel.

Roger seemed to sense her hesitation, and she felt a hand reach out and squeeze her shoulder.

It might've made her angry in another place, another time, but here, as they walked into the darkness, she was glad to have him with her.

Barry's flashlight led the way, and the debris that was stored at the mouth of the tunnel started to lessen as they moved farther in. The blue glow from the entrance, like a television left on at night, was still visible, but the useful light didn't penetrate as far as Dan, and her only view was the cone cast by her headlamp and those of her companions.

The brick around her became rough. No finish had been applied to this part of the tunnel, and the walls were as they'd been when chunks of chalk had been dug out by hand.

Dan could see the pick marks Barry had talked about, clean imprints from where the tools had been swung to break stone away. She also saw the seams of dark flint running around the tunnel, lending a marble effect.

Barry stopped ahead of her, and although she could have passed, she didn't. He pulled something from his pocket, and when it came to life, Dan could see that it was a small battery-powered T-lamp. He turned back to her.

"These little ledges"—he pointed to a tiny flat section in the rock, no bigger than a saucer for a teacup—"these were what the navvies used to put their candles on while they worked. I'll do the same."

He placed the light there and turned away.

The light shone up the wall, not at it, and it made the wall look stranger, highlighting the deep dark welts between the rough chunks of wall.

Dan stepped forward, toward the wall, but Barry stepped back and caught her.

"It looks weird," he whispered. "The shadows look too dark, but it's not shadow." He shone his light directly into one of the gaps.

"The bats," said Dan.

"Yes. They live in the crevices in the walls." He shone his flashlight around him, over the ceiling and down the other wall.

Dan saw that all of the gaps were filled with the small black shapes, and it made her shiver. Her own light followed her vision, and as she looked down toward the bottom of the wall and onto the floor, she saw that she was standing in something.

"Bat poop," whispered Barry, but Dan had figured that out. What she was looking at were the indentations that ran down one side of the pathway, footprints that were still clearly formed.

She turned back to Roger.

He nodded and stepped forward toward Barry.

"Who was last in here, Barry?" he asked.

Barry stuttered, having seen the prints himself now.

"Only me, maybe one of the other guides," he whispered.

Dan was listening, but she was also looking at the prints now, seeing that they ran both ways and that there was a pathway worn down one side, as if a person had hugged the wall for guidance, walking the same route time and time again.

Dan reached into her pocket for a telescopic police baton and extended it with a flick of her wrist. She heard Roger do the same.

"Stay behind me," said Roger, moving up beside Dan and trying to step past her.

She looked up at him, her face incredulous, though she realized he couldn't see it. She elbowed him in the ribs.

"When was the last time you used a baton in anger?" she whispered. "You stay behind me."

She stepped forward, feeling him follow, and headed farther into the tunnel.

She could see that there was a cavern ahead now. Some light was seeping toward her, dull and weak, but she knew they were coming to the end of the tunnel and could see the entrance to the Defiance gun emplacement.

Roger moved up beside her and she could tell that Barry had dropped farther behind.

They moved as silently as they could and eventually stepped down into a multilevel chamber. It was separated into sections, like huge pigeonholes, where guns would have been mounted, with space for their crews, ammunition, and supplies.

Dan had her baton raised and resting on her shoulder, ready to be brought down into action. She hugged the wall to her left and felt Roger do the same off to the right. There was a deeper darkness away to her left, a storage chamber behind the gun emplacements, clearly windowless, no light seeping in through cracks. Dan shivered but headed that way. She walked slowly, her senses on alert, and the smell was the first thing she noticed. She halted, breathing through her mouth, and took a moment to suppress the gag reflex.

Behind her, not far away, she could see Roger's light moving around in other areas, and she snapped her fingers. His light turned toward her and then moved closer.

"Jesus," he whispered, as he came close enough to smell it; he, too, recognized the scent of death.

Dan stepped forward toward the chamber, tense, her baton ready, and as she stepped into the doorway and shone the light inside, she felt her stomach lurch and flip as flies buzzed around her.

There were hooks around the walls, set there during the war to hang coats, rifles, and equipment, but now they were hung with the carcasses of animals in various states of decomposition.

Nearest to Dan was what looked like a fox, its front legs tied together above its head so it hung like a prisoner ready for interrogation. Its body had been ravaged, cut, and burned, and the marks on the wall behind it, the scratches and gouges, told Dan that the animal had lived through some of this torture and that its death hadn't been quick.

She shone her light around the rest of the room and stopped.

In the far corner was a human, skin and bone, naked.

"We're too late," said Dan, feeling tears well in her eyes.

"Shhhh," said Roger, his flashlight beam also focused there now.

Dan couldn't look away, couldn't help but notice the blond hair that was still visible, trapped between the skull and the wall.

"That's not her," said Roger, "that's much older, far too decayed."

Dan looked again, taking her time. He was right, the body had been there awhile, the blond hair drawing Dan's eye away from the decomposed skeleton.

"It's the girl who went overboard from *Defiance*," said Dan, certain she was right. "Cox must have taken her and faked the report to the bridge. The girl never went overboard at all. Cox managed to hide her and get her here."

Dan turned away, unable to look any longer, when her own flashlight beam caught something else. She looked back, bending forward and retching.

Sitting back against the wall on one side, almost hidden in the corner, was a male body, naked and skinny, blood congealed around the neck, the head nowhere to be seen.

45

Dan watched as the two bodies were stretchered and taken away. She was as sure as she could be that the small blond corpse was Stephanie James, the young sailor thought to be lost overboard from *Defiance* a year or so before. Sarah Cox had been the one to see her fall, to report her overboard and start the recovery actions, but the woman's body was never recovered, and no wonder.

The corpse looked so skinny underneath the blankets, barely making a bump in them.

The decapitated body came out second, Roger walking a few paces behind the gurney. He looked gray and strained as he walked; neither of them had any idea at all who this was.

The police and crime scene techs were still working in the area inside the Defiance gun emplacement as other people discussed how to enter the tunnel from the far end to avoid disturbing the bats any more than necessary.

Her phone rang, and she knew without looking it was her dad again. He'd called already and she wanted to speak to him, but now wasn't the time, not with all this going on around her.

"You know," Roger said from behind her, "this place never saw action in any of the wars. It never even got its full quota of guns delivered, because they weren't needed, and so, really, there shouldn't be any death here."

Dan looked at him, trying to understand what he meant.

"I mean there's a place up top called the killing field. A place meant for death, designed to gun down invading forces so they couldn't take this position and then attack and control Portsmouth Harbor. You expect death there, in a place like that, and maybe you expect it in a wartime gun emplacement, but it never happened, so there shouldn't be any, and now we find this. Remains of one unidentified young girl, a whole host of animals, a headless corpse . . . It looks like some kind of ritualistic killing room."

"I think she was practicing," said Dan. "Anyone who'd ever watched American crime drama could see that. She'd been bringing them in and practicing."

"Then she graduated to the next level?" he said, and Dan shot him a look.

"Graduated? Hardly a proud and successful day."

Roger rolled his eyes at her. "You know what I meant, but torturing animals and even the young woman is one thing. Straight-up beheading an adult male, that's something very different."

She turned away and looked back into the mouth of the tunnel.

"I don't think so," said Dan. "I don't think she graduated, I just don't think doing it herself was what got her off. I think she tried it, but I think she wanted to watch, not do."

Roger looked at her closely, squinting as though trying to read something more.

"That's an interesting insight," he said, finally looking away. "I'd be interested to know how you made that leap given the information we all have."

Dan looked away.

"You know, if she'd disposed of those bodies," Roger said, his voice strained, "we'd likely never have known. Even if we'd gone in there on an anonymous tip." He stared at Dan as he said this. "Even then, we wouldn't have known what we'd found. We just wouldn't have known to look harder. We'd never have gone in there forensically."

Dan nodded. Roger was right, and she knew it.

"That's how Hamilton did it for so long," she said.

He nodded.

"I don't understand it, though," said Dan. "I don't get what we're seeing. Her house looks as though she was running, so why take the time to come here and drop a body off? It's pretty fresh—why not take it to the yacht along with whoever the other body is? It doesn't make sense."

"No, it doesn't," agreed Roger.

"And where's the head?" said Dan. "I bet beheading someone takes a lot of strength."

"Sarah Cox is strong," said Roger. "You and John can testify to that."

Dan nodded and was silent for a moment.

"So what now?" she asked. "How do we catch her? We don't know where she is, or where she might have gone. She's a flight risk by land and sea, and likely with a lot of cash. I'm guessing that, anyway, assuming she had an escape plan."

Roger sat down next to Dan.

The wall she was sitting on was quite high, and the stone was cold beneath her.

He jumped up and sat closer to her, their legs touching and his broad shoulders making her lean off to one side a bit.

"Budge up, fatty," she said, pushing him, but he didn't move. Instead, he put one arm round her shoulders and held her toward him.

Then he pointed to the entrance to the tunnel.

"Look," he said. "Look at where she was working. It's private and remote, but look at the state of it. She'd little or no light to work with. It's risky getting victims, animal or human, in and out. You saw the tools she was using. Most of them picked up from her garden shed. This place is perfect if you're William Knight and you want to bring girls here, before they sealed up the upper access. You can come in quickly along the ridge there."

He pointed along the top of the mound that connected the gun emplacements.

"You take the girls in and then you're out of sight and you can do as you please. You don't want light, not much, anyway, because you want them to have few memories of where they are, of who you are, and so you do what you want to do, then you bring them back out, unconscious, and drop them wherever. It's perfect for someone like that. But for Cox, this place isn't perfect at all. You saw that second body, the foxes, cats, dogs, badgers, and whatever else was in there. She wanted to experiment, to do things to people, and you're possibly right, a lot of the pleasure for her has to be in the seeing. The top of the emplacement is closed off now, not even moonlight can get in, so she manages to get a copy of the key made and accesses the site through the tunnel, leaving traces and increasing her chance of discovery with every coming and going. Taking them in there's risky, but she can check for cars, scout ahead for flashlights and other people, but bringing a dead body out of the tunnel . . . She used a location that's also the site of a number of other crimes, maybe that added to it?"

"She used to come here with Knight and watch him," said Dan. "I'm not sure what the relationship was, whether she became more powerful than him or what, but that's how she knew this was here."

He nodded.

"You can tell me the truth later about how you know all this, though I think I can figure it out, but, that aside, there's nothing about this that tells me this woman's prepared. Everything about it tells me she's up and down, one minute fighting what she is and the next trying to embrace it. She used only what she had lying around and was doing it with equal parts of impulse, emotion, and guilt. She's trying to be in control, maybe even believes that she is, but the fact that she kept Natasha Moore at her house at all tells me she didn't know what to do. Here, Moore would have frozen to death eventually; at home she's preserved, but a constant risk. Sarah Cox hasn't yet fully understood what she wants, and that's her undoing. It sounds like we already have a good starting point in identifying the older victim—Stephanie James, from what you're saying—and we'll confirm that soon. I think Natasha was to be her second, and I think we'll identify the beheaded body very quickly. It's a male, the body's not in great condition, but he died recently, his head removed postmortem. I think we'll probably have some ideas from the local missing persons list or from the navy defaulters and absentees list. I also think Natasha was a crime of passion, or impulse, done in the moment, forced. I think Cox saw Black and believed she could manipulate him, and Natasha was already in her sights, so she went with it to try and rope him in. I think she was forced to act on board the ship and bring Natasha off, and the fact that she had to do that, that she felt it necessary to take that huge risk again, means she doesn't think through what she does, isn't as clever as she thinks she is. But one thing I'm really certain of is that she doesn't have an escape plan. She's in the wind and doesn't know what to do. She needs help, but she won't know where to get it. We'll find her soon, because she'll have no idea where to go."

Dan looked at Roger, then jumped down off the wall, moving away from him.

"We can't just wait," she said. "She could hurt someone else. We need to go and speak to people who know where she might go."

"You off for another séance, then?" asked Roger, looking at her hard now. "Seems to me you've got information that can only come from a dead man."

Dan shrugged and turned to walk away.

"Don't start hiding things from me, Danny," said Roger, his tone making her turn round. "We've always been close, you and I, and you know how important it is to confide, to share."

She stopped and thought, looking at her friend, boss, and mentor as he swung his legs, kicking his heels against the wall like a small, bored child.

"I'll share. I promise. I'm not going to speak to the dead, not again, but there's someone else who knows way more than they should about all of this, and they're very much alive."

"No," said Roger. "I won't allow it, not again."

"You can't stop it, Roger."

"Watch me," he said.

Dan stepped toward him, feeling her temper rise.

"And why are you so against it?" she asked.

"Because Chris Hamilton does nothing to help anyone, ever. He only serves himself, only has his own agenda, and even if it feels like he's helped you, even if it looks like he might have helped you by accident, he hasn't. You can't manipulate Chris Hamilton, because he lives only to manipulate others. Whatever he told you, whatever you're holding back from me—"

"I'm not holding anything back," said Dan. "I don't know why you'd think that. It's like you're paranoid. I told you everything he said to me. I went and saw Jimmy Nash and he gave me information about William Knight and that led me here. But I thought I was following up on the NCA case, then it turns out that I'm not, that Hamilton actually led me here.

So he knew about Cox, knew I was working the case, knew what she was doing, who she was. How's that even possible? In the time frame he had, how can he know all that he knows? Is there a page on social media somewhere where the worst of the military's villains get together and discuss their days? Trade secrets? What?"

"Hamilton only helps himself," said Roger, seeming to ignore all Dan had said. "You don't know what his end goal is, Danny, you don't know what he's trying to achieve, and I forbid you to speak to him again."

Dan looked at Roger, saw the defiance melt out of him as he looked back at her.

"Come with me again. Wait in the viewing room like last time and I'll come and debrief you the second I'm out. Okay?"

He jumped down and faced her.

"I need to go back in before we leave," he said, gesturing with his head toward the tunnel. "You can come with, or wait here for me."

Dan looked into the dark mouth of the tunnel and shivered.

"I'll wait," she said. "I'm not going back in there."

He put a hand on her shoulder.

"You told me that about the shop in the New Forest, too, said you'd never go back there, but you know, that's not how I think of you, I always think of you as someone who faces her fears, not shies away from them."

"I face the fears I need to face," she said, her mind drifting toward memories of her last meeting with Hamilton. "But the ones I don't need to—places I don't ever *need* to go again—I'm cutting myself some slack on those. I'll wait here."

46

Dan felt the pressure on her back disappear and be replaced with pain as she was picked up, bodily heaved off the floor by the seat of her trousers and the scruff of her neck and carried to another pallet across from where Chris Hamilton's body lay motionless. She was dumped on the floor.

Now, much closer to him, Dan felt a surge of relief that brought tears to her eyes because she was sure she could see Chris's chest moving; he was alive, at least.

She shuffled round and looked at the men, kneeling upright, tattoos revealed, the Armed Forces apparent in every one of them.

Then she looked at Matt Carson.

He was standing, ignoring her, looking at the men he'd assembled here. He paced toward a man at the end, a man Dan could now see was significantly older than the others.

"How you doing there, Malc?" Carson said, leaning down toward the man's face. "How's the breathing? Age isn't helping is it, making you weak?"

The man Malc said nothing. Was unable to speak.

"D'you remember," Carson began, "in week two? We'd had a tough first week, and I think we can all honestly agree that I was struggling a bit. I was young, wasn't I? Only sixteen, and just turned at that. The youngest in the regiment, I'd have been, if I'd been allowed to pass out with my class."

Carson pulled over a chair; the sound of the legs dragging along the floor echoed around the rafters and bounced off the walls. He unslung the SA-80 rifle that was across his chest and laid it on a crate. Then he sat down in the center of the circle.

"You must remember, Jimbo," he said, directing the words at another man. "In week two, when I was struggling a bit and I didn't shower after one of the beasting sessions in the gym. I had to get to the next serial and I didn't have time, so I turned up still sweating."

None of the men moved or reacted in any way, and Dan began to watch them carefully, each in turn, watching for small signs of movement to tell her they were still alive.

"So anyway, I remember." Carson smiled. "I remember when we got back from the parade square. I think it was you who grabbed me first, Jimbo, I think it was you, anyway. You grabbed me from behind, so I wasn't totally sure, because I didn't see. Anyways, the one thing I do remember, while you all held me down and two of you nearly took my skin off, scrubbing me with hard brooms, was you, Malc. I don't know if you knew that I saw you, but I did, you was watching through the glass panel in the door to the showers, watching while they made me bleed."

Dan saw Malc move, his eyes flicker, and for a moment she felt relieved that he was alive, until she remembered the crime scene where they'd found the last four bodies of the men Carson believed had wronged him. She remembered the blood that ran so far up the walls of Carson's deserted home that she'd been unable to comprehend what he'd done to the bodies, the carcasses, that he'd left behind; maybe a quick death was the best outcome for these men, unless help came soon, unless help could get into this building before Carson could pull the trigger.

She shifted her weight quietly, aware that Carson's focus was elsewhere and determined to keep it that way. She felt her hands move a little and wondered how tight he'd pulled the plastic zip-ties around her wrists. She had small hands, had been a nightmare for her sister to truss up when they played as children, and now she started to pull and twist at her bonds.

They were tight, biting into her skin at first, but as she worked at them, aligning her palms and then twisting to work the plastic apart, Dan wondered whether she might be able to get free.

Carson laughed, loud and fake.

"So there I am, sixteen years old, being held down by my mates, 'cuz that's what you were all supposed to be, bleeding from where the hard brooms literally scratched patches of skin off me, fucking flayed me, and we're all laughing, aren't we lads? Weren't we, Malc? Laughing, 'cuz that's funny. Then, you remember, Malc? When I cried? Because that's when things got bad, wasn't it, Jimbo?"

Carson was looking from one man to another.

Dan heard a sound, a sob, from one of the other men, and she watched as Carson stood up and walked toward him.

"Yeah, like that," he said, towering over one of the kneeling men. "Well done, Shads, trust you to improve a story with an appropriate soundtrack."

Carson reached toward the man, who flinched in panic and lost his balance, falling hard onto his side.

Dan saw the man fall, saw how as soon as he was no longer kneeling, he lacked the strength to hold his ankles up far enough behind his back.

The weight of the man's own feet and legs began to pull on the rope that was tied around his neck, and Dan could hear choking sounds as it slowly strangled him.

"But I know why you're really crying," said Carson, squatting beside him. "And it's appropriate to the story, really, 'cuz I can't remember who it was that said I 'couldn't take it.' Or who then said that I needed to learn to take it. But I do remember you, Shads, turning the broom around . . ."

Carson jerked to his feet, dragging the man called Shads to the center of the circle and dropping his body there so that the others could see as he choked under the weight of his own lower legs.

Shads was on his belly and he was fighting hard to keep his knees bent and his heels tucked up close to his back, but he was failing.

Dan worked at the bonds behind her and looked away, for just a second, to see that Chris Hamilton was now awake.

He smiled at her, blinking as he did, and Dan smiled back.

"So, to teach a young lad, at barely sixteen years of age, how to 'take it,' you made me take it, didn't you, Shads?"

The man on the floor continued to gasp and gurgle as his body fought its fatigue and his cold, dead muscles failed him.

"And you, Malc, the man with the duty of care—not that we gave a shit about that back then—you watched, smiling, while they raped me with a broom handle. But then we didn't use that word back then, neither, did we?"

Carson turned toward Malc, fixed the man with a stare, and then pushed his boot down against the side of Shad's head, twisting his foot and then increasing the weight as though he were stubbing a cigarette into the ground, as though determined to obliterate it, to force it deep into the earth.

Carson was a big man, heavyset, and Shad's body went limp, his legs relaxing back and the choking sound ceasing, Carson took a few paces back, two to the left, and bent forward.

"It's the final moments of the game," said Carson. "This penalty kick could secure the regimental title. If Carson can place this between the uprights, the trophy is his."

He moved forward a few paces, drew his leg back, and swung through, his steel-toe-capped boot striking the side of Shad's head, his skull splitting open with a crack that made Dan gag.

"And it's good!" shouted Carson, like a television sports commentator. "The title is his! Carson will be a regimental hero now, there's no question about that."

Shad's body was limp.

Carson looked at the men around him.

"Doesn't look like he could take it, does it?"

Dan looked at them again, thinking back and trying to recognize who the men were.

Carson's life had been a train wreck. He'd barely lasted three months in the army before he'd been discharged for "self harming." He was a "cutter," so his files said, and there were some faded Polaroids showing his arms and torso like a textured tapestry. Within two weeks of leaving the British Army, he'd been in an accident on a moped, which had cost him his left leg.

The details on Carson were sketchy for a while after that.

He'd eventually surfaced on the streets making a living by begging, passing himself off as an injured veteran. He'd been picked up by a charity that supported homeless veterans and told them that he'd lost his leg in Afghanistan. He'd told stories of bravery, both his and others', and had obtained numerous medals, both campaign medals and some that are only awarded for valor, which he sourced from online stores and proudly displayed on a secondhand blazer gifted to him by an elderly member of the Parachute Regiment, a man who'd been among the first troops to land at Normandy.

The scales were tipped for Matt Carson when, as part of his masquerade as an injured veteran, he attended the armistice parade in central London, marching with the British legion.

He was recognized by a member of his old troop, the first man to die at his hand, Patrick "Paddy" O'Connell. O'Connell had spotted him and denounced him openly. In an open argument he'd faced Carson down in front of many who thought they knew the man, many who thought they'd helped a fellow soldier get back on his feet. Carson had run from the parade, but photographs were taken, and articles in some of the national press over the coming days had meant that there was nowhere he could hide from his lies and deception.

Carson dropped off the grid and his killing spree started.

Dan looked over at Chris.

He smiled again, but weakly.

She watched him look around, taking in the scene, spotting the blood spreading out across the dusty gray stone floor and the faces of the men who'd yet to die. She pulled harder against the bindings on her wrist as she tried to get a hand free. Her skin split and blood started to seep from where the bonds dug in. Dan closed her eyes, wincing at the pain, but the blood was lubricating her hands and she felt the plastic tie slide beneath one of them. She wasn't free yet, but she might be soon.

Chris Hamilton was watching her. He mouthed something at her and nodded slowly.

It took a second for Dan to realize that he was telling her to be calm.

"Doesn't look like old Shads can take it at all," said Carson. "And look at my boots, Malc," he said, turning back to the old man who'd once been his training sergeant. "They were clean, immaculate, I promise you they were. You said I'd never make it as a soldier, but yet here I am, with all you lot, you professional soldiers on your knees waiting to die. All of you from the beginning, some of you from the end."

As Dan heard that she looked again at the men and realized who some of them were, other soldiers who'd been in the homeless program with him, those he'd befriended and known, who'd thought him to be the hero he told them all he was.

"You all spout off about loyalty, but you didn't show me any," said Carson, his voice beginning to rise, his eyes blinking and face twitching.

A movement caught Dan's eye.

Over by the window, not the one she'd looked in through, but one near it, she saw a tiny black shape move, then stay still, then it seemed to have gone, or maybe just dropped down to rest on the windowsill. It was no fatter than a pencil, and Dan knew that it had to be a remote viewing device.

Someone was outside looking in, and when they saw the body on the floor, it'd only be a matter of minutes before they'd move in and take Carson out. Eight, now nine dead meant there'd be no appetite to negotiate.

She looked across at Chris, who nodded to acknowledge he'd spotted it, too.

"Loyalty," said Carson as he scanned the men. Then he reached for his pistol and looked at each in turn, stopping at each one, the pistol held out in front of him, his eye squinting as he paused and took aim.

"I don't think you should do that, Matthew," said Chris, his tone light, upbeat, and cordial, jarring with the scene around them and the confusion in his eyes.

Dan looked at him, eyes wide.

"Honestly, I really don't think you should. Is it okay if I call you Matthew? It's what your mum must have called you, am I right? Always nice to use people's proper names."

Carson turned slowly and looked over at Chris Hamilton.

"I told you that if you talked again, I'd cut your tongue out," said Carson.

"Yes, but I notice that my colleague over there got some tape on her mouth, and while I agree she's a talker, it does make me feel like you might want to hear what I have to say, at least on a subconscious level."

Carson turned fully toward Chris and took a few steps toward him, stopping halfway between Chris and the semicircle of condemned men.

Dan pulled hard at her right hand, the pain excruciating, but the blood and plastic sliding as the bond went as far as her knuckles. She wondered how an assault team would breach this area without allowing Carson to reach his rifle and strafe bullets into them all. Carson was blinking again, twitching, looking agitated and stressed as he stared at Chris Hamilton, as though killing one of his former colleagues had calmed him some but hadn't lasted.

"Come and talk to me, Matthew," said Hamilton. "Not like this, come close, so we can't be heard. I've got some things to tell you that I really think might help you, that I really think might save your life, just yours, mind."

Dan looked at Chris, his voice soothing and slow.

He was smiling at Carson, smiling as though he wasn't concerned that his hands were bound, that there was a corpse on the floor with its skull cracked open, that the man who'd done it was walking toward him now, an old Browning pistol in one hand and his boots leaving moist red prints on the floor as he traveled.

"Come on, Matthew, talk to me for just a second, what harm can it do? Then you can go back to slaughtering these bastards in any way you think they deserve."

Chris's voice was calm and slow, rising slightly at the end, on the word "deserve," as though he'd just said, "And of course there'll be cake, you can't have tea without cake."

Dan watched, her breathing slowing as Carson approached Chris, as though he were sleepwalking.

"Come and talk to me," said Chris. "You recognize me, don't you?"

Carson was near him now, staring down at him.

"Come on, closer. I've something to tell you. Something to help you really make them suffer for what they did. And the ones who think they didn't do anything, they need to suffer, too, because what we allow, what we're prepared to walk past, is what we condone. We both know that there were those who did, and those who condoned, and they'll all die today if you'll just listen to me, and each one of them will deserve what they get."

Carson was still, looking down.

"I do recognize you," he said, his voice stilted. "I wasn't sure it was you."

"It's me," said Chris, "but I need to talk to you privately."

Carson nodded and knelt, his back to everything else. He leaned in toward Chris and they whispered together.

She looked at the window; the small pencil-like camera was gone. She looked at the huge metal doors, heavy, slow, and hard to breach. She looked at the man in a pool of blood that seemed to have found its shape. Then she looked over at Carson, kneeling, whispering with Chris Hamilton, engrossed.

Carson stood up suddenly. He turned around, looking first at Dan and then in all directions, and then raised his pistol. He roared, a sound that contained no words, and spun around again. He ran for the rifle he'd set down on the pallet and swung it up, pointing it at the men in front of him, readying it to fire.

Dan pulled one last time and felt her right hand slip free as she watched the rifle come up. She leaned forward as hard as she could, stumbled up onto her feet, and launched herself at the back of Matt Carson's legs.

The sound of the first shot rang out as he stumbled forward.

Dan fell facefirst onto the floor and rolled onto her back, trying to get away but needing to see.

Carson spun toward her, the rifle tracking toward her chest.

She grabbed the second baton from her pocket, an instinctive movement, but she couldn't grip it properly, the blood on her hands making it impossible to flick out the telescope sections, so she threw it at Carson, making him flinch, making the bullet he fired pull off to the right and hit the wall somewhere behind her.

An explosion sounded behind him that shook the room.

The force of it pushed Dan's head back against the floor, fireworks exploding in her skull as the room suddenly became lighter and a hole appeared in the wall opposite her.

The hole was immediately filled by men in black suits, faces covered, and in a burst of sound that seemed to last for only a second, before Dan could only hear ringing, she saw holes appear in Matt Carson's chest. One, two, then a third, as Carson looked at her, confusion replaced by nothing, and toppled over toward her.

He was pulled off her in an instant and the room was filled with bodies.

Weapons were pointed at Carson's corpse, and others, in the hands of anonymous police, moved into the room to secure it.

"Clear!" someone shouted. The sound echoed, dreamlike.

Then there was more noise and bustle that Dan couldn't make out as she looked at Carson's face, relaxed now, unmoving, his eyes staring through her, off into the distance.

Roger Blackett was there now, his lips moving, but no sound making it through the ringing in Dan's ears. He touched her face, wiping something off, and then called over his shoulder, words that Dan couldn't make out. He pulled her forward into a sitting position and rubbed her back, though Dan didn't know why.

Dan felt his hands under her arms as he pulled her to her feet and then began to walk her slowly away from the blood and bodies.

"Danny?" he was saying, the words starting to penetrate.

She turned to look at him as Chris Hamilton came into view, calm and still smiling, as though he'd met them both in the booze aisle of a local supermarket.

"What did you say to him?" said Dan, staring at Chris. "How did he recognize you?"

The corners of Hamilton's mouth twisted up into a knowing grin.

"He's never seen me before in his life. Don't believe anything you hear from a crazy person. I knew they were going to breach quickly. I just tried to keep him talking."

"It worked," said Roger, patting Hamilton on the shoulder. "Well done, but I can't help thinking that Danny saved all of you at the end there."

Roger and Hamilton looked at each other, the smile fading from Hamilton's face.

"Considering the past scenes, I doubt he'd have left anyone alive," said Roger. "You included. Danny saved your life, Chris, saved all of you."

Hamilton looked at Dan and reached out, patting her on the arm.

"So, you saved my life," he said, smiling again. "Who knows, maybe one day I'll be able to pay you back."

47

Dan didn't hesitate before she walked into the interview room this time.

Hamilton's solicitor was in the next room again, watching on the video stream and checking that no audio was taken, in accordance with Hamilton's rules. He'd been only too happy to ensure this meeting was set up quickly, choosing to believe that his client's cooperation was starting to bear fruit.

Felicity was on her way, had asked to Dan to wait for her, but Dan couldn't do that, because her questions weren't about Felicity's case.

"Danny," said Hamilton, half rising, as before, as far as his cuffs would allow, when she came into the room. "I honestly hadn't dreamed that I'd get to see you again so soon. The images of you that I committed to memory for those times when I'm alone in my cell have barely faded, and yet here I'm already getting some more."

He blinked his eyes a few times, mimicking the sound of a camera as he did, as though snapping photos of her in his mind.

"And your face, *ooof*, looks sore. It's like you came all made up as one of my short-term lovers. Have the usual jokes been made? What do you say to a woman with two black eyes?"

He waited, but Dan ignored him.

"Nothing at all, she's been told twice."

He chuckled and raised his eyebrows as though hoping for a reaction.

"Nothing? Not a titter? What's the first thing a woman does when she's been released from the battered wives' shelter?"

Dan ignored him again, breathing out deeply and pursing her lips as though bored.

"The dishes, if she knows what's good for her."

"Cut the shit, Chris," said Dan, knowing she had to be strong, had to try to at least take some control in all this. "If you keep on with any of that vile crap, then I walk and we don't talk again. I didn't need to put up with that while you were outside, and I certainly won't while you're locked up in here."

He leaned back in his chair, his eyes wide, as though a strong wind had blasted against him.

"You feeling a little tired there, Danny? Feeling a little short-tempered?"

Dan stared at him across the table.

"Wait. Is it that time of the month?" he asked, with a sad look as though sympathizing with her. "Doth the red flag fly between thy thighs?"

Dan stood up and shrugged.

"If I want to hear childish misogynist crap like this I'll go speak my mind on Twitter."

She made for the door without looking back.

He said nothing, just watched her, Dan could feel it and knew he'd be looking for any hesitation, that was how he worked. He'd be watching for body language, weakness, anything at all that would tell him she *needed* to talk, that she needed not to walk out that door.

Dan never broke stride, except to look up at the cameras and shrug toward them, as though she'd done her best. She reached the door and knocked twice, hard and loud.

"Not even a good-bye?" he said from behind her, but Dan didn't turn back to look at him.

She waited, looking through the vertical glass pane to see where the guard was, and then knocked again when she didn't see him coming.

The guard walked into view, unlocked the door, and Dan stepped through it.

Her heart was beating fast. Had she given in too soon and blown her chance to talk with him, and all over a few stupid comments? She forced herself to walk quickly through the door without looking back, making sure her shoulders were low and relaxed and her gait nonchalant, as if she hadn't wanted to go in there anyway and so he'd saved her a chore.

The door was almost shut behind her, the guard fiddling with the key, when she heard him call.

"Okay, Danny," shouted Hamilton. "Okay."

Dan kept walking, aware that the guard had stopped the door from shutting properly.

"Miss," said the guard. "Mr. Hamilton says he wants to talk?"

Dan didn't stop walking, seeing the next door and knowing that once she passed through it, the chance really was gone.

"If he wants to talk, he knows what to do. He didn't have the world's greatest upbringing, but the navy taught him manners," said Dan, reaching for the handle and closing her eyes.

The latch clicked and she began to pull the door open.

"Sorry, Danny," shouted Hamilton, and Dan paused. "I'm sorry."

She turned and looked back at the guard, who raised his eyebrows as though unsure what was going on.

"He said he was sorry, miss," said the guard.

Dan paused, waiting, not sure how quickly to go back. Then she released the door and walked slowly toward the interview room, aware that her footsteps echoed, marking her progress.

She waited at the door, smiled at the guard, and then leaned round and looked at Hamilton.

"I. Am. Sorry," he said, looking straight at her. "My behavior was unacceptable and, frankly, I think I was just crying out for attention. It won't happen again today."

Dan paused as though considering this, then walked back into the room, thanking the guard, and sat down opposite Hamilton.

She looked at him, wondering whether it'd get easier each time she saw him but thinking that it likely wouldn't, as she dropped her hands beneath the table so he wouldn't see them shaking.

"You came back to talk," he said. "So what's up?"

"I've got more questions," said Dan, "but I think you know what some of them are going to be, don't you?"

He smiled and spread his fingers out on the table in front of her.

"How did you know?" she asked.

He laughed. "I said that to you once, do you remember?"

Dan just stared at him, saying nothing.

He stopped and rolled his eyes, as though she were a boring friend refusing to relax and have fun.

"How did I know what, Danny? You must be clearer when you phrase your questions."

"How did you know what investigation I was working? You didn't help with the NCA investigation we talked about at all, you helped me with my case."

"I'm sure I said I'd only help *you*," he said, as though this were obvious, pulling a face as though trying to recall a previous conversation to make sure he was correct. "Yup, I remember now. You were there, I was here, I was wearing these bracelets"—he paused—"do they make me look fat, Danny, you can tell me? Anyway, you asked me some questions and I said that I'd help you, specifically you, and no one else. And did I?"

Dan wasn't sure what to say, wasn't sure which answer showed strength and which showed weakness, whether there was even a line drawn between them.

"Yes, you did," she said, opting for honesty.

His eyes opened wide and he smiled broadly, like a child being told exciting news.

"Did you find my old friend William?" he asked, leaning toward her, eager to hear.

"I did," said Dan.

"Well, I really wasn't sure you would, you know. He's a nasty piece of work, but I thought you'd figure out where he'd had his fun before long, once you had the name. How was he?"

"Not good," said Dan.

Hamilton shook his head slowly. "Such a waste. He had real talent, that one, could have gone all the way, but crimes that leave live victims, I always thought they were higher risk."

"He was a rapist, not a footballer who showed promise," said Dan.

Hamilton seemed to have been thinking about something else and now snapped back to look at her.

"But if you saw him, that means they've kept him alive. Was it awful?"

Dan nodded, just once.

"But you'll go and get him now, won't you, Danny? You won't be able to help yourself. Regardless of what he's done, you'll hunt for where he is and go and fetch him. It'll worry at you constantly, just like the case on *Tenacity*; I'm reliably informed you're still pursuing that, too."

Dan looked down at Hamilton's hands, still flat on the table in front of him, the fingers spread out and steady.

Those hands had murdered so many people and yet they looked so normal, so ordinary, the skin gathered between the knuckles, the veins raised.

"Why did you put me onto him? You don't do anything without reason."

He smiled again, saw her looking at his hands and tapped each fingertip against the table once, starting with his left pinkie and working across to the other before he spoke.

"Well, you know one reason now," he said, and Dan realized that freeing Knight was something Hamilton knew she would try to do, something he knew she would think about, an injustice she wouldn't be able to let pass. "Other reasons, well, it's more complicated, I grant you that." He paused, looked away from her, his brow furrowing, and then he looked back. "Or is it? Honestly, Danny, I get so little intelligent conversation in here that I rather forget what women like you are capable of. Did you bring a chess set? I offered to coach you. I think you'd be good if you tried, though you know that even in chess, the women don't play in the men's tournaments, and with good reason. Did you know that the top-rated woman in the world is ranked fifty-ninth overall? If that doesn't tell you what you need to know about gender equality, then I really don't know what will."

Dan drew in another deep breath and let it out slowly.

"Okay, okay, but Danny, please, one day, talk gender equality with me. It's something I've wanted to discuss for years, and I know my views and yours won't match, but we can have a rigorous discussion about it, right? An intellectual joust and still be friends?"

"What was the reason?" asked Dan.

"Chess set?"

Dan knew he was jousting with her for power again, trying to take back what she'd won in the opening exchange, trying to make his early loss nothing more than a gambit. She considered it, watching him closely.

"I make no promises," she said.

He nodded at that, seemingly appeased.

"The key reason, Danny, is this. I need you to trust me, to know just how much I know and how much I can help you. Because at some point, possibly soon, I'm going to want to trade, and I will need you to understand, and to convince the Morlocks out there, that I have something of value to offer."

"Why don't you start by telling me where the bodies of your victims are?"

"Oh, Danny," he said, and rolled his eyes again. "Stop with the bodies, for God's sake."

Dan noticed that he didn't deny that there were bodies this time, a first as far as she could remember.

"Then what?" asked Dan. "If that's not what you have to trade, then tell me what it is."

He shook his head, and his eyes darkened. "Not yet, Danny, but when the time comes and I do tell you what I have to offer, you'll know for sure I'm not lying. Trust me on that. You'll know the value of what I have."

He spoke in riddles, as always, and Dan would've written off what he'd said, if only he hadn't led her to Knight and from there to the lair Cox had operated from. He'd proved that he knew more than she'd thought, more than should be possible. He was right, Dan wouldn't be able to live knowing that Knight was being held the way he was, but he'd also shown his hand, just a fleeting glimpse of it, and Dan wondered if he realized how much.

The pool of people who knew what Dan was working on, who knew about Cox and all that had happened in the time since Natasha disappeared, wasn't small, not by any means, but it was finite, and though it could have been any number of civilian police, the obvious link here went right back to Hamilton's roots in the Armed Forces. There was someone he was close to. There was a trust between them, and a method of communicating, a deep knowledge of both what Hamilton might know and what he would want to know. Someone that close, someone that far inside Hamilton's head, could easily be the same person who might know where Hamilton kept his victims' bodies. Someone that close might even be able to send parts of them to the National Crime Agency, though why remained a mystery.

"Well, no one can hear us," said Dan, looking around at the cameras. "I can cover the debrief and tell them that you told me not much, just chatter and nonsense, but what I want to know is if you know how to find Sarah Cox."

He leaned back at this, smiling at her as though he'd found some new respect for Dan, or maybe seen a side of her that he hadn't expected to.

"Are we speaking so directly now?" he asked, his face bemused. "Aren't we supposed to talk in circles? I'm not sure how comfortable I feel being asked an incriminating question outright. Frankly, I'm hurt you think I might even have that information."

Dan leaned forward and drummed her fingers on the table, watching Hamilton as he watched her. She was trying to read him, though she knew it was a pointless exercise—the man had spent almost his whole life pretending to be something that he wasn't, pretending to be someone he wasn't.

He'd carried this off in life generally, but also as a policeman, even when surrounded by those same people who were trying to identify him for his crimes. He was worrying at the inside of his lip now, nibbling at the skin as though trying to tear a tiny piece of it away. He licked his lips, his tongue just poking into view.

"I don't think I can answer that, Danny."

He reacted to the way she let her shoulders slump, as though he could see that she was disappointed in him and he wanted to turn that around, to get her interest back.

"Not necessarily because I wouldn't, but I simply don't have that information."

Dan sighed and let her eyes fall back down toward her hands, which were flat on the table, mirroring his.

He turned his hands over and made them into fists, only his index fingers remaining straight as he pointed at her. "But I do have some ideas. You see, Cox likes them small and blond, doesn't she? She's taken on Knight's tastes?"

Dan nodded.

"And she's big? Not obese, but sturdy?"

Dan shrugged and nodded again.

"Do you think she's attractive to men?"

"She's not ugly," said Dan.

"But she's not feminine, is she? She's not the sort that William Knight would go for?"

"No, she's not."

He leaned back.

"She'll have known all about you, Danny. You're petite and in a position of power, a direct threat to her, in her mind at least. I'm sure you've endeared yourself to her with your wit and charm, too, so she'll have done her research on you, that much I'm certain of. So, while I don't know where she is, I can tell you a few places she might be. One would be your home, where she knows you'll definitely go. Maybe have that checked before you go in. She'll have watched it, know where it is, seen you come and go. Maybe not often, but you're too high-profile for someone like her not to be interested in."

"Okay," said Dan. "I'd get my house checked anyway, so hardly a revelation."

"Well, the other place she'd go will be the opposite. If she's scared of you now, thinks you've brought this on her and she's running, then she may go somewhere she thinks you'd definitely never go. I genuinely don't know where that might be, but she'll have her own ideas."

Dan paused, thinking.

"I think you just managed to talk for two whole minutes and say absolutely nothing of use at all," she said.

Hamilton's face turned dark and his eyes narrowed again.

"Oh, Danny, you're such a disappointment. It's part of who you are, of course, the focus, the single-mindedness and self-obsession, but it really does you no good sometimes. Like your submarine, *Tenacity*, sometimes you have to stick your head up and look around."

"I don't think I'm with you," said Dan.

"No, you never really were. But at the very least, ask some questions, try to become informed. Ignorance, this level of it, really doesn't suit you."

Dan looked at him and couldn't help but feel rebuked. She needed to change the subject, to see how he reacted, to move away from this line of conversation.

"Someone's sending fingers from your victims to the NCA," said Dan.

"I know. Isn't it terribly exciting!" said Hamilton, and Dan noted that, again, he hadn't denied the victims were his.

"Do you know who it is?"

"Yes."

"Will you tell me?"

"No."

"Do you know why they're doing it?"

"Of course."

"Will you tell me?"

"Of course . . . I will not," said Hamilton, and laughed at his own joke.

"Do you think you've helped me in some other way than locating Cox?"

"Yes."

"Will you tell me how?"

"I hear your slot on the investigation has become vacant again. How's Stewart? Will he recover?"

Dan watched him, desperately trying to think whether he could have managed to hurt Stewart Mackenzie, the investigator assigned to the NCA case in Dan's stead, or whether he'd simply found out about it and was trying to exaggerate his reach.

"Tell me how you helped me," said Dan, ignoring his comments about Mackenzie.

He looked at her and didn't reply.

"When we found the place where Natasha Moore had been kept, someone had cut off her ring finger. That's the same finger that's been sent to the NCA from your other victims. I don't think it was Cox. Do you know who did it?"

"Yes," he said, smiling, as though they were finally making some progress. "Did you find out who at the NCA the fingers were addressed to?"

Dan shook her head.

"Jesus, Danny," said Hamilton, trying to throw his hands in the air. "This is painful, like pulling teeth. I really thought you were better than this."

"Help me, then. I can't see the link."

He leaned back, his smile broader than she'd ever seen it.

"And so you finally ask me outright for help. Help which I will gift to you, though only a push, Danny, a nudge in the right direction and no more."

Dan nodded.

"Thank you," she said.

"Tell me, Danny, at this moment, what do you want more than anything else? Be honest with me, only you and I can hear, tell me the things you want."

"I want to find Sarah Cox, because I believe—"

"No need for explanations, Danny, it matters not to me *why* you want these things, only that you do."

"Okay, I want to find Sarah Cox. I want William Knight to be freed and face a proper trial for his crimes."

Hamilton was nodding as she spoke.

"I want to find Ryan Taylor and bring the people who used *Tenacity* to smuggle drugs into the country to proper justice. I want to find the person sending women's ring fingers to the NCA, and I want to find out who cut Natasha Moore's ring finger off, and why. Then I want to bring them to justice, too."

He laughed and clapped, his chains rattling as he did.

"Damn, you're good. So selfless, so committed to justice. You know what? I believe you, too, because your life is so devoid of meaning and purpose that you want nothing personal at all, just crimes to be solved and justice to be served. What a grand person you are, Lieutenant Danielle Lewis, so utterly selfless and yet so completely selfish and self-centered at the same time. But what if all of those things, that list of things, what if they weren't so different after all? What if some threads loomed them together like different scenes on the same tapestry? What if many, if not all, were connected in some way?"

"Then . . ."

Dan stopped, she didn't know what to say.

"Yes, Danny, go on."

"Then I'd need to find out what the connection was."

He clapped again. "You would indeed. But what could possibly connect all these different silken threads, Danny? What beast might live at the hub?"

"I don't know," she said, looking at him. "It can't be me. So if you're going for that, then don't. Natasha Moore and Sarah Cox had nothing to do with me at all, I was just assigned to the investigation."

"That's true, you were. It was random chance, but now, at the end here, things changed, no? Two investigations began to merge."

"The fingers?" asked Dan.

"The fingers," repeated Hamilton. "An interception, an intruder, someone with a cameo in the wrong crime, but they're stealing the show, don't you think, Danny?"

Dan thought about that, thought about her feeling that Cox hadn't been the one who'd cut off Natasha's finger. Why would she do that? It made no sense. But then who had?

"So I'm the link?" said Dan, turning up the corner of her mouth and scrunching her nose. "Chris, if my life was that exciting, I'd be delighted, honestly I would. The excitement of being at the center of intrigue and conspiracy—but alas, I think we both know I'm not."

Dan stood up, readying herself to leave.

"Well, let's see," said Hamilton. "I'm fairly certain we'll speak again, once you've had time to think this all through."

Dan walked to the door.

"Chess set, Danny, for next time?"

Dan looked at him and then nodded.

"I ordered one online, should be delivered soon."

He smiled.

"Thank you. I look forward to that very much. Your mail does seem erratic, though, don't you think? Are you sure it'll arrive?"

"Of course," said Dan. "It's not likely to go anywhere else."

Dan knocked on the door and then turned.

"You said you'd tell me how Matt Carson found you and what you whispered to him back in the hangar near Aldershot."

"I did, Danny, I did. He didn't find me; I walked in there as soon as you were gone. A little guidance from me and he'd have been a lot more effective, maybe even escaped. Unfortunately, he overreacted before I could really talk to him, and you saw the results when you arrived."

Dan nodded.

"And what did you whisper to him when you did speak?"

"I told him to kill them all while he still had time," said Hamilton, smiling, "and I asked him to spare you, or at least kill you last. I like to think that maybe you never saved my life that day after all, maybe it was I who saved you; ironic, don't you think?"

Dan looked into his eyes and knew that what he said was true.

She turned to the glass while she waited for the guard.

Hamilton was drumming his fingers on the desk.

"Deuteronomy 24:16," said Hamilton as the guard arrived at the door. "I really can't help you any more than to tell you that the Bible is, in this case as in many others, very wrong. Tell no one that I said this to you. As to the rest, say what you like, but keep that to yourself, please, agreed?"

The door opened.

"Miss?"

Dan turned to see the guard waiting for her.

"Say that again?" she said to Hamilton.

"We're done for now, Mr. Darzada," said Hamilton to the guard, though he was looking straight ahead. "Good-bye, Danny. See you soon. Be safe and keep your hand on your ha'penny, as my mother would never have said, nor done."

48

"Not overly helpful, then," said Felicity, still breathless from running down the corridors trying to get there before Dan went in. "Interesting that his language has changed around accepting that there are victims, we'll keep an ear on that and see if it continues. And thanks for going back in there, I really do appreciate it, though I'd really have liked you to wait; I don't understand the rush."

Roger was silent as he watched them both.

"There wasn't a rush, I promise," said Dan, "Just . . . once I'd made up my mind to go back in, I didn't want to wait and risk that I might change it."

Felicity nodded.

"And I believe Roger had some good news for you," said Felicity.

Dan turned and looked confused.

"Roger?" she asked.

"You haven't told her?" asked Felicity, reproach in her voice.

"I've been a bit busy," said Roger, with a pointed smile at Dan. "You've been seconded, part-time and in a probationary arrangement only, for now at least, to the NCA to assist in their investigation."

Dan watched Roger carefully.

"We need to make sure you're safe though, Danny," he said, reaching for his phone. "That bit about Cox sounds like a threat, and . . ." Roger's words faded off and Dan and Felicity both stopped to look at him.

The implication was that Hamilton's threats had come off before, that the last time he'd spoken to Dan, he'd admitted to knowing about the attack against her several years before.

Roger looked away. "I know Hamilton can be full of shit, but he might be right this time," he continued. "We'll take some reasonable precautions. I'm going to ask the locals to check your house and the surrounding area and to do stops past it at intervals for the next few days."

"Her address is already on the watch list," said Felicity.

Dan and Roger turned to look at her.

"I mean, it should be, we can get it added as soon as possible," Felicity said, turning to Dan, "so if you dial emergency, they'll know it's to be taken very seriously and they'll be there in a flash."

Dan paused for a while, thinking, before she looked from one to the other.

"Maybe one of you could move in and drive me to work and pick me up and bring me home again? Being an adult's a real drag."

Roger laughed, but Felicity just scrunched up her nose and whispered, "Quit your bellyaching" slowly and quietly, overenunciating each word.

"Well, we need to do things right," said Roger, "but we also need a proper strategy if Dan's going to be speaking to Hamilton again. Having no audio isn't going to work forever, it was a power play by Hamilton and his legal representative, but we all need to know what he's saying."

"He'll never agree to that," said Dan.

"Can't we get a judge to order it?" asked Roger.

Felicity frowned, thinking. "I doubt it. Well, I mean, yes, we could, but I doubt we could do it without Hamilton's legal team knowing, because although he clearly wanted to speak to you, Danny, he agreed only to do it under this framework, and I doubt we can break that and record what he says in case he then incriminates himself. I'll run it past legal and see, but I'm not hopeful."

"Okay," said Roger, "but I'm not happy for this to continue in its current form, I'm stating that now." He turned toward Dan. "I assume you're going to accept the liaison place on the NCA investigation?"

Roger and Felicity both looked at her now, and the way they were standing, with Roger next to Felicity and both of them facing her, Dan felt as if she was looking up at expectant parents, as if they were waiting for an answer and they both knew what the right one was but were unsure whether she did.

"I'll talk to you about it tomorrow," said Dan.

She grabbed her bag and coat and looked at them; they were both still watching.

"We have three cars and we're all going in roughly the same direction," said Dan. "So, not great for the environment, but I'm out of here. You two walking out?"

"I'm going to chat with some folks I know here," said Felicity.

"I'll come," said Roger, grabbing his jacket and walking to the door.

Dan leaned in and gave Felicity a kiss on each cheek before joining Roger.

They walked in silence along the corridor for a few paces before Dan turned.

"Wait here for me," she said to Roger, turning back into the room and shutting the door behind her.

Felicity looked up, surprised.

"He mentioned the parcels again," said Dan. "Asked me if I knew who they were being delivered to. You have any luck with that?"

Felicity shook her head.

"Odd," said Dan. "I'd have thought that'd be easy to find out."

Felicity stood straight and looked Dan in the eye but said nothing.

Dan watched her friend and knew she had finally seen.

"You lied to me," said Dan. "You lied right to my face, and more than once."

"We're professionals, Danny, you know it and I know it. I'd tell you anything I could, I'd do anything I'm able to do to protect you, but I wasn't cleared to tell you, and so I didn't. It's not lying, it's professional conduct, and you'd have done the same."

Dan was taken aback by the response, the lack of apology, the truth in what Felicity said.

"Tell me now, then," asked Dan. "Is it just the parcels, or has he been sending other stuff to me?"

Felicity swallowed.

"The fingers of those women were sent to your home address," Felicity said. "The first one was picked up when it leaked and triggered a biological contamination investigation. We intercepted all of your mail after that, but had no reason that would allow us to open anything other than the subsequent parcels."

"That's why you wanted to read the letter," said Dan.

Felicity nodded.

"Do you know why he's having someone send them to me?" Dan asked.

Felicity shook her head.

"We're hoping that'll come from your contact with him."

"And that's why my house is on the watch list?"

"It is," confirmed Felicity.

"If I had known . . ." she began.

"If you had known, then he might have been bored with you and stopped speaking to you a long time ago. This seems to be as much about playing games for him as anything else. Now, though, you do know. I can't apologize, and you should know that I fully supported the decision not to tell you, but does it change anything about what he's said so far? Could we go over the notes and see if it jogs anything?"

Dan thought about what Hamilton had said, what he seemed to know, that there was an intruder in her crime, someone who shouldn't be there.

None of it made any sense.

She shook her head and turned to leave.

"See you tomorrow?" Felicity asked.

Dan nodded, leaving the room and seeing Roger frown as he waited.

They walked out in silence, following the guard who led them through doors and along corridors until finally they handed in their passes at the visitor desk and left the prison.

"I think you should join the investigation team," said Roger, not looking at her, just speaking out into the air, as though he'd been certain she was thinking about it anyway. "I don't know why you're even pretending you might need to think about it. It's exactly where you want to be. Unless that's what you were speaking to Felicity about?"

"I don't know where I want to be," said Dan, ignoring his second question. "It's always black-and-white for you, but I don't know if I want to stay in the environment we're in. Where petty assholes like Harrow-Brown can make the wrong decision based solely on a personal grudge.

I don't know if I want to work the way we do, with our hierarchy and structure."

Roger snorted.

Dan clenched her jaw. The sound irritated her.

"Like you ever give a crap about the hierarchy and structure," he said, pushing Danny on the shoulder, chiding her and trying to be playful.

She shook her head.

"You know what I mean, Roger."

"I do," he grumbled. "But look at it this way. Do the liaison role. Work with the civvies for a while. Get away from the navy for a few weeks or months and think it through, okay? Don't walk away because of Harrow-Brown. The man's a dick, we both know it, don't let him decide your future. He'll never act in your best interests."

"Yeah, you're right," said Dan, feeling herself relax.

"But, Danny, neither will he," said Roger, pointing back into the prison as though they could still see Christopher Hamilton.

"I know," said Dan.

"What did he say right at the end?" asked Roger. "When you were at the door about to leave, it looked like he spoke, but he was facing away from the camera."

Dan shook her head.

"Just the usual crap," she said, shrugging. "See you soon, Danny, bring a chess set . . ."

He watched her and then smiled.

"He usually looks at you when he says that stuff."

Roger fumbled in his pockets.

"Did you see my notebook in the room before we left?" he asked.

"No."

"Bollocks," he said, checking his jacket pocket. "I need to go back in and find it. I'm staying down in Portsmouth tonight, so I'll see you tomorrow. Where's your car?"

Dan pointed to it across the parking lot.

"Okay, be careful, take precautions."

"Yes, Dad," said Dan, shaking her head, but not really angry.

He leaned over and gave her a peck on the cheek.

Dan tensed up, not reacting quickly enough to return the unexpected gesture.

"Drive safe," he said, and turned back toward the prison entrance.

Dan watched him go, thinking about what he'd said and then walking to her car.

It was dark now, but the lights were all on and the parking lot was well lit.

Dan knew there were cameras all around the place and she walked slowly, rummaging in her bag for her phone and turning it on.

The screen flashed into life and she pulled up a Web browser as she walked, typing in "Deuteronomy 24:16" as she did. The search came back quickly and Dan selected the top result and read it:

> The fathers shall not be put to death for the children, neither shall the children be put to death for the fathers: every man shall be put to death for his own sin.

She read it again and again.

Hamilton had said the Bible was wrong, but as she read it, she couldn't make sense of it at all. Then she stopped and thought.

The Bible was wrong . . .

She read the line again and remembered the card that had dropped through her door, tried to remember if there'd only been one of them or whether she'd shredded more than one with the junk mail.

"The sins of the father will be visited upon the children," she whispered, unsure where she'd heard that before, or why it'd come to her.

She stared at the screen as a text message arrived. She opened it, to see that it was informing her of a missed call from her dad.

Hamilton had said she was selfish, self-centered, needed to wake up and look around.

Jimmy Nash knew her father.

Marcus knew her father.

But that meant nothing, they were Royal Marines, it was a small corps, reasonable that they would know one another.

Then Hamilton said that things were linked, joined, that she was too selfish to see it. Could it be that the thing that bound them all wasn't her, but her dad?

She thought about Ryan Taylor and *Tenacity*, could think of no link between them and her father at all. She thought of Roger's warning about how Hamilton only served himself. Perhaps sowing seeds of doubt about her father was just a way of screwing with her, trying to see if he could confuse her. But then Jimmy Nash's closing words echoed in her mind.

"I've got nothing at all on your old dad."

Dan considered Jimmy Nash, the man who knew her father, the man who could grab a rapist from a naval base before the police could get their act together and get there. A man with organized crime links across the south coast and into London. A man who made his living through intimidation, illegality, and drugs, who confined and tortured people, who'd said he might do that to someone like Ryan Taylor. A man who knew her father and claimed to have nothing on him.

Dan stopped, thinking quickly. She needed to go and speak to Hamilton again, but she knew it wouldn't be possible now. She needed more information than she had, more guidance, more of a nudge.

She didn't know where to start, but then she thought again about what Hamilton had said. If it was all connected, then whichever lead she followed would lead her to where she wanted to go.

Sarah Cox—where would she go?

Dan's mind flitted to her house, how she'd felt as though she were being watched there, that feeling when you look around to see who's there and there's no one. She couldn't believe Cox would go there now. It was too secure, and if she'd been to look, she'd know it. She'd have to take Dan in the parking lot, and then what? She'd know that the police would be around. It made no sense.

Hamilton had said, "Somewhere she thinks you'd definitely never go. I genuinely don't know where that might be, but she'll have her own ideas."

Dan thought about that, and only one place came to mind that Cox might think she'd never go again.

The conversation they'd had in her cabin when they'd first met, when Cox had congratulated her on catching Simmons and asked her about the shop.

Cox had talked about how remote it was, how awful and secluded.

"I'd never go back there," Dan had said to her.

She opened her car and got in, thinking about Hamilton and how he'd pushed her so far, pretending to know things when he didn't, pretending not to know things that he did. She wondered at the difference between being helped and being manipulated, but she'd only go to look, to prove to herself that Hamilton was wrong and maybe, as Roger had said outside the tunnels, to face down that fear. She started the car and headed for the abandoned shop in the New Forest.

49

All was in darkness, and though Dan had a flashlight and desperately wanted to use it, she braced herself for the dark and stepped into it.

She didn't have to do it, didn't have to go in there, not now, not again, not alone, but she needed to. To prove to herself that Hamilton wasn't right, didn't know everything, hadn't guessed where Cox would be when Dan couldn't.

She walked toward the door that led to the shop's storeroom, shivered again as she thought of David Simmons dragging Evelyn in there, almost killing her. Dan listened outside the door, but there was nothing, no car, no light, no sign of life. She could turn around now, walk back down the dark lane to her own car, and drive home; she'd been here, returned to the building and faced the darkness, and she could go now. Except she would have done it all for nothing. Without looking inside the shop, without checking that Cox really wasn't there, it would all have been for naught.

The memories of when she'd last done this, while Simmons was up on the roof threatening to kill his wife, who was trussed up below, gave Dan a sense of what she would see once she opened the door.

She flashed her light on quickly once inside, shone it straight at the far door that led to the front shop area. The door was shut, and so she switched it on again and scanned the storeroom. Nothing had changed and it was empty. No signs of life.

She moved across the storeroom quickly, moving straight to the door, then doubling back and shining her light into the office area to make sure there was no one hiding in there; there wasn't.

She moved to the door that would lead through to the main shop and listened.

Nothing.

She felt the way she had as a child, daring herself to go to the toilet in the dead of night. Each time, nothing attacked her, yet every night she was just as terrified as she'd been the night before.

She waited by the door.

She knew there were shelves directly opposite her, running the whole length of the shop. If she went right, that took her to the fire escape; left headed down toward the tills and was closer to where she'd fought with Simmons.

She looked down at the handle, opened it quickly; no point in hesitating or messing around.

The door came open easily and she stepped back and out of the way, grabbing her baton from her pocket and extending it in a single movement.

Nothing came through the door save a stream of light.

The shop's main lights were on and they made Dan blink as she looked out into the brightly lit space. Those lights hadn't been on a few minutes ago. They hadn't been on a few seconds ago.

Her heart thumped and she took a step backward, edging toward the door.

She heard a noise, a whimper like a trapped animal, and listened again, her senses hyperaware. She moved back to the door and leaned her head to look as far through it as possible in one direction, seeing nothing but shelves and stock. Then she moved into the doorway and looked the other way and waited. Animals didn't turn lights on.

She turned and moved quickly back to the door she'd entered the storeroom through. She'd go back, phone for help from the car, get other people up here, Roger, Josie, and some of the team. They'd go in together.

As she reached the door her heart skipped a beat.

It was shut.

She tried the handle. It was wedged shut, the door wouldn't move at all.

Dan turned, put her back to it, and held the baton out in front of her.

No one was coming, no one was sneaking up behind her, so she turned again, took a deep breath, and tried the door, pushed it, pulled it, levered the handle. It was wedged tight; she wouldn't be going out that way.

She had two choices, the fire exit and up onto the roof, and trying to get out one of the front windows and doors. Both meant heading back through the main shop.

She walked over, her baton resting on her shoulder, her flashlight on but becoming less useful as she approached the lights in the main shop.

She looked in again. There was nothing there—well, nothing that shouldn't have been there. The shop looked dusty but ordered, identical to how it'd looked the last time she'd been here, though this aisle hadn't seen any of the action.

She looked to the right, toward the fire escape door, and saw it was shut. The bar was there and she knew it should open from the inside, but she also knew how easy it would be to block it. Then she looked to the left, considering whether to check out the shop first, but the door was there, tempting, and she needed to know if it was locked, needed to eliminate that route from her mind before she spent time looking elsewhere.

Whoever turned the lights on knew she was coming anyway.

She stepped through the door and turned right, walking slowly along the aisle and listening to the sounds around her as she took each step.

The shelves ended about six feet from the far wall, and the fire escape door was set into it. As Dan reached the end, she changed course, moving away from the shelves, swinging out wide toward the exit, so anyone waiting at the end of the shelves would need to show themselves before they could be on her. She had the baton raised, and became aware of the aching and tension in her shoulders, suddenly feeling weak and tired, thoughts creeping into her mind telling her to just sit down, get some rest, put her back to a wall and wait.

She flexed the baton down, stretching out her shoulders and taking a deep breath; then, raising it again, she steeled herself, ready for anything, and stepped away from the cover of the shelves and into the area at the end of the shop, heading for the fire exit.

It hit her instantly, but not from close, not from behind the shelves as she'd expected.

Dan stumbled back, dazed, dropping her left arm as pain shot through her shoulder. She gasped. The impact of something heavy and hard, combined with a clattering noise and another human screaming, was over-loading her senses and her vision blurred for a moment, the room whirling around her. Her legs felt weak, as though she might go down, might collapse there and then.

She staggered back behind the shelves and looked down, rubbing her shoulder. It felt dead, as though she'd been punched hard, and it'd left her with no feeling in that arm. She looked at the floor and against the wall, saw a can of food lying there that hadn't been there before.

She took some deep breaths and tried to listen above the sound of her own breathing, her own heartbeat, and a screaming in her body, from her head and her shoulder, that was degrading all of her senses. She readied the baton in case someone rushed her, but her left arm wouldn't go up past her shoulder now, and so she held the baton ready with her right arm and listened.

Nothing.

"Who is that?" shouted Dan.

She edged closer to the end of the aisle and turned her head so she could peek in the direction that the projectile had come from. She readied herself to recoil quickly in case another tin was coming down the same flight path, but there was nothing there, no one there.

Footsteps sounded, but she couldn't place them. They stopped again and there was silence.

50

Dan froze, the baton raised in her right hand, and waited.

There was nothing now, no sound, not even breathing.

She looked at the fire exit, so close yet now seeming impossibly far away. She'd try it again, but first she needed to know for sure who she was in here with. She'd prefer a straight-up confrontation to all the sneaking around; if it's coming, let it come.

Turning slowly, glancing back over her shoulder at every step, she moved silently toward the tills.

There was nothing there that shouldn't have been. No one there at all. Dan took the corner wide again, tensed and ready for another attack.

She looked at the tills and at the shuttered window across from her. She'd looked in that window last time and seen a woman trapped and beaten. Now she was that woman.

She turned and looked along the aisles.

There were several to choose from, but waiting wasn't an option; she had to move forward.

One way stood out to her, familiar, and Dan went that way first, recognizing that she was going the same way she had when she'd come to find Evelyn Simmons. She looked ahead and saw the gap where the gift section had been, on the left-hand side. Dan remembered the rocking chair beneath the gift sign and leaned her head around a set of shelves to look.

Her stomach tightened, forcing a gush of air out of her mouth, and her arm fell limp, the baton hitting the floor as she almost dropped it.

She stepped around quickly, moving until the whole chair was in view.

The gift section sign was still there, but beneath it, arranged on the chair like a fetal baby, was Natasha Moore.

Dan looked around her, raising the baton again, ready to fight. She edged closer to Natasha, and when she could, she reached down and touched the girl, seeming to wait for an eternity to feel some warmth, some faint movement or sign of life.

It was there, though, something inside the girl was still fighting for her life, and Dan heard Natasha stir, wheezing as she drew in a breath.

Dan spun as she heard a sound, her mouth dropping open as she looked.

Sarah Cox was standing halfway up the aisle looking at Dan and Natasha, her mouth open as though she, too, was stunned to see them.

Cox was still in her clothes from when she'd fought with Dan and John at the marina. Her shirt was literally soaked in blood, some of it dry, but on her right side, Dan could see a sheen of red moisture glisten as fresh blood poured from her ear and down her face and joined the dark patches of her shirt.

"You?" said Cox, her voice sounding thick and slurred.

She raised her arm to throw another object at Dan.

Dan stepped back, turning to shield Natasha with her body, to protect her.

The movement made Cox's missile go wide, and Dan heard a scream as Cox charged toward her.

Standing up, Dan spun to face Cox, losing her footing as she stepped on something round. She was on her backside in an instant, scuffling away, her eyes flicking to Natasha.

"Sarah!" she shouted, but the reply was a glass jar exploding on the floor next to Dan's hand, a red sauce splattering the floor and causing Dan to recoil and wipe her eyes as she tried to clear her vision.

Cox was almost on her, and Dan spun on the floor, trying to get her legs toward the woman so that she could kick her away, but Cox was there in a heartbeat, standing over her, her arm raised, and Dan could do little more than flinch away, covering her face and body as Cox hurled something hard and heavy at her from close range.

It hit the side of Dan's shoulder, the pain was blinding, and Dan screamed as lightning shot down her arm. She turned away, her eyes shut, and she heard a dragging sound before she was hit by multiple falling items as Cox swept her arms across the nearest shelf.

Dan tried to roll away but felt a boot catch her on the back, and then something heavy against her head, and she felt her body go limp for a moment, on the edge of passing out.

Cox was standing over her. Dan could feel the weight of her shadow looming.

Natasha's hand was at the edge of Dan's vision, hanging limp off the edge of the chair, the ring finger missing, a bleeding stump where it should be.

Dan kicked out, her legs flailing wildly, and she turned to see Cox step away from her, her eyes wide.

Dan followed her eyes and saw Natasha look back at her, her eyes only just open.

"Natasha," said Dan, kicking out at Cox's knee, forcing her to take a step back.

Then Cox stumbled on some of the detritus she'd strewn around the floor. Her leg slid from under her, and Dan, acting on instinct, looked for her baton, grabbed it, and swung it hard at Cox's supporting leg, striking hard at the side of her knee.

The baton made contact with a loud thwacking sound, and Cox cried out before she went to the ground.

Dan swung the baton again, aiming for Cox's outstretched leg but landing only a glancing blow. She tried to push herself up, to get to her feet, but her left arm wouldn't do it, seemed to have lost all of its strength, and before she could try again, Cox was on top of her.

Dan had been here before, knew she was in a lot of trouble, and scrabbled round, trying to grip her baton so she could swing it at Cox.

She felt Cox grab one wrist and then the other, stretching Dan's arms out above her head like a playground bully.

"How did you find me?" said Cox, her voice odd, thick, muffled. "Why did you bring me here?"

"What?" said Dan as the questions sank in.

Dan struggled and kicked out, writhed and arched her back, but Cox was on top and holding her tight. She could feel her strength draining away as the heavier woman leaned down on her wrist and kept her pinned to the floor.

Dan stopped, looked up for just a second to see Natasha Moore grab the baton from the floor and swing it at the back of Cox's head.

Cox rolled off as Natasha collapsed to the ground beside her, spent, all her energy used up in the one effort.

Cox looked as though she'd landed hard. She was lying on her back, her arms beside her, her body open and unprotected, her eyes wide in shock. She was already regaining her senses, her fingers working, clenching and flexing, and Dan moved quickly.

She stood up, grabbed the baton from Natasha's open hand, and stepped to Cox's side. She drew back her boot and made to kick Cox in the ribs.

Cox saw it coming and put her arms down, turning slightly to absorb the kick, but Dan had taken no chances, hadn't overreached, and she raised the baton above her head and brought it down as hard as she could onto the front of Cox's exposed shoulder, near her neck.

The sound of Cox's collarbone breaking sent a sickening shudder through Dan.

Cox didn't even scream.

The pain seemed to put her into shock, her face turning pale, her mouth opening wide, and her pupils dilating as Dan watched her.

Dan stood over Cox, holding the baton in her right hand and panting as she looked down.

"You're done," Dan said.

Cox's eyes barely flickered, and Dan looked more closely at her, at her ear, where the blood was still trickling down. Something had been done there, Cox's ear was a mess, it looked as though someone had attacked the side of her head with a cheese grater.

"What happened to you?" shouted Dan, assuming that Cox's hearing had been affected by whatever had happened to her. "Who did that to you?"

Cox looked at her, rolling her head to look up into Dan's face. Then she smiled at Dan and quietly laughed.

Dan watched and waited, saying nothing, not sure what was going on in Cox's mind and waiting for clarity to come back.

"How did you find me?" said Cox, her voice a whisper, as though she were on the edge of passing out. "How did you find her?"

"I didn't," said Dan. "I didn't."

"You've no idea what you've done," whispered Cox.

Dan looked into her eyes and saw a reflection flash across Cox's wide pupils as something moved behind her.

In an instant, Dan felt an arm around her neck, the crook of the elbow underneath her chin, and she was picked up clean off the floor.

Her hands went to her neck, trying to free herself from the grip, but whoever had her, had her tight. She kicked, scratched, felt her legs clear the ground, before colored dots appeared across her vision and the strength drained out of her.

51

Dan was lying on the floor again, but comfortably now, on her back, something beneath her head and something draped over her to keep her warm. She tried to open her eyes, but then she heard a voice, not too far away, and froze, keeping her eyes tight shut, not moving at all.

"Dan's in a bad way, but she's going to recover."

Dan recognized the voice, though her head was pounding and she couldn't place it.

"The others?"

A second voice; she recognized this one, too.

"Whoever took them out wasn't messing about. They hit the big one hard, she won't come to for a while." He paused. "They're alive, and all three need help; the little one, though, whoever it was banged her, too, and she looked as though she was already in a bad way; she really won't last forever."

Dan's body was inanimate, frozen in place, but her mind was whirling. Where had she heard those voices before she knew they were talking about Cox, who had to be "the big one," and Natasha, who sounded as though she was barely hanging on?

"He's here," said the first voice.

"Fuck," said the second, and Dan heard feet shuffling, and a sound that she was sure was a cigarette being sucked on one last time, and then being ground out under a shoe.

There was movement, a cold draft, and then more footsteps.

"Where's my daughter?"

Dan didn't know how to feel, what to feel, how to react. She now heard the voice she'd known since childhood, would recognize anywhere, and she was hearing it somewhere it just shouldn't be.

"She's over there, Taz, she's okay."

Footsteps approached.

"Taz, wait. She's fine, I promise. She's unconscious, looks like someone choked her out, but she'll be fine."

Dan felt her father's presence near her and the warmth of his familiar hand on her face, as he looked down at her.

"I told you what would happen if either of my girls was hurt," he said, standing up, his voice changing in tone. "I warned you, Jimmy."

"It wasn't us," said the second voice, and Dan recognized Jimmy Nash's cockney twang and gruff accent.

"It really wasn't, Taz," said the first voice, polite and well-spoken. Marcus.

"We were watching her," said Jimmy, "just making sure she stopped looking into the business, that's all, but this mess wasn't us."

"Then who?"

"We don't know."

"So why did you call me down here?" asked Taz, his tone clipped.

"I didn't. I got a message from you to meet here. Wasn't till I got here and found her that I knew you hadn't sent it. I didn't call this meeting," said Jimmy.

They stood for a moment in uneasy silence.

"So who called us, then?" asked Taz, his voice quiet.

"I. Don't. Know," said Jimmy, and Dan detected something in his voice as he answered her father, a mixture of threat and maybe fear, the sound of a man who would only go so far.

"Tell me what happened," said Taz.

"I got a message claiming to be from you," said Jimmy. "Said to be here ASAP. So I came ASAP. Found your girl on the floor round there, unconscious. Found another one over there, on her front, cuffed. Found a little blond one, looked just like my girl, out cold on a rocking chair round the corner. Her finger's missing."

Jimmy paused.

"Which one?" asked Taz.

"You know which one," said Jimmy. "And that's it. We checked they're alive, made Dan comfortable, and waited. You?"

"I got a message from you," said Taz.

There was silence again.

Dan began to feel cold, to feel she might drift away again, back into a dream state instead of this crazy dream she was in now.

"There's something you need to know." It was Marcus speaking. "One of our contacts at the NCA says that fingers have been arriving for a few months now. The NCA intercepted them and they've got seven or eight."

"Intercepted them from where?" asked Taz.

"They were being sent to Danny's house."

Dan heard a scuffle, movement, and grunting.

"Pack it in!" shouted Marcus. "Jesus."

"And you never thought to tell me?" shouted Taz.

"I only recently found out myself," said Jimmy, breathless. "We got good contacts, but it takes time."

"Are they his?" asked Taz. "Hamilton's?"

Silence again.

"Yes," said Marcus. "We think so, and so does the NCA. Who else's could they be? Dan's been speaking to him. Spoke to him last night before she came here, too," said Marcus.

"What does he want?" The question came from Taz. "I warned you that we were out, Jimmy. Fuck, I was never in, but I warned you to leave my girls alone. I told you the consequences if you didn't—"

"And I left them alone. Both of them. Even when your girl cost me money, took down a whole shipment and broke a supply line, I still stayed away from her."

"She cost you pennies, Jimmy. We both know that what you were really after still got through, didn't it?"

There was a pause.

"She came to me," said Jimmy. "We needed to know she'd stopped sniffing around *Tenacity*, that's why we're watching her, but whoever set this up tonight put two of my best lads in the hospital. They must've known we were tailing her. It wasn't us."

There was a long silence and the sound of footsteps.

"There's more," said Jimmy. "One of our establishments was broken into yesterday. Two of our guests were taken. One you won't know: a local rapist who's been with us a long time. We don't know where he is."

Dan felt herself tense and a wave of nausea passed over her.

They could only mean Knight, who else could it be? And he was out, released and unaccounted for.

"And the one I will know?" asked Taz.

"The other guest of ours was a young man called Ryan Taylor, one of the *Tenacity* mules. Your girl's been looking for him for months, thinking he'd help her find out about us."

"You, Jimmy, not us. There's no us. I don't want to know anything about it," said Taz.

"Well, you might, because his fucking head is currently in the fridge around the corner."

Dan felt her breath catch as she heard the words.

"Underneath a sign that says LAST CHANCE. Dan was out cold when we got here, but it looked like she'd been dragged round and positioned so she'd see it when she came to."

"Or so we'd see it," said Jimmy. "Why else bring us here?"

"Dragged by whom?" asked Taz.

"We don't know," answered Marcus.

"This is a warning, pure and simple," said Jimmy. "Outside of us three, there's only one other person who knows about what happened, and he's locked away."

"So who did it, then?"

"He must have people helping him on the outside."

"Then what does he want?" asked Taz again, his voice growing angrier.

"Who fucking knows what Hamilton wants?" said Jimmy. "He's a sick bastard. Maybe he wants what he always wanted, to watch the world burn and see people die."

"No. He did enough of that," said Taz. "He's deliberately brought this together. He's had one of your places hit, letting you know that he knows where it is and how to do it. He's taken people from you, at least that's all you're admitting to at the moment. He's sent the fingers, and we all know that's a reference to only one thing, and he's aimed it squarely at Danny. He's linking us all together, warning us, not her, he's warning us all at once."

"How do we sort this out now, tonight?" asked Jimmy.

"We have to put it back like we found it and call it in," said Marcus. "Let the police come and sort it out. They're looking for the big girl round the corner, so it'll look like Danny got her and she'll be a hero."

"Okay," said Taz. "If that's what we have to do, then let's do it. We need to talk again, though, we need to know what he wants, why he's doing this now, after all this time. What can he possibly think he'll gain from it?"

They were all silent, until Dan heard movement and Marcus spoke.

"I'll get the blankets," he said.

"No," said Taz. "She's my little girl. I'll fix her."

Danny felt her father approach, felt him lean in and lift her head as he removed the padding from beneath it.

"Don't open your eyes. Don't even stir," he whispered, so quietly that Dan wasn't sure at first that she'd heard it.

Her heart missed a beat.

"I'll be waiting for you, okay? I'm going to call Roger as soon as I leave. I'll be outside watching you until he gets here. I won't let anyone hurt you."

He leaned forward and kissed her on the forehead.

"More than anything else in this world, I love you," he whispered, and gently took the blanket from over her.

52

Saturday, February 7 (early hours)

"Danny?"

Roger edged open the door to Dan's hospital room.

"Are you awake, Danny?"

Dan turned her head toward the door and saw him silhouetted against the dim lights in the corridor.

"I'm awake," she said, surprised at how weak her voice sounded and how dry her throat felt.

John was hesitant in the doorway, stepping back out before he came through the door again, but backward.

There was some bumping, and Dan lifted her head to see what he was doing.

A moment later she realized that he wasn't alone, that he'd brought someone in in a wheelchair. She saw a flash of blond hair and a tiny frame sitting in the chair.

"Sorry," said Roger, "but this young lady was desperate to see you. I doubt we have long before the nurse tracks me down and kills me, but she really wanted to come and see you."

Roger let the door close with a quiet bump and wheeled the chair closer.

Dan watched as the ghostly-white figure of Natasha Moore came into view.

It was dim, but not dark, as plenty of light was spilling in from the corridor through the glass panel in the door, which let Dan see a small, tired smile cross Natasha's face as she neared the bed.

"Hey," said Dan. "How are you feeling?"

Natasha's eyes welled up and her mouth began to quiver.

Dan reached out, looking for Natasha's right hand, the one that wasn't heavily bandaged, and resting her hand atop it with a small squeeze.

"You'll be okay," said Dan, squeezing her hand again. "You're strong and driven and you're a survivor. You'll be okay, I promise," said Dan.

"Thank you," said Natasha. "I just wanted to say thank you. I don't remember much, but I remember you coming for me. I don't know what would have happened if you hadn't."

Dan smiled.

"I remember you coming for me, too," said Dan. "And I really don't know what would have happened if you hadn't. So I think we're even."

Natasha smiled through her tears.

"Who came and got you from Cox's house?" asked Dan. "Did you see them? Was it a man or a woman?"

"Danny," said Roger, his tone gruff. "We'll get to that later. Not now."

Dan said nothing. She continued looking at Natasha, seeing the strength in the girl's features and knowing she'd be willing to help.

"I never saw their face," she said, "but I'd say it was a man, just because of the size and physical strength."

"Stop it," said Roger, not angry, but sounding like a parent frustrated at two arguing teenagers.

"I'll think hard," said Natasha. "When you can, when I can, I'll tell you everything I know."

Dan squeezed her hand again.

"Thank you," she said. "I met Jason."

Natasha smiled at that and said, "He's on his way. He's going to pick me up when I'm allowed out and maybe stay with me for a few days." Natasha paused. "Not together," she added. "That ship's sailed, but I think we can be friends. I don't really have anyone else anyway, except Mark, and we can't get hold of him yet."

Dan looked up at Roger, who stared back at her, and she realized that Natasha hadn't been told yet that the body of Mark Coker had been identified from the charred remains on Cox's yacht.

"Well, he seems like someone who'd be a good friend, but if you need someone else to talk to about all this, call me."

Natasha smiled, though it quickly turned into tears again.

"Thank you," she whispered.

There was a knock at the door and it swung open.

A nurse walked in and stopped, hands on her hips.

"This young lady needs rest," the nurse said, her accent foreign but hard to place.

"Sorry," said Roger, sounding suitably chastised. He hung his head for emphasis.

The nurse stepped forward and took control of Natasha's chair.

"Any more nonsense, sir, and you'll be asked to leave. Understand? And that includes questions and all that."

"I understand," said Roger.

He glanced over at Dan and she was sure she saw him wink.

"I'll see you soon," said Dan as Natasha was wheeled out of the room and she was left alone with Roger.

"What other nonsense have you done tonight then?" she asked.

"I tried to get in to talk to Cox," he said, "but the sphincter police wouldn't let me. I just wanted to get a feel for how she was, but her parents were notified and are on their way, along with an uncle, I think, who's some big-shot law type. So I reckon that chance has gone. I wonder at what some people will do to protect their kids, you know. They'll mount a defense and try to keep her free, when they've no chance at all."

"When are you going to tell Natasha that Mark Coker's dead?"

Roger sighed and shook his head.

"Tomorrow, once we've informed the family. It's not something I'm relishing, but Naval Personnel and Family Services will appoint a worker and that'll help her deal with it. She's been through enough. I don't think I could tell her tonight, even if I was allowed to."

Dan realized that there was no answer that seemed right, no way to break the news that would soften the blow.

Roger pulled up a chair and sat next to the bed.

"Your dad's on his way," he said, his eyes flitting away from hers. "I called him and let him know."

Dan watched him, surprised at how easily he was lying to her and yet how bad at it he was.

"He'll be a while, then?"

"Down by midmorning, I think. It's a good eight hours if the traffic's okay."

Dan nodded.

"Thanks. I'm really looking forward to speaking to him."

Roger stood up.

"I better go," he said.

He reached out and gently touched her brow, brushing her hair aside.

"You're going to be released tomorrow. I spoke to the doctor. She just wanted you in to check for concussion, but she's saying she'll be happy for you to go after morning rounds. If your dad's not here, then I'll come and get you, okay?"

"Did we get an identification on the second body to come out of the armories?"

"The one who'd lost his head?" said Roger, immediately realizing it wasn't the time or place for gallows humor. "No, not yet," he said, his eyes flitting away as he lied.

"It's Ryan Taylor," said Dan. "His head was at the shop."

Roger froze, and then looked a bit embarrassed.

"I didn't think you knew that," he said. "I was going to tell you tomorrow."

"It wasn't Cox who killed him," said Dan, watching as Roger started to protest. "I'm telling you now, she killed Stephanie James, the young girl who was supposedly lost overboard from *Defiance*, she killed Mark Coker, and she would've killed Natasha, but she didn't kill Taylor."

Roger glanced back at the door as though worried the nurse would burst in and blame him for the topic of conversation.

"Danny," he said, his voice low and almost begging. "His body was with her other victims, he'd been decapitated with one of her weapons, her prints are all over the knife and the shop, and his blood is all over her."

Dan looked away from him.

"Let's talk tomorrow, okay?" he said, patting her shoulder. "You rest up. It's been a tough few months, and if you look too tired and beat up when Taz arrives, he might never move out of your house again."

Roger laughed, but it sounded forced.

She watched him head for the door.

"It's all linked into *Tenacity*, you know," she said, watching him as

he reached for the door, sensing that out of her line of sight he was closing his eyes in frustration, sighing and trying to summon patience.

He turned back.

"Just rest up, okay?"

"What's your link between Cox and Taylor?" she asked. "There's nothing, I'd have spotted it if there was. But I'll tell you where the link is, it's
Tenacity and Jimmy Nash. I said to you repeatedly that it'd be too hard
for a few guys to move that volume of narcotics without an established
network behind them, and all the time there's a known network with links
that go all the way back into the Armed Forces, a network built exclu-
sively from the Armed Forces."

He waited, saying nothing, before he shook his head slightly.

"Jimmy Nash is a two-bit drug dealer and a thug," Roger finally said.
"It's no more likely to be him than any of the other dealers around, if
there's a network at all, but even if we accept that, what's the link between
Taylor and Cox? Or *Tenacity* and Cox?"

"I don't know yet," said Dan.

"Just leave it, Danny," he said, turning back to the door. "Live your
life for a while, enjoy something, but leave this alone. Just for a few months.
It'd be great to see you smile again one day soon, and you could if you'd
stop carrying the weight of the world on your shoulders."

He walked out without saying another word, and Dan turned her head
away from the light that shone in through the glass panel in the door.

She lay there, thinking, when she heard the door open again. At first
she thought it was Roger returning, but as the figure stepped through
and blocked the light, she felt a familiar presence.

"Hey, Danny," said her dad, as he closed the door behind him.

"You were supposed to be eight hours away," she said.

"I couldn't wait any longer, I needed to know you were okay, and to
see you."

Dan looked toward him, at the huge silhouette he cast with the light
behind him. She felt as if she might cry, and then as if she might fly into
a rage, and then she just felt so tired she could barely keep her head turned
toward him.

"What have you done, Dad?" she said, closing her eyes. "What the
hell did you do?"

ACKNOWLEDGMENTS

Thanks to Elizabeth and Sammy, my mum, dad, Vicky, and Alan.

Thanks to my friends Steph B, Martin and Mary, and Liz and Sara for reading and critiquing, in the nicest possible way, and to my friend Matt Seldon for all his creative endeavors. Thanks also to Trev, Paul, Sheapy, Mitch, and Mac for their naval knowledge, and to John Smith of the Royal Armouries for an excellent tour.

Thanks to Esther Newberg at ICM Partner; to Michael Signorelli, Kanyin Ajayi, Stephen Rubin, and Chris O'Connell at Henry Holt; and to Jonny Geller and Catherine Cho at Curtis Brown.

All your help and support is very much appreciated.

And finally . . .

To all my brothers and sisters in the Armed Forces who are deployed around the globe, away from their loved ones—be safe, look out for each other, and remember: never let the truth get in the way of a good story!

ABOUT THE AUTHOR

J. S. Law served in the Royal Navy Submarine Service, rising through the ranks to become a senior nuclear engineer. *The Fear Within* is his second novel. He lives in Portsmouth, England.